RANDOM SH*T FLYING THROUGH THE AIR

Nic stands with his arms folded, a grim expression on his face. When I make my way over to him, he gives me an utterly blank look. Like he doesn't know who I am.

"Nic?"

"What?"

"What is it? Is everything . . . ?"

The rain has picked up even more – I hadn't realised it, but I'm soaked through, my hands patterned with grime.

"San Bernardino," Nic says. It's a spot to the east of LA, near Riverside. Around here they call that area the Inland Empire, although I don't know why.

"I don't understand . . ."

"It's gone." His voice is as dull as his gaze. "Wiped out."

BY JACKSON FORD

The Girl Who Cold Move Sh*t With Her Mind

Random Sh*t Flying Through the Air

RANDOM
SH*T FLYING
THROUGH
THE AIR

JACKSON FORD

orbit

www.orbitbooks.net

ORBIT

First published in Great Britain in 2020 by Orbit

1 3 5 7 9 10 8 6 4 2

Typeset in Bembo by M Rules
Printed and bound in Great Britain by Clays Ltd, Elcograf S.p.A.

Papers used by Orbit are from well-managed forests
and other responsible sources.

Orbit
An imprint of
Little, Brown Book Group
Carmelite House
50 Victoria Embankment
London EC4Y 0DZ

An Hachette UK Company
www.hachette.co.uk

www.orbitbooks.net

Dedicated to Jay Rock, Watts,
and paella.

Also to Nipsey Hussle. RIP.
The marathon continues.

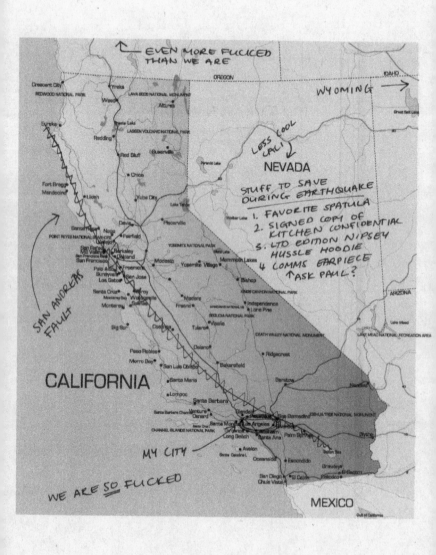

ONE

The State Trooper

Ninety-nine per cent of traffic stops are completely routine.

Rudy Daniels knows the stats. He's been doing this job for a while. All the same, that pesky one per cent is never too far from his thoughts, close as the sidearm on his left hip.

Not that he's worried about *this* stop. In his learned opinion, it fits squarely in the ninety-nine per cent. He caught a glimpse of the driver as she shot past in her red pickup – she's not the one per cent type.

Daniels pushes the accelerator, coming in close behind her and blipping the siren. The pickup swerves slightly, as if the driver had been on the verge of falling asleep. There's the flash of an indicator, and the truck comes to a stop on the hard shoulder, the tyres sending up a burst of fine desert dust.

Daniels brings his cruiser to a halt twenty feet behind the pickup. He squints into the harsh afternoon sun, reading the plate, scratching it out on his notepad in case the driver decides to take off. Not that he's expecting it. The worst he's ever encountered on this particular road was the time a couple of kids got into a drag race, and thought they could outrun him. Spoiler alert – as his daughter Kyla would say – they couldn't.

He keys his mic. "Dispatch, Charlie C3."

Connie's voice comes over the line cleanly. "Copy Charlie, what's up?"

"Got an 11-95 out on the 10."

"Anything serious?"

"Naw. Just letting you know what's what." Daniels reads her the pickup's plate from his notepad.

"Goddamn slow-ass computer," Connie mutters. "Sorry, Rudy. Give it a second to run."

Daniels sighs. If he waits, he'll be here for ever. "I'll go have a look-see. Doesn't seem like trouble."

"Copy that."

He grabs his hat from the dash, slipping it on as he clambers out of the cruiser. He wishes he didn't need it – he's six-two with shoulders like a linebacker, already scary enough without his shades and the wide-brimmed Highway Patrol hat. But both are essential out here, in the shitting-hot, baking hardpan of the Arizona–California border.

The sunlit sky above is completely empty. So is the highway: no traffic in either direction. Daniels adjusts his nametag, making sure it's visible, knowing it is but doing it from habit anyway. Traffic stops go a lot easier if the subject has a name to hold onto. He's heard of other patrolmen, even LA cops, taking their badges off before they head into action. It's the kind of thing that makes him curl his lip every time he hears about it. God above knows, he's not perfect, but even the thought of it makes him angry.

The truck has New Mexico plates, yellow on blue. The window is already down, which is good. The driver's hands come into view as he approaches, still tight on the wheel. No rings – just a single gold bangle on her left wrist. The hands are veiny, fingers thin, the skin baggy around the knuckles.

Daniels can't properly make out the interior yet, let alone the driver, but the hands tell him plenty.

The rest of her comes into view as his eyes adjust. She's younger than her hands suggest – a lot younger. Early twenties, maybe. Bleached-blonde hair with the brown roots showing tied up in a messy ponytail. High cheekbones, a splash of freckles across tanned skin. Daniels would peg her for a college senior heading out on Spring Break, if it wasn't for the hands. And her eyes. They're a little too big for her face, and she's blinking too much.

For a second, Daniels is on edge – if she's high, this is going to get a lot more complicated – but then he relaxes. She's just nervous.

"Afternoon, ma'am. I'm Officer Daniels, California Highway Patrol. You coming from Arizona?"

"That's right." Said with a little upward tilt of the chin, like he'd accused her of something.

"May I see your licence, please?"

She starts, digs in her purse. Daniels flashes a quick smile at her passenger, the little boy sitting on a booster in the front seat. His tanned skin is dotted with freckles, untidy brown hair hanging down past his neck. He's wearing an oversized white T-shirt with a bright hot-air balloon on the front, advertising the Albuquerque International Balloon Fiesta. His head, which is a little too large for his scrawny body, is bent towards the iPad on his lap.

Usually, kids get interested when Daniels asks for a licence, ask if he's a real police officer or if he can arrest them. *Yes I am, and only if you're mean to your mom.* The answers are ready, but the boy barely glances at him.

"Here," the woman says.

Daniels squints at the licence. Amber-Leigh Schenke, and

she looks as nervous in the photo as she does in real life. "You folks on vacation?"

"That's right. We're visiting LA. I wasn't speeding, officer . . . "

"No, ma'am, you weren't speeding." He leans down, hands on his knees, looking across the car. "What's your name, young man?"

The young man in question says nothing. He ignores both of them, fingers tapping at the tablet screen. He's reading an ebook, and not one with pictures. His finger traces along the text, his mouth moving silently. Daniels blinks – the kid can't be more than four. He's reading already? At that age, his Kyla had only just figured out the sounds of the different letters.

"Say hi, Matthew." Amber-Leigh rests a hand on the boy's leg. He doesn't look up.

Daniels has always relied on his gut in the past, relied on it to send up a little warning signal when something isn't quite right. It's just given him the very slightest twitch.

He lets it go, annoyed with himself. His brains must be cooking. He's stopped hundreds of drivers since he started the job, and he recognises the type. Law-abiding, nervous-as-hell, head filled with scare stories about rural cops.

"Well," he says, hitching his belt, "you might not know this, being from out of state, but your son's too young ride in the front seat."

"He can't?"

"No, ma'am. Against the law in California."

"I want to sit up front," Matthew says. He has a thin voice, high and reedy. He still hasn't looked up from the iPad.

"He likes to sit in the front," says Amber-Leigh.

"Sorry. No can do, my young friend." He taps the pickup's roof. "Better move on over to the back."

"We're sorry, officer." Amber-Leigh glances at her son. "Would it be all right if he stayed? I'll drive real careful."

Rudy Daniels frowns. He's not in the habit of letting traffic stops negotiate with him. And technically, he should be writing her up – something he wasn't intending to do, until she started arguing with him.

His stomach rumbles. There are some nuts in the cruiser's glove compartment, packed by his wife, who says they're good for his cholesterol. Daniels happens to think that they taste like salted sand, and he'd be better served by a burger over at the diner in Ripley. He'll have a salad instead of fries, though, to keep Stella happy.

He hands back the licence. "Just put him in the back seat, OK?"

"Is there no way we could—?"

"Have a good day, ma'am. Drive safe now." He gives the pickup's roof another tap, turning to head back to his cruiser. By now, Connie's system will have turned over. Odds are Ms Amber-Leigh Schenke doesn't have any violations, but—

Officer Rudy Daniels gets three yards from the pickup before the ground opens up and swallows him.

One moment, he's mid-stride, mind already on his burger, wondering if maybe he should skip the salad and just have the fries anyway, Stella isn't going to know. The next, there's nothing but air beneath his foot.

It's as if the ground is the surface of a pond – one that's just had a heavy stone dropped into it, right where Daniels is standing. A depression forms instantly, a huge hole that grows deeper by the second. The displaced earth rises on either side of it in two enormous waves, the rocks and dirt and dust rushing outwards and upwards. He falls face-down into a gaping pit, mouth open in a scream that doesn't quite make it out of his throat. His left wrist snaps on impact, a horrid burst of pain ripping up his arm. His ears ring, and above the sound, there's a horrible, shivering roar.

Daniels rolls onto his back, gasping, getting a split-second glimpse of sky beyond the rearing waves of dirt. He has time to think one thought – a memory of playing on the beach in Santa Cruz with Kyla, holding her tight as they bodysurfed – then the earth crashes down.

Plumes of white dust drift away. The only evidence of what just happened is a vaguely ovular depression, as if a giant had briefly ground the sole of his boot into the dirt. There's no sign of Rudy Daniels. His cruiser sits quietly on the shoulder, blinkers on, engine ticking as it cools.

In the pickup, Amber Schenke has her hands back on the wheel, ten and two. Knuckles white.

"You didn't have to do that," she says, staring straight ahead. Her voice is brittle.

Matthew shrugs, still not looking up from the iPad. "I didn't want to sit in the back."

After a moment, Amber turns the key and pulls away.

TWO

Teagan

Oh, I fucked up.

I fucked up *bad*.

Sweat pours down my forehead, sliding into my eyes. I wipe it away with a knuckle, but that just makes it worse. Goddamnit, how could I be so stupid?

I lick my lips. OK. I can fix this. No biggie. I already have everything I need. Holding my breath, I manoeuvre the little wedge of metal into view, floating it through the air with my psychokinesis. Just as well – my hands are *way* too sweaty to hold it right now.

"Come on, baby," I whisper. "Momma needs a new pair of shoes ..."

Moving very, *very* freaking carefully, I wedge it into the gap. Wiggle it gently back and forth.

With a slight *skritch*, the metal spatula slips underneath the burnt rice, levering it up from the non-stick surface of the pan.

I almost squeal with anxiety, hardly daring to look. When I do, I let out a relieved groan. I didn't scratch the pan. It's the one good piece of kitchen equipment I own, outside of my knife, and I really didn't want to fuck it up because I don't know how to make paella.

I'd already transferred the top layer of unburnt rice to a fresh pan, so at least I have that to work with later. I keep at it, gently prying up the edge of the burnt crust. Yes, I know you're not supposed to use metal on non-stick. I've lost my plastic spatula. It's somewhere, in the messy clusterfuck that is my apartment, and I haven't been able to find it.

The key to a good dinner party is to cook something you're familiar with. That way, you can do it on autopilot, casually reducing sauces and sautéing onions while chatting to your guests and looking like a total pro.

So of course, for tonight's dinner, I got it into my head to cook a dish I've never attempted before. Paella. It's Spanish, and it's yummy. Chicken, mussels, peppers, chorizo, jumbo shrimp. Bound together in creamy, *al dente* risotto rice, stained yellow with saffron. It's one of my favourite things to eat in the world. Even the ones I've had here in Los Angeles, which is obviously not Spain, are pretty badass.

After reading the recipe, I figured it didn't look too difficult. I don't exactly know why I thought the best time to attempt it would be on a night I'm trying to impress a certain someone, but I did. I'm smart like that.

Paella needs to be cooked over fire, in a wide, shallow pan. That's how you make sure the rice is soft and squidgy on top, and crusty and awesome on the bottom. I do not have a fire, or a special paella pan. I have a shitty four-ring burner in my postage-stamp kitchen.

My mistake was turning the heat too high. The pan couldn't cut it. It's baking hot around the stove, and as I dig in with the spatula to get the rest of the burnt rice, a couple of drops of sweat launch themselves off my forehead and land right on top of the only properly cooked shrimp in the entire pan.

Perfect. Just what every dish needs. Teagan's secret sauce.

I push the spatula in deeper, going past the edge into the central part of the paella. "Come *on*, you stupid piece of shit."

The burnt crust does not come on. The burnt crust is a little bitch and stays put, even with my pinpoint-precise mental movements of the spatula.

Yes: having psychokinesis – PK, as I call it – is really useful in the kitchen. It doesn't help with actual ingredients – I can't lift anything carbon- or hydrogen-based, so food is a no-go. But it's great for implements. Not that I can reveal my ability to anyone. If I ever *do* make it into a professional kitchen – something that is absolutely going to happen, by the way – I'll be on my own.

Of course, to cook for a living, you probably have to know how to make decent paella. Right now, I am so fired.

It might be better if the meal actually *looked* nice – trust me, a glowing pan of orangey-yellow paella is an orgasmic sight. Mine is . . . not. It's an off-white sludge of creamy rice and proteins and overcooking peppers. As it turns out, you need a ton of saffron to make any real difference to the colour, and saffron is fucking expensive. Shockingly, the government agency I work for wouldn't let me expense four grams of the stuff.

I run my finger down the oil-spattered page of the cookbook next to my stove, take a swig of beer. It's my third, and I only started drinking an hour ago, but screw it. I put the bottle down and go back to scraping, which is when the smoke alarm goes off.

What the actual fuck? I know I let the rice burn, but the thing can't be *that* sensitive. Except . . . Jesus, there's a lot of smoke. My little apartment has high-ish ceilings, and it's all collected there, turning the air hazy. It looks like someone hot-boxed the place.

I send out my PK in a wild burst of energy, hunting for the off switch on the alarm. As I do so, my foot lands on a wet patch on the kitchen tiles. I grab at the counter for balance, arms whirling. My flailing hand *just* nicks the half-full beer bottle, knocking it off the counter to shatter in a bazillion pieces across the floor.

I stand, breathing through my nose, listening to the blaring alarm, doing my best to think very hard about nothing at all.

I somehow manage to shut the noise off, and grab a dustpan and mop out from under the sink with my PK to handle the shattered bottle. Then I go back to scraping, keeping what's left of my poor mind on the beer clean-up.

PK is great for multitasking, but I do sometimes my wish my parents had given me other abilities. Super-powered cooking skills would have been nice. The ability to sense burning before it begins. Not exactly useful when you're trying to create the perfect soldier, but definitely more applicable to everyday life.

The central part of the burnt rice still won't budge. It's tempting to just rip the stove and oven out of the wall with my PK and send them smashing through a window. I can do it, too. I used to think I could only lift around three hundred pounds, but a few months ago I discovered I was ... Well, let's just say I'm a lot stronger than that now.

There's a knock at the door.

No way is it seven-thirty already. It can't be. A look at the oven clock tells me otherwise. Goddamn it, he was supposed to text when he was getting close.

I grab my phone from its charger by the fridge, and of course, he did. I just didn't hear it because I was too focused on not destroying dinner.

There's a horrible moment of frozen panic, where I'm not sure if I should keep cooking, open the windows for the smoke, answer the door, get him a drink or just fall over.

I settle for the door. I badly wish I had time to smarten up – when your crush is coming over for dinner, these things matter. I'd planned to put on something a little less gross than the 2Pac tank I'm wearing, and fix my hair. I've been growing it out lately, and it's pulled back in a short, messy ponytail, black strands going every which way.

I take a deep breath, tell myself to calm the fuck down, and open the door.

THREE

Matthew

The book's gotten boring. Matthew's already figured out who committed the murder. Part of him is pleased that he managed to outsmart the writer, even as he's equally annoyed that there's no point in finishing the story now.

For the first time in hours, he lifts his gaze from the iPad, blinking. It's gotten dark outside the truck. Clouds have just started to gather, deep and black, scudding across the sky. The dashboard clock reads 6:02.

"I'm hungry," he tells his mother.

"OK," Amber says carefully, not taking her eyes off the road. "There's some chips in the back, I think?"

"I don't want chips. I want a tuna sandwich."

"We'll be at San Bernardino in a little bit. We'll stop for some dinner there."

"I don't want it in a little bit." His voice has gotten louder. Why does she always try to calm him down? "I'm hungry *now*."

"Baby, don't get mad. I'll find you some food soon, OK?"

She should have gotten snacks. He can't buy food – he's too little, even if he knows a lot more than most grown-up people. The annoyance turns to anger, boiling up inside him, his chin trembling. A tear pricks at the edge of his left eye. He lets it drop – grown-ups hate it when kids cry.

He reaches out with his mind, grabs hold of a small rock from the side of the road. It's harder to do if he's in a moving car than if he's standing still, but he manages to snag it, whipping it at the window as they rumble past. It collides with a crack, making his mom yelp.

"Baby, please . . ."

In response, he grabs another rock, cracking the back window. "I'm not a baby," he yells.

"Mattie, I'm sorry, I—"

A chunk of soil spatters across the windshield on her side, and she has to fight not to swerve. Matthew's anger grows and grows. He'll make her get out the car and stand still so he can teach her a lesson. The thought of pelting her with dirt, of finding the smallest, sharpest rocks he can, fills him with a slippery little jolt of glee. It's the kind of glee most children feel when they do something bad, when they draw on a wall or pour a full glass of milk on the floor. Most children have the sense to back away from it, aware that they're taking a risk – not just the wrath of a grown-up, but something much more primal.

Deep inside Matthew, there's a twitch of worry – a little vestigial tail, weak and helpless. The worry that this time, he might have pushed it too far. He ignores it, as he always does. He's done *way* worse than this before, and hasn't gotten in trouble, not really. Not even at the School. Definitely not with Amber.

Thinking of the School makes him angrier. Matthew wishes he'd stayed. So what if the government was coming to shut the place down? He wouldn't have let them. Ajay and the other teachers knew what he could do – they'd tested his powers a bunch of times. He was the smartest person there, everybody knew it, so he didn't get what the big deal was. He shouldn't have let Ajay talk him into running.

He howls, tears gushing down his cheeks now, mouth twisted in a snarl as his mother begs and pleads. Dirt and rocks hammer the car, cracking the rear window, scudding against the tyres. No one else can do what he can do, no one else knows how, they're not smart enough. What would happen if he threw something bigger? Concentrated a little bit more, grabbed a rock or a boulder, smashed it right into Amber's stupid face? Is she saying he *can't*? Does she really think he won't do it?

A building looms out of the darkness. A gas station, just ahead, the awning visible around a sloping hillock. Amber gasps with relief. "There! We'll stop quick, OK? Get some dinner."

For a moment, Matthew wants to keep going. Just smash the car to pieces, see what she does. But he *is* hungry. He wasn't making that up. Slowly, the anger fades. Not gone completely – just smaller now.

Maybe they'll have *toasted* tuna sandwiches.

Despite the fact that they're in the middle of nowhere, the gas station is a big one, a huge Chevron sign perched on a massive awning. The concrete apron is old, worn in spots, but clean. There's movement behind the windows of the station's store, a clerk stacking a shelf already loaded with potato chips. To the right of the store, a man wearing overalls tied around his waist fiddles with a cage of propane tanks. A green Toyota idles at the pumps, the driver getting ready to pull away.

At that moment, Matthew feels a twitch, deep in his gut. It makes his eyes go wide, banishes the anger and hunger.

"Stop the car," he says.

"Just going to park, baby."

"*STOP THE CAR NOW!*"

She slams the brakes, face twisted in confusion and fear. Matthew leaps out before they've even come to a halt, popping the door and shooting across the grey tarmac.

He's always been able to feel the ground – the dirt, the rocks, the soil. He can feel them all in his mind, like he's holding them in his hand. He's so used to it he barely notices, but *this* . . . this is different. This is big. Bigger than the biggest rock he's ever lifted. It's like the ground is calling to him, from very far down. He's never felt anything like it before.

The Toyota has just begun to pull out from the pumps, and it comes to a screeching halt as Matthew crosses its path. He ignores the driver's angry hand gesture. He just side-steps, sprinting for the edge of the concrete apron. Behind him, Amber comes round the other side of the truck, shouting his name.

He skids to his knees, hands exploring the desert dirt. There's not a breath of wind. The tears on his cheeks haven't even dried yet.

"Matthew!" Amber reaches her son, coming to a halt a few feet away.

It's energy. Not the smooth, even energy he gets in a rock, or a clod of soil. It's pulled tight, stretched like guitar string. It's deep, almost too big for him to wrap his mind around. He's directly over it.

"What—?" Amber stops, coughs. "Sweetie, what's going on?"

The propane guy shouts something from back by the building. Matthew ignores him. "I can't even feel the end of it," he says. "It goes on *for ever*."

The energy line runs north to south, going further than he

can touch. For the first time in his four years of life, Matthew feels something other than joy, or anger, or annoyance.

What he feels is awe.

Genuine, ice-cold awe.

"It's deep," he says. "It's real deep. But I think ... OK, I'm just going to try something ... "

He places his hands flat on the ground, lowers his head. Around them, the loose rocks in the topsoil begin to shake.

FOUR

Teagan

A lot of lawyers don't know how to dress down. Nic Delacourt isn't one of them.

He's wearing a crisp, grey V-neck T-shirt over dark jeans. It's been threatening rain all day, and it looks like it just started: a few drops glisten on his bald head. Yes, we do occasionally get rain in LA.

Nic coughs from the smoke. "Bad time?"

"Perfect, actually. Come on in."

He waves a hand in front of his face. "Think I'll stay outside. Where there's air."

"Shut up." I pull him into a hug, making sure to keep it quick and friendly. His shoulders are tight under his shirt – he's toned, rather than ripped, but he spends a lot of his spare time outdoors. Nic's a surfer, and snowboarder, and rock climber, with a knack for finding the best spots to do those things in.

But listen, you think you've had awkward break-ups? Try this. Girl has psychokinetic abilities. She works for the government doing bad-ass secret-agent shit, and they refuse to let her reveal those abilities to anyone. That means she doesn't dare have a boyfriend because said abilities go haywire during sex.

(Oh, your teenage years were awkward? Imagine tearing your room apart every time you masturbate).

Then, a really cool guy she's friends with asks her out, and she has to be a dick and say no. Then she's framed for murder, and has to go on the run. She ends up asking the cool guy for help, and in the process, reveals her powers to him.

Cue major freak-out, *I'm-living-in-an-Avengers-movie*, *holy-shit-superheroes-are-real*, blah blah. It didn't help that right after, we got ambushed by a group of special forces commandos, and I ended up wrecking Nic's apartment in the escape. That was before we all got chased down Wilshire Boulevard by one of the commandos, a psychopath named Burr who had a real hard-on for taking me out.

Anyway, he got over it – Nic, I mean, not Burr; Burr is a flaming ass-clown who will never get over himself, let alone me. The day was saved. Well, *saved* might be a little strong. I made it out, but lost another friend in the process. Our wheel-man slash grease-monkey, Carlos Morales. Also known as Chuy. Also known as the asshole who fucked us over, framed me for murder and nearly got us all killed. Also known as my former best friend in the entire world.

The less I think about him, the better.

Bad guys dead, injuries healing, back to normal. Psychokinetic girl asks cool guy out. Even kisses him. And cool guy turns her down.

Sad trombone.

Don't get me wrong: Nic doesn't owe me anything. He's got every right to think things through, and make his own decisions. It just . . . sucked.

Shock horror, I don't define my self-worth by what someone else thinks of me – definitely not what a man thinks. Never have, never will. And after Nic decided he didn't want to be with me, I went through a period of real anger. It was a self-righteous, high-horse kind of anger. I didn't need Nic, I didn't need anybody.

It didn't last long. Mostly because I missed him.

I missed hanging out with him. I hated not being able to call him up after I got a tip on a new food truck, or to zip over to the other side of LA to try out a new pho place.

And sometimes, two people can't stay apart. Ask anybody who hooked up with an ex, even though they knew it was a bad idea. We started texting. Then we started meeting up for coffee. I was careful. He knew how I felt about him, and I didn't want to scare him off. Tonight is the first time he's been back to my place since we kissed.

I still want to date him. But I also know it's going to take a while to convince him that we'd be good together, especially given what I do for a living. The old me might not have been so careful, but let's just say that the past few months have taught me a little bit about being careful.

"Hope you like paella," I say, stepping aside to let him in.

He wrinkles his nose. "I like it when it's not on fire."

"Shut up. I'll deal with the food, you open a window. I've got awnings, the rain shouldn't get in."

"Can you turn the music down a little?"

"What? Oh. Sure." I have two massive, ancient speakers in my lounge, currently playing some very loud rap. Jay Rock – the *Follow Me Home* album. I reach out with PK and turn the volume down.

"I brought beer." He drops a damp cardboard box on the counter and heads over to the window.

"Is it that hoppy shit you like?"

"Different kind. Not as strong."

"So I'll be tasting hops for days then, not weeks."

He gives an awkward laugh. For a few seconds, neither of us say anything.

"Here." I toss him a beer from his six-pack, desperate to break the moment, and crack one for myself. "Cheers."

"Cheers." He takes a sip that is just a little too deep. The kind you take when you're waiting for the other person to say something.

We crash on the ratty couch. Like everything else in here, it's seen better days, and like everything else, I can't bear to get rid of it. At least I managed to tidy the place. Sort of. I didn't really have shelf space for all my cookbooks, so they're currently in a stack taller than I am, over by my bedroom door. My plastic spatula is probably underneath them.

I draw my legs up. "How's the caseload?" Nic's a special assistant in the District Attorney's office.

He rolls his eyes. "I see briefs when I go to sleep at night."

"Fun."

"Anyway, it's the usual boring shit. What about you? How's work?"

He tries so hard to make it sound like a casual question that it ends up sounding really awkward. Not exactly surprising. For most people, work is sitting in an office or drilling stuff on a construction site or waiting tables. For me, it's using my PK to break into places and put tracking devices on briefcases and lift important objects out of moving cars.

"Work's good. We're prepping for a mission in a couple days."

A flicker of a smile. "Paul still making you guys do moving jobs?"

"Ugh. Yeah." The little outfit we work for has a cover: a removals company called China Shop Movers. Our logistics guy, Paul Marino, is the Daniel Day-Lewis of secret agents. He loves getting into character.

"He still dating . . . ?" Nic frowns.

"Annie."

"Right, Annie. I can't believe that – they seem really different."

"They are." Annie Cruz is the point person on our ops, which is a fancy way of saying she's my babysitter. She has a sense of humour so small you'd need an electron microscope to detect it.

"How do they actually make that work?"

"I hear he's really good in bed."

He forces another laugh, even more awkward than the first. Of course I had to make a joke about sex. Why do I even bother trying to stop myself?

"Hungry?" I say, desperate to change the subject.

"Kind of. I don't mind waiting if . . . "

"No, it's cool, I don't want it to get cold."

Bowls. Paella. I give the rice a big squeeze of lemon, which should take care of any carbonised aftertaste. I dish up, giving Nic a few extra shrimp, then bring the bowls back to the couch.

Our relationship doesn't hinge on whether I can make paella or not. All the same, I just want him to like it. All the good things in life happen over food – or at least, they begin there. Nic and I first started hanging out because we both loved eating, and with tonight's meal, I kind of want to remind him why we work so well together. Why we should *be* together. In the past few months, I haven't thought about much else.

He looks down at the mess of paella, and takes a cautious bite.

I search his expression for a hint of a grimace, a sign that he's not enjoying it. He chews it slowly, swallows – then quickly takes another forkful, jamming it into his mouth. I take a bite of my own – and I'm stunned to find that it's actually OK. Not amazing – more Guy Fieri than Ferran Adria – but definitely edible. If you were stuck in the wilderness with only a bowl of my paella to keep you going, you wouldn't be all that mad.

For a minute or so, we eat in surprisingly comfortable silence. Jay Rock is still playing in the background, rapping about how you ain't gotta like it cos the hood gon' love it. I'm about to mention to Nic that I want to go see him at the Coliseum next month when he says, "So you talked to Reggie yet?"

"Hmm?"

"About chef school?"

"Not yet. *But*," I say, when I spot him starting to reply, "I'm planning on talking to her tomorrow, actually. She's heading off to Washington on Thursday."

"To meet with Tanner?" he asks.

"Yeah. Better her than me."

"You think they'll go for it?"

"It's gonna be more of an FYI than a request."

And it is. They can't stop me – what's Tanner going to do, get rid of her prize black-ops asset because the asset wants to learn how to cook like a pro?

All the same, there's asking, and there's asking. If I want Tanner's sign-off with minimal hassle, I need Reggie's first. Reggie is the boss at China Shop. As well as running our little band of losers, she does all the hacking work for us: killing security cameras, opening doors, digging up dirt.

She reports to Moira Tanner, the government spook who founded China Shop. The deal Tanner and I have is that I work for her, and she keeps the government off my back. There are people who really, really want to cut me open and see if they can figure out how I do what I do, and I'd prefer that not to happen. Hence, our arrangement.

Tanner won't exactly be thrilled with me saying I want to train as a chef. Reggie's a sweetheart – seriously, she's awesome – but it's going to take one hell of a job to convince her boss to let me plan a life outside China Shop.

"Anyway, yes, I'm doing it." I fork my paella, mixing it up some more.

"Kind of surprised you haven't done it already."

"What do you mean?"

"They don't know what you do after work, right? Why not just go do . . . I don't know, night school? Something like that."

"I thought about it, but like, that's not . . . It's not sustainable. I don't want it to just be something I'm sneaking away to do. That's not cool."

I've thought a lot about this. Just going ahead and signing up for night cooking classes was tempting, sure . . . but it didn't feel right. There's more to it than I'm willing to tell Nic.

"Sustainable," he says with a mouthful of paella. "Look at you, with the big words."

I kick him. "Close your mouth when you talk."

"How am I supposed to close my mouth when I talk?" He laughs.

"When you *chew*. Fuck you, you know what I mean."

He waves his fork at me, swallows. "I'm glad you're finally asking them, though." He gestures to his bowl. "This is really good, by the way."

"Yeah?" I sit up a little straighter.

"There's like a charred flavor, but I think it works? I'm not just saying that either."

I recover quickly, like it's no big thing. "Cool. There's more if you want."

The awkwardness from before is gone. Soon, we're talking and laughing and giving each other shit like we used to do. He gets a second bowl, dishes up some for me, cracks us a couple more beers. We argue over background music, eventually settling on Lizzo. I'm a little drunk, and not nearly as nervous as I thought I'd be. This feels good. This feels ... *right*.

How can he say no to this? To us? Being with me means dealing with a lot of strange shit, but surely it's all worth it if we get more nights like tonight?

After the chaos with the paella, I'm glad I went simple for dessert. Salted caramel ice cream, from Carmela's in Pasadena. I'm dishing up, my back to the couch, listening to Nic telling a story about a case he and his boss were working on. He can't reveal specific details – attorney-client privilege and all that jazz – but he's got some fun stories nonetheless. " ... And then she realises she's been doodling all over the brief," he says.

"Doodling? What do you mean, doodling?"

"Like actual doodling! While they've been talking. Rocket ships and dinosaurs and weird squiggly letters, not even thinking about it. Just drawing while she talks."

On the table, his phone buzzes. He ignores it.

"The Central Operations Bureau Director for the whole of LA, and now she's got to hand this brief to the opposing—"

Unlike Nic, my phone isn't set respectfully on silent. It bleeps very loudly, cutting him off.

"Shit, sorry," I mutter, reaching across to the table for it.

"No worries. Anyway, then the council goes—hey, what's wrong?"

I frown at my phone. I wanted to put it on silent, but the message on screen caught my eye.

Nic puts his bowl down. "China Shop?"

"No." I open the message up so I can read it properly. "It's an automated warning. Says there's been an earthquake."

"Oh, yeah. They send them out automatically. Probably just a six-pointer, or . . . "

He's trailed off because the room has started to sway. The couch cushion underneath my butt is moving. A couple of glasses dance off the counter, shattering.

"Jesus," I say.

Nic rolls his eyes. "It'll pass. That's California for you."

"Wait – do you hear that?"

"What?"

A rumble. Slow, steady, building. Like a distant train approaching.

I haven't been in LA for all that long – just a couple of years – but I know what a six-point quake feels like. Six points sounds violent, but it really isn't all that bad. This is different. This *sounds* different. And the room is starting to sway a *lot*.

On the coffee table, my beer bottle begins to dance. It tips over, gushing amber. The pans in the kitchen start to rattle. The whole house is shaking now, the rumble getting louder and louder. One of my speakers tips over, wires ripping out of it.

I meet Nic's eyes – and then the rumbling turns up to eleven. It hurls me off the couch – hurls both of us. A shower of paella splatters across me.

"Under the table!" Nic doesn't wait for me to follow instructions. He grabs me, pulls me close to him. The table is way too low to the ground to lie under, but Nic's got some strength to him. He shoves it upwards, pulls us both underneath, holding on tight to the table so it forms a shield over us. I can't help – it's made of wood, and I can hardly get a fix on anything with my PK anyway. The whole apartment is going crazy.

When I'm in danger, and those wonderful fight-or-flight

chemicals start rocketing around my brain, my PK goes super-charged. I'm able to lift much heavier objects, and more of them, than I can normally. My range gets larger. It's definitely happening now – I can feel all the way out to the cars on the street, which are bouncing and rocking on their wheels. But there's nothing I can do with it. It doesn't matter how strong I am; I can't stop an earthquake.

The Big One. It's been talked about for years – the quake to end all quakes, stored up in the San Andreas fault. I don't know if this is it, but if it isn't, then I'm going to move state. Maybe country. This is ... *insane.*

Nic pulls me in tight to him, his big body folding around mine. I don't mind very much. Because of course, I'm having romantic thoughts in the middle of a terrifying earthquake.

It's amazing I can think at all. The noise just gets worse and worse, like a freight train roaring past outside my window. Something in my apartment falls over – the fridge, I think – and Nic grunts, as if it came down right on top of us. There's a smaller crash on the other side of the coffee table, directly over our heads – the ceiling fan coming down.

Nic pulls me closer, holds on tight ...

FIVE

Teagan

If I'm being real, the shaking only lasts about twenty seconds. But that twenty seconds is enough to completely destroy everything in my apartment.

Smashed glass and furniture. Toppled speakers. Scattered food. I blink, and it seems to take as long as the quake did. My ears are ringing.

I try to wiggle out, and Nic squeezes me tight. "Don't. There might be aftershocks."

The world is still. Slowly, the ringing in my ears fades, replaced by distant shouts, sirens, running feet.

Nic makes us wait five minutes before we crawl out. The damage is worse than I thought. My fridge is on its side, food and beer disgorged across my carpet. Every cabinet in the kitchen has spilled its guts. My speakers, my records, my books ... it looks like a giant toddler had a temper tantrum. Worst of all is the crack. It zig-zags up my living room wall, winds its way across the ceiling.

The blood rushes to my head. Nic has to put out a hand to steady me. "Easy." He's got a haunted look in his eyes, and his hands are shaking ever so slightly. "Where's your gas?"

"My . . . what?"

"Your gas. We have to turn it off. Fire."

"I don't have gas." Is that true? I think so – my stove burners are electric. But what if . . . Fuck, I don't know. This is going to make one hell of an insurance claim. Shit – insurance. Did I even get renter's insurance? I can't remember . . .

Nic accepts my gas explanation with a distracted nod. For a long moment, we both stand in my wrecked living room, looking around. Outside, the noise has gotten worse.

"Let's go look," I say, heading for the door. It's still an effort to put one foot in front of the other.

My apartment is at the back of an existing property, the street reached through a short passageway. My landlord and his family are on vacation, but they're going to have to cut it short. The outer walls of their house are cracked, like the inside of mine. A lawnmower lies overturned in the back yard, blade still turning, and pots lie smashed, bleeding soil. Fat, icy drops of rain speckle my shoulders – the drizzle has picked up, a cold wind whipping it back and forth.

When I reach the sidewalk, I come to a dead stop.

"Definitely not a six-pointer," I murmur.

It's like a street party for the end of the world. Everyone is out: standing in small groups, sitting cross-legged on the pavement. The road surface is a wreck – not just cracked, but *shattered*, like glass. Parts of it have been forced upward, as if tree roots were pushing from underneath.

Roxton Avenue used to be lined with jacaranda trees every few feet; several of them have toppled, their roots ripped up. Harry, a homeless guy I know from around the neighbourhood, is on the far curb. Wide, shocked eyes over an unkempt beard. His cart with its cans and black bags lies scattered across the tarmac.

Amazingly, the houses are still standing. Or not so amazingly – they're made of wood, and I think I read somewhere once that wood does better in a quake. It bends, instead of breaking. But they're in bad shape, several leaning to one side. One is actually on fire, spewing dark smoke into the sky. The groups of people trying to fight the flames don't appear to know what do, yelling confused instructions at each other and frantically tapping at their phones. All across the street, power lines are down – there's a ripped wire fifty yards away from us. It's not jumping, like you see in the movies, but every few seconds it emits a flash of blue sparks.

"Are the cops coming?" someone shouts from behind us. They're gone before we turn around, racing down the street.

I feel sick. Because it's not just Leimert Park, my neighbourhood, that got hit. There's distant smoke on the horizon, everywhere I look.

Nic points. "Oh, shit."

A hundred yards away, a grey Prius has plowed right into a jacaranda tree. The hood has been bent in two by the trunk, smoke gushing from the engine. The wheels are cocked at odd angles, bowed outward; the high-beams are still on. Other cars have stopped at random on the street, as if they too swerved to a halt once the quake hit.

Nic starts running towards the wrecked car. "Wait!" I yell after him.

He ignores me. And he's got long legs, so it takes me a minute to catch up with him. He's at the edge of the wreckage, pulling at the door, his shirt starting to soak through from the drizzle. My stomach gives a sick wrench – there are two people inside the car. An unconscious man, slumped over the steering wheel, blood matting his long black hair. And a kid. A teenage boy, thirteen or fourteen, blinking out from the passenger seat.

Nic can't get the door open. The impact has crunched it shut. It's the same thing on the other side, where two people – a burly guy who looks like a construction worker, and a woman in a business suit – are trying to haul it open. The black smoke from the ruined engine is getting worse, and there's the very first flicker of flame.

An ambulance shoots past the intersection, siren wailing, swerving to avoid a rucked-up section of the road. It doesn't slow, not even when the construction worker sprints off to flag it down.

"Teagan."

Nic has stepped away from the car. He puts his hands on his knees, hangs his head for a second. But when he looks back up, there's steel in his eyes. He wipes his mouth, then spits, dirty saliva arcing through the air. "I need your help. We gotta take the door off."

"I don't—"

"It's jammed shut. Can you lift it? I'm going to need you to . . . Teagan, look at me. We have to get them out, right now."

I can't move.

It's not just the shock of the quake. It's what he's asking.

He's asking me to use my ability in front of other people.

It's the one thing I am absolutely not supposed to do. Not ever. It's Tanner's big golden rule, part of the deal I have with her. Break it, and she steps aside, letting the government have me. It's a rule I've had to break before, and it's only through sheer dumb luck and circumstance that I survived the first time. Doing it here, in front of all these people . . .

But hang on. Hang on one goddamn second. I don't have to make it obvious. I don't have to float shit through the air.

All I have to do is snap the hinges. Tweak the frame a little, so the door can pop out. It's nothing. I can do it in about three seconds.

Except . . .

What if I mess it up?

What if someone sees? Or figures it out? If that happens, China Shop goes away. I'll lose everything. The life I've created here – gone.

"Teagan, are you hearing me?" Nic grabs my shoulder. "You gotta help us."

My whole life stretches in front of me. Nic. Cooking school. Los Angeles. China Shop.

No. Fuck that. Fuck it right in the ass. I'm not just going to stand by when I could help.

But that's exactly what I do. I don't move. I stare at the car, my breath coming way too fast. The more I tell myself not to be ridiculous, that I can help out without revealing my ability, the harder it becomes to do it.

"What's wrong with you?" Nic says, desperation edging his voice.

At that moment, the teenager groans – a horrifying, agonised sound. Nic shakes his head, staring at me in disbelief, then turns to help. There are more people now, at least six. They surround the car, Nic directing operations, telling them where to grab hold. He doesn't look at me. The smoke is gushing now, swamping the body of the car, flames licking at the paintwork. Nic and the others have to step away, coughing, yanking clothing over their mouths before plunging back in. The boy is hammering on the windows.

And while all this is going on, I stand frozen, terrified, unable to move a goddamn muscle.

Finally, after what seems like hours, I kick myself into gear.

Exposure be damned. There are people in that car, and if I don't start helping, they're dead.

But as I refocus my PK, getting ready to lift, they manage to move the door. It comes loose with a grinding squeal of metal, so suddenly that Nic actually stumbles backwards. Hands reach into the gap, dragging the man and the boy out. The kid's left leg is a bloody ruin, the man unconscious.

"I can help," I say. Nobody hears me.

Then we're being hustled away from the burning car, stumbling across the wrecked street. I lose track of the injured man and his kid, spinning in place, hunting for something I can lift, burning with shame and wanting to fix it.

But all the other buildings are wood, and they've managed to stay upright. There are downed power lines, but nobody's trapped underneath them. I don't see any more burning cars.

I sit down heavily on the curb, my head swimming. The oddest thought: *You didn't put enough liquid in your rice. That's why the paella burned.*

I don't know how long I sit there for. When I look up, Nic is huddled with another group of people, clustered around a phone. The man who owns it flicks his finger rapidly, scrolling. The woman on his right is the one in the business suit, the one from before who was helping Nic out with the car. She's wearing a lone red stiletto, and is staring in horror at the phone screen, hand over her mouth.

Nic stands with his arms folded, a grim expression on his face. When I make my way over to him, he gives me an utterly blank look. Like he doesn't know who I am.

"Nic?"

"What?"

"What is it? Is everything . . . ?"

The rain has picked up even more – I hadn't realised it, but I'm soaked through, my hands patterned with grime.

"San Bernardino," Nic says. It's a spot to the east of LA, near Riverside. Around here they call that area the Inland Empire, although I don't know why.

"I don't understand . . ."

"It's gone." His voice is as dull as his gaze. "Wiped out."

SIX

Teagan

Nobody can make any calls. The lines are jammed. Amazingly, some of the networks still have data – slow-as-shit data, but it's working. It's how we found out about San Bernardino.

A man I don't know – a dude wearing horn-rimmed glasses and a ponytail who looks about a thousand years old – explains to anyone who will listen that every time a quake increases by a single point, it releases thirty-two times as much energy as before. It's from him that we find out the quake was actually a 7.1.

"Seismic events this big are actually quite rare," he says. He sounds like the preachers you sometimes get outside malls. "You might only get twenty a year worldwide. We had one in Ridgecrest last year, but that wasn't nearly as bad as Northridge in '94. Hoo-ee! That was a bad one. Although there was a 3.3 in 2014 where one person died . . ."

His eyes shine as he talks about orders of magnitude and Richter scales and seismic events. After a while, he goes off to talk to someone else.

There's surprisingly little to do. If the quake had happened during fire season in October, with the Santa Ana winds kicking up, we would be well and truly fucked. But it's the middle of winter now – or what passes for winter in LA, anyway. The rain keeps the few fires on my street under control, and after an ambulance finally arrives to treat the two people from the car, we all end up just standing around. The streetlights don't come on – power is down across the city, apparently – but people turn their headlights on, bathing the street in a yellow, rain-flecked glow.

Harry is pushing his cart of bags and bottles down the sidewalk like nothing has happened. Chunks of broken concrete are everywhere, cracks zigzagging, but he just moves his cart around them. When I ask him if he's OK, I get a vague smile, and he waves me away. He's never said a word to me, not one, although I don't know if it's because he prefers not to talk, or if he's actually mute.

I lose Nic for a while. It's full dark before I find him, sitting on the hood of a car, scrolling through his phone. He has an old Clippers hoodie on over his T-shirt – I have no idea who gave it to him.

I slide in next to him. "Hey."

He looks up. Back down.

"I'm really sorry about before," I say quietly. "I didn't how to help, and then you had the door off, and . . . I was just scared, that's all."

"Don't worry about it."

I don't know what to say to that. There's nothing I *can* say.

"You check in with your Mom and Dad?" I try, after a few moments.

"What? Oh. Yeah, they're fine. Pico Rivera's about the same as here. No power, but the buildings're all up to code, so . . . "

It's not hard to fill in the gaps. The neighbourhood around us has taken a hit – plenty of cracks in the street, the odd fire, downed power lines. But as scary as it seemed at first, it's not a killing blow. It's damage that can be repaired, that can be worked around. From the few conversations I've had with neighbours, it seems like most of LA is the same. Hit ... but not all that hard.

Can't say the same for San Bernardino. Something went wrong there. Buildings that weren't up to code. Misplaced funds. Apparently it's been a problem for years. I guess it finally caught up with them.

"A few of us were talking," Nic says, as if sensing my thoughts. "We're going out to San Bern, see if we can help. I don't know what's going on with you, but we could use you there."

I pull out my own phone. I found it when I went back into my house earlier – through some weird miracle, it was still on the kitchen counter, about the only thing that didn't get thrown around my living room. There are a bunch of messages on the China Shop group chat. Reggie, asking whether everyone is OK. Paul, wanting to know the power status of everyone's neighbourhoods, warning us about aftershocks, demanding we check in hourly. Annie, sending picture after picture of Watts, her neighbourhood, including a shot of a weird scaffolding-sculpture-artwork thing. She sends three thumbs-ups afterwards, so I assume it's important.

Those aren't the messages I'm after though. The one I show Nic is from a contact labelled HAIL SATAN. It simply says, *Do not go near San Bernardino. Stay within the city limits.*

"Tanner?"

"Uh-huh."

He lets out a low breath. "The people in SB were right near the epicentre, and it just ... They're saying there's over two hundred dead."

"Jesus."

"Yeah. You in or not?"

He tries to make it sound casual, but his voice is tight.

"I can't," I say softly.

"Can't? Or won't?"

"Nic . . ."

"Help me understand, Teags."

"If Tanner sees me, on the news or whatever, then who knows what she'll do? Even if I just use my abilities a little . . ."

"So you could help save a bunch of people, but you're not going to do it because your *boss* might be watching?"

"That's not fair. You know that's not fair."

"You don't have to throw shit around – just put a little of your . . . your PK or whatever it is into the heavy stuff. She won't even know."

"She will."

He mutters something.

"What?"

"Nothing." He won't look at me.

I just stare at him. When he does meet my eyes, the careful blankness in them is like a physical thing. Diamond-hard, edges sharp enough to draw blood.

"Come on," I say. "Don't be like that."

He pushes himself off the car. "You've got a couple hundred dead, who knows how many injured and a situation where you might actually be able to do some good. Then you've got your job, your life and your fucking boss. It's . . . it's *amazing* to me that you haven't figured out what's more important."

"You think I don't *want* to help those people? I do. It's just . . ."

"What? Just what, Teagan?" He digs the heel of one hand into his right eye. "Fuck it. They need people out in SB, and I don't have time to stand here arguing with you about this. You change your mind, you come find us."

"Nic, wait."

But he's gone.

I sit there, in the rain, listening to distant sirens. Thinking of a million things I could have said. I should have made him apologise, say he was wrong, get him to admit that it's more complicated than he thinks it is.

But Nic's a lawyer. He *lives* complicated. If it was this simple for him, then what does it mean for me?

If I went out to San Bernardino, and Tanner saw me, everything would be over. Any good I'd be able to do in the future, any bad guys I could take down through China Shop . . . all that would vanish.

Two hundred dead.

I hang my head, knuckles white on the edge of the car hood. Maybe I might be able to help somewhere, lift the guilt that has settled on me like a heavy blanket. But there's nothing for me to do here. There are no more people trapped under rubble. The fires are out – at least from what I can see. Maybe I should hop into the Batmobile – my black Jeep, still parked up the street from my house – and cruise around. But where would I go? What would I look for? And what if I accidentally *do* reveal my ability? The thoughts paralyse me, lock my feet to the ground, just like before.

"Did you know the San Andreas fault maxes out at 8.3?"

I didn't see the earthquake preacher come up behind me, but he's in full flow. "It doesn't have the capacity to store more energy than that. Not like Cascadia – hoo boy, if that ever goes, we are really in trouble. Well, I say *we*, but it's more like everybody in Oregon and Washington. We probably don't have to worry too much. And people think quakes like these relieve pressure on the fault lines, but actually—"

"Dude."

"—it's only a ten-thousandth of the total—"

"Dude."

" . . . Yes?"

My mouth can't decide between *Go fuck yourself* and *Stick your dick in a blender*, so what comes out is, "Go fuck your dick in a blender."

Not my strongest comeback, I know. He gawps at me as I trudge back to my house.

The power's still out. The ambient light from outside my windows just barely makes things visible. I sit in the dark, eating direct from the tub of salted caramel ice cream. It was on its side on the floor when I came in, but in a rare moment of clarity, I'd put the lid back on after I'd finished serving us. It's mostly melted by now, but fuck it. Maybe this is how the night was always going to end: sitting in the dark, alone, eating a tub of ice cream.

It's not the quake. Nic just used that as an excuse. He doesn't want to be with you.

It's a nasty thought. Poisonous. And utter bullshit – because really, how self-absorbed do I have to be to put my own hang-ups over a goddamn earthquake? But that's the thing about poisonous thoughts. Sometimes, you can't stop yourself taking another bite. I follow this one all the way to its conclusion, relishing the bitter taste. I don't know why I thought I could pull off tonight. Did I really think I was going to win him back using . . . what, some stupid fucking Spanish rice?

My phone buzzes – a text from Reggie. *Glad all safe. Most roads and freeways unaffected AFAIK. Would like to see everybody at office tomorrow 9 sharp. Biz as usual!!!*

"Biz as usual," I murmur.

I sit in the dark for a long time.

SEVEN

Amber

Amber tries to light her second cigarette. Can't do it. Her hands are shaking too hard.

She takes a deep breath, tries to steady them. She's already dropped the first smoke, which spiralled away into the dark motel parking lot below the balcony, vanishing from sight. They're not hard up for cash – Ajay took care of them – but it wouldn't be a good idea to waste what they have. That would bring nothing but trouble.

It's full dark. In the room behind Amber, Matthew is asleep. Finally. Passed out on the mussed-up covers, the iPad still propped on his chest.

A fault line. That's what it was called. He'd looked it up afterwards, when they were back in the car, feverishly scanning the internet to find out more about what he just did. In the stunned moments following the earthquake, Amber had wondered why it had never happened before – why Matthew had never come across another fault line. None in New Mexico, she supposed. Until a few days ago, neither of them had ever left the state, a state where they were still known as Diamond and Lucas Taylor, instead of Amber-Leigh and

Matthew Schenke. The new names are more of a mouthful, harder to remember, which was probably Ajay's intention when he made up their new IDs.

Still, the new names had stuck. Then again, who is she kidding? Lucas (*Matthew*, she reminds herself) had insisted on sticking to them. Amber had called him by his birth name just the once, a few hours after they'd left Albuquerque, and he ... he'd ... been angry with her.

Distracted, she lets the lit cigarette fall from her lips. It tumbles off the balcony, the wind catching it, blowing it out of sight. She doesn't move to light another one, has already forgotten it. She can't stop thinking about the moments after the quake.

When the shaking started, he'd cocooned them in a sphere of earth – sealed them in a protective barrier. The terror Amber had felt was unbelievable, holding her in a vice-like grip. Trapped in the dark, the thick air choking her, Matthew cackling with glee as the world roared outside. And afterwards, when he opened the cocoon ...

The gas station building was gone. Collapsed in on itself. One wall remained standing, steel bars sticking up like flag-poles. The awning above the pumps had wrenched loose off its supports, tilted to one side like a ramp, the big Chevron sign hanging by no more than a few shreds of metal. A puddle was spreading out from the pumps, the air above it shimmering. Propane containers rolled loose, their cage torn open. The man who had been filling them was dead. Crushed. The sky above was dark and thunderous, and chill wind had picked up, raising the hairs on Amber's arms.

The ground was different. Not torn or broken up; it was if it had been rearranged while her back was turned. There were mounds and bumps where there were none before, small depressions, the earth caving in on itself. The gas station's concrete apron was cracked and pitted.

Matthew had started laughing.

It was the delighted laugh of a child discovering a new toy. He'd spun in fast circles, as if he didn't know where to look. Hands up to his face, palms plastered against his cheeks. It reminded Amber of a game she used to play with him, when he was very little, before he started to show signs of being different. She'd puff out her cheeks, pretend to squeeze the air out with her hands, and he'd giggle until he was out of breath.

The light hadn't changed, the ground bathed in bright sun even though the sky was dark with clouds. Inside the destroyed building, a woman was wailing.

As she started to grasp what he'd done, Amber had felt the bottom drop out of her stomach. Matthew could move anything natural – wood, leaves, grass – but only a little. Soil, though? Earth and dirt? That was no problem for him. Sometimes, she'd daydream about what it would be like if he wasn't the way he was. If he was ... good. How they'd buy a little plot of land, create a garden, moving earth from place to place like it was lighter than air.

She had no idea he could do what he did this afternoon. That was something else.

"It's a connection," he'd told her breathlessly. "There's all this stored energy. I could connect right to it, and let it go. Amber –" he hadn't called her *Mom* in over a year "– it was amazing!" She'd never seen him so happy. His whole face was one huge, bright smile.

Their pickup truck was toast. On its side, axles dented and smashed, one wheel still spinning. Broken glass, picking up the light like uncut diamonds. They found another vehicle around the side of the building – a second pickup, a much bigger one, battered and ancient but somehow miraculously still upright. They had to smash the window to get in, but at least starting it was no problem. The truck was old, which was good – easier to hotwire. She'd done it in a daze, barely aware of what her hands were doing. Amber hadn't boosted a car in a long time, but it was amazing how quickly it came back to her.

The road was a ruin, the tarmac folded and cracked like the icing on a cake. Amber had worried they wouldn't be able to drive, but the pickup had a high wheel-base, and it managed the broken tarmac without an issue.

It took them a good few hours to reach San Bernardino.

Or what was left of it.

They'd been turned back a mile or two from the city, the road blocked by emergency services. Matthew had gaped at the broken buildings on the skyline, at the pall of smoke that was almost blacker than the clouds above them. It had to started to rain – fat, icy drops thudding against the windshield. It was like the end of the world.

"What happened?" Matthew said to the first fire marshal, as soon as Amber rolled down the window. His face was completely innocent, his voice curious. He was good at that.

"Earthquake." The marshal bellowed over his shoulder at an unseen colleague: "Sixteen! I said sixteen!" He turned back. "Sorry – you can't get into the city."

"Did people die?" Matthew said.

The marshal gave him a fleeting look, as if seeing him for the first time. "Go around over there," he said to Amber, pointing. "That'll put you on the freeway south, OK?" Then he was gone.

He did that, she had thought, staring at the horizon. *Matthew. And no one will ever know.*

They'd been directed towards San Jacinto, which the marshals told them was still fine. It took them more than three hours to get there, the new pickup almost out of gas by the time they reached the city limits. For the first part of the drive, Matthew had been almost incoherent with excitement. He was jumping between screens on the iPad, reports and Twitter feeds and pictures. The occasional loud blast of news footage. Matthew kept the volume on high, and several times, it made Amber jump.

The answer to the question he'd asked the marshal came quickly: two hundred dead, maybe more. She expected Matthew to squeal in delight, even laugh – that's what normally happened when he hurt people. But instead, he went strangely quiet. As if even he was having trouble processing the number.

He's in the motel room behind her. He roused briefly to eat half of one of the cheeseburgers she'd gotten them from a Burger King near the motel, and had tried to do some more reading on the iPad. When he started talking again, it was almost to himself.

"I shouldn't have been able to do it," he'd said. "The fault was way too far underground. It was like it was calling to me though . . . Hey, do you think there'll be aftershocks?"

"I'm not sure, honey," she'd said carefully. It felt someone else was speaking through her, controlling her mouth. "Are those . . . That's when there are little smaller quakes, right?"

He'd glanced at her, as if slightly surprised that she'd spoken. Then he'd smiled, just a quick one, his eyes brightening. Amber had felt a hot, guilty rush of pleasure.

"That's right," he'd said. "They happen when an earthquake changes the stresses on a fault, and some more sections let go. I was reading about it. I knew about earthquakes of course, and

I knew they happened a lot in California, but I never thought I'd be able to actually *make* them."

He kept trying to stifle yawns, and failing, and he'd spent longer and longer looking at the same page on the iPad. Soon, he'd fallen asleep, the tablet on the pillow and the burger wrapper trapped under one bare foot.

She'd looked at him, wanting to reach out and stroke his hair, a muscle memory she couldn't excise. Her delight at how he'd smiled at her hadn't faded. She tucked it away, deep in her mind. It didn't matter *what* he was smiling about – just that he was smiling.

She fumbles with another cigarette, but her hands are shaking too hard to light it. This time, she has to bite her lower lip to stop the shakes, using the pain to make them quiet down.

She hasn't had to do that for a while. Not since the time one of her marks turned out to be a cop, and she had to make a run for it. He'd chased her for what felt like ten blocks. By the time she finally lost him, she was so terrified that biting her lip was the only way she could calm herself down.

The con usually worked flawlessly: the old Flop trick, with a twist. She could fake a convincing hit really well – she had a knack for picking the right moment, choosing an angle where the hit from the oncoming car would leave her uninjured. Amateurs stopped there, hoping to scare the driver into paying up to avoid court. Not her. Diamond Taylor was smarter than that. Instead of pretending to be hurt, she'd tell the startled driver she was fine – shaken, sure, but all good, sir, don't you fret. Only, the collision had smashed her iPad. She'd hold it up, distraught. *Goddamnit, it's for work, they're going to kill me . . .*

Usually, that was all it took for some money to change hands. Sometimes she threw in another wrinkle, refusing to take payment, saying it was all right, it was her fault anyway.

At which point, a nearby pedestrian would march over, say he'd seen everything, accuse the driver of negligence, threaten to call the cops, trying to convince her to sue.

Later, she and the pedestrian would split the cash.

A good con involved seeing the angles – adjusting a plan on the fly, always looking for the next mark. Amber's problem was that her ability to see the angles only went so far. There never seemed to be enough money, and it never seemed to last as long as it should. The big plans she'd had and the larger cons she wanted to run never quite came together.

It wasn't like she didn't *try*. She'd known she'd have to get out of the game sooner or later – you couldn't work the same cons in the same city for your entire life. She tried to read as many self-help books as she could, getting them from the only library that was near her little shithole apartment in Barelas. She'd read them all: *The 7 Habits of Highly Effective People*. *Awaken the Giant Within*. *As A Man Thinketh* (Almost hadn't picked up that one – what most men think didn't amount to much – but it was pretty good). And of course, *Think and Grow Rich!*

It all seemed so smart when it was written down on paper. But she could never quite work out how to apply it to her life, how to break out of the endless cycle of tiny, piss-bucket cons.

And then she got pregnant.

She'd always dreamed about having a baby. But it had been something for later, not when she was running around in Albuquerque trying to make a buck. She'd forgotten her pills, or run out, she can't remember, and that had been that. The guy she was seeing at the time, Wade, had taken the news like a hammer blow. He was gone the next day, and she wasn't the least bit surprised. She didn't even bother looking for him.

Well, fuck Wade, and fuck everyone else. She could find an

angle in a con, and she can find an angle now, no matter how bad her hands are shaking. All she has to do is think.

It isn't Matthew's fault, what happened with the quake. It *isn't*. You can't blame a little kid for wanting to explore the world. And even if he really did mean to hurt people – she acknowledges this grudgingly, as if it's an unwelcome visitor asking for food and a spot to crash – so what? Just because he's super smart or whatever doesn't mean he understands what he's doing. He's *four*, for God's sake. She can't just yell at him, or turn him into the cops – like they'd even believe her! Anyway this is on her as much as it's on him.

She may not have given Matthew his powers – the people at the School did that, even if they didn't know exactly what those powers were going to be. She wasn't the one who killed the highway patrolman, or the ones before him, and she didn't set off the San Andreas fault line. And yet, she's done nothing to stop it. She's responsible. If she'd been a better mother ... if she'd just gotten food for the car, or ... Well, she couldn't have done anything about the patrolman and Matthew sitting in the front seat, but ...

And that's the angle. Right there. That's how she controls the situation. She doesn't give up on her boy. She'll never abandon him, no matter what he's done. He won't stay four for ever. The tantrums, and the times when he hurts her ... they'll stop. Whatever he is now, he can change. She can do what a mom is supposed to do: steer him, teach him. Protect him. *Be better.*

Her hands have finally stopped shaking. She takes a drag, turns – and Matthew is standing right behind her.

Amber yelps, taking a step backward. "Sweetie, you scared me."

"What are you doing?" he says. He's barefoot, wearing

pyjama pants and the same balloon T-shirt from earlier. His eyes are as blank as deep space. "You weren't there when I woke up."

The old terror grows in her chest, familiar as breathing. She reminds herself that he's her son, and she's his mom, and she shouldn't be scared of him. Even in her head, the words sound very small.

Suddenly he yawns. A huge, python stretch. He actually shivers after it ends. His shoulders relax, and he gazes out into the rain.

"You need to drive me somewhere tomorrow," he says.

"OK?"

"The Meitzen Museum. 803 Exposition Park Drive, Los Angeles, California 90037. 10 a.m. to 5 p.m."

"What's . . . ?" She clears her throat. "What's there, sweetie?"

He rubs his nose. "The burger's cold. I want another one."

" . . . It's late. I don't know if they're open, so—"

"They are. I looked." He pads past her, still barefoot, then looks back at her quizzically. "Come on."

EIGHT

Teagan

As I reach our office in Venice Beach, the morning after the quake, I take the time to ponder a potent metaphysical question: how bad would it be if I just turned around and went home and pulled the blankets over my head and kept them there until the heat death of the universe?

But of course, I know what would happen. Paul and Reggie would send Annie to get me, which would make Annie even more pissed than usual.

I take a sip of my coffee – a takeaway one, my third today. At least LA looked OK this morning. Mostly. Reggie was right: biz as usual. Freeways still upright, most buildings still standing, fires mostly contained. It's not what you'd call a regular day, and I definitely saw plenty of damage on the way over here – cracked roads, fallen signs and billboards, the odd downed power line. But people were still going to work. Most of the buildings in LA, it seems, have been brought up to code. It's a relief, I guess. Knowing we can take a hit, and keep on trucking.

Can't say the same for San Bernardino.

I'm still trying to process it. It *should* be a gut punch. It's part of Greater Los Angeles, and having it fall should be ... awful. But I've only been to the place a few times. I don't know anyone there. I feel the same way about it as I would about a disaster in Djibouti, or the Ukraine. Which makes *me* feel like kind of a class-A douche-nozzle, because this is my city. But it's not as if there's someone to blame. Earthquakes aren't anybody's fault. You can't swear revenge on a tectonic plate.

I must have sent Nic a dozen texts. I'm still mad at him for what he said, but I also want to make sure he's OK, after he headed out to SB. In some way, I was hoping he'd call me, and we could talk. I've gotten exactly one text from him: *We're fine. Helping at emergency shelter.* That made me feel even worse. I told myself I should go out there, fuck what Tanner said. But of course, I didn't.

It's not raining any more, but it was when I woke up, and the air is sharp and chilly. I take another slug of coffee, promise to exact bloody revenge on the people who decided 9 a.m. was an acceptable time to start work and push open the door to Paul's Boutique.

It's a small wood-frame house in Venice Beach, a few blocks from the ocean. On a clear day, you can sit on the roof and drink a beer and watch the sun sink into the Pacific, the scent of surf wax and weed on the breeze. We work out of the ground floor. I named the office Paul's Boutique after I went on a month-long Beastie Boys jag. Of course, our own Paul accused me of being immature and not taking the operation seriously, but then, he can be a *genuine* class-A douche-nozzle.

"Look at this mess," he's saying when I walk inside. The ground floor of the Boutique is a big open-plan living area, and Paul is on his knees in the middle of the floor, sorting through a pile of paper and stationery and thumbtacks and overturned coffee mugs.

Paul is in his forties, balding, with a paunch and horn-rimmed glasses. His desk is still upright, but it's been knocked out of position, and the whiteboard he uses to plan our jobs lies flat on the floor. The L-shaped leather couch has been jolted away from the wall.

"Teagan," he says, waving me over. "Great. You can help me clean this up."

Before I can answer him, a thought whacks me upside the head — one I should have had a long time ago. "Reggie! Is she—?"

"She's fine," Paul says. "Monitors and towers were bolted to the wall." He nods towards Reggie's door. "She's in there."

"Hoo boy. OK. Cool."

"Now come on." He gestures to the mess. "Time's a-wasting."

He is way too chipper for this early in the a.m. Then again, he's a former Navy quartermaster. They're used to getting up at sparrow's fart.

My foot crunches down on glass. "Back up," says Annie Cruz, leading with a broom, hustling me backwards. Jesus, I didn't even see her there.

The kitchen is trashed, cabinet doors yawning, plates scattered across the floor. The ridiculous ornamental mirror that hangs above the couch lies in pieces. The fridge has danced away from the wall, and Annie has to squeeze past it to get at the glass I stepped on. Fortunately, she's thin enough. Annie is tall and willowy, built like a gymnast, if a gymnast could kill a person at ten paces with a single raised eyebrow.

"Don't just stand there," Annie says, stabbing at the floor with her broom. "Grab a sweeper. Help out."

"Sweeper?"

"You know what I mean. Come on, man, let's go."

I raise an eyebrow, then pull all the debris towards me with my PK. Annie steps backwards, startled, as I collect the glass and crockery in a large ball. I float it over to the giant trash can they hauled in from the garage, and drop it inside.

"I keep forgetting you can do that," Annie says.

"You're welcome." I take another sip of coffee. "Any major damage? Beyond a few plates and shit?"

"Trash cans round back are all over the place. Hey, what's with the get-up?"

"What get-up?"

"Your get-up." She waves a hand at me. "You look different."

Right. The get-up she's referring to is an actual collared shirt – a white one, the only one I actually own, and which I've only worn about once before. I don't even remember where it came from. I've paired it with the second-smartest thing I own, a pair of khaki slacks. I even made sure to put on a little more make-up than usual. If I was the kind of person who owned a pencil skirt, I'd probably be rocking that too.

I give a twirl, showing off. Maybe if I pretend I'm in a good mood, it'll trick my brain into actually doing it. "You like?" I look at Annie over my shoulder, pull a duck face.

I'm expecting her to make a crack. Instead, she tilts her head, looking me up and down. "Eh. Suits you."

I blink, surprised. "Thanks."

"No problem."

"Also, I see what you did there."

"What?"

"Suits you? As in a suit? Cos . . . never mind."

Normally, I'd take a huge swerve around an outfit like this.

But today is Good Impressions Day. It's all part of the plan, for when I ask Reggie to ask Tanner if I could do some pro-cooking school. I certainly wasn't planning on getting a compliment from Annie, but fuck it. You take 'em when you get 'em.

"Hey, can you help me with these papers?" Paul says.

"Can't. They're organic."

"I meant by using your hands, Teagan. Like the rest of us mere mortals."

"Nah. I don't know what order you want them in. I might mess up your system."

Paul frowns. "It's messed up anyway. If you—"

"She's just fucking with you, babe," Annie says, giving me a meaningful look.

"That's OK," Paul grumbles. "I think I got it."

"Hold on, white boy, I'm coming." She props the broom against the counter.

"Are you sure? I don't want you to hurt the baby."

I'm halfway through swallowing, and nearly choke to death on hot coffee. "I'm sorry, what?"

Then I see the look on Paul's face. "Oh. Ha ha. Hysterical."

He turns back to his papers, grinning. "You're not the only one who can mess with people."

"You *really* need to work on your jokes."

"For once, she's right." Annie cuffs Paul on the back of the head. "You joke about that again, we gonna have a problem."

"I'm sorry. You're right. I *don't* want to have a baby with you."

Annie rolls her eyes, dropping to her knees to help. She slowly brushes her hand across his shoulders as she does so – a gesture I'm not even sure she's aware of. When she gets to his level, he plants a quick kiss on her forehead, murmurs something in her ear.

I will never understand how Annie and Paul got together. Not in a billion years. The tight-ass, white-bread Navy quartermaster and the former gangster from Watts. Then again, maybe Paul's tight ass *did* have something to do with it – I wouldn't know, I haven't ever seen him naked, thank God, but . . .

I shudder. There are things that one should never have to imagine, and our logistics man's naked butt is one of them.

Anyway, they've been together for a few months now, and if anything they are *more* disgusting than they were when they started. They've also relaxed a little. Paul has gotten less uptight – not a lot, but some – and I may or may not have been unfair when I said that Annie's default setting is angry. Mildly irked, maybe.

She's definitely loosened up around me. We've been through a lot together in the last few months. What can I say – police chases and murder plots and stand-offs with black ops teams have a way of bringing coworkers together. And she is probably just as essential to China Shop as I am, with her ridiculous network of connections across LA. Annie's Army, we call them. If you need a security pass, a camera tilted out of whack a little or info on how the mayor likes his coffee, you ask Annie. She'll ask a few people, and have an answer in about twenty minutes.

I bring myself back. "Tell me the coffee machine made it through the—"

"*Teggan!*"

In the next instant, I'm swept off the ground, squeezed from behind by two enormous arms. My coffee cup goes flying, the contents spattering across the counter.

I manage to force words out. "Can't . . . breathe . . ."

From behind me, Africa lets loose a gust of laughter, gives one squeeze for luck and releases. Then he spins me around, huge hands gripping my shoulders, looking me up and down. Like he's checking for damage. I'm surprised when he doesn't find any.

"You *dëma*," he says. "You made it out the shaking! I thought maybe something fall on you. You so small, they never find you."

Africa is Senegalese, seven feet tall, with a voice that can travel for miles on a clear day, and I was kind of hoping he'd decide to stay home. He's wearing orange sweatpants so vivid they should be banned under international law. On top, he has a purple-and-gold Lakers starter jacket that looks like it last saw action when Magic Johnson was playing. On his feet, pristine Timberlands, the suede clean and crisp.

He smashes a fist into an open palm, the sound like a thunder clap. "I was at Home Depot with Jeannette. I was buying jars for my kitchen, and everything started falling everywhere. We have to hide in the checkout."

"Yo," I say. "You spilled my coffee."

"Oh!" His eyebrows shoot up, and he thunders past me, grabbing a wad of paper towels, slamming them down on the counter. "OK, I fix. No problems."

Here's another fun story. A few months ago, I was on the run after being framed for murder. Africa – real name Idriss Kouamé – was a homeless dude who hung around the area the poor bastard died in.

Actually, calling Africa a homeless dude was selling him short. Less homeless, more dude. He was a guy who knew a guy, a man with a million stories, a hardened survivor of downtown LA and a thousand other places across the world.

No joke: if he hadn't helped me out, I'd be strapped to a table at a government black site right now. I managed to clear my name, but not before Carlos betrayed me.

After the shit-show that led to Carlos's death, I thought Tanner would fill his spot with someone safe. A spec ops guy, a CIA agent, another bureaucrat to keep us in line. I jokingly suggested we should hire Africa, and was – how can I put this? – a little surprised when Reggie and Annie actually took me seriously.

Their argument? That he was unconventional, and that our job required unconventional thinking. He knew a shit-ton of people in LA – not as many as Annie, it's true, but he still has plenty of useful contacts that she doesn't. He can drive – amazingly, the big lunk has a current licence. He's also huge, and good at looking scary when he has to.

For once, I was the voice of reason. Africa was cool, and I owed him big time, but I did *not* think he'd be a good fit. I was worried he was going to do something stupid – try and sell us out, or tell someone about my ability. And when *I* am worried about a person doing something stupid, that's when the red flags start going up.

I told the guys they didn't know him like I did; I loved him to pieces and I had his back, but I also wasn't going to put him in a position where he could hurt us. It would be like making Lil Wayne the US ambassador to Germany.

I was overruled. Tanner and Reggie bought him dinner, and the next thing I knew, I had a new teammate.

I'd forgotten how our boss operates, of course. I should have seen it coming. Tanner could, in fact, get Lil Wayne to be an upstanding and respected diplomat – if she actually knew who Lil Wayne was. It's not just unconventional thinking she likes. She likes leverage. She likes getting people to act against their own self-interest, usually by holding something over them.

In my case, it's her protection against those in the government who want to cut me open and take out the important parts. Paul has a ton of debt he can't get out from under, and Annie has a criminal record that would make her unemployed for the rest of her life. I don't know what secrets Africa has, but they're ones he wants kept that way. He emerged from the meeting with Tanner ashen-faced, shaking his enormous head, muttering Senegalese swear words.

Tanner had briefed him on my ability, and when I showed him – dancing a coffee cup through the air – he didn't even flinch. Just grinned, and called me a *dëma*. A witch. Only he could turn a word like that into a term of endearment. Then he told us a long story about how he once knew a woman in Mali who could make plants grow just by touching them. I'll admit: I sort of lost track of the plot halfway through, but the key takeaway here is that my freaky-deaky abilities didn't stress him out.

He also seems to genuinely like the job. It's helped him get off the streets, move into an actual apartment with his girl-friend Jeannette. She used to be homeless too, and she doesn't like me very much. I smashed her tent to pieces by accident when we first met. It's a long story.

"Looking good, *yaaw*," Africa says to me as his giant hands scrub the counter, ignoring the waterfall of coffee still cascading off the side. "You never dress this nice before."

"Good enough for government work," I mutter. Ugh, I was hoping to keep my little good mood balloon up for a while longer.

"Huh?"

"Never mind." I grab a fistful of towels to help, mourning the death of my coffee.

"Hey, Africa." Paul tried to call him Idriss at first, but Africa refuses to answer to his actual name. "Little help?"

"Yes boss!"

"You really don't have to call me boss. We've talked about this."

"OK, boss. Sorry. Not boss."

You'll be shocked to hear that Paul didn't want Africa on the team. He said he was a loose cannon, not to be trusted, and wouldn't hear any arguments. He was flabbergasted when Annie voted against him – I think he genuinely believed that because they were dating, she'd back him up. His gast was flabbered even more when *I* sided with him. He was the only one who seemed to get that I was kidding when I suggested Africa as a new driver.

I'll be honest: I could have done without the big guy today. Turns out that the key to getting along with Africa is to do it in small doses. Before, I saw him once every few months. Maybe. Now I see him every day. Imagine hanging out with a really hyper pit bull for hours at a time, only the pit bull is seven feet tall and has a bark that can be heard from space.

The coffee machine is still on the counter. "Thank fuck," I say, sliding past Africa and heading over to it. "Anybody else want?"

"Can't." Annie doesn't look up from her paper-gathering. "No water."

"No—what?"

"There's no water."

"What do you mean, there's no water?"

"I mean, it's been replaced with Miller Lite. The fuck you think I mean?"

"Are you serious?"

"Water's out to the whole of Venice. Burst main somewhere. Bunch of other places too."

"Are you *serious*?"

"How many cups you drink?" Africa says. "You have too much coffee, Teggan. Your heart go pop."

"Hey, I have had no more than two cups, OK?" Four, but whatever, I'm fine.

I head over to Reggie's door, figuring I'd better get this done before the lack of caffeine causes permanent damage. I'm about to knock when I realise Annie is staring daggers into my back – I can feel her from here. Leaving before helping with the clean-up probably isn't going to win me many brownie points. It might only be Reggie's permission I need, but it can't hurt to have the rest of the crew feeling positive about me.

So I take a deep breath and pitch in, working with both my hands and my PK, piling paper, turning chairs the right way up, flipping the whiteboard onto its feet.

It's not long before the office starts looking like its old self, minus a few glasses and plates. I stand, dusting off my hands, and am about to head over to Reggie's room when Paul says, "OK, thanks, guys. Everybody gather round."

I pause, my handle on the doorknob. "Why?"

"Briefing. It was on the Google calendar."

"Oh, come—"

Annie clears her throat. Behind her, Africa smiles witlessly.

"How are we even still doing Tanner jobs?" I sit down on the couch with a thump. "You know we just suffered a massive earthquake, right?"

"Yep." Paul gets to his feet, his knees popping. "We still have work to do – the world hasn't ended."

"Tell that to San Bernardino."

Africa lets out a hissing breath. "All gone, huh? S'not good. Very sad."

I flick a glance over at my backpack, wanting to check my

phone, knowing it's pointless. Nic hasn't responded to any of my texts — I can tell, because I have the ringer set on high. All the same, the urge to check is almost overwhelming. I haven't completely killed the poisonous thoughts from the night before, but they at least have the decency to stay in the background.

"But," Paul says, grabbing his laptop and lowering himself to the couch, "most places held up OK. They're working to turn the water and power back on. I remember after the Northridge quake in '94, the 10 went down, and it took them three months to get it moving again. They've done a bunch of work since then. More importantly —" he opens his laptop "— the airports went back to normal this morning. That means our target is still on schedule for arrival tomorrow."

"Mister Germany," Africa says, nodding, as if he's answered a tough question in a test.

Paul gives him a pointed look. "His name's Jonas Schmidt."

"Ya. Him."

"What about Reggie?" I say. "Shouldn't she be here?"

"She's researching something on the quake," Annie says. "You know how she is when she gets an idea in her head."

"I get ideas in my head all the time. Why don't I get to skip the briefings?"

"Because you didn't do a bunch of prep work and research beforehand, and you actually have to go out on the job." Paul taps a few keys, and a picture of Schmidt appears on screen.

He's one of those young tech billionaires who you want to both marry, and punch repeatedly in the face. He is disgustingly good-looking. The photo Paul has of him was taken somewhere sunny; Schmidt is wearing mirrored aviator sunglasses, smiling a very expensive smile, his shoulders bare and his hair tousled by a light breeze.

Not that his good looks are going to help him. Once you get onto Moira Tanner's radar, nothing can save you.

Schmidt made his money by taking risks, betting big on start-ups and wild business ideas. His latest one is real good: attempting to sell a list of American overseas deep-cover assets to the highest bidder. It's not going to make him nearly as much money as his other business ventures, but that's OK, because he's trying to get into politics. And by *get into politics*, I mean become a behind-the-scenes power broker who enjoys causing the fall of three governments before breakfast.

Schmidt is landing his private jet at Van Nuys airport tomorrow morning, and he'll be heading into the city to meet with a buyer. Tanner's sources say the list is going to be on-board. It's an actual piece of paper in a safe, or possibly a USB stick — no way Schmidt is going to put something that sensitive on a computer with an internet connection.

If all goes to plan, he won't have anything to sell. Reggie will get us onto the airport property, and it's up to me to get on board the plane, sneaking inside while it's parked in the hangar. I'll use my mad PK skillz to crack the safe, snatch the goods and then get the hell out of there.

"Wait, wait, wait." Africa points at Paul's whiteboard. "He just gonna have his list on the plane? Maybe he keep it in his pocket?"

"Nah," Annie says. "Dude wouldn't just walk around with it."

"Not even with, like, a briefcase cuffed to his wrist?" I say.

"You do know people don't do that in real life, right?" Annie replies.

"It actually makes sense for him to keep the list on his jet." Paul taps a finger on his chin. "An airport is a high-security area anyway, and he'll have his own hangar, with his own guards. Better than a jacket pocket, or a hotel safe. Those things are real easy to bust open."

Paul does this thing when he's focusing hard where he very gently bites the tip of his tongue. It's ridiculously annoying at the best of times; this morning, it makes me want to destroy the office all over again. "Schmidt's used the same firm of limo drivers for the past five years," he says. "Island Limos. They'll be picking him up at 10:15 precisely, and if I look at the driver records . . . here. They don't tend to be more than three minutes late, when they aren't on time. I have to crunch some numbers to know for sure, but—"

"Fascinating." I push myself off the couch, straightening my stiff shirt. "You do that."

"Where are you going?" Annie says.

"Gotta talk to Reggie about something." I look for the wall mirror to give myself a once-over, before remembering that it was smashed to pieces.

"Is it about the budget?" Africa levers himself off the couch, limbs unfolding. "I need a raise, *yaaw*. Jeannette wants to buy a new oven, even though she can't cook anything." He snorts.

"What are you talking about?" Paul says. "You literally just joined the team. You can't get a pay rise until you've been working for six months. It's in the contract – clause six, if I remember."

"But, boss—"

While they're bickering, I push through the door into Reggie's office.

NINE

Teagan

The space is the nicest in the house, easily. The drapes are as thick as comforters, the walls painted a tasteful turquoise. They're decorated with abstract art, chosen by Reggie – or rather, they would be, if the canvasses weren't all stacked in a messy pile in the corner, surrounded by ripples of shattered glass.

Reggie's computer setup is still bolted to the wall: six massive monitors, and three towers. She calls the collection her Rig, and when she's working, it looks like an extension of her chair, Reggie seated in the middle of it all like the pilot of a giant, kaiju-crushing mech.

Her hands dance across two specially designed trackballs, all while she mutters commands into the microphone mounted on the headrest of her chair. Alongside the big, curved monitors, there are at least three laptops open on the table in front of her. They're all displaying a zillion black-and-white text boxes on the screens, moving way too fast to follow

She doesn't look up when I enter, but I know her eyes will be dancing like she's in REM sleep, navigating through whatever system she's locked into. The helicopter crash in

Afghanistan might have taken her body – she's an incomplete quadriplegic – but it didn't take her mind. Or her ability to get shit done. Or her love of acting – she's part of a theatre company out in Anaheim. I've never actually been to one of her shows, because I am a horrible person. God, why didn't I get off my ass and go? It would have been the perfect way to start a conversation today, and then I could smoothly change the subject to other artistic pursuits, like cooking, and—

Nic's voice in my head: *It's amazing to me that you haven't figured out what's more important.*

I shake it off, clearing my throat and shutting the door quietly behind me. No response. One of the laptop screens is running multiple news reports on the quake, grainy footage of the LA skyline belching smoke.

"Reggie," I say, when she still doesn't look round. "You got a sec?"

She ignores me.

"Uh, hi? Reggie?"

I creep closer, coming round into her field of view. Her eyes are narrowed, locked on one of the screens, which looks to be displaying more data from the quake. For a long moment, she doesn't move: just stares at the screen, mouth slightly open. She's only in her forties, but there are already deep wrinkles around her eyes, tugging at the corner of her mouth.

I lift my hand, waving it near her face. "Anyone in there?"

"If you don't move your hand," she says slowly, not looking away from the screen, "I'm going to bite your little finger off."

"Sorry." I yank it back.

I stand there for a second, expecting her to continue. She doesn't.

"So it looks like we're set for the job tomorrow," I say. "If

Schmidt lands on schedule, we should be able to get inside the plane."

"Mm."

"It looks like the best way to go in is through the roof? Apparently the hangers at Van Nuys have skylights, so . . . "

"Yes, I know, Teagan." Her Louisiana accent is thicker than normal. "I was the one who dug up the schematics."

"Oh. OK. Right."

She starts moving the trackball again. Her fingers don't work as they should, but she's got enough movement in her arm to manipulate the ball with her hand. A map of the quake appears on screen, with a red bull's-eye centred on the Arizona border.

I clear my throat. "I was wondering—"

"Damndest thing," she murmurs.

"What?"

It's a few moments before she replies. "Someone called in a missing state trooper. They found his car in the middle of nowhere, outside Mesa Verde. Door open, key in the ignition, phone still in the charger. No sign of him."

"The hell is Mesa Verde?"

"Our side of the Arizona border." From out of nowhere, she pulls up a photo: an older guy in a tan police uniform, wearing one of those ridiculous cowboy hats rural cops like. He has the slightest smile on his face, and wrinkles around his eyes that remind me of Reggie herself. He looks like somebody's grandpa.

"Rudy Daniels. I did some digging. Career officer, wife and kid, flying colours on his last psych eval. No reason for him to go missing."

"OK but, no offence, why do we care? Not exactly our jurisdiction is it?"

"Maybe not. Seems kind of strange though, don't you think? It's not like Mesa Verde's a crime hotspot."

"OK . . . but I just don't see—"

"That's because you aren't looking hard enough."

Her tone is sharp, irritated. It's so unlike her that I actually take a step back.

Her face softens. "Sorry, honey. Didn't mean to snap at you."

"Are . . . you OK?"

She sags back in her chair. "Just worried about Washington."

Reggie's heading to DC tomorrow – she's due to leave right after we wrap things up with Schmidt. I still can't believe I left it this late to talk to her.

"Moira's been in one hell of a mood lately," she says. "Can't say I'm all that excited to meet up with her this time round."

"Tell her that I'm being a total bitch, as usual. It'll give you guys something to talk about."

She smirks. "You're only a total bitch when you barge into my room uninvited."

"Oh, I knocked. You just ignored me."

"By choice." She nods towards her paintings, mouth twisting in annoyance. "Gonna take us for ever to clean *that* up." She turns back to me, as if seeing me for the first time. "Speaking of cleaning up – you're looking good today. Nice to see you making an effort."

Perfect opening. "Thanks. Hey, so I wanted to ask—"

The door opens behind me. "Oh, Annie," Reggie says. "Good. You're here. Do you know anybody out in Mesa Verde?"

"Out in where now?" Annie stands in the doorway, looking as confused as I am.

Reggie explains about her missing state trooper. "So, do you?"

"Do I . . . what?" Annie glances at me, like she's expecting me to step in and help.

"Do you have anybody out in Mesa Verde?"

"Uh . . . no."

"What about Paul, then?" Reggie swings back to her Rig, distracted. "Or Africa?"

"I'm here!" Africa bellows from the lounge. Then he's striding in, ducking his head to get through the door. "What you need?"

"You must know *somebody*," Reggie says to Annie.

"Reggie, Mesa Verde's like five hours from here."

Africa frowns. "Messa Ved? What is that?"

"Town on the Arizona border," Paul shouts from the main room.

"I thought we were at the airport tomorrow. For Mister Germany."

"So *nobody* has any contacts out there? Not even in law enforcement?" Reggie sounds irritated. "Well, get on it. Start making calls."

"OK, why are you being weird?" Annie says. I'm really glad I didn't have to ask the question, because I need Reggie on my side right now.

"I'm not being weird."

"Sure you are." Annie folds her arms. "Who gives a fuck about Mesa Verde? Or some missing cop? Probably just ditched his wife and went to Vegas."

A look of real anger crosses Reggie's face. It deepens, threatening to explode . . . then subsides. She closes her eyes. "You're right. Forget it."

Africa tilts his head to one side. "You OK?"

"If one more person asks me that, I'm going to . . . " She takes a very deep breath. "Never mind. Go back to what you were doing. Go do the Joseph Schmidt thing."

"Jonas Schmidt," I say, before I can stop myself.

"Yes. That. Now, please."

"You sure you OK?" Africa says. "I can make some food or something if you want?"

"Come on, dude." Annie pulls him away. "Let's help Boss Man clean up."

"You needed something, Teagan?" Reggie says.

Her question catches me off guard. I open my mouth to ask her about cooking school, to pop the big question . . .

But the words won't come.

"No," I say. "We're good."

"All right then." She gives me a nod. "Give me a call if you find anything."

She turns back to her Rig. I linger for a second, willing myself to say something, *anything*. I open my mouth, close it again, then head for the door, cursing myself and my stupid brain and my stupid life and my ability and Moira Tanner and all of it.

"So you know where to come tonight?" Annie asks, as I close the door behind me.

It's the second time today that I missed her standing next to me. "Jesus. Yes. No. I don't know. What?"

"Tonight. Dinner at my mom's. Remember? I texted you the address a while back."

"Oh. Sure."

"You don't remember, do you?"

"Of course I did. I just forgot that it was tonight, that's all. Is she still doing it though? I mean, with the quake and everything?"

Annie gives me a pained look. "Take a lot more than a little quake to stop my mom. I don't bring you clowns over tonight, she'll never let me forget it."

Dinner at Annie's – let alone her mom's – would have been

inconceivable a few months ago. Annie was more likely to eat Big Macs with Donald Trump than invite me into her life. But she's thawed a little since the whole Carlos thing, and a couple of weeks ago, she grudgingly announced to the office that her mom wanted to have us all over for dinner in Watts.

"1773 East 107th," she reminds me. "Just be there six-thirty. And wear something nice."

I point at my outfit. "This is literally the smartest thing I own."

"You know what I mean. More dinner-datey."

"Sure. I'll pull out my ballgown."

"Could we *please* get back on track?" Paul says. He and Africa have righted the whiteboard, and he's already sketching a diagram of Van Nuys Airport, his Sharpie dancing. "Before every American asset in the free world gets compromised?"

TEN

Matthew

The Meitzen Museum occupies a large building in Exposition Park, southwest of Downtown. Matthew and Amber arrive just as the doors open for the day.

The entrance is a huge, airy rotunda of steel and glass, bordered by wings made of red brick. The earthquake from the night before doesn't appear to have damaged the museum, although there's a section of steps with a major crack in it, surrounded by plastic orange cones. Matthew sidesteps them, hardly able to contain his excitement. He feels like he's journeyed off the edge of the map into bright blue seas, speckled with islands to plunder for hidden treasure.

"Amber, come on!" he yells over his shoulder. He's wearing a short-sleeved green button-down with jeans and sneakers, and he made Amber comb his hair. He hates getting his hair combed, but he needs to look good today.

The inside of the museum is hushed and cool. There's almost nobody in the entrance rotunda – a few security guards, a small group of Asian tourists. Matthew skids to a halt, head tilted, as if sniffing the air. Then he spots what he's looking for – a stairway, heading up to the second level – and bolts for it. He's brought up short by a security guard, a stocky man with cornrows who steps in front of him. "Hold up, son. Gotta get a ticket first." He spots Amber, jogging up. She's wearing jeans and a green tank top, with a faded denim jacket. Her scraggly blond hair hangs loose around her shoulders. "Over by the window, ma'am. Entrance is free, but I need to see a wristband."

The urge to grab some soil out of one of the nearby plant pots and attack the guard with it is almost overpowering. Matthew makes himself wait, dancing from foot to foot. He can't just make the people here do what he wants – well, he *could*, but he'd get in trouble. Real trouble, not just the kind where Amber tries to get mad at him. He's got to be more careful here. He hates playing pretend – it always makes him think of the other kids at the School, who acted like babies. But he can do it if he has to.

When Amber *finally* brings him his wristband, he all but snatches it from her, flashing it to the security guard and bolting up the stairs.

There are exhibit signs everywhere. *Secrets of the Pharaohs*; *Earth's Changing Climate*; *Pollution Solution*; *Mission to Mars*. Amber lingers at this last one, staring longingly through the open double doors, where there's a glimpse of a NASA logo.

Finally, he finds what he's looking for.

The California Earthquake Exhibit has an air of permanence, a lived-in look that speaks of a lot of foot traffic and not a lot of maintenance. It's a big, dimly lit room filled with dilapidated exhibits. There's a shake table, holding plastic blocks designed to be formed into miniature buildings; a giant globe showing tectonic plates; a model of the Earth's core.

Matthew stops by the shake table, hands on his hips. Amber

comes up behind, stifling a yawn. "You want to build something?" she asks.

He doesn't look round. "It's for little kids. I want to talk to someone who knows about—"

And then he's gone again, heading towards a volunteer in a blue shirt, working on what looks to be a wind tunnel.

The volunteer is Amber's age, an Asian woman with brown hair pulled back in a neat ponytail. She looks up as Matthew skids to a halt in front of her. "Hi," he says, his voice bright and alert. "Do you know about earthquakes?"

"Well, hello there," the volunteer replies, straightening.

"Do you?"

"As a matter of fact, I do." The volunteer's name tag reads *Mia*. Her skin is awash with freckles, and she has a quick smile. "I'm in charge of that exhibit you were just at – the shake table." A flicker of worry crosses her face, and she bends down, hands on her knees. "Is this because of yesterday? I thought it was pretty scary too."

"Yeah." Matthew shivers – an exaggerated motion that sets his whole body wobbling. "My mom and I were OK though. We went to a motel."

Mia mouths a quick *hi* at Amber, gives her a little wave.

"I wanted to know about how plates work," Matthew says. "And fault lines."

Mia frowns. "How old are you?"

"Four. I'm smart for my age."

Mia looks up at Amber, who shrugs. "He's gifted. He was reading by the time he was two." The words are long-practised – Matthew's heard her use them many times before.

"Is that right?" Mia says. "Well, I love people who ask questions. Fire away."

"So how much *do* you know about earthquakes?" Matthew says.

"Quite a lot. I'm doing my grad school work here – there's a whole research lab attached to this exhibit."

"I know. I wanted to go there, but you have to be a scientist to get in. Can you get me in?"

She laughs. "I don't know about that ... "

"But you're a scientist, right?"

"Oh, absolutely," she says, as if he'd questioned her ability. "But not like a professor – not yet, anyway. I'm just a research assistant. Although you're pretty smart, so I think you might get there before I do."

Matthew makes himself giggle.

"Why can't we predict earthquakes?" he says.

Mia leans back against the wall of the wind tunnel. "Good question. One of my professors told me that every earthquake is a surprise to a seismologist. That's a person who—"

"Studies seismic waves," Matthew says. Why does everybody think he's *stupid*? Just because he's four. He keeps the smile plastered on his face; he can actually feel the individual muscles pulling his lips back, the ones that widen his eyes.

Mia flashes Amber an impressed look. "Correct. We know quite a bit about fault lines, but it's still tough to figure out what they're going to do." She lifts her hands in front of her face. "So imagine you have a pencil, and you start bending it. You know that at some point it will break, but you don't exactly know when. It depends on the stuff inside. You don't know where the strong and weak points are."

"You can't find out?"

"Well, the Earth is a lot bigger than a pencil, and there's a lot of stuff down there. The San Andreas fault – that was what caused the little rumble yesterday – goes for miles and miles."

"So there's no way to predict them? At all?"

Mia tilts a flattened hand back and forth. "Sometimes. It's not what we'd call an exact science."

It's all he can do not to scream. *Not an exact science*? She just said she was a scientist, so why is she pretending she isn't?

Fine. He'll play along – there are plenty of ways to get grown-ups to do what you want, even without hurting them. Matthew frowns, looking around him, as if scanning for another volunteer.

"But," Mia says, crouching down so she's at his level, "we do know quite a lot about fault lines, especially San Andreas."

Matthew's eyes light up. "Yeah! So why wasn't the earthquake yesterday bigger? Why was it a 7.1 and not an 8.3?"

For a second, he thinks she sees flash of suspicion in Mia's eyes. Just a hint of it, a slight narrowing. "Been reading a lot, huh?"

"I found this podcast." Matthew looks down at his feet, pretending to be embarrassed. He hates to admit it, but he's pretty good at playing pretend.

"Well. That's . . . wow. Anyway, it was only a 7.1 because of where it happened. The plates only shifted a little bit."

"So if they moved somewhere else, the quake would be bigger?"

"Matthew, honey," Amber says. "Do you want to get juice or something? Maybe we should leave the nice lady alone . . . "

"No, that's OK." Mia flashes her a bemused smile. "I don't mind at all. I don't usually get to talk to people this clever." She winks at Matthew. "In fact, you know what? How would you like to come and see some of the research we're working on? Both of you?"

"In the lab?"

"We'd need to stay here, but I do have some stuff I could

show you. I don't know though, you might find it pretty boring; it's just graphs and charts."

He could kill her. Tear off her stupid head. In like five seconds. He'd make sure she knew what was happening, too. He clenches his fists, lets them go, forces himself to stay calm.

"That's OK," he says. "I don't mind."

Amber is still there, standing behind them. She knows what he did yesterday. Matthew looks her up and down, drinking in the familiar flash of fear in her eyes. She's stupid too, so she probably won't understand what Mia tells him about quakes. But what if she does? What if she figures out what he wants to do next?

She can't stop him. No one can. But that doesn't mean he has to tell her what he's doing. He might need her to drive him around and buy food and stuff, but it's better if she doesn't know his plans. *In the dark* – his mind readily supplies the phrase. He likes that one, remembers it from a book about the Mafia he once read. Yeah. Better if she's in the dark.

"Actually," he says to Amber, "can I have a soda please?"

"Oh. Um. OK. I think I saw the cafeteria at the—"

"No, I mean, can you bring me back a soda? Mountain Dew Red. Please," he adds, for the benefit of Mia.

Amber bites her lower lip, which annoys him. A lot, actually. Why does she always think she can make him do stuff? She always tries, and it never works. He can't use the dirt on her here, but later, maybe he could—

Her shoulders sag. "OK, honey. Mountain Dew. Sure."

"Hey." Mia's forehead creases, which makes her look a little older than she is. "We're not really supposed to supervise kids by themselves. I don't know—"

"She'll only be gone a few minutes," Matthew says. "And there are security guards everywhere. See?" He points to the far end of the exhibition hall, where an elderly guard is slumped on a chair.

"Yeah, but still . . . I'd get in a lot of trouble if—"

"We're in the middle of a museum. If you wanted to kidnap me or whatever, there are cameras everywhere, right? And I bet you've had, like, first aid training, so if I have a seizure or something, you know what do already."

Mia blinks in the face of Matthew's logic.

"I mean, it's kind of up to your mom . . . " she says.

Amber looks like she's about to protest. Matthew glares at her, making her eyes meet his.

Amber's expression becomes a very careful blank. "I don't mind. The cafeteria's just down the hall. I promise he won't be a bother . . . "

"I should probably get my supervisor to OK it . . . "

"Your supervisor?" Matthew's eyes go wide. "Like from the lab? Can I ask him stuff too?"

Mia gives him a cautious smile. "That's right. I just want to make sure he's OK with—"

"See?" Matthew says, as if that settles it. "I'll be with *two* grown-ups. Please?"

"It's really no problem," Amber murmurs.

Mia nods. "Well, if you're sure – *oh*."

Matthew has taken her hand, his little fingers intertwined in hers. Mia gives Amber an apologetic look, but Matthew is already pulling her away, peppering her with questions.

ELEVEN

Teagan

Alien spaceships have landed in Watts.

They're on the opposite side of the road from Annie's mom's house, at the end of 107th Street, the cul-de-sac forming a diagonal with Santa Ana Boulevard. Right where the roads meet, in the middle of a tree-lined park, there are several spiralling, cone-shaped towers, each one taller than the last. The tallest one must rise a hundred feet, skeletal scaffolding clad in grey concrete.

There's evidence of yesterday's quake everywhere. The road surface is cracked and bruised, and a building next door to the spaceship-like towers has collapsed in on itself, its roof leaning drunkenly. But the towers themselves stand tall and proud, looming over the street in the still air. It's stopped drizzling, for now, but the clouds are low and grey in the dusk. They make the towers look like alien monoliths. The air around us is still, as if wind is scared to blow too hard in this part of town. Like it might wake them up.

"Gonna take more than an earthquake to bring those down," Annie says. She's just climbing out Paul's truck behind me. Reggie is in the back seat, looking at something on her phone. We followed Annie here from the office – data is still spotty, which means no GPS. As Annie put it, she didn't want us late for dinner because we forgot how to use paper maps. I decided not to tell her that I've never actually owned a paper map.

"Wait, you can see them too?" I point to the structures. "I'm not hallucinating?"

"Hilarious. They're the Watts Towers, man."

"Think I saw that group at Coachella once."

"It's actually pretty fascinating." Paul pops out the passenger side. "The person who built them was an Italian immigrant, and he—"

"Come on," Annie says. "If we're late, I'm the one she'll be giving an earful to." She glances at me. "'Sides, why you acting so surprised? I've told you about them before. *And* I sent you that photo of them yesterday."

"No, seriously. How did I not know these were here?"

The towers are surrounded by a high concrete wall, which itself is surrounded by a big metal fence. The towers and the wall are undamaged, but the fence has been knocked over by the earthquake. I step inside to take a closer look. There are strange objects embedded in the concrete: shells, chips of glass, bits of broken pot. They cover the towers, as well as the wall itself.

There's something else that feels odd about the towers, and it takes me a second to spot it: no graffiti.

This is Watts, where every surface is covered in tags. But there's not a single one anywhere on the inner wall. Even when the fence was intact, I can't imagine that would've stopped anyone who wanted to tag the wall, and it must be a pretty enticing target. Does paint not stick to the concrete? Maybe they've coated it with—

"*Sho*." Africa's exclamation makes me jump. He's standing in the middle of the street, ham-hock hands on his hips, gazing in undisguised awe at the towers.

I didn't hear him pull up. His green Nissan sits at the curb, the door still open. It's even more beat-up than the Batmobile, with a major case of rust on the rocker panels. It's also the messiest car I've ever ridden in – and the Batmobile could win prizes for being untidy.

"Really?" Paul gazes at us in astonishment. "Neither of you have seen these before?"

"What you expect?" Annie clambers up into the truck's cargo well, hefting Reggie's chair. "Most people live in LA all their lives, they don't know about the towers."

"That's absurd. Why wouldn't they?"

She gives him a slightly pitying look. "Because they never come to Watts. Let's go. We're gonna be late."

She and Paul help Reggie into her chair. Our fearless leader smiles thanks, but says nothing. She is deep in thought, tapping at something on her phone, which is secured to one hand with a special ring. I still haven't asked her about chef's school. Maybe I should—

The world goes wavy.

You know tinnitus? That ringing in your ears because you spent too long sitting in the car blasting NWA at top volume? You know how sometimes specific frequencies will set it off – someone closing a door or laughing in a particular tone or the voice of a character on TV? It'll be in the background of your hearing, and then suddenly it'll be really loud and annoying, blocking out all other sounds.

This is exactly like that, only it's in my mind.

I lose my PK entirely, get it back, lose it again. The sensation is bizarre: like someone has filled my head with water, and is now shaking me back and forth, sloshing it around. It's not painful. It's just . . . *weird*.

"Teagan?" Annie says. She sounds very far away.

I do that stupid thing where you squeeze your eyes shut, then open them wide. It doesn't help. Whoever put the water in my head is shaking really hard now, back and forth, back and—

Gone.

Just like that, everything is normal.

"You OK?" Africa asks.

I spin in a slow circle, blinking hard, trying to see what the fuck just caused . . . whatever that was. But there's nothing. The towers. The trees around them, the uppermost branches swaying back and forth. The rucked-up tarmac. A couple of kids walking down the sidewalk.

Something's different.

But I can't figure it out. My PK is exactly the same as it's always been. I've got a firm grip on everything in a fifty-foot radius. My head is clear. So what—?

"Yo." Annie snaps her fingers in front of me. "Space cadet. You good?"

"Um. Yeah. Yeah, I'm fine. Let's go."

The five of us make our way across the street. A bunch of little kids have started a basketball game, throwing the ball up at an ancient hoop someone has erected in their driveway. There are a surprising number of people around, milling on the sidewalk in groups. We get a few curious looks, but nobody approaches us. A couple of people yell Annie's name, and she responds with a distracted wave. A car drives past, bass thumping loudly. On a wall nearby, someone has painted a huge mural – twenty feet wide, at least. It's a memorial to Nipsey Hussle, a rapper who died a while back – he made some incredible shit. Whoever did the mural really took their time – Nipsey's giant face is almost photorealistic. I half expect him to wink at me.

A thought occurs to me as we reach the sidewalk. "Where's Jeannette tonight?" I ask Africa.

"Huh?"

"Jeannette? Your girlfr—"

"Oh! Ya ya. Busy." He steps over a puddle in a single huge step – I have to go the long way round. Weird; I could have sworn he said Jeannette was coming tonight. In fact, I know she was, because I was psyching myself up to be nice to her.

"Maybe she come later," Africa mutters. "Annie, my dear, am I smart enough?" He's wearing a threadbare brown suit that only barely fits his enormous frame, over a Mandela shirt with a pattern of psychedelic green swirls.

She rolls her eyes. "You're good, dude. Relax."

The power lines are down, but the lights in the houses around us are still on. There are some cracks in the walls, but I guess whoever built the homes did them to code. There's no power, though: the clatter of generators is an undercurrent to the noise of the neighbourhood.

Annie leads us to a small bungalow, badly in need of a paint job, set back from the street behind a chain-link fence. As she pushes through the gate, a huge monster explodes out of the shadow of the porch, roaring, desperate for blood.

"Jesus fuck!" I take a quick step back, glad that I'm not the first one through. The monster is a Rottweiler the size of an SUV. It launches itself at Annie, almost bowls her over. But Annie has clearly been through this dance before. She braces her legs, catches the dog's paws on her shoulders, then quickly pushes it back down before it can slobber on her. The beasts's barks are loud enough to drown out the generators.

"Hey, Rocko." Paul isn't quite as skilled as Annie, and the

dog nearly does knock him over. Then it's off him, heading right for Reggie.

There's a horrible second where I think the dog is going to knock her right out of her chair. Instead, it skids to a halt in front of her, tongue lolling, head tilted to one side.

"Well, hello there," Reggie says. A delighted smile crosses her face – the first I've seen all day – and then Rocko is gone, leaping towards me.

All the restraint he showed with Reggie vanishes. He actually leaves the ground, front paws outstretched, pink tongue flicking out flecks of saliva.

I don't have a great history with dogs. I like them just fine, but they don't always like me back – I regularly have nightmares about a little terrier from a job we did in Long Beach, who I am convinced wanted to eat my kidneys.

"Annie," I manage to get out. And then I'm on my back in the grass, Rocko slobbering right in my mouth, plastering me with delighted licks. I decided that it wasn't worth pissing off Annie, or her mom, so I actually did make an effort with my clothes. I'm wearing a summer dress with a floaty skirt, and no sooner does Rocko have me down than he grabs hold of the hem and pulls.

I am a government agent who can hurl a car with the power of thought, and there is absolutely nothing I can do.

"Rocko!" Annie shouts. "No!"

She has to yell twice before Rocko lets go. He bounds away and starts humping Africa's leg. I push myself up on my elbows, blinking in embarrassment.

A whistle pierces the air. The dog about-turns instantly, huge paws scrabbling at the ground, heading for the porch. He comes to a stop and sits immediately, next to the woman who's just come out the front door.

She's tiny – half Annie's size, even smaller than I am. She's wearing slacks and a polo-neck sweater, her greying hair pulled back in a tight bun. She's in her early fifties, with full lips and huge, milky-blue eyes. She has a cannula inserted in her nostrils. A cart trails behind her, holding a small tank that looks like a beer cooler, connected to the cannula.

"Stay," she says to Rocko – even sitting, he comes to halfway up her arm. He woofs delightedly, nuzzles her hand.

Annie straightens up. "Hey, Ma."

"Did you bring my Paul?" The woman's voice is curiously wheezy.

"Over here, Mrs Cruz," Paul waves.

Annie's mom makes her way down the front steps, lifting the tank, moving with surprising speed. Rocko stays where he is, still slobbering. "Look at you," Mrs Cruz says, pulling Paul into a massive hug.

Paul hands her a bottle of wine when she lets him go. "I brought your favourite."

"That's so sweet. Thank you, my dear. We'll have to drink it together. How's your little boy?"

"Up in Arizona for a few days," Paul says. He keeps his smile plastered to his face. His son Cole is six or seven or possibly ten, I don't really remember. I know Cole likes soccer and Pokémon and that his mom is, as Paul calls her, a "difficult person", but I admit to blanking on a lot of the other stories Paul's told us.

Mrs Cruz pats Paul's cheek. "I bet he misses you. And he's always welcome here, you know that."

Annie's smile is a rictus. "Hi, Mom. Nice to see you. Remember me? Your daughter?"

"Yes, hello, dear. Aren't you going to introduce me to your friends? You must be Regina. I've heard so much about you."

She doesn't offer Reggie a hand, or bend down, like most people do when they meet her — just gives her a nod, along with a wide, welcoming smile.

Annie gestures to me. "This is Teagan."

Mrs Cruz's eyes narrow. "Aren't you the one always giving my daughter trouble at work?"

"Uh . . ."

"Every time Annie comes home it's Teagan this, Teagan that, Teagan said some such or other."

"Mom!" Annie looks like she wants the ground to open up and swallow her, which is fine, because I'll jump right in after her.

"Well, you did! Anyway, Teagan, happy to have you. Ignore my Annie, she can be a little touchy sometimes." She turns to Africa, ignoring Annie's protests. "And you are?"

And Africa does the oddest thing. He swoops into a low bow, one arm at his stomach, the other spread wide.

"I am Idriss Kouamé, madam," he says to the ground. "It is a pleasure to make your acquaintance."

Annie and I share a glance, and Annie mouths *What the fuck?* I just shrug.

"Such a nice name!" Mrs Cruz tells him. "And I'm Sandra-May. You might not want to bow to me, though. My late husband did that when he asked me to dance for the first time, and our marriage didn't turn out so good."

"Um, *hello*?" Annie says.

"Oh please, Annie, you know what I mean. Come on in, come on in. Paul, I've been meaning to ask you, could you take a look at the cabinet again? It's still sticking a little, which makes me think the hinges need some more oil, but I'm not really sure." She marches Paul up the steps, his arm in hers, Rocko trotting at their heels.

"Mom likes the boyfriend," I say to Annie, as we lift Reggie's chair up the steps. "That's half the battle, right?"

"Yeah. The other half would be convincing her not to disown me if we ever broke up. She thinks Paul's gonna be the one to straighten me out."

"Annie!" Mrs Cruz's wheezing voice reaches us. "Take your shoes off before you come in the house, haven't I told you enough?"

The outside of the house might need attention, but the inside is warm and clean. There's hardly a speck of dirt on the carpet, and absolutely zero dust on the shelves. It has nothing to do with that old piece of shit about poor people being proud of their homes: it's because Sandra-May Cruz can't tolerate any dust. It kills her lungs. Ditto for cologne or perfume – Annie specifically asked us not to wear any tonight. Somewhere out of sight, a generator is running.

Sandra-May has to stop several times before she gets to the kitchen, wheezing and coughing. She waves away all offers of help. "Be damned if I can't make it to the kitchen in my own house. Annie, dear, get down the good glasses. Not those ones – the ones in the cupboard over."

The kitchen is cramped, with ancient appliances and a broken clock on one wall, but whatever is cooking smells amazing. Meat and sizzling oil and gravy and spices, all mixed together. Pots bubble away on the stove.

"You have a wonderful house," Africa says.

"Like hell. It's small and noisy. Those youngsters from next door never stop their racket. Parties till six in the morning!"

"That's why I keep telling you to move," Annie says.

"Out of *Watts*?"

"To a bigger house, away from the towers. We've had this conversation."

"No, I am serious," Africa nods his head slowly, gazing around him. "It is beautiful. I used to have a house like this, when I was living in France."

"You lived in France?"

"Oh ya! I was a policeman in Lyons. I have a house in the country, very nice, maybe two stories."

"Thought you ran a bookshop in Lyons," I mutter.

"I was bookshop man *and* a policeman." He puffs out his chest. "I tell you already, Teggan. You know this."

"You're very welcome." Sandra-May says, utterly ignoring the bullshit story Africa just told. "That's what I keep telling Annie. Move out of Watts, she says. I been here twenty-five years, I ain't going anywhere. I thought I might have to sell the house at one point – damn health insurance wouldn't cover my lungs. Annie takes care of me, though. She's a good daughter."

"Nice to hear you admit it," Annie says, ignoring the look that passes between me and Reggie.

Sandra-May's emphysema and her lack of insurance led Annie to do some pretty crazy shit a few months ago. And by pretty crazy, I mean shipping a bunch of heroin up north for the MS-13 gang. It went horribly, ridiculously, stupidly wrong, and almost got her killed.

I don't know why I should be so surprised that Annie takes care of her mom the way she does. People aren't just one thing – and while that's a goddamn trite statement if I ever heard one, it also happens to be true. I guess it's just because the Annie I know did some seriously foul shit back in the day. It's hard to put that together with the house she grew up in, the mom that still cooks her for – let alone how she's now involved with a straight-laced Navy boy.

"Long as you keep this one around," Sandra-May tells Annie, swatting the straight-laced Navy boy on the behind.

"Your taste in men is better than mine used to be, I'll give you that."

"*Mom!*"

"Now, dinner will be ready shortly – Teagan, Idriss, be honeys and set the table. I'm afraid the bump we had last night knocked some of my china out the cabinet, so we'll have to use the old plates. At least the house stayed standing. Most of Watts and Compton were fine. Hell of a thing, what happened out in San Bernardino. Hell of a thing."

"My utensils are in the bag on the right," Reggie tells me. She uses a special fork and knife to eat, which strap to her wrists. I dig them out of the compartment on the back of her chair. "I'm not going to be much help, I'm afraid," she says, as Africa walks past with an armful of plates.

"Nonsense. You can stay and talk to me while the youngsters do the heavy lifting. You run the office for the moving company, right?"

"That's right."

"And you're a vet?"

Reggie purses her lips – she's never liked talking about the chopper crash that paralysed her. Sandra-May takes another wheezing huff of oxygen. "Both Bushes were damn fools, sending you folks over there. And my fool of a husband voted for him! Drove me to the cigarettes, and now look at us. I'm guessing you've got a few lung problems of your own. It's on hot days, right? When the smog gets real low?"

Reggie blinks, then laughs. "Like trying to lift a truck off your chest."

"Damn straight! Difference is, I only got myself to blame for *my* condition. I got no excuse. And I *still* want to sneak one now and then, even though I haven't smoked in three years. You believe that?"

Africa and I leave them to it, heading through to the living room. To my surprise, there's a massive dining table – the kind of thing you'd see in Downton Abbey, all ornate curlicues and fine-grained wood. It takes up nearly two-thirds of the living room, squashing the plastic-covered couch up against the window. A big TV plays silently in one corner, showing football reruns. Rocko wanders in, snuffling around the edge of the couch, ignoring us.

"Teggan – where your boyfriend tonight?" Africa says, as we set the table.

"What's that now?"

"Nathan?"

"Nic." I actually feel myself blush, a little.

"Ya ya. Where he now? You two OK?"

"He's not my boyfriend."

"Ah, you break up?" He kisses his teeth. "Shame. But if he hurt you, he must learn. I will talk to him . . ."

"No! Jesus, Africa, calm the fuck down. We were never actually together."

He nods, like he suspected all along. Goes back to sliding plates into position.

We set the rest of the table in silence. Which is a hundred per cent A-OK with me. Despite the smell of good food, despite Sandra-May, I don't really want to be around people. Maybe I should have blown off tonight . . .

"Hey, Teggan," Africa says, straightening forks. "We must talk about something, huh? Can you tell me—?"

"OK." Sandra-May waddles through, trailing Paul and Annie, both of whom hold big pots in oven-gloved hands. "Paul's fixed the cabinet, and the gravy's ready, so let's get to eating."

Oh, thank God.

Turns out, we all have to pitch in to help. Sandra-May made a *lot* of food, like she was expecting the whole neighbourhood to come calling. Baked ham, studded with cloves. Gravy thick enough to stand a spoon up in. Platters of rice and mashed potato. A huge crock of green beans. Annie's told us before how tired her mother gets, so she must have gone to huge trouble to make it all. I feel instantly bad for wanting to blow tonight off. Fortunately, this time my guilt is going to be rewarded with good stuff to eat. I didn't realise how hungry I was, and by the time we all sit down, I'm salivating. The rain has started outside, spattering the windows with thick drops, but it feels a million miles away.

"Now," Sandra-May says, once we're all seated. "We don't do grace here. I'm not a big God person. But we *do* give thanks."

"Mom, are we still doing this?" Annie says.

"You're damn right we're still doing it." Sandra-May's tone is steak-knife sharp. "And you best remember that, you wanna keep coming by for my ham."

She reaches out, takes her daughter's hand. "I'm thankful my only daughter has found such a good man to take care of her."

"*Mom.* Please, enough."

"No, I'll have my say, and give my thanks. I'm grateful for Paul, for who he is and how he respects Annie, and how he keeps her from leading the life she did when she was younger."

"This is so embarrassing," Annie mutters, hiding her face with the one hand her mom has left her. "It's the twenty-first century, Mom, not the eighteenth."

"*And,*" Sandra-May says, "I'm grateful to all of you for coming to visit me. It's hard for me to get out the house sometimes, and Rocko ain't much for civilised discussion."

At her feet under the table, Rocko is busy licking his balls.

"Well," Paul says, lifting his glass, "I'm grateful to you, Sandra-May, for your hospitality. We all are. And I'm grateful to Annie." He takes her free hand. "For letting me be in her life."

Africa applauds, grinning wildly. Paul leans over, kisses Annie on the cheek. She rolls her eyes, then cracks a smile, leaning over and kissing him back, to cheers from the rest of us. "Well, I'm grateful you two got the sappy stuff out of the way," Annie says, laughing. "You know I wasn't gonna say it."

Nic's face comes into my head. The argument we had last night ... and how good it was before, when we were eating dinner and it all looked like it was going to be OK. Annie kisses Paul again, whispers something in his ear.

"And you, Idriss?" Sandra-May says.

"Mmmmm." He nods to himself, brow knotted. "My job, I think. Ya. It get me off the street. It was hard, *yaaw*, very hard." More nodding, his eyes down, as if he's trying to contain himself. "No money, police causing trouble. But Teggan and Reggie, they ask me for help, and Idriss always help, ya, so now we here."

Reggie gives him an encouraging smile. He wipes his face, and continues. "I have plenty jobs before. I work for police in France. I cut trees. I wash dishes. I smuggle gold. I work security for Barack."

Sandra-May raises an eyebrow at this, but says nothing.

"But I think, ya, this is the best job I ever have," says Africa. "It has the best people."

"*This* is the best job you ever had?" Annie says. "Damn, dude, you need to put yourself out more."

"Hush," Sandra-May says.

Reggie clears her throat. "I'm grateful we all survived the earthquake, when so many others didn't. I'm grateful for the roof over our heads, and the people round this table."

"Amen," Annie's mom murmurs.

"Thought you didn't believe in God, Mrs Cruz," I say.

"*Amen!*" She has to take a deep breath to say it, fighting through the wheezing, but there's a huge grin on her face. More cheers, this time with Paul and Annie joining in.

"What about you, Teagan?" Reggie says.

"Hell no," I say, laughing. "I'll go after—"

Carlos.

I was about to say, *I'll go after Carlos.*

Africa gives me a strange look. The table is silent, the others waiting for me to speak. I stare down at my empty plate, thinking hard.

What do I have to be thankful for?

I have a job. I have friends. I have a house – one that hasn't been destroyed by fire, or the quake. My lungs aren't fried like Sandra-May, and I have two legs to walk around on, unlike Reggie. I have Los Angeles. I have a past that doesn't haunt me, because I know exactly who I am, and where I come from.

And yet, when I try to tell everyone that, nothing comes out.

If I've got so much to be thankful for, why am I trying to change it? Why do I want to go to chef school? Why am I fighting with Nic? Why can't I get Carlos out of my head? If my life is so perfect; if I have so many good things; then why do I feel so ... stuck?

After everything that happened with me being framed for murder, I'd convinced myself I had something good in China Shop. That these people were my friends. And they are ... up to a point. A meal like tonight's doesn't happen every week, or even every month. During work hours, we're friendly enough to each other, and I know they've got my back. But outside work, it's different. Paul and Annie spend all their time with each other. Reggie prefers settling down with a book or a movie. I'm not exactly begging to hang out with Africa. The few other friends I have outside of work aren't close enough to make a real difference, and as for Nic . . .

"I'm thankful for the food," I say, still looking at my empty plate. "And for us. You know?"

Polite smiles. An encouraging nod from Paul, as if expecting me to go on.

"Hear hear," Reggie murmurs, when it becomes clear that I'm done.

"Can we eat now, Mommie dearest?" Annie says sweetly.

"Why yes, sugar plum." Sandra-May reaches for the mashed potatoes. "We can eat now. Paul, be a dear and pass me the gravy."

TWELVE

Teagan

Van Nuys Airport isn't as busy as LAX, which is essentially a sprawling self-contained city that just happens to have runways attached. But it still gets plenty of traffic, and when we pull up to the security gate at 10:15 a.m. precisely, we have to wait behind a line of cars.

"Come on." Paul cranes to look out the window. He's more fidgety than normal, which is crazy annoying. The back of the China Shop van is cramped, with racks of equipment and tools that line one side. A thick sheet of metal sits propped against the rear door. The low bench on the other is just wide enough for Paul, Annie and myself to sit on, but if he doesn't stop jumping up every five seconds, I'm going to brain him.

"Relax, babe." Annie rolls her shoulders. "Schmidt got in right on schedule this morning. We got plenty of time."

"That we know of. He's flying private. That means he could take off whenever he wants."

"Reggie says he hasn't even left the hotel where he's meeting the buyer." She stifles a yawn.

"All the same . . ."

Africa jerks the van forward, fighting with the clutch. Paul thumps back down, his glasses knocking themselves askew.

I don't know why Paul's on edge. In theory, this should be an easy job. Schmidt might be meeting buyers, but he won't be carrying the list of our deep-cover assets around with him. That would be very dumb. No, he'll keep it locked in a safe, on *his* plane, surrounded by *his* guards, in an airport filled with trigger-happy TSA, until such a time as an exchange can be made. Reggie found out that Schmidt has booked the Presidential Suite at the Hotel Bel-Air to meet his buyer, which is fine by us. One of Annie's Army was prepared to add our licence plate to the TSA's *Cleared* list so we could get inside. Probably cost a shit-ton, but what the hell; Tanner can afford it.

We're all dressed in Homeland Security uniforms. Dark blue short-sleeve shirts, open at the collar, and navy slacks. Also toolbelts that hold enough gadgets and gizmos to give Batman a hard-on. Plus mirror shades, and a hot, heavy bulletproof vest. Like wearing a turtle shell.

The uniforms are pretty cool, as uniforms go, but I've always found it kind of stupid that airport officials wear them. They dress like they're about to breach a paramilitary compound in Columbia, when ninety-nine per cent of their job is asking jet-lagged tourists from Turkey how long they plan on staying in the United States and if they're members of a terrorist organisation. At least I got to wear my black Air Jordans for this mission – with what I have to do, heavy boots would be a bad idea.

Africa finally clears the gate. "Everybody OK?" he says through the van partition. He sounds surprisingly nervous.

"You learn clutch control, I'd be better," Annie mutters. Our van is manual – when Carlos was our driver, he insisted on it. Africa has learned quickly, I'll give him that, but he still can't pull away without jerking the car.

I'd rather not have Carlos intruding on my thoughts today. I'm feeling surprisingly good. Maybe it was the ginger ale Sandra-May served, which she jacked with bourbon, or her speech about gratitude actually penetrating my subconscious, because I slept surprisingly well. I only needed two coffees to get going this morning.

There was no time to talk to Reggie about chef school this morning – hardly surprising, as it's always a little crazy before our jobs. But she wants a full debrief back at the Boutique later, and even taking that into account, there'll be a couple of hours before she has to leave for her flight to Washington. If the job goes well, she'll be in a good mood. Yesterday was ... hard. But it looks like today might be a little better.

"Hangar 22, ya?" Africa asks.

"Yep. It was in the briefing," I say.

Annie cackles. "You wanna be careful, Africa. When Teagan remembers stuff from the briefing that you can't, you are *way* behind."

"Bite me," I tell her.

"No, no, no, I know, I know." Africa shakes his head, like we're the ones being ridiculous.

Paul leans into the partition window. "Remember: stay on this side of the solid yellow line. You can't cross into the movement area without ATC permission."

"Hey, Africa," I say. "Can you put on some music?"

"*No*, Teagan." Paul gives me an irritated look. "We've talked about this."

"Come on. It'll be a while before we get there, and we already know what we have to do."

"We should be focused. Like I've said before—"

"You mean you've never been tempted to play, like, the *A-Team* theme song in this thing? Not even once?"

Annie screws up her face. "What?"

"*The A-Team?* Bunch of dudes in a van on secret missions? Big guy with biceps the size of tree trunks?"

"I know who the A-Team are, dumbass. I just think you're weird."

"I'll show you weird." I lower my voice. "In 2020, a crack commando unit was sent to prison by a military court for a crime they didn't commit."

"Oh my God." Annie rolls her eyes.

"These men – well, these men and these significantly badass women promptly escaped from a maximum security stockade to the Los Angeles underground. Today, they are used by the government as soldiers of fortune. If you have a problem, if no one else can help, and if you can find them, maybe you can hire . . . the T-Team."

"The *T*-Team?" Annie says.

"Well, I'm just saying—"

"It literally has an A in the name. If anything, we the Annie Team."

"Could we please just—?" Paul's words are cut off when the van fills with machine-gun fire. No – not guns. Drums. And then a voice much deeper than mine, also talking about crack commando units. It's the actual theme song. Playing, right now.

Annie groans. Paul frantically bangs on the partition glass. All of which is drowned out by my shout of triumph. "Yes! Thank you, Africa!"

"I found it online! I use the Bluetooth!" he yells back, just as the main theme kicks in.

"Come on, Annie, sing it with me," I say. "You too, Paul."

"This is embarrassing," Annie says. But there's a sly smile on her face. Before long, even Paul has given up protesting, as Annie, Africa and I harmonise.

Yeah. I feel good. Scratch that – for the first time in a while, I feel fucking *great*.

A few minutes later, Africa pulls us to a stop in the shadow of a hangar.

I put a hand on the side door handle, only to be stopped by Paul. "Teagan, hold. Let's do a comms check."

"They work fine. They always do."

"All the same." He keys his earpiece. "Paul here, you hearing me?"

"From two places at once." I point at him, then my own earpiece. "It's my worst nightmare."

Annie rolls her eyes, touches her ear. "Annie here."

"Africa. I am here."

"And this your friendly neighbourhood psychokinetic. Can we go already?"

"Wait." Paul holds up a finger.

"What now?"

He ignores me, touching his black earpiece. "OK, copy that. Over." He looks up at me. "Reggie's taken care of the cameras. You're good."

Our comms system is short-range only – I don't know the specifics, exactly, but we have group chat up to about half a mile. Paul also has a direct line to Reggie, which we can't hear, so she can provide him with intel that he can then spread to us. I once told him it would be a lot more efficient to include Reggie on the group chat too, but he started talking about command and control and lines of communication and I blacked out from sheer boredom.

"Can I have some more music to hop out the van to?" I ask him.

In response, Annie reaches over and pops the door, shoving me through. It's not exactly the exit I imagined – in my head, I had Africa playing Nipsey Hussle's "Last Time That I Checc'd" while the rest of us jumped out the van in slow-motion, shades on, looking dangerous. Oh well. At least I get to wear a cool uniform while I do it. Even if the heavy bulletproof vest makes me stumble on the landing.

We're parked at the back of Hangar 22, its rear wall looming above the van, a vast expanse of metal sheeting. The air is filled with the sound of planes landing and taking off, the beeping of reversing trucks and baggage carts. It's not sunny – the clouds still hang low over the city – but it's warmed up a little since yesterday. The rain is holding off, for now.

"All right," Annie says. "See you in a sec." She starts walking, heading towards the front of the hangar.

Another snag to my slow-mo-movie-exit stunt: Paul didn't actually leave the van. He's still inside, hefting the sheet of thick steel that was leaning up against the rear door. I help him with it, manoeuvring it out onto the concrete surface. In the distance, one of the weird little tug vehicles they use for moving planes to their parking spots is buzzing around the corner of a hangar.

Paul puts an arm on the open driver-side window. "Africa, you know what to do?"

"Ya ya."

"Teagan?"

"I literally suggested this part of the plan. Yes, I know what to do." I nudge the metal sheet with my sneaker. It's around four feet square, and has a high weight tolerance. "All aboard."

"I still don't think this is a good idea."

"Yeah, it's gonna look pretty stupid. But it's the quickest way to get up on the roof."

He scowls, but steps onto the steel, which clanks under his weight. I join him.

"Annie," I say. "How're we doing?"

"You're supposed to say *over* at the end of a transmission," Paul grumbles.

"Hold." Annie's voice is crisp and sharp in my ear. "All right, I see Schmidt's goons. They're looking in my direction. Go."

"Snuggle up." I grab hold of Paul, then wrap my PK around the sheet.

When you're psychokinetic, you don't need ladders, or elevators. If you're strong enough – and over the past few months, I've gotten plenty strong – you can float yourself up to wherever you're going. It makes infiltration missions a cinch, and would also be super-handy if you lived in a second- or third-storey apartment. Who needs keys?

It's also why *we're* being sent on this mission, instead of a special forces unit with guns and terrible beards. When you can move things with your mind, it's very easy to get in and out of a place without being seen. Why risk the chaos and potential lawsuits of knocking down the door when you can be quick and quiet? Also fabulously good-looking, if I do say so myself.

It's about fifty feet to the roof of the hangar. Paul and I bend our knees for balance as my PK lifts the metal sheet. The weight might not be a problem, but keeping it steady is tricky. I was worried about incoming pilots spotting us – after all, they are literally right over our heads – but according to Paul, we're far enough from the actual runways. They won't see us.

Normally, Annie is point on our missions, with Paul handling comms and logistics. Not on this one. Annie's scared of heights, and point-blank refused to join me on my amazing improvised lift. I believe her exact words were "The fuck I wanna do that for?" I can't blame her – on the night I was framed for murder, I had to throw both of us out the window of a skyscraper. She's never let me forget it, either.

While Paul and I get high, Annie's going to be around the

front, pretending to be an anal Homeland Security official, demanding to see the papers for Schmidt's guards and pilot.

Paul and I ascend in silence, the sheet beneath us rocking slightly as it moves. Below us, Africa has his head tilted up out the window, shading his eyes, watching us with a kind of awe. I have to resist the urge to flip him a lazy salute.

I'm concentrating hard on keeping us airborne, so it takes me a few seconds to realise that Paul is doing something ... kind of strange.

"Are you humming?" I say.

"No." He doesn't look at me.

"You so were. Wait ... " My eyes go wide as I recognise the tune. "That's from *Aladdin*."

"Well ... "

"That was 'A Whole New World'. You were humming 'A Whole New World'!"

He shrugs. "It's a good film." He lets go of me, stepping carefully onto the roof.

"Wait – Will Smith remake or Robin Williams original?"

"Um ... "

"Animated or real life, dude?"

"Oh. The first one."

"And I just gave you a magic carpet ride. You do know that makes you Jasmine in this situation, right?"

I step off the plate – and my foot meets nothing but air.

While I was talking, I let the steel plate drift a little too far from the edge. I wasn't looking down at it, didn't think.

Paul moves faster than I've ever seen him. He grabs my wrist, the other hand going around my opposite forearm, leaping onto the roof and yanking me just far forward enough for my toes to catch the surface.

For a horrible second, both of us teeter on the edge of the

roof, fifty feet of nothing below us. I've still got hold of the sheet with my PK – it's now drifting a good two feet away from the edge – but terror has wiped my mind clean.

With a grunt, Paul hauls me all the way onto the roof. I end up collapsed on top of him, my rapid breath feeling like it's going to tear a hole in my throat.

"Christ." Paul steadies me. "You OK?"

I can't answer just yet. I'm still trying to convince myself that I'm not about to die.

"What were you thinking?" he says, helping me to my feet.

I find my voice. "Shut up, Jasmine."

He's right, though. I *do* need to focus. This mission has to go well – I don't want to risk putting Reggie in a bad mood. Or, you know, letting the list of super-secret deep-cover assets fall into the wrong hands. That would also be bad.

I rest the steel plate quietly on the roof, for our exit later. There's not much to see from up here: the ugly sprawl of Northridge and Granada Hills, hunkering under the low-hanging clouds. A gust of wind plays with my hair, flicking strands into my face.

"Hey," I say to Paul. "Thanks."

He flashes me a half-smile. "Somebody's got to look out for you. Come on."

In the blueprints Reggie dug up, there was an access hatch in the hangar roof. That's where we head now, picking our way along the metal surface. Before we even reach it, I've popped the combination lock. It's big and heavy, thick enough to defeat bolt-cutters. I open it in about four seconds. By now, Annie will have engaged Schmidt's guards in conversation, giving them hell on behalf of Homeland Security. She'll be demanding that pilots and crew disembark, too, which means the cabin will be nice and empty.

Paul gives me a nod. Very slowly, I ease the hatch up, wary for the creak of rusty hinges. They don't come.

Paul and I crouch by the hatch, peering into the hangar. The plane is just below us – a Bombardier Global 8000, if I remember Paul's briefing. As expected, there are several security guards on the hangar floor below us. They're all clustered in one spot: near the entrance, where a tiny figure in uniform is making pointed gestures.

"You see it?" Paul points to the jet, and the emergency escape hatch above the cockpit. That's the way in.

Paul digs in his backpack, unloading rope and carabiners. Much as I'd love to magic-carpet my way down, it's not a good idea. Not when a guard might get bored with Annie, and casually glance upwards. If I'm going to be caught, better it *not* happen right when I'm using my ability.

"Remember: the safe should be in the master bedroom." Paul climbs into a harness, passes one to me. "You don't need to do anything on the way down – I'll lower you. Copy?"

"I'm not on the radio. I'm standing right in front of you. You don't need to say *copy*."

"Do you understand this part of the plan or not?"

"*Yes*, I get it. Let's go."

Paul moves quickly, connecting up the rope to our harnesses and threading it through a complicated series of pulleys and carabiners. Annie is still talking, haranguing the pilot and crew about visas. At least, I think that what she's doing. I don't care if she starts singing them "Baa Baa Black Sheep", as long as she keeps them distracted.

Paul pulls on a pair of thick leather gloves. "Try not to move too much."

"Ooh yeah, baby, talk dirty to me."

He doesn't deign to respond to that. I sit on the edge, then push myself off. The rope takes my weight immediately. No training needed – I just need to hold still while Paul lowers me down.

The inside of the hangar is dark, thank fuck, especially up here – but all the same, I keep a close eye on Annie and her crowd. The pilot is to her right, a big man in uniform. Looks like there are two crew members with him.

I look down, eyeing the plane below me. I'll have to be careful – it's directly below the roof hatch, but parked at a slight diagonal. I'll hit the body slightly off-centre.

Ten feet. Five.

Here we go.

Touchdown.

My Jordans barely make a sound as they kiss the body of the plane, leaning into it, cat-walking my way up onto the body. I glance at the entrance, but nobody's looking. So far, so good.

The cockpit escape hatch is less than twenty feet away. I unclip quickly, just like Paul and I practiced, and flash him a thumbs-up before starting my walk over. I stay low, quiet, placing my feet carefully.

"Teagan," Paul whispers in my ear. "Be *damn* careful."

The hatch is only meant to open from the inside, and when it does, there are reels that pop out, so the pilot and co-pilot can descend from the plane without breaking their legs. I reach out with my PK, focusing, wrapping it around the hatch . . .

I move the internal mechanism and slide it upwards, holding the reels in place. Smooth and easy – the hatch pops in under two seconds. I don't waste time, lowering my legs inside, and dropping into the cockpit.

Action-hero ninja landings are crazy tough to pull off in real life. But if I do say so myself, I give it a pretty good go. I only wobble a little bit on the landing, coming down into a crouch, arms up, just behind the pilot seats. Above me, my PK seals the hatch.

"I'm in."

THIRTEEN

Teagan

OK, private jets are awesome.

This plane is bigger than my apartment. And it's way more comfortable: buttery leather seats, muted silver accents, tables that I'm pretty sure are real wood. Also a full bar, with some *seriously* good whiskey stacked behind it.

Forget being a chef. Hell, forget being a government agent. I should try find work as a German tech billionaire.

The soft carpet muffles my footsteps as I pad towards what looks like the bedroom door, fine-grained wood with a steel handle. It's locked, of course, but I'm through in seconds, my PK making short work of the mechanism.

The first thing I notice is the contraption hanging from the bedroom ceiling. When I realise what it is, I whistle, long and low.

"What is it? Over," Paul says.

"Dude has a sex swing bolted to the ceiling. Like a bondage sex swing. On his *plane*."

"Focus, Teagan," Paul says. "*Now.* Over."

Sex swing aside, the bedroom is rad, with a huge double bed and an enormous flatscreen TV. There's an oversized window on the other side of the room, letting Schmidt look out at the clouds from his pillow. An en-suite bathroom to my left, the door ajar, reveals an expanse of smooth white tile. The mother-fucker has an actual shower in there.

He hasn't gone to any trouble to hide the safe – why would he? It's on the lower half of a bedside cabinet, secured with a hefty biometric lock.

Come to think of it, I'm not sure I want to see what's actually in there, now that I know what Herr Schmidt gets up to on transatlantic flights.

I feel at the lock with my PK, driving my mind into the mechanism. It's a little bit more complicated than ones I've seen in the past. I have to focus, teasing out the right pieces to manipulate. It would be a lot easier just to rip out the entire door, but I believe the idea is to not alert Mister Germany that someone was all up in his shit.

I can feel the solution on the tip of my mind when Paul comes on the comms. "Hold. We have an unidentified vehicle on scene. Over."

"I see it," Annie mutters. I have to restrain the urge to reply, *Of course you do, you're right there.*

"Do I need to do anything now?" Africa says.

"No." Paul pauses. "Hold position."

A moment later, he sucks in a breath. "It's Schmidt. Schmidt is here."

"What the fuck do you mean, Schmidt is here?" I hiss.

"It's him all right," Annie murmurs. "I can see him getting out."

"Reggie?" Paul sounds frantic. He must have forgotten he was still on the group channel. There's a buzz of static, Paul adjusting something, and then Reggie's voice in my ear.

"That's impossible," she says. "I've been monitoring the hotel, he's still . . . "

There's a second of silence. Then she sucks in a horrified breath. "Oh, shit. Paul, I got it wrong. He left the hotel. He's there. He's with you."

"He didn't make the sale?" I say. "Is anybody with him?"

"I don't know. Working on it!"

Paul doesn't hesitate. "Team: abort. *Abort mission*."

"What—?" I scramble to my feet. "No!"

"Annie – keep them distracted, just a little longer. Teagan, I want you back up on top of the jet for extraction. And Africa, keep the engine running."

"But I haven't got the goods yet!" I hiss.

"Doesn't matter. We—"

"It's just him," Annie says quietly. "I don't see a buyer."

"Annie," I say. "Keep them distracted. I need, like, two more minutes." Reggie has gone completely silent as if she doesn't want to make anything worse.

"Teagan," Paul says. "The jet isn't rented. Schmidt owns it. He'll send the pilot back on board and deal with TSA himself."

"Oh. Fuck."

"Exactly. You need to exit, qu—oh god*dammit*."

"What now?"

"The pilot's coming back now. Repeat, pilot inbound. They'll be onboard in the next twenty seconds."

I close my eyes for a second, then rocket out of Schmidt's love den, cursing. If I can get to the cockpit quickly, I can be out the top of the plane before they know I was there. Except ... shit, it's not going to be enough. There's no way I can get up, out, and then lock everything down before the pilot comes into the cockpit.

Not like I have a choice. As my feet hit the plush carpet of the main cabin, there's a squeal of tyres from outside the plane, closely followed by Paul saying, "Africa, what in the hell are you doing?"

"It's OK." Africa sounds more excited than I've ever heard him. "I will keep them busy."

There's the sound of a door opening over the comms, and then Africa's voice again – not just in my ears, but echoing across the tarmac. "Hey! You! Mister Germany! You bloody *toubab*!"

"Uh, Paul?" I say, hovering, frozen. "What exactly is happening out there?"

He ignores me. "Africa, *stand down*."

"No worries," he says, speaking quickly and quietly. "I give Teggan time." Then another roar: "Ya, you! I'm talking to you. This is the Homeland Security, I will put you in Guantanamo Bay!"

I have to bite down on a laugh. The thought of Africa striding across the tarmac, a seven-foot-tall behemoth in a Gestapo outfit and mirror shades, looming over the little German tech bro and his entourage, is hysterical. Also useful, because it'll buy me the time I need. I risk a peek out the plane's open door; the pilots have stopped on the tarmac, staring at the huge, gesticulating monster in their midst.

Africa, you hero. I will never get mad at him again, not ever.

I turn towards the cockpit . . . and stop.

The list is here. I'm sure of it. It's in the safe, right behind me. What if, instead of getting the hell out, I stayed on board? What if I used the time Africa bought me?

Hide. Wait. When the coast is clear, open the safe, grab the goods, get the hell out. Come back a legend.

I don't bother with closets, or the en-suite bathroom. The first thing Schmidt is likely to do is hang up his jacket, then take a piss. Besides, I pride myself on thinking laterally in these situations. I throw out my PK, tendrils of mental energy running along the floor and walls.

Africa and Annie are still tag-teaming everyone on the tarmac. "Teagan, where are you?" Paul says. "I'm ready to pull you back up. Over."

"OK, don't get mad . . . "

"What do you mean, *don't get mad*?"

"I've got an idea."

"Get out of there *now*. That's an order."

It'll take me a little time to crack the safe, but if I can find a hiding place, I can do it mid-flight, while Schmidt and his goons are drinking schnapps in the main cabin. I *could* risk opening the safe up now . . . but I'd still have to get out, and I might not be able to do it without running into someone nasty. "Sorry, Paul," I murmur. "We're doing this."

"*Teagan!*"

There. Three panels in the floor, on the other side of the bed, covered with thick carpet. The carpet is glued down, but it's synthetic fibre. I have it up in about five seconds, rolled like a yoga mat, exposing the panels beneath. I pop one, revealing a crawlspace thick with wires and electronics. It will be a hell of a tight fit, but there's just enough room for me to climb inside. In my earpiece, Africa is still yelling incomprehensible nonsense at Schmidt, and it sounds as if Annie is trying to calm him down. Paul is going fucking nuts. I'm pretty sure he's about to have a heart attack.

Tight fit. That's like describing Antarctica as a tiny bit chilly. I have to curl into a ball, knees jammed under my chin, and even then I'm not sure I'm going to be able to put everything back where I found it. At least I don't have to use my hands. I push the panel down on top of me, grunting as it squashes me even further into the space, locking me in darkness. Dust tickles my nose as I roll the carpet back over the panel. It probably doesn't look nearly as good as it did before, but I doubt Schmidt will notice.

A few seconds later, someone – the pilots and crew, I assume – board the plane.

Thumping footsteps, in the room above me. I stay still as I can, hardly daring to breathe. There are voices, but I can't make out the words.

A sneeze tries to worm its way into my nostrils. I don't let it, using this trick I know where you squash your tongue against the roof of your mouth. *Not going out like that. No way. Not with a fucking sneeze.*

Africa and Annie stall for as long as they can – demanding passports, visas, background checks. But eventually, Annie comes over the line. "I had to clear him. He was about to send someone to get a supervisor. Teagan, where are you?"

"Kind of a funny story," I mutter.

"She OK?" Africa sounds out of breath. "Teggan?"

"They've cleared the plane for taxi," Reggie says quietly. There's a lot of static on the comms now.

Around me, the plane's engines and internal systems begin to kick in, vibrations rattling through my tiny hidey-hole. There's a jolt, and I bang my head against a strut. I have to bite my lip to stop myself from swearing very loudly. It's only been a couple of minutes, but my muscles are already aching, throbbing with pain that doesn't go away no matter how much I shift my weight.

The rumbling gets louder as the plane starts to move, taxi-ing out of the hangar. A sudden, horrible thought occurs: they insulate the cabin, but they do nothing about the rest of the plane. What if I have to hide out here for the whole flight? I may badly want to complete this mission, but I've got absolutely no desire to freeze to death while doing it.

More footsteps, the voices moving away. I take a deep breath, and send my PK out as far as I can. This time, I'm not trying to move anything.

You can't live with my ability without figuring out some very useful tricks, and one of those is what I like to think of as echolocation. It has nothing to do with sound, of course. When I move an object, I can sense how it fits into the world: size, velocity, position in space. What that means is that when I focus, I can build up a picture of the world around me, even with my eyes closed.

This doesn't work with people, who are organic and complicated and annoying. But human beings tend to carry lots of inanimate objects around with them. Phones. Keys. Watches. Jewellery. Pacemakers. Artificial hips. Butt plugs. It's very easy to build up a fine-grained picture of the world, just by tracking the things people have on them.

I concentrate, trying to pick up as much information as I can. There are two people in the cockpit – or, if I'm being accurate, a couple of smartphones, two upright pens in shirt pockets, and what feels like a very expensive Rolex. Four in the main cabin, their positions flagged by a bunch of other watches and metal wallets and stud earrings. And guns. At least two guns. There's nobody in the bedroom above me.

The engines ratchet up to a roar, the vibrations rattling my crawlspace as the plane thunders down the runway. *Shit.* Oh well: I've always wanted to see New York. Apparently they have great pizza. Paul and Annie are speaking in my ear, but I can't hear them over the noise of the engines.

A takeoff means everybody in the plane will be in their seats in the main cabin, at least for a few minutes. That gives me a window of opportunity. I send out another burst of PK, ensuring there are no keys or coins making their way towards the bedroom, then peel back the carpet and crack the hatch.

Uncoiling myself, rolling out onto the floor of the bedroom, is better than anything the people who land up in Herr Schmidt's sex swing have ever experienced. I have to resist the urge to purr like a cat. The ache in my muscles goes from horrible-owey-yikes pain to oh-my-God-don't-you-dare-stop pain.

My good mood lasts precisely three seconds. Because when I'm done with the safe, I'll have to go back into the floor. Not only will I have to be there for hours and hours, but I also have to do it while the passengers are sipping vodka tonics and eating cocktail olives. And then probably getting freaky in the bondage swing, right where I can hear them.

It's a good thing I'm flat on my back, because right then, the plane takes off, the floor tilting underneath me. Slowly, I get to my feet.

"Paul? Annie? Come in?"

Nothing. Just a slight hiss of static. A little knot of worry forms in between my shoulder blades.

I shake it off, going back to work on the safe lock. I drop to my knees in front of it, mind half on the objects and the rest of the cabin. Still no movement. Good. I zero in on the lock components, isolating them with my PK, working out which parts do what. A few moments later, the sequence clicks together in my head, and the lock pops. *Bam.* In.

The safe is full of paperwork. Stacks of it: bearer bonds and contracts and notebooks. My heart sinks. It's going to take me too long to hunt through this mess. Should I just take it all? What if he opens the safe during the flight? Then again, he might do that anyway, even if I just take the list. What will happen if he finds it missing? Will he turn and head back to LA? Book it for Germany? Much as I want to see

Europe, I'm not sure I can take a full night beneath Schmidt's floorboards ...

I haven't thought this through. There are too many elements, too many things to juggle. I have to stop, take a breath, actually figure out how to—

A soft footstep. Behind me. I whirl, and Jonas Schmidt is standing in the doorway.

He looks younger in person, in his early thirties, with a mop of floppy blond hair over a smooth-cheeked face. His eyes, a piercing blue, are wide with surprise. He wears a tight, white V-neck T-shirt over cream linen pants, and he's taken off his shoes.

I stare back him, blinking in shock. It's impossible for him to be here. I might have been concentrating on the safe, but I kept some of my PK focused on the main cabin, and none of the pens and coins and watches had—

But Schmidt isn't wearing a watch. There's nothing in his pockets: not a phone, not a wallet, not even a zipper on his pants. If he had them earlier, he's put them aside somewhere. He wears no jewellery. Doesn't even have any fillings. His clothes are lightweight linen and cotton. There is absolutely nothing on him that my PK could latch onto.

Teagan, you fucking idiot.

I give him a wide smile. "Um. Hi. So you've been selected for a random security screening ... "

"Mikhail," he shouts. "Gerhard. *Komm schnell!*"

FOURTEEN

Amber

Amber doesn't dare ask Matthew to put on his seatbelt. Not when he's this quiet. He stares out the window of the pickup, hands folded in his lap, still as a statue. Inside the car, there's no sound but the hum of the engine, the rumble of the road. When she'd put on the radio, he'd snapped at her to turn it off.

His silence isn't the sullen, irritated type that he gets when he's hungry, or needs the bathroom. It's a calm silence. Focused. His face is a total blank. Amber knows this silence well. It's what happens before he hurts someone.

No. He's just tired, that's all. We were up late last night, and we spent a long time at the museum so . . .

It's taken them over two hours to get out of Los Angeles. The 2 was jammed with traffic, and multiple detours have added to the journey. Now, they're deep in what's supposed to be the Angeles National Forest, north of the city. Amber doesn't know why they call it a forest; the few trees she does see are scraggly things, widely spaced and burnt-brown.

Her son had still been talking with Mia, the museum volunteer, when Amber had returned with his Mountain Dew. The young woman had grown more and more amazed at his questions, and after a while, Matthew had a crowd gathered around him, volunteers and scientific staff both, enthusiastically talking about fault lines and aftershocks and tectonic activity.

Amber had tried to follow along. She knew she should be paying attention, trying to pick up clues to what her son was planning. But the conversation went down rabbit holes, twisting and turning, playing with concepts she couldn't even begin to fathom. The longer she'd stayed there, trying to listen, the more confused she'd become. And what was she going to do? Drag her son away? He'd just punish her later.

One of the staff – an older man with a ring of white hair below a shiny, bald scalp – had taken her aside, handed her his card. "We can't employ children – obviously," he'd said, grinning. "But when he gets old enough, we'd love to have him intern here, even if it's only on the weekends. You've raised one hell of a good kid. And of course, you're both welcome back any time."

Hell of a good kid. Amber had found herself guiltily pleased. Even at the Facility, she'd never gotten that kind of praise. They, of course, knew better too. Even Ajay, as they lay in bed together while Matthew had been off on one of his tests or in one of the classes, had never told her she was a good parent. He'd talked excitedly about Matthew's potential, about the Director's hopes for him and the other children. But he'd never said she'd been doing a good job as a mom. Hearing it from this stranger, someone who'd only had the barest impression of her, gave her a queer pride.

It isn't what you have or who you are or where you are or what you are doing that makes you happy or unhappy. It is what you think about it. She remembered that one from *How to Win Friends & Influence People.* So she'd let herself be happy. Let herself be proud.

Matthew had finally said his goodbyes to the museum staff, and he'd told her, "I know where to go next."

They'd loaded up on burritos and bottled water, Matthew poring over Google Maps while she ordered, then headed north. Matthew hasn't said a word since they left La Cañada Flintridge. He'd said to head for Big Pines, a town at the north-eastern edge of the park, but Amber has a sense that that's a direction, not a final destination. Someone at the museum had found him a California Earthquake Exhibit T-shirt, which he's now wearing. Big red letters on white fabric, slightly too big for him.

The light on the highway is cold, all colour driven off by the low-hanging clouds. If not for the dashboard clock telling her it's almost 11:30, Amber wouldn't know what time of day it was. She keeps a steady speed, both hands on the wheel, not daring to look at her son. Trying to think of a way to stop him.

Nothing comes. And so they drive.

There's hardly any traffic, but as they climb a short hill, they pass a green Prius stopped on the shoulder, the driver tapping away at her phone behind the wheel. The colour makes Amber shiver. It was a green car that hit her on her last Flop attempt, the one she should have known better than to try. You didn't *do* that shit when you had a baby – but nothing else had been working, and she'd already had to run from the cops once, and she was desperate. And that's all there was to it.

When she woke up, she wasn't in the hospital. She was at the School.

She was angry. Confused. But they'd told her they could save her baby, bring him to term. And they *had*.

The moment her son was born had been the most shining, most glorious moment of her life. As she held him in her arms, as the heat and life and sheer *presence* of him washed

over her, she experienced – for the first time in for ever –
true bliss.

She'd rocked him softly, and knew she'd die for him. He'd
saved her. And they'd told her she could stay at the School, that
she'd be taken care of. *They* would be taken care of.

The setup didn't make sense to her, at first. The School –
that was what everyone called it – was a well-built complex
in a nondescript building on the outskirts of Albuequerque,
on the very edge of the desert. It wasn't like any school
she'd ever come across. There weren't any students for one
thing – or at least, none that weren't babies, no more than a
few months old.

And the Director . . . she was *young*. Amber's age. Far too
young to justify the title. And yet, she was clearly in charge: a
focused, calm, determined presence, familiar with every inch
of the building, commanding total respect from Ajay and the
other doctors.

She tried to see their angle, tried to figure out if the Director
and Ajay and all the others were playing their own con. Then
again: what exactly did she have to gain by heading back
to the streets? What was she going to do, go back to running the Flop?

That was before . . . everything else. Before they realised
how smart Matthew was.

By age two, he was speaking – full words and sentences.
By three, he was reading. He would get utterly absorbed in it,
blocking out everything around him. He'd slept like – well,
like a baby when he was very young, but as soon as he started
talking, he hardly slept at all. Two or three hours a night
wasn't unusual.

She still remembers when he started moving the earth with
his mind. She remembers standing in the doorway of their

little room, gaping as he made chunks of dirt from the window box dance. She'd leaned against the door frame, shaking, trying to process what she was seeing.

She'd confronted the Director, of course. The Director had listened, and then fixed her with a level gaze. "He would have died if we hadn't taken you in. If you've got a problem with his new abilities, you're free to leave him with us."

Amber could read between the lines on that one. She didn't think the Director would have her killed – at least, she hoped not – but she also knew there was no paper trail. If she left, she'd lose her son.

She'd raged. Screamed. Threatened. Wept. None of it made a difference. And in the end, it wasn't the Director's calm expression that had convinced her. It was Ajay, and the other doctors. When they saw what her son could do, they'd congratulated her. Congratulated *her*.

The ground was shifting under her feet. The Director and Ajay and the Facility were the only stable thing for miles. So she held on.

Gifted – that was the word Ajay had used to describe Matthew. Others, too: prodigy, precocious, unusual. Her son had a kind of terrifying intelligence that made her wonder, briefly, if there'd been a mistake – if they'd handed her the wrong baby. People like her were not supposed to have bright kids. Dirt-poor con-artist trailer trash from Barelas weren't supposed to give birth to geniuses.

But he wasn't just a genius, like the Director explained. It wasn't just his powers.

He read endlessly, was curious about everything he saw. But he never laughed. Almost never smiled. He wouldn't respond to jokes – and he got angry when he was teased, even a little bit. He had to be kept apart from the other children – he'd try use his ability to hurt them, and no amount of persuasion or threats would stop him.

Once, she had come into the Facility's courtyard, where the children played under the blazing New Mexico sun, and found him packing one of the other children in dirt. Holding it in place with his mind, ripping it from the planters around the edge, smiling as the other child writhed and pleaded and cried.

She had grabbed him, shaken him, genuinely angry and – for the first time – not bothering to hide it. She'd screamed at him to stop, and he had, but the strange smile had never left his face.

That was the first time he'd hurt her, too. The first time he'd turned his powers on her. In the end, they had to inject him with a sedative.

She digs the heel of her hand into her forehead. She can't think about the Facility now. The government's taken it over – it was a miracle Ajay got them out when he did. Ajay. God, what she wouldn't give to have him here. If only *he* had been the father.

A short while later, they reach an intersection – hardly worthy of the name, really, a wide dirt track bordering the highway on two sides.

Matthew stirs, straightening. "Stop here."

Amber pulls the pickup onto the right shoulder, dirt crunching, little whirlwinds of dust swirling around them. When she cuts the engine, the whole world holds its breath.

Her son pops the door, climbs out. "Bring the water. And my burrito."

He leads them to the dirt track, heading south from the road, marching with purpose down the middle of it. Amber follows in his wake. It's a struggle to breathe, as if the clouds are a heavy blanket, smothering her. A few times, her son crouches down, head bent, as if listening intently. No sooner does she reach him than he jumps to his feet, striding away.

It's going to happen again. Another earthquake.

Something inside Amber hardens, a core of steel she didn't know she had and she clings to it. This time, she knows what's coming. If she can find the angle, control the situation, she can stop it.

A few minutes later, Matthew abruptly turns left, leading her off the track and into the scrubland. The trees are a little thicker here, and the air smells of dust and dry leaves. There are several burnt stumps, and before long, Amber's legs and shoes are smudged with soot. "Matthew?" she says. "Honey?"

He ignores her.

Distract him. "Do you want some water? Or food? I brought a bag of chips, too, and there's your . . . the rest of your burrito. In fact, you know what? Why don't we go get burgers in Big Pines? I read yesterday there's a *great* cheeseburger place in—"

"Be quiet." He's stopped at the base of a thick pine tree, down on one knee, patting the earth. He nods to himself once, straightens up. "This is the place. This is where the most energy is stored."

He turns to her. The smile he wears is completely genuine: self-satisfied, delighted, *ecstatic.*

The man at the museum was right. She *is* a good parent. And good parents don't let their children walk all over them. If she can't distract him, she'll show him who's boss.

"That's enough," she says, startled at how harsh her voice is.

He blinks at her, his smile faltering.

"We're going back to the car now." Her fists aren't clenched. Her voice isn't strained. She's working very hard to make sure neither of those things happen. She needs to be firm, quiet, calm. "We're going back to the car, and we're going to go to Big Pines and get cheeseburgers. That's what's going to happen." She holds a hand out to him. "Come on."

He doesn't move. His smile has curdled.

"Did you hear me, Matthew? I said—"

The clod of dirt hits her in the face.

It's dry, crumbly, spewing red dust. But it's the size of a closed fist, hardened by the sun, and it sends her stumbling. She almost falls, catches herself, startled at the numb, swollen feeling in her cheek.

"No," she says. "*Stop.*"

It's not a plea. It's a firm command. She is his mother, and he is her son, and he's going to *listen to*—

More clods fly at her face. She bats away the first, but the second smacks into her mouth. Blood and dust mingle on her tongue, and this time, she does fall.

Matthew watches, not moving. Usually, when she doesn't do what he says, he throws a tantrum. Yells. Cries fat, ugly tears. Not this time. He's done this before, and there's a not a damn thing Amber can do about it.

Except, she has to. He's going to kill hundreds of people. Thousands maybe. And there is no one coming, no police, no Facility staff with sedatives and first aid kits. No Ajay. Just her. He is her responsibility.

"Matthew, that's *enough.*" Her words are fat, clumsy. "If you don't stop right now, I'm gonna—"

He throws more dirt at her. This time, it's a hailstorm, a tornado, soil spattering her skin, jagged rock slicing it. She covers her face, rolls away, but the dirt comes from everywhere. Every time she tries to suck in a breath, she inhales more of it. It coats her mouth, burns her throat. Blood runs down her arms and neck from a dozen wounds, mixing with the dirt, turning black.

This is worse than it's ever been, worse than anything he's done to her. *He's going to kill me.*

All the courage she'd dredged up leaks away, leaving a roaring emptiness in its wake. She's sorry, she's sorry, she's so goddamn sorry and right now all she needs to do is let him know, tell him, but she can't, her mouth is numb and bleeding and she can't see and he's going to kill her kill her kill

But he doesn't.

By the time she realises the dirt storm has stopped, Amber is curled in on herself, sobbing. Matthew stands over her, the dark clouds appearing to swirl around his head. He looks satisfied.

"You shouldn't try to stop me. Are you going to do it again?"

She shakes her head.

"Are you?"

"No." Barely a whisper. Blood on her lips.

"Are you?"

"*No.*"

"Good." He turns, heads back towards the base of the pine. "Stay still, Amber. I can shield us more easily if you just stay there."

"*Why*? Matthew, why?"

He looks back at her, shrugs. Still smiling. Inside Amber, a tiny light winks to life – a mother's instinctual brightening at seeing her child smile. Then it's gone. Snuffed out by a cold so sharp and biting that she almost gasps.

"Why not?" he says.

He drops to his knees. Puts both hands on the ground. His shoulders rise and fall, rise and fall.

FIFTEEN

Teagan

I'm a little surprised Jonas Schmidt doesn't break out the cuffs.
He probably has a few lying around.

Instead, his goons march me out into the body of the plane,
push me down onto a leather chair. It's more comfortable than
the spot under his floorboards, but at least there, I didn't have
guns pointed at me. The weapons in question are twin Heckler
& Koch handguns, good German steel. One is held by a rat-
faced little twerp in a *Men in Black* suit, standing next to me;
the other by a dude with shoulders like ham hocks, straining
at his suit jacket. Schmidt addresses rat-face as Mikhail, ham
hock as Gerhard. And that's not counting the beefy flight
attendant, minding his own business at the back of the plane.

Guns aren't a problem for me. I can jam them into holsters
and lock the safety shut and take them away from their owners.
There are a million ways I could use my PK in this situation –
hell, I could take the guns, hijack the plane, force it to turn
back. Of course, doing so would involve revealing my PK to
everyone. Not exactly the best option.

Schmidt sits opposite me, in an identical chair. His electric-
blue eyes search mine, his hands folded neatly in his lap.

There's a very slight smile on his face. He says nothing. And keeps saying nothing for a good two minutes.

The silence gets to me. I lean forward, causing Mikhail to stand a little straighter. "I think this is where you say, 'We have ways of making you talk'?"

He actually laughs. It's deep and genuine, and his eyes crinkle when he does. "Well, you are definitely not BND."

"And they are?"

"*Bundesnachrichtendienst*. The Federal Intelligence Service of Germany. They are not known for their joking. Although, if I am fair, I knew you were not them when I found you in my bedroom. They would never have been so clumsy."

"Hey, man, you didn't even know I was on board until you walked in on me."

"*Ja*, I am curious about that." He nods to the window. "The Homeland Security agents who were bothering my men. Yours, yes? I imagine that is when you snuck aboard the plane."

I don't say a damn thing.

"If you are indeed American, then you will be CIA. No? Perhaps the Department of Military Sciences? Are you one of Church's people?"

"I literally don't know who that is."

"One of your SEAL teams, then?" he says, sounding faintly bored. "They have been known to carry out missions such as this . . ."

"Yeah, well, my people know I'm on this plane. Any second now, you're gonna have F-16s off your port bow." Shit, is that a plane thing, or a ship thing?

"I think not." He settles back in his chair. "We still have communications. All I must do is let my intelligence contacts in Germany know that we have had hostile action from an

American agent, and there will be an international incident.
Your government does not want that. I think your F-16s are
not coming. Drink?"

" . . . What?"

"You do drink, yes? We have a good selection on board."
The flight attendant appears at his elbow, smiling. "Beer,
Rodrigo, thank you. And for you, miss . . . ?"

Fuck it. "I'll take a beer too."

It arrives quickly, tall and frosty. I suddenly realise how
parched I am, and I'm about to take a chug when I stop, eyeing
the glass.

Schmidt raises an eyebrow. "You cannot be serious."

"Hold on—"

He throws up his hands. "Fine. You caught me. I have
dosed your beer with a deadly serum that was concocted by
the Illuminati at a Bilderberg Group meeting at Sacred Oaks.
All true billionaires know these secrets – it is the way we run
the world. Now that I have told you, you must die."

He reaches across and takes my beer from me, sipping from
it. The slick bastard keeps eye contact the entire time. A crust
of foam has settled on his top lip, and he wipes it off with his
hand, not bothering to reach for the serviette on the armrest.
"There. See? No poison. Unless, of course, I am immune,
thanks to my daily infusions of infant blood."

A smile creeps across my face before I can stop it.

"So. She is human after all," he says. Schmidt passes my
beer back, takes a sip of his own. Good thing too, because he
doesn't notice my slight shiver. *If only you knew, dude.*

"Now." He leans forward elbows on his knees. "Perhaps
you will tell me your name. Or *a* name. Something I must
call you."

"Jay." It's the first thing that comes to my mind, mostly

because Jay Rock – one of the best LA rappers ever – has been doing rotations in my brain for the past three days. Plus, Jay can be a guy or a girl.

"And I am Jonas. A pleasure, truly. You are here for the list, yes?"

He doesn't wait for my response, just nods to where the safe is. "It is not there. You would have done better to intercept my limousine on my way to the airport."

"What are you talking about?"

He reaches inside his jacket, pulls out a neatly folded slip of paper. To my right, Mikhail tenses.

It doesn't make sense. If Schmidt was going to sell the list, then having it on him while he negotiates with a buyer is about the dumbest thing I can think of. I've only known him for five minutes, and I can tell he's smarter than that.

"You know what the most ironic thing is about technology?" It's the first mispronunciation he's made, twisting the first syllable of *ironic*, so it sounds like the vowel in *hit*. "Those of us who make our money from it do not trust it. It is not so easy to control. You see this everywhere. The CEO of a large social media company will not let his children join it. A programmer for a piece of software that handles Amazon payments will suddenly leave her position, talking to the media about data and privacy. But a piece of paper ... it cannot be hacked, and it is hard to steal."

He unfolds the list, flicks it with a finger. "Your assets in the Balkans. Moscow. Shanghai, Islamabad. I even have the name of the operatives you have in the Mossad. This list will be copied and placed in several secure locations across the world. If anything should happen to me—"

I've had enough. He can joke all he wants, offer me a drink and a comfy chair, but I shouldn't forget what this asshole came to my city to do. Fortunately, I have a few tricks of my own, and not just ones that involve moving shit with my mind. You can't hang around Moira Tanner for long without learning a thing or two.

I lean forward, look him dead in the eyes. "Cut the shit, Schmidt."

OK, that sounded kind of stupid, but I don't dare quit now. "We know about the list. We know you were in LA to sell it to the highest bidder. When you land in New York to refuel, my agency will board this plane and take you into custody. The only way you stop that happening is if you give me the list, and let me walk away. Maybe, just maybe, I convince my bosses to let you crawl back into your million-dollar mansion and never appear in public again."

I expected defiance. Anger. Hell, I was hoping for fear. I would even have settled for slight discomfort. What I don't expect is confusion.

"I do not understand," he says.

"Do I need to spell it out for you? Do you need flashcards?"

"I was not in Los Angeles to sell the list."

"Bullshit."

"No." Now he looks even more confused. "You did not know this? Jay, I came to Los Angeles to *buy* it."

I blink at him. That can't be right.

"It appears your agency does not have good intelligence all the time, hmm? But yes, I bought the list in Los Angeles. I will not tell you the name of the seller, of course – he is a good man, and I do not wish him harmed."

If it's true, then someone, somewhere got something wrong. I refuse to believe it's Tanner, or Reggie – there's no way they would make a fuck-up like this. The info must have been bad.

"I have no intention of releasing this list, unless I am forced to. Do you think I want your spies in these countries hurt? No – not unless there is no other option. I bought this list as an insurance policy, in the case of your government deciding that I am too dangerous."

"Because putting down cash for a list of our deep-cover assets is a great way to stay off their radar? Seems logical to me."

A sad smile creeps onto his lips. "I am already on their radar. There are things I have seen . . . "

"Oh, please."

He stares out the window. The clouds have parted, and the LA sprawl is visible below us, stretching to the horizon.

"Did you know your government is engaged in a biological weapons research programme at several bases in the Arctic Circle?" he says. "Research that breaks a hundred different international treaties?"

"That's not a—"

"Or that they help finance slave labour in West Africa, for the mining of uranium? And there is more still. I am aware, for instance, that they once engaged in a genetic research programme for persons with special abilities. There was a facility in Waco, in Texas, where they once tested a live subject who showed demonstrable ability to move objects without touching them."

His words freeze me to my seat.

That's impossible. He can't know that.

Waco was the highest level of secrecy, minimal staff, absolutely zero contact with the outside world. I may not know everything, but I *do* know something about how government secrets work, and that one? That one they are *very* careful about.

If he really does know about Waco, then he knows about me. Did he mention it to unsettle me? See what I would do?

Except: he's not even looking at me. He's still staring out the window, rattling off more things the US government has done. The Waco facility was just one thing on his list. It doesn't matter how he found out; he has no idea that I was the person at that facility.

So why tell me? Why mention it at all? Either he's pulling off a massive, triple-layer Jedi mind trick on me, or . . .

Or he's telling the truth.

"Hang on," I say. "If you know about all this stuff – and I'm not saying it is true, because it sounds pretty fucking far-fetched, to be honest – if you know about it, why not expose the government? Why keep it a secret?"

"These things are not so easy to prove. I do not have possession of the documents I have seen, or the whereabouts of the people I have spoken to. It is *possible* to prove them . . . but it is difficult. What your government is afraid of is that I may start speaking publicly about these things.

"No doubt they will paint me as a mad person. What is the word? A crackpot. But in these days we live in, people do not believe what is based on facts only. They believe what they want to believe. And so perhaps, they will start looking a bit closer at the things I have told them about. They could uncover . . . well, anything. You know the story of Pandora's Box?"

"OK. So why don't they just kill you?"

"I have survived several assassination attempts." He says it like he's mentioning he takes sugar in his coffee. "Including several incidents of tampering with my plane, or my cars. Fortunately, I pay my staff much more than they were offered to kill me, and they are very good at their jobs. Besides, I have somewhat of a high profile, even in the United States. Killing me is not so easy." A shrug. "Perhaps they will try again soon.

Maybe you were even sent here to kill me, after you retrieved the list."

He taps his breast pocket. "This document is not a conspiracy theory. It is real. Verifiable. I do not even have to release it publicly – just pass it to my friends in Israel, or in the Kremlin. That is what your government is truly scared of. As I say, the list is my insurance policy, and what it buys me is not just my life. It buys me time. Time to find concrete proof of these things, so they will no longer be secret."

"Why tell me all this? Why not just kill me yourself? Or toss me off the plane in New York and just go?"

That sad smile again, the crinkling around the eyes. "You will laugh at me."

"Buddy, I think your whole story is pretty fucking hysterical." But is it? Waco is true. It all happened. What about the rest of it? What if he really does want to protect himself from the government?

"I am not very good at being rich," he says slowly. "I am too curious. Others will invest in things, and not ask about where they come from – or if they do, they do not care. If I did the same, I would be much richer. But I ask too many questions, and the things I find out ..."

He takes another slug of his beer, wipes his mouth. "It is wrong to stay silent when others are being hurt. That is why I tell you all this. I look into your eyes, and I do not see a killer. An assassin. No. I see someone who may understand."

"So you're the good guy in all this, huh?"

He doesn't get a chance to answer. There's a burst of German from behind him, loud and urgent. Rodrigo, the flight attendant, is looking out one of the windows, his mouth open in horror.

"*Was ist es?*" Schmidt says, just as the pilot comes over the intercom, spitting another barrage of hurried German.

Mikhail and Gerhard scramble, keeping their guns on me as they drop into leather chairs of their own. I raise an eyebrow. "Something wrong?"

"*Mein Gott.*"

Schmidt has a face to the window. He's gone a blood-less white.

The plane banks hard. We're high up, but haven't hit cruising altitude yet, so we can still see the ground below.

At first, I think someone is letting off fireworks. Big, crackling, white ones.

But they aren't fireworks. They're power lines, ripping apart. It's happening everywhere, every place I look. The traffic on the roads has stopped, the ant-like cars coming to a shaking halt.

That's not all. There's something wrong with the ground. It's hard to see at first, but when I catch it, my stomach drops three inches. It's vibrating. No: *shaking*. Buildings swaying from side to side. Then, as I watch, they start to collapse, exploding in tiny puffs of dust. Fires bloom, explosions joining the white sparks of the power lines.

"*Erdbeden.*" Gerhard says slowly, his voice low. "*Das grosse Erdbeben.*"

I don't have speak German to know that one. Earthquake.
The Big One.

SIXTEEN

Teagan

I can't move. Can't look away from the window. Directly below us, a freeway collapses – just falls apart, sending cars tumbling. There's smoke everywhere, billowing in huge clouds.

As I watch, a street cracks down the middle – slowly, like a loaf of bread being pulled apart. An entire house crashes into the abyss. It's not the only one – everywhere I look, buildings are being torn apart, cloaked in fire and ash.

My people are down there. Reggie. Annie. Paul. Even Africa. Holy fuck – *Nic*. Where will he be now? He'll be at work, which means the courthouse in Inglewood. That's to our southwest ... but how far? Where does this thing reach?

A taller building, not quite a skyscraper but close to it, shakes itself to pieces. It happens in silence. There should be a roar, a crack, a volcano of sound. There's nothing but the plane's engines, rumbling away.

I'm going to throw up.

The words from the earthquake preacher, from two nights ago: *Did you know the San Andreas fault maxes out at 8.3?* This is it. The 8.3. The biggest earthquake possible. There's no way I can know that for sure, but I'm certain. And I'm in a metal tube in the sky, forced to watch it all.

"... unconfirmed reports of a massive seismic event in California." Someone has turned the plane's TV on. The news anchor's head is bent, her finger to her earpiece. It makes me think of Paul, on the roof of the hangar. *God*, I think. *Keep them safe. I know I don't believe in you, and if you are real this is probably all your fault, but please please please keep my people safe.* It's not much of a prayer, but it's better than nothing.

Schmidt pushes himself away from the window, starts barking at his guards in rapid-fire German. I can't even begin to follow the exchange. Nobody's looking at me. They've forgotten I exist. Gerhard is arguing with Schmidt, his face taut and pale. I could take the list. Right now. Just reach out and ...

And what? Fuck the list. It doesn't matter any more. It's just my brain hunting for something familiar, some semblance of order. And the list is in Schmidt's pocket, so there's no way I'm getting it – not if I don't want Gerhard to break my face.

Do something. But what? What in the world of blue fuck am I supposed to do?

The window draws my gaze again. I can't help it. There's more smoke now, a lot more, blanketing the city. Has the shaking stopped? Impossible to tell. Behind me, the news anchor's voice catches. "We're just getting reports that ... yes, a magnitude eight or higher earthquake has hit the city of Los Angeles. We're told it's emanating from the part of the San Andreas fault north of the city, somewhere in the Angeles National Forest."

Something is poking into my hip. My phone – *my phone!* I nearly rip my stupid uniform pants pulling it out, shaking fingers tapping at it. The phone's clock reads 11:42. There are messages from Paul, a dozen of them – but they're all old, stopping ten minutes ago. Most of them are just him shouting at me, telling me to contact him ASAP. None of them mention the quake.

I write a quick *Are you OK???*, hit send. Nothing. No signal at all.

"Come on, you *piece of shit*." I try again, same result. It's all I can do not to hurl the phone across the plane. No point even trying my comms earpiece – we'll be way out of range.

"You are going to need to strap in." Schmidt, buckling himself into his seat. Gerhard, Mikhail and Rodrigo are doing the same. The plane has banked even harder than before, turning in a tight circle.

My brain is having trouble catching up. The plane levels out, engines rising to a high whine. It might just be my imagination, but I could swear we've turned around completely, which means . . .

"We're going back?"

"We have to." He tightens his belt, fingers shaking. "We have some basic medical supplies, food, satellite communications. The plane will have power. It will not be a large amount of help, but even a small amount is good, yes?"

It's all I can do not to leap out of my seat and hug him. We're going back. Forget whatever humanitarian mission he's on – I can find the others, make sure they're safe.

My ears pop as I fumble with my belt. I haven't been on many planes in my life, but I remember the popping. It means we're descending. Before long, we'll be on the ground, and we can—

"Wait, wait, wait," I say to Schmidt. "We can land, right? There'll be a runway for us to land on?"

"Well, in theory . . ."

"What do you mean, *in theory*?"

"We will be able to see when we get close. My pilot is

very good – very highly paid. He will be able to see the condition—"

"I don't give a flying fuck how much you pay him. Do we have a runway or not?"

"It does not matter. Even if there is damage, the shock absorbers on the landing gear are built for big impacts. We can handle the runway if there is damage to it. We circle until the earthquake stops, then we go down."

"What about air traffic control?"

He shakes his head. It's like he's aged ten years in the past ten minutes. "There is no air traffic control. There is nothing."

"So to be clear: we're trying to land on a runway that may or may not exist, with no one to tell us if other planes are doing the same thing at the same time, all because you wanna play Good Samaritan?"

His gaze hardens. "It is my plane. My decision."

"Uh, yeah, you aren't the only person on this plane." I turn to Mikhail. "Dude, I know we haven't seen eye-to-eye yet on account of me breaking in here, but you *cannot* think this is a good idea?"

Mikhail stares back at me, stony-faced. Great. A loyal employee. This would be so much easier if Schmidt was a terrible boss.

"So land further away," I tell Schmidt. "Find an airport with ATC still working."

"That will take too much time," he replies. "The longer we are in the air, the worse things on the ground may be."

I can see from the look on his face that he's never going to listen to me. He's a billionaire. He doesn't just accept risks – he enjoys them. His intuition has brought him money and supermodels and private jets, so I have precisely zero chance of convincing him.

I close my eyes. *Are you there, God? It's me again. I wanted to tell you that you're a giant, flaming asshole.*

If we don't stick the landing, I guess I'll be able to tell him right to his face.

SEVENTEEN

Teagan

You'd think that the moments before a deadly plane crash would be insane. People screaming, oxygen masks flying, bags tumbling out of overhead lockers. You know, the stuff that makes life worth living.

Turns out, if you're on a private jet, it gets very quiet. Everyone is in their seats, white knuckles gripping armrests. Looking out the windows, or at the TV, which has the volume turned down low. I have a real sudden urge to scream at them about why they aren't screaming, because Jesus fucking Christ we're all going to die in a plane crash in the middle of an earthquake.

I don't. I just sit quietly, and make myself breathe. The rain has started up again, silent drops speckling the windows.

"How do you know other planes aren't doing the same thing we are?" I ask Schmidt again. "If there's no air traffic control, how would we tell—?"

"Quiet," Mikhail barks at me.

Schmidt shushes him with a gesture. "We don't know," he says.

"Oh, perfect."

"Indeed. But it is a risk we must take," he says.

"No, it's a risk *you* must take. I'd rather just grab one of your parachutes."

"There are no parachutes on board."

" . . . Are you serious?"

The ghost of a smile, strained and hard. "That is not how jet aircraft work. It is not practical."

"Well, it would be pretty fucking practical right now, don't you think?"

"You are the one who stole aboard my plane, Jay. You do not get a say in how or where it is flown."

Behind me, the harried news anchor is saying, "Molly Zuckerman has more from Los Angeles, where we go now, live. Molly?"

The reporter is in a helicopter, the windows showing much the same view as we have. Her frizzy brown hair is squashed awkwardly by her bulky headset. "Gina, words almost can't describe what I'm seeing. The devastation is . . . total. We haven't been able to land anywhere and our sources on the ground are completely unresponsive. From our vantage point here, the first earthquake appears to have run its course, but there's every expectation that there will be aftershocks . . . "

"See?" I say. "They're being smart. They're not landing."

Schmidt doesn't bother to respond. He's talking quietly in German to Gerhard. As I watch, he reaches out and grips the big man's hand, squeezing tight.

The digital clock on the corner of the news channel reads 11:58. A little over an hour since I came on board. An hour since I was standing on solid, steady, very-much-unbroken LA ground. It feels like something that happened in another life.

The plane is very low now. I make myself breathe. My palms are sweaty, and wiping them on my pants doesn't help.

Schmidt turns to me. "Tell me, do you pray?"

"Tried a few times. Didn't work."

"I do not either. My mother does – she is still active in her church in Berlin. Do you have family?"

There are ... too many ways to answer that question. I shake my head, trying to make sense of the tumbled, chaotic, gut-wrenching thoughts.

I'm saved from having to answer when he says, "You should be thinking about them, not about parachutes. When we are on the ground, you will need to find a way to let them know you are safe. Your family, and your friends, if spies have such a thing."

Friends.

It's impossible not to see Carlos. See him sitting at the bar, knocking back whiskey, cackling as he described the sexual peculiarities of his latest ex. See him in the passenger seat of the China Shop van, offering me jerky to recharge my energy levels after a tough mission.

See him impaled on a steel pole, with a fire raging closer, begging me to help him.

Death never used to scare me. I didn't want to die, because why the fuck would I, but I wasn't scared of it. I figured I'd been through so much bad shit, death couldn't possibly be any worse. But what if when I die, I have to face Carlos? We didn't find his body after the fire, but that doesn't mean anything. He could have burned to ash. What if the first thing I see in the afterlife is him, and he asks me why I didn't save him?

The plane banks again. The ground is closer than ever before.

Fuck this. I'm not going to die. I don't care if I have to reveal my abilities: this is not the end of me. I don't know if I'm strong enough to lift a plane with my mind, but I'd say now would be an excellent time to find out. I send out my PK, wrapping it around the body ...

Only, what the hell am I supposed to do? Am I really going to be able to land this thing better than Schmidt's pilot? I'll just get in the way, end up fighting with him. If the plane is damaged by the landing, I can try hold it together ... but how will I know which pieces to use my PK on?

"*Macht euch bereit!*" the pilot says, clipped and urgent. Schmidt immediately bends at the waist, hands on the back of his head. No translation needed here.

Brace for impact.

EIGHTEEN

Teagan

I always thought airplane seatbelts were next to useless. Because if I ever *was* in a plane crash, there was no way a piddly little strip of fabric was going to save my ass.

Either I was wrong, or private jet seatbelts are made of titanium.

When we touch down, it's with a bang that shudders through the cabin, my seat bucking underneath me. If it wasn't for the belt, I'd have been thrown right out. The plane hits something – a jagged chunk of raised ground, maybe. It kicks back up into the air, listing crazily. The TV reporter is drowned out by the hideous whine of jet engines. Gerhard bellows, his belt straining. Schmidt's knuckles have gone white.

We slam back to earth. This time, we tilt far enough for the right wing tip to just touch the ground. The belt isn't helping any more; I have to use every muscle I have to stay in my seat, bracing my arms against the armrests. My teeth are clenched so hard my jaw creaks. I don't care what kind of shock absorbers are built into the landing gear – they can't take much more of this. It's like the plane is trying to twist itself in half.

There's muted beeping from the cockpit, the world outside

rushing past, fire and smoke and ruined buildings. What might be another plane, burning, turned on its side.

The shaking should have stopped by now. We should have come to a halt. Instead, I swear we start to move *faster*, the engines roaring. What does that mean? Is the pilot trying to outrace something? Another plane? Not knowing is killing me, but I don't dare get out of my seat. Even if I did, I wouldn't be able to keep my balance for more than half a second.

And then, just like that, the engines start to slow.

The plane is still shaking, but not quite as badly. Outside the window, the runway is flying torn to pieces, cracked and jagged. Smoke drifts on the breeze, the clouds hanging low.

Schmidt laughs. Softly at first, but then he breaks out in huge, loud, gusting laughter. It makes him look like a teenager, shaving years off his face.

I stare at him. The words *Have you lost your fucking mind?* are right there, but I don't have the energy to get them out.

There's a crackle, and the pilot's voice comes over the intercom. I don't catch what he's saying, which is still in German, but the reaction in the cabin is immediate. Schmidt reaches across the aisle, high-fiving Gerhard. Rodrigo clambers up from his seat, envelops Mikhail in a shaking hug.

Schmidt unbuckles, staggers over to the cockpit, delivering shaky instructions in rapid German. Moving very slowly, I unbuckle my seatbelt. It takes more than one try to stand up. My eyes feel curiously gritty, like I've just woken up after a long sleep.

"We will taxi off the runway," Schmidt says, reappearing from the cockpit. "I do not think that the air traffic control will mind. The tower . . ." He runs a hand through his hair. "It's not there any more."

Fuck me.

The plane is still moving, trundling down the runway. Hopefully trying to get off of it as fast as possible. I have to find China Shop – like, right now. My phone still has zero signal – not exactly surprising. What about my earpiece? It wasn't working before, but now that we're on the ground . . .

I tap it. There's a very faint burst of static, then nothing. "Paul? You reading me, dude?"

"Paul? This is your handler?"

It's Schmidt. He has two glasses in his hand – plastic flutes, filled with pale yellow liquid.

"Something like that," I say.

"I see." He hands one of the glasses to me. "Champagne?"

"Uh . . . what?"

He looks faintly embarrassed. "One of the bottles survived our landing. Champagne is not useful in a disaster zone, and since we are all still alive, I thought . . . "

I don't listen to the rest. I down the glass, the bubbles sharp on my tongue. The drink wakes me up, gives me the kick I need. I have to get the fuck out of here.

"That was Krug Private Cuvée," he says, staring at me. "Seventeen hundred euro a bottle."

"And it was delicious." I point at the door. "Pull over. I gotta go find my friends."

"Friends?" He takes a sip of his champagne, smacks his lips. "I have met spies before, and they do not describe their colleagues as friends. It is a strange agency you work for."

"We're more like a moving company."

"I am not understanding?"

"Never mind. You gonna let me off, or not?"

"Shortly. We are taxiing to a safe space, where another plane will not hit us."

Gerhard overhears. He jabs a finger at me, looming over

Schmidt, speaking rapidly. Too fast for me to follow – not that I understand German anyway, most of the time – but I get the gist. *Hey, boss, do you not remember this lady trying to steal your shit? You should totally not let her go because she'll, like, completely ruin your day.*

Schmidt listens to his bodyguard, expressionless. Mikhail joins in, and it's not hard to see he feels the same way as Gerhard. Great. Just what I need right now – to be imprisoned on a private plane in the aftermath of a deadly quake.

If that happens, then I'm totally drinking the rest of the seventeen-hundred-euro champagne.

The plane bumps and jerks as it trundles over what is presumably pretty fucked-up tarmac. Schmidt and his goons go back and forth for a minute before he shuts it all down, turning away from the glowering bodyguards with a muttered snatch of German. He sips his champagne, removes his jacket. He has a pretty nifty tattoo, sneaking out from under his T-shirt sleeve: a pattern of geometric dots, swirling around his bicep. "I must ask a favour of you, Jay."

"Oh yeah? What's that?"

He leans on the back of his seat. "I cannot detain you. No – excuse my English. I am able to, but I cannot. Gerhard and Mikhail wish me to do so, but I do not think they understand our situation. Soon, we will have people coming to this plane who need help. They will need food, or medical supplies, or communications. We cannot have a prisoner that we must watch."

His eyes find mine. "We will be vulnerable when this is happening. It would be easy for you or your agency to come on board and take my list." He pats his breast pocket.

I say nothing.

"I must ask you, as someone who helped get you back on the ground safely. Let us work. Leave us in peace."

For a second, I have a real urge to just grab the list and run. Disable him, get it from his pocket, take out his goons, and get the hell out. It'll be tricky, maybe even almost impossible, but . . .

Fuck it. Who cares about the stupid list? If he's telling the truth, he doesn't plan to release it anyway, and I'd say there are bigger things to worry about.

"It's cool," I say. "I'll tell them . . . you didn't have it. That our intel was wrong."

Another ghost of a smile. It only lasts for a second, and surprisingly, I find that I miss it when it's gone. "Thank you."

We come to a shuddering halt, the floor tilting slightly. As the engines power down, Schmidt directs Gerhard to pop the exit door for me. The bodyguard gives me a scowl that could freeze Niagara Falls, but does as his boss asks.

The door opens, and there's a hiss as the evacuation slide inflates, a ballooning expanse of orange rubber. Spitting rain gusts in, carried on air that is hot and angry, stinking of smoke.

Schmidt gives me a nod of thanks, already turning away, firing instructions at Mikhail.

"Hey," I say.

He looks over his shoulder.

"That was pretty awesome. Coming back to help. You didn't have to do that."

This time, the smile stays. "You are kind to say so."

As I'm halfway out the door, he speaks again. "What is your real name?"

"Huh?"

"You are not named Jay, are you?"

I stare at him, not sure what I want to say. If there's even any point in lying about it.

"Never mind," he says, looking ever so slightly disappointed.

"Maybe you will tell me another time. If we meet in better circumstances, perhaps."

Then he's gone, heading to the back of the plane. Gerhard taps me on the shoulder, jerks his head at the slide and I'm gone.

Straight into hell.

NINETEEN

Matthew

The first time Matthew caused an earthquake, he'd had to react fast. He had an *idea* of what would happen, but he wasn't prepared for how sudden it all was. He'd only just managed to shield himself and Amber in a cocoon of dirt. It kept them safe from the worst of it.

Today is different.

It's even *better*.

The earth beneath him drops a full foot in under a second, spilling him onto his backside. Amber does better – she's prone already, bloody and shaking from when he had to throw stuff at her. He scrabbles towards her on all fours, falls, gets to his knees. He starts laughing, goofy with joy.

The giant pine tree above him snaps in two, the top half falling towards them with a hissing, crunching roar. Amber gets a hand up, as if she can stop the tree herself. Matthew yelps, thrusting his hands into the soil. There's an explosion of dirt, a giant pillar of it rocketing upwards, leaving a gash in the ground. The dirt slams into the falling tree, knocks it sideways. It lands a few feet away, boughs snapping, just as Matthew hurls himself onto his mom. Despite how he hurt her, what he had to do when she wouldn't listen, she holds him. Tight.

Another blast of dirt, dropping them into the earth. Matthew cocoons them in a sphere of it. The world goes dark, the smell of damp and rot invading his nostrils.

In the cramped space, under the insane noise from outside, the sound is a dead, muffled thing. He laughs, delighted, horrified, his breathing hot and heavy as he tries to hold their prison together. They are tossed about like a beachball in stormy seas. Amber sobs, her body shaking against his. The terror and excitement he feels is cut with annoyance. *Just like her to start crying now.*

He doesn't know how long the shaking lasts. A while. Either way, when he finally lets the light in, the world is still. No sound but the wind.

He clambers out of Amber's grip, crawling under the last wisps of floating dirt. He lets them drop, dust and rocks and roots raining down on them. Amber lies there, hitching in cold, agonising breaths, as her son gets to his feet.

"That was awesome," he breathes. He turns to her, his eyes shining. "That was *awesome*."

He punches the air, his feet actually leaving the ground. "I found a ton of stored energy down there," he says, his words coming so fast he fumbles some of them. "They were right. At the museum? There was all this pressure that hadn't gone anywhere. And I just . . . it just let go, the second I touched it."

Nobody could stop him. Not even Amber. She tried, and he did it anyway, and it was the best thing ever. He giggles, wanting to look everywhere at once.

One of his teeth is loose. He jabs it with his tongue – aren't they supposed to start dropping out soon? The thought is a distraction, unwelcome, and he shoves it away. Maybe he just hit his face somewhere. And who cares, anyway?

"The whole Pacific Plate . . . *boom!*" He claps his hands together, delight glowing on his dirt-streaked face. "That was two whole plates sliding past one another. All that pressure went all at once, the second I touched it!" He spins in a circle. "We gotta go see. That must have hit the whole of LA! Maybe even San Francisco!"

He rushes over, pulls her to her feet. Her blonde hair is crusted with dirt, blood drying on her face. Cuts and scratches mark her cheeks.

The landscape around them has changed. Most of the trees have been toppled like dominos, roots moving in the wind. The dirt track is gone. There are new hills everywhere, new rocks, still crusted with the dirt that held them deep in the earth. Fissures zig-zag across the ground, some pencil-thin, others a foot wide, more, their interiors black as night.

Matthew hardly registers the choked sob that bursts out of his mother. He turns in another circle, slower this time, taking in the details. The heights at which the tree trunks snapped – most lower to the ground, but some halfway up, as if they were better able to withstand the energy release. Perhaps because of their roots, spread wider through the soil. The sky above them is filled with great flocks of honking birds, whirling in confused, terrified circles. Matthew beams up at them.

OK. Enough little stuff. He leads them back to the pickup, dancing across the cracked dirt.

The quake tore the road in half. When they reach the tarmac, the pickup is lying half-inside a huge fissure. Its engine compartment is crushed, the air stinking of oil. A tyre spins on a bent axle, creaking gently.

For the first time, Matthew slows down, considering the pickup. He forgot about it entirely – he should have figured out how to shield it during the quake. For some reason, he doesn't feel like admitting this – not to Amber, that's for sure.

"I tried to shield it, like I did for us," he says, the lie

slipping out of him with no trouble at all. "I must not have aimed right."

Out of nowhere, he yawns, his mouth gaping. He's tired – like, *really* tired. Not surprising, given what he just did. He squeezes his eyes shut, opens them again, trying to clear his head. "You need to get us a new car," he tells Amber. "And I bet it was *more* than an 8.3! That's supposed to be the max for San Andreas, but I bet I pushed it even further!"

The interior of the truck is a wreck, their possessions and supplies thrown around the cabin. A few bottles of water have split open, but the rest looks OK. The blood on Amber's cheeks has dried to a thin crust.

He's glad she isn't badly hurt. It would be a real pain in the ass if he had to walk to Big Pines alone, carrying all their stuff. He has a momentary image of himself teetering down the road with a pack twice his size, and giggles again. The giggle changes to another yawn, one which brings irritation in its wake. Ugh, why does this stuff make him so tired?

Maybe it won't be that way when he gets older. *When I get my big teeth*, he thinks, suddenly bitter. He wishes he *was* bigger. He wouldn't even need Amber then. He wouldn't need anyone.

Amber is staring at him. Dull horror on her face.

"What?" he says.

She doesn't reply, turning to gather the water, the last of their food. Packing clothes in a backpack. Matthew sits down against the side of the pickup. He'll just rest. Just for a second.

He wakes briefly when Amber snuggles in beside him, wrapping her arms around his chest. In that moment, he's angry with himself for falling asleep – what if she'd tried to run? She could've just left him here, and he wouldn't have been able to stop her.

Then again, she didn't. She knows he'd find her.

Matthew smiles, and gives a long, contented sigh.

TWENTY

Teagan

The world outside Schmidt's plane isn't as bad as I thought it was going to be.

It's worse.

Much worse.

I get to my feet at the bottom of the slide, gaping. A little, involuntary sound sneaks out of my throat, half-moan, half-whimper.

We're off to one side of the runway. From here, I can see clear across to the terminal building. Every plane that was on the ground during the quake has been tossed and tumbled around like childrens' toys. They lie on their sides, sunken into the earth, crashed, burning. Wrecked airport vehicles are everywhere – trucks and tugs and luggage carts.

The ground itself is ... It looks like the ocean in rough weather, frozen in time. The tarmac is cracked and bruised, thrust up in some places, fallen away in others. The runway we came in on is a nightmare. How in the hell did we manage to land on that?

The terminal building – what's left of it – is on fire. *Everything* is on fire. It's raining, but not nearly hard enough to make a difference. The chill drizzle soaks my shoulders through the thin Homeland uniform.

The 7.1 from two nights ago was a glancing jab; this is a haymaker, a knockout punch, one that sends teeth flying and blood spattering the canvas. I put my hand to my mouth, a horrible, sick nausea filling up my gut.

There's nothing I can do.

Not against this. Not against something this huge and violent. I can lift things and throw them around, maybe help clear some rubble – if I can actually convince myself to reveal my ability. But there will be thousands of other people to help, thousands of buildings and cars and trucks and houses and offices. I won't be able to do more than make the smallest dent.

Standing there, on the tarmac of the burning airport, I have never felt so small.

I lift a shaking hand to my earpiece. "Paul? Annie? Anybody?" I swallow. "This is Teagan. You there?"

Not even static. Just dead air.

I start walking, not really caring about the direction, just knowing that I have to move or I'm going to collapse. Was Nic at work when it happened? Did he get out OK? What about Reggie? "This is Teagan, *please* come in. Over."

Is it my imagination, or was there the very faintest hint of something other than static? I freeze, speak the words again, like they're a magic spell.

Nothing. No response. I keep moving, making my way across the uneven ground. I'm starting to see people now: customs agents and runway workers and fire fighters, swarming like ants. A fire engine shoots past me, siren blaring, loud enough to make me stick my hands over my ears. I don't know where it's going – it's heading for the runway in the opposite direction to the fires. *Maybe it's trying to get away.*

I almost collide with a man as he weaves onto the tarmac. He's wearing a high-vis jacket that used to be yellow. It's a dark brown now, covered in drying blood from the horrific gash on his forehead. I gape at him, not sure if I should yell for assistance, help him myself or just run.

"There's a fire," he says, clear and calm. "Someone should call 911."

Then he collapses. Like he's been shot.

That same horrible indecision. Do I help him? Find someone?

My body moves for me. In seconds, I'm kneeling beside him, scrabbling for his wrist. I can't find a pulse, no matter where I put my fingers. But I've always been bad at finding pulses, so I stick a finger under his chin, and that's when I see he's gone. I don't need a pulse to know that. His eyes stare at nothing, glazed and empty.

Oh, shit.

My earpiece crackles. "—over where the—"

"Paul?" I hit the earpiece so hard I almost wedge it into my ear canal. We must be back in range – there's interference, but I can hear him. I can hear him! "*Paul?* Are you there?"

"—gan, we're—"

"Paul, I'm OK. Tell me where you are." My legs start moving on their own, taking me away from the dead man. Who was he? Did he have a family? A girlfriend? Did he—?

Nope. Stop that right now. There's nothing you can do.

I keep walking towards the terminal building, pausing every so often to cough, the smoke burning my throat. My uniform pants are covered in dirt – I don't even know how that happened.

"—peat, we are by the tower. If you can—will be waiting for y—"

The tower. It's almost impossible to pick out in the billowing smoke, but I find it. Or what's left of it. It looks like a tree that's been felled by a lightning strike, a jagged lance jutting into the sky. It's maybe a third of a mile away.

I'm halfway there when the aftershock hits. It's a jolt, rocketing up through the soles of my feet. Then a shaking that sends me stumbling onto all fours. I flatten myself on the ground, hands stinging from where I fell, thinking: *Stop. Please stop. You have to stop.*

And it does. After a few more seconds, the rumbling fades. I stagger to my feet, keep walking.

It's the van I see first. It's on its side, wheels still spinning. Smoke gushes from the hood. Annie, Paul and Africa are huddled behind it. When he spots me, Africa gives a yell, exploding to his feet and sweeping me up in his arms. He squeezes tight enough to make the muscles in my shoulders creak.

"What happen to you, Teggan?" he says. "You were up on the plane, *yaaw*?"

"They turned around," I say, when he lets me go.

"How the hell you pull that off?" Annie's dark skin has gone ash-grey. She's dirty, but outside of a scrape on her forehead, she looks unharmed. Paul, on the other hand—

"Fuck." I drop to my knees in front of him. "What happened to your arm?"

He's holding it tight to his chest. Midway down his right forearm, there's an angle where there shouldn't be one.

"Hit the door frame when we crashed," he says through gritted teeth. "I'll be fine."

"You do *not* look fine."

"He hit his head too," Africa says. "I think maybe he has concussion."

"Teagan," Annie says, insistent. "How'd you get back?"

"Like I said, they turned the plane around."

"What? Why?"

"Long story."

"And the list?"

"He didn't have it."

"Are you sure?"

"Yeah. Look, forget the list, we need to get out of here."

Africa straightens up. "I must go to Redondo. Jeannette is there."

Paul swallows, his Adam's apple bobbing. "I already told you what Reggie said. We have to go back to Venice, right now."

I frown. "Why? What did Reggie say?"

Africa ignores him. "It's nonsense. We don't know what she said."

"I need to get to Inglewood," I say, sidestepping whatever this conversation is. "Nic's there, so—"

Another fire engine roars past us, siren deafening – and then there's a huge, dull thud. At first, I think it's another aftershock, but it doesn't sound the same. We all turn to see a gout of fire blooming at the end of the runway – a big one, belching smoke.

"That was a plane." Annie's voice is almost inaudible.

"Two," says Paul. "I saw it. They hit each other."

"*Yaaw.*" Africa sounds like he's just shrunk two feet.

"Shit, Teagan, you came in that same way?" Annie says. "Same runway?"

That does it. I turn, and retch up my breakfast. It's been threatening for a while, and I can't hold it off any longer. Coffee and digested energy bar and very expensive champagne spatter my uniform boots. I'm suddenly embarrassed, for no good reason, and stumble away. That only makes it worse – now I'm walking and vomiting, gruel painting my shins. I can't stop shaking.

Africa is crouched down, hands dug in underneath the overturned van.

"The fuck are you doing?" Annie mutters.

Africa sees me looking. "Come help."

" . . . What?"

"The van. You can use your *dëma* powers, huh? Get it up."

"The engine's fried," Paul says.

"Teggan – flip the van. *Flip the fuck van.*"

I don't think I've ever heard Africa swear. The way he speaks doesn't permit it – he has too many other words to draw on, three languages of amazing slang. And he's not the kind of person who gets angry. Hearing him say *fuck* gives the word its power back. He lumbers over to me, grabbing me by the shoulder, as if he can make me do what he says.

I whack his hand away. "Don't touch me."

He steps back, a look of shock on his face. But he backs up.

I don't normally mind him touching me. God knows, he hugs me enough. Then again, this wasn't a relieved hug – this was him ordering me to do something, treating me like a tool. We don't have that kind of relationship. We never will.

Carlos would know what do. Carlos could fix the engine. He could—

I don't have Carlos. All I have is Africa, and he's no Carlos. And now is not the fucking time, Teagan, by the way.

Not that Carlos deserves any of my time. Not one god-damn second.

"Come," Africa says, pleading. "You got these powers. You must use them. Flip the fuck van. Then we find the man who make the earthquake."

I blink at him. "I'm sorry, the what now?"

"*Hey.*" The shout takes all the strength Paul has. He collapses back against the side of the van. "Let's just all . . . just all think for a second."

"Don't move, baby." Annie crouches by him. "Stay still. I'll go get help."

"No, listen," Paul says. "Listen to me. We have to go back to Venice, OK?"

"Baby, I heard what Reggie said too, but that doesn't mean—"

"What the hell are you two talking about?" I wipe my mouth, flicking away a speck of vomit. I'm a little light-headed, and it has nothing to do with the quake.

Paul gazes at Annie, an unsettling look passing between them, which doesn't help my state of mind.

"What does Africa mean?" I say. "*The man who made the earthquake?*"

Paul's eyes meet mine. "Just before it all went crazy, Reggie called in. She said she knew who had caused the San Bernardino quake."

"Wait, Paul, I'm sorry, hold on a second." I close my eyes. "I'm pretty sure I just heard you say the word *who* there. Not what."

He grimaces in pain. "Correct. She said the earthquake was caused by someone with abilities like yours. Then the comms went dead. I can't raise her."

Silence.

"Bullshit," I say.

"I'm just telling you what Reggie—"

"Nope. Bullshit. I call bullshit. Bull. Shit. Your comms were faulty."

"I heard it too," Annie says quietly.

"Well, you fucking heard wrong. OK?"

"I don't get it – what's so impossible about this for you?"

"Because ... because it just can't happen. There's no way."

Annie looks over at Paul and Africa, as if asking them to back her up. "You can move shit with your mind. And six months ago, you met a guy who was even stronger than you. Is someone who can cause earthquakes really that much of a stretch?"

"OK, I'm pretty strong. And Jake was stronger. But neither of us could break an *entire fucking city*. So yeah: you heard wrong."

I try not to talk about things being *impossible*, or *far-fetched*. I can move shit with my mind, after all. But this ... no. It's so far beyond what even I have experienced that I just can't see it.

But, what if that's not true? If the guys heard Reggie right, there's someone else with abilities, and he just destroyed a city in a single morning. How am I supposed to fight that?

"Teagan, you're not ... " Paul's been trying to get to his feet, and collapses backwards mid-sentence. I don't know a whole hell of a lot about concussions, but I do know that not being able to stand is a pretty sure sign you have one.

Africa spits a torrent of angry, rapid-fire French, before slipping into English. "I must go to Jeannette." He sounds desperate. "She cannot take care of herself."

"Be cool," Annie says.

"Ah, you tell me I must be cool, *yaaw*?" His voice rises again, his eyes bugging out of his head. "What about your mother, huh? Where she, now? You not gonna go find her?"

"She can handle herself," Annie snarls back. But she sounds unsure.

Africa's in shock. Worse than the rest of us. But all the same, I can't help thinking of Nic. He'd be in Inglewood, at the courthouse ... maybe even still helping out in San Bernardino, because he's the kind of person who would totally still be there two days after a quake. I pull out my phone to text him, then angrily jam it back in my pocket. I don't think I've ever felt this helpless.

"Why is the guy with the concussion the only one thinking straight?" Paul is sweating, despite the chill, his shoulders set very tight. "We *have* to go back to Venice. Or the rest of you do, anyway."

"Why you need me?" Africa says. "I'm the driver, *yaaw*? What am I gonna drive now?"

Paul's face is white. "Idr—Africa. Listen to me. I know you want to find your girlfriend. If my son was in town, I'd probably do the same."

"They're not?" I say.

"No, they're in Arizona this week, at his grandparents. But Africa: what if you get down to Redondo, and she isn't there?"

Redondo? Don't they live in Venice? I push the thought aside, irritated.

Africa says nothing. Just stares, stony-faced.

"Why wouldn't Jeannette be there?" Annie says.

"She's not just going to stay and wait for us," Paul says. "There'll be emergency relief coming in – and if she got out OK, she won't hang around waiting for us. She'll go to wherever there's shelter, medical attention."

"She would wait for me!" Africa bellows.

"*Christ*, Africa. Right now, we have no idea where anybody is. What if she wasn't in Redondo today? What if she went somewhere? Or Annie – what if Sandra-May went to the store? Or had Marshawn from next door take her down to the clinic? *We don't know.* They might be anywhere."

"That doesn't mean—"

"The office is quake-proof. Tanner and I fixed it up – we didn't want Reggie in a situation where she couldn't get out.

It's up to code. Her power might be down – you can fix that, get a generator up and running. There'll be food and water, and you'll be able to use her systems."

"Up to *code*?" I point at the runway. "That was an 8.3. That just set the code on fire and pissed on the ashes."

I work very hard not to look in the direction of the crashed planes. There's a rumble, and behind us, part of the control tower collapses, sending up another cloud of dust. The sirens are everywhere now.

"Are we just not gonna talk about the fact that you're hurt?" Annie says.

"I'm fine," Paul mutters. He tries to push himself up with his good arm, can't do it. When he thumps back down, a horrible, pained noise hisses out of him.

"I can help with that," I say, pointing back towards Schmidt's plane. "He's got some supplies."

"He?" Annie narrows her eyes. "Who's he?"

"Schmidt. On his plane."

"The target?"

"Yeah. He can help."

"You out of your damn mind?"

"What the fuck difference does it make?" I gesture at the destroyed airport, the cracked tarmac. My muscles feel loose and hot, almost liquid. Another shockwave of nausea slams into me, one I have to force back down. "I'd say mission is officially aborted."

"Oh, so we're just gonna go ahead and reveal our-selves to the—"

"The van." Paul sounds like he's trying to swallow glass. "First aid kit. There's a sling. And there's painkillers."

"The plane will have better—"

"No, it won't." He doesn't quite smile, but his lips twitch

upwards at the corners. "They didn't have me ... packing their kit."

"They'll have doctors on board. Schmidt said he was going to—"

"Not for ... a while yet. Chaos right now. The break will need to be set, eventually ... but we have a kit here. In the van."

"You are *such* a nerd," I say. It's meant to be an attempt at humour. On any other day, it might have actually succeeded.

"How are we even supposed to get to Venice, anyway?" Africa says, sullen.

Paul grunts. "Freeway. The 405. We get a truck—"

"The 405." Annie puts a hand on her hip. "The most congested road in America. *That's* how you wanna get to Venice?"

"Dude," I say. "It's bad enough at like 3 a.m. on a Tuesday morning. After a quake? We won't make it ten feet."

"Just *listen* to me. You get a truck, head out west of the airport. There's a store we passed on the way over here."

Annie blinks at him. "What kind of store?"

"Bikes."

We fall silent, digesting what Paul said. I can see it – just. It would mean traffic wasn't an issue ... and once we got going, it wouldn't take much longer to get to Venice than it would by car.

"You know it makes sense." Paul shifts position against the van, grimacing. "You can all ride down to Venice. It's ..." He turns his wrist to look at his watch, a wave of pain rolling across his face. "... Christ. OK. It's almost half-twelve, I'd say. You can make it to Venice in three hours – four at the most. Then—"

"What about you?" Annie says.

His eyes find hers. For a second, it looks like he's about to tell her he's fine, he'll come. Then his shoulders slump. "Last thing you need is me losing consciousness. And I won't be able to keep my balance on a bike. I'd just slow you down."

"The fuck you will. I'm not leaving you here."

"*Annie.* You have to. There'll be doctors soon, or they'll take us to an emergency shelter. You can patch my arm for now, and they can treat my concussion – or at least find me a dark room to rest in." He winces again.

She wipes her mouth.

"If I fall off a bike," Paul continues, "I'm no good to anybody. You need to get to Reggie ... but you don't need me there. That's the quickest way to find out what's going on. Maybe to find your families too. If anybody can track them, Reggie can."

Annie's face contorts, her expression going from worried to scared to angry, and back to worried again. "Baby, no ... "

"*I'll be fine.* I promise."

She trails off, staring into the distance.

Oh boy. I want to tell myself Paul heard Reggie wrong – that she said *what*, not *who*, that the idea that a person caused all this is bugshit crazy. But the problem is, if he heard right, then we can't afford to do nothing.

"Teagan," Paul says, bringing me back. "Find us a vehicle. Preferably an SUV or a pickup. Annie: you and Africa crack the van. Get the first aid kit."

TWENTY-ONE

Teagan

It's surprisingly easy to find a car during an earthquake. People just leave them standing there, doors open, keys in the ignition. Sometimes they've even left the engine on. If you run a chop shop, an earthquake is a serious growth opportunity.

I probably shouldn't be making jokes right now. Sorry not sorry. It's either that, or throw up again.

It takes me a while to find the kind of car Paul asked for, though. It's a Ford F150, just inside the boom of a staff parking lot, on the other side of the terminal building. The engine is on, the truck beeping softly to let everyone know a door is open.

My legs are jelly, but I somehow manage to climb in. The windshield is cracked on the driver's side, spiderwebbing out from the bottom-left corner. A smear of blood on the wheel, too. No sign of the driver, but there's an airport laminate badge on the passenger seat, the photo showing a smiling, bald man in his fifties, with a scruffy beard. *Ralph Lorencz. Crew Schedule Coordinator.* "Thanks, Ralph," I mutter, shifting the truck into drive. "Hope you got out OK, bud."

I wish I could believe that.

It's less than five hundred yards back to the van, but it takes me a good ten minutes to get there. It's not just the cracked, chopped-up ground. It's the smoke, drifting on the breeze and obscuring my view out the windshield, forcing me to drive slow. It's the other cars, abandoned, many upside down. More than one has a dead body inside, with blood-spattered windows and wrecked bodywork. I do my best not to look, feeling absurdly guilty. Like I should climb out and apologise to them.

When I reach the guys, Paul's arm is in a makeshift sling. He's on his feet, unsteady but OK. Africa and Annie are fussing over a backpack, loading it up with a couple of water bottles we had in the van. Snacks too: there are some bags of beef jerky on the runway next to them. I know exactly where they were, in the van's glove box. Right where Carlos used to keep them, so I could eat after missions.

Fuck you. Not now.

Africa eyes the truck's broken windshield, looking queasy, but says nothing. The tarmac is slick from the drizzle.

"OK," Annie says to Paul. "We're gonna drop you off at the terminal, and—"

"No." He shakes his head, then winces, his eyes squeezed shut. His hand strays to his neck, rubs it. "You can't ... can't risk someone commandeering the truck. I'll be fine. I can't ride a bike, but I can still walk."

Africa and I load everything up, leaving Annie with Paul. As I sling my backpack into the passenger footwell, Annie is still arguing with him, gesticulating.

"Teagan," Africa says. "Please. I *must* find Jeannette."

"Dude, Paul was right. By the time you get to Redondo—"

His expression hardens. "I will take one bike. You cannot stop me."

I bite back what I really want to tell him, which is that he sounds like a little kid having a tantrum. "True. But you know Paul's right."

Africa holds my gaze for second. Then his shoulders sag, his huge hands at his sides. "And no list, huh?"

"What?"

"On the plane. You say Mister Germany not have the list."

"Yeah. Well."

"I think I might be in trouble," he mumbles. "With Paul, you know? He and Reggie wanted me to stay with the van, but when things went bad for you on the plane, I just think, maybe I can help."

"Don't even worry about it."

He continues like I hadn't spoken. "You back me up, huh? If I get in trouble?"

"What?" I'm barely listening. "Oh. Sure. Whatever."

"Thanks. I really don't want—"

"Annie!"

Paul's shout is ignored. Annie walks away from him, not looking back, face set as she climbs into the truck.

I waver, not sure what to do. After a moment, Paul's shoulders sag. His bald head gleams in the wet.

He walks up to us, moving gingerly, like he's walking on broken glass. When he leans in the window, his face is very pale.

"Nuclear Bikes, on Valerio Street," he says, addressing me. "Just head west out the airport – you'll find it. I've given Annie my ex-wife's number – make sure she calls it from the office, OK? Let her know I'm fine."

Annie, in the backseat, doesn't look at him.

I chew on my bottom lip, not wanting to leave him there. "Can I not at least give you a ride to—?"

"*No.* We can't risk a first responder taking the truck. I'll be fine – just go."

This sucks.

But it doesn't stop me from giving him a wave, clambering into the truck and heading to the western edge of the airport. In the rear-view mirror, Paul stands alone, a dwindling silhouette in the rain.

TWENTY-TWO

Teagan

Whoever Crew Schedule Coordinator Ralph Lorencz is – or was – he had good taste in trucks.

The F150 is clunky but powerful, and we manage to cross the tarmac without too much trouble. The truck mounts the torn-up sections easily, although I have to steer it around several of the larger cracks. I'm worried about getting past the airport fence, unable to stop thinking of armed guards, alarms, landmines, whatever hell else the TSA protects airports with.

It turns out not to be a problem. Because the fence isn't there any more.

It's worse outside the airport. There, things were spread out – the broken planes and broken buildings were far enough apart that it felt like I could ignore them. Here? It's zombie apocalypse. Nuclear winter. Day of the dead. Broken buildings, sirens, burst water pipes, downed power lines spitting like firecrackers. The few people we see look barely alive: covered in dust and blood, with dazed looks, as if they've just woken from a long sleep.

That same feeling again: total helplessness. There is no

way – at all, ever – that a single human being caused this. No freaking way. I don't believe it.

It's around one-thirty by the time we reach the bike store, which is exactly where Paul said it would be. Most of it, anyway. Like just about every other building we pass, it's collapsed in on itself – not helped by the fact that an electric pole has crashed right through the ceiling.

I snag us three bikes out of the rubble, winding my PK inside the wrecked building and pulling them out. I have to psych myself up to do it; there's that same hitch, the same almost-physical resistance against using my powers. Not in public. Then again, the few people I do see aren't paying attention to us anyway. At the far end of the block, a woman wanders in uneven circles, staring at the sky like it's changed colour.

The bikes are identical black BMXs, with balding tyres and slightly rusty gears. Even after I get them onto the sidewalk, I can't help feeling anxious – like Tanner herself is going to step out from behind a building and whisk me away to a black site lab.

"Keep an eye out," Annie says. It's the first words any of us have spoken since we left Paul.

"For what?" Africa asks, shrugging on his backpack. He straddles the bike – it's way too small for him, making him look like something out of a circus.

Annie swings her leg over. "Everybody else. Bikes are gonna be hot property."

"I can't get Google Maps." I cycle my phone to airplane mode and back, hoping against hope. Google Maps is an excuse. It's Nic I want to get hold of. I keep thinking of how he yanked me under the table during the first quake, back at my apartment. That instinctive, unquestioned move to protect me.

My apartment. Gone, probably. Vaporised, sucked down into the earth, felled by a power line. The thought doesn't make me feel anything. Maybe I'm in shock, too.

"Don't need GPS," Annie says. "I know the way. Let's go."

It hurts to leave the truck. It feels like rejecting a gift. More than that: it was warm inside the truck. Dry. Outside, the rain that started up while I was in Schmidt's plane has gotten heavier, drops spattering my skin. But Paul was right – we'll get nowhere on the 405 in a regular car.

I leave the keys in the truck's ignition. Maybe someone else can make use of it. I also pull a few more bikes out of the wreckage of the shop, leaving them on the sidewalk. Somehow, I don't think whoever runs Nuclear Cycles is going to mind.

The 405 doesn't actually start until you get of the Valley. We have to go through the Sepulveda Pass first – a kind of chokepoint through the Santa Monica Mountains. By the time we reach it, I'm both freezing and out of breath. We're riding right into the rain, and it soaks me to my skin, which is already drenched in sweat. I can't find a rhythm on the bike. The constant changes in the terrain and the cracks in the road surface make for hard going.

There are more people the closer we get to the Pass. The entry ramp, at the south edge of the Sepulveda Basin, is choked with cars – many of them with their front or rear pointed skyward, half-swallowed by cracks. One or two of the cars are on fire, slowly being consumed by flames.

"Ayo," someone shouts as we pass – an enormously fat man with a white T turned transparent from rain. "Where'd you get the bikes?"

"Up on Valerio," Annie replies. "In Balboa."

"Y'all got anything to eat?" he fires back. She doesn't reply to that – just peddles harder, pushing her bike up the on-ramp, weaving between abandoned cars.

The man doesn't follow us. Neither does anybody else. I guess we haven't reached full-on apocalypse-looting stage yet. The thought is cynical, way too bitter. Should I share some of the water in my backpack with these people? I stop myself just in time. As much as I want to help, it's too risky. Someone might decide to snatch our bikes, or *all* of our water. A confrontation right now is the last thing we need.

Thank fuck the freeway isn't elevated, or it would have collapsed completely. Paul was a hundred per cent right about the bikes. There's a ton of traffic, cars and trucks blocking the road in all directions, but weaving between them isn't too tricky. Ahead of us, Annie hunches over her handlebars, and Africa looks miserable. I'm shivering now, blinking away the steady rain.

Holy fuck. In a weird way, like with the last quake, I think we got lucky. It's all too easy to picture this happening in the fall at the height of fire season – a thousand small blazes blossoming as the quake ripped open gas mains, the fires fanned by the winds, consuming everything.

The thought gives me another jab of nausea. My parents were killed in a fire at our farm in Wyoming. The fire was set by my brother Adam. He died too, along with my sister, Chloe. The only reason I escaped was because I'd been outside, chopping wood. I've made it a point to avoid fires since then. It hasn't always worked – I had to fight Jake, the only other psychokinetic I've ever met, in the middle of one last year. It was exactly as much fun as it sounds. The thought of a quake, followed by a city-wide firestorm, is too awful to think about.

Then again, it's not like what we have now is much better. The crowds get thicker the further south we get, people milling in large groups at the edge of the highway. Everybody seems to have a wound of some kind: a broken arm or leg, a bloody nose, a gash in a shoulder or hip. Even the ones who escaped injury look dull, exhausted, watching us pass with slack expressions.

Some of the dead are under blankets. Most aren't. I do my best not to look at them – *just keep peddling*, I tell myself, keeping my head down, making myself breathe. I'm in agony, my thigh muscles burning, and there's not a damn thing I can do about. Well, I could stop peddling, but that would strand me on this highway, this junkyard of broken cars and broken people.

I pull out my phone again as we peddle, desperate for signal. Zip. Nada. Dick-all. And – holy fuck, it's almost two-thirty. Have we really been peddling for an hour already? I feel like we've gotten nowhere.

It's not long before we hit something even the bikes won't help with. As we reach the southern end of Bel Air, the freeway tops an overpass. One which has collapsed in on itself, cutting off the road ahead. Annie comes to a halt, looking left and right, then abruptly peddles for the side of the freeway. She dismounts, lifting her bike and clambering over the barrier onto the hard shoulder.

"Um, Annie?" I say. "Where are you going?"

She vanishes over the other side. I take a breath, biting back against the stitch in my side, then do the same. Africa follows, mute and shivering.

Turns out, Annie knows what she's doing. There's a road on the other side of the embankment, a smaller one, winding up into the hills. It's not easy to get to – we have to scoot down on our backsides, awkwardly holding the bikes. Africa manages better than we do, his long legs spidering down the slope.

By the time we reach the broken tarmac, we're all covered in freezing mud. There's a building on the hill above us. A huge, white structure, towers and domes and angular blocks, like a hospital designed by a crazy person.

"Getty Center," Annie mutters.

"Uh-huh." Africa brightens for a moment, before his face drops back into its dull, sullen stupor.

I know the Getty, but I've never been inside. It's an LA landmark – a massive art museum, high above the city. I get a better look at it as we bike up the road, my thighs straining against the steep gradient. It's hard to tell from here, but it looks like it survived the quake. The thought actually cheers me up a little – until we crest a rise at the base of the Center.

Africa lets out a horrified breath. I can't even do that. All the air has been sucked from my lungs.

There was terrible movie about an earthquake I saw once – *San Andreas*, maybe. The movie, whatever it was, had this one shot of a huge, miles-wide section of Los Angeles tilting up and sliding into the Pacific.

It was an amazing shot. I mean, it was a very stupid one – the kind of thing best experienced with popcorn and several beers and a bunch of friends who don't mind yelling drunken comments at the screen – but still amazing.

That shot has nothing – *nothing* – on the view from the Getty Center right now. Beyond the fact that it makes me wish I really *was* black-out drunk.

From here, we can see the whole of Los Angeles, from the Westside to Downtown. I saw a tiny bit out of the window of Schmidt's plane, but that was like watching a movie on a phone. This is IMAX, with Dolby Surround and 3-D picture.

The city hasn't slid into the Pacific. Instead, it looks as if a giant ripped the whole of LA up from the bedrock, then let it crash back down. Fires everywhere, smoke growing like tumours. Torn buildings, toppled trees. A freeway – the 10, I think – wrenched from its supports, which stick up from the ground like broken teeth. Several of the skyscrapers in downtown are gone, and the usual rumble of the city has been replaced by a thousand distant sirens. Helicopters hover everywhere, like flies buzzing around a corpse.

How could they build a city here? How can a million people live right over a fault line and act like that's normal?

Annie's voice is steady. "Let's go."

We descend, the road winding alongside the freeway, and rejoin it just where it crosses Wilshire Boulevard. This time, it's different. People are moving, not standing in small groups, all of them marching south. Ahead of us, there's an Army truck, soldiers with assault rifles waving people past, yelling instructions at each other. They look exhausted, overwhelmed.

News choppers buzz overhead. It's kind of unbelievable they haven't collided. Then again, maybe that's already happened, and I just haven't noticed.

You know what gets me? Nobody's really talking. Everybody's quiet. I didn't notice it before, but the further we go, the more it bothers me. I guess with something this big, there's nothing to talk about. There's no story to tell – not when everyone around you is living through it too. Telling stories can come later. Right now, it's just about getting out.

"Where you headed?" I ask a woman, as I peddle alongside. She's young, carrying a little girl in her arms, leading another by the hand. The walking girl looks stoned. She's got a black eye, a healthy purple shiner. Like someone socked her.

"Dodger," the woman says, distracted.

"What?"

"Dodger Stadium. There's a camp there, I think."

She's barely paying attention to me. I accelerate, ignoring the flare of pain in my thighs, pulling in alongside Annie and Africa. When I tell them where the crowds are going, Annie frowns. "We should get back off the freeway. Last thing we need is to get caught up in all that."

"What's happening at the stadium?" Africa asks.

"That's where FEMA'll be. My guess is they probably don't want it to be another Katrina situation, so they'll be on this quick."

"Will it make a difference?" I say.

"Fuck if I know, man. But LA makes a whole lot more money for America than New Orleans ever did."

Cold. Also true.

There's got to be something I can do to help. Find Reggie, sure, maybe even find Nic, but after? Am I just going to sit around an emergency camp somewhere? See if my house is still standing? Nic was right. I can help, and I should be out there doing it.

Except: how much help could I be, really? I'm strong. I can lift concrete and cars. But how long will it be before word gets out about what I'm doing? What happens then? It's the same worry I had back in Leimert Park, on the night of the first quake – only worse. Way worse.

And even if I did do all those things, what happens after? When the quake starts to become ancient history, when the people of LA return to their lives – either here, or somewhere else? What will Tanner and the nameless agency she works for do about me?

Of course, I already know the answer to that one.

We slip away from the freeway, peddling further south into Sawtelle. It used to be a pretty nice area: decent bungalows, small apartment blocks, trees and Priuses. It's a wasteland now.

It's even worse because this is where Nic lives – his apartment is on Westholme, to the north-east. He probably won't be there, but it doesn't stop an urge to turn tail and peddle like hell. I'm not even sure I'd make it: my feet are completely numb. Fingers, too. I have to grind my teeth together to stop them from clacking.

Annie takes us down Cloverfield Boulevard. At the point where it crosses Olympic, she pulls up. We've been pedalling for a couple of hours now, and my legs are more than happy to let me know it.

"Everything OK?" I say, trying to stop my voice from shaking with cold.

"Just thinking." She points. "We should head for the pier. We can take the boardwalk down to Venice – there won't be as many cars."

Strange. She didn't need to stop and tell us that. Africa and I have been blindly following her for a while now. Then I look closer – she's exhausted, too, bent over the handlebars. She wanted an excuse to rest, and is trying not to show it.

"Good call," I tell her. "I could really use some beach time."

"Say what?"

" . . . Some beach time? I've been under a lot of stress lately. Just, with the quake and the whole ... You know what? Never mind."

"I don't understand," Africa says.

"Just trying to lighten the mood."

"We can't go to the beach now, *yaaw*."

"It's a dumb-ass joke, man." Annie shakes her head. "T makes them when she's nervous. Thought you'd have that figured out by now – you guys known each other long enough."

Africa looks away, and I flip Annie a middle finger. She doesn't even notice.

"What about the big waves?" Africa asks, squinting into the rain.

I look over at him. "The . . . what, the tsunamis?"

"Ya ya. I thought earthquakes made them happen."

"San Andreas fault is inland," Annie tells him. "Tsunamis only pop up when a fault is underwater. Paul said—"

She stops abruptly, her mouth snapping closed.

"He'll be OK," I tell her. "I'm pretty sure he's not gonna die. He's way too smart for that shit."

Annie is about to ask me to stop being an insensitive dumb-dumb – I can tell just from the look on her face – when a very scary man walks around the corner of Olympic.

He's tall, six-five or six-six, with the broad shoulders and chest of a bodybuilder. He wears a blue and yellow Warriors starter jacket, zipped all the way up, over jeans that have been absolutely torn to shreds. The skin underneath is dotted with grazes and scabs, the denim bloody. Despite the wounds, he's walking – well, limping would be more accurate. He's got a facial tat, a dark scribble on pale skin that I can't make out at a distance. His mouth is twisted in what he probably thinks is a friendly smile.

"Where y'all headed?" he says. His voice is higher than his body would suggest.

Annie says nothing, eyes locked on his. A line of water trickles down my back, making me shudder.

Beside us, Africa is silent. The man notices him, looks him up and down, but doesn't back off.

"I said, where y'all—"

"Heard you." Annie's voice is calm, non-threatening.

"Y'all ain't answer, though." His chin twitches, like a rat's. "What's in the backpacks?"

"Nothing."

The smile gets wider. "Come on. I can tell y'all from around here. We gotta look after each other, you know?"

There's the sound of a very soft footstep at my five o'clock. Two – no, *three* more. Lining up behind us like a firing squad. They're not as big as the dude in front, but they don't look friendly. One of them wears a Rams football jersey, and there's even one guy in a suit, tie pulled down.

Come on, man.

"That's how it is?" Annie says, fiddling with something on her handlebars.

"That's how it is," says the big one. And just like that, he has a gun in his hand.

TWENTY-THREE

Teagan

I see the pistol before I feel it, my PK registering the shape in his waistband as he reaches for it. If I wasn't so goddamn freezing, I might have picked it up earlier. Behind me, one of the others draws a second gun.

"This ain't gotta be hard," Warriors Jacket says, sauntering towards us. "Just redistributing the wealth, that's all."

"*Redistributing the wealth?*" Annie glares at him.

He shrugs. "Saw it on CNN once."

"Eh, eh, eh," Africa says. It comes out like an animal growl, a bear clearing its throat. But his eyes are wide, his Adam's apple bobbing in his thin neck. "Go away, *yaaw?*"

"Look at you, man." Warriors Jacket tilts his head, appraising Africa. "You their bodyguard, right?"

"Hey, Teagan," Annie says. "You got us covered?"

"What, her?" His gaze lands on me. "She packing?"

"Yeah, we're good," I say. I hate guns. Fortunately, they are made of metal, with lots of moving parts. Like safety catches, which can be held in place. Like firing pins that can be twisted and bent.

I'm not planning on revealing what I'm doing. The last

time I used my powers in self-defence, Moira Tanner ended up sending a black-ops team to bring me in. I only escaped because they didn't realise how powerful I'd gotten – and if I hadn't taken out the other psychokinetic who had framed me for murder, she would have made them keep at it until they succeeded. But a locked safety won't arouse suspicion, and really, what the hell else are they going to do?

Footsteps, behind me – and then there's cold metal against the back of my neck. "Off the bike. Now."

Slowly, I raise my hands. "Buddy, take it from me. This isn't gonna work out well for you."

"I *said*, off the bike," the man behind me growls.

Ugh. I've already got his gun locked down, so this is just a waste of time. I'm kind of tempted to do something stupid, let him hear the impotent little click as he pulls the trigger. See that stupid look in his eyes.

Which is when Africa throws his bike.

He just launches it. Yells like a goddamn banshee, and hurls the damn thing. It careens through the air, peddles whizzing. For a split-second, everybody just stares at it.

Then it hits the guy in the Warriors Jacket, sends him sprawling ass-first into the mud.

The guy holding the gun to my head pulls the trigger.

I admit it: I flinch. You would too. Fortunately, I'm good at my job, so the safety catch stays locked. The dude doesn't even realise it's on, because he's been wandering around with the safety off. He's lucky he didn't shoot himself in the dick. He pulls the trigger again – just as Africa crashes into him.

"No!" Annie yells.

I may have mentioned that Africa is a big dude. The other guy doesn't know what hit him. The only thing he can do is try to get his arms up to protect himself from Africa's flailing telephone-pole limbs.

Which doesn't stop the man in the Warriors Jacket from stepping forward, cocking his arm back, and pistol-whipping Africa across the face.

He's smart. Smarter than the others maybe. He's figured out something is wrong with his gun, and he's adjusted. Africa happens to have his mouth open, yelling furious Wolof curse words into his victim's face, when the gun hits him. His head snaps sideways, a spray of blood arcing through the air.

All of this happens in the space of about three seconds.

The blood spatters onto the rain-soaked pavement, Africa going down like a felled tree, face screwed up in agony, more blood gushing from his mouth. Annie takes a step towards him, only to be stopped by one of the others. Warriors Jacket tries to grab Annie's backpack, darting out of range, laughing as she takes a swing at him. She's exhausted, haggard, not nearly as quick as she normally is.

That does it.

Every rational thought I have about not revealing my power is pushed to one side by a blinding, furious rage. No more subtlety. No more keeping my ability under wraps. Moira Tanner is a very long way away. I am cold and tired and worried and pissed off and ready to wreck something.

I take their guns away. They don't even resist when my PK rips the weapons out of their grip. It takes their blown minds a full second to catch up, to understand that the guns they'd previously been holding in their sweaty palms are now floating on either side of my head, barrels to the grey sky.

I release the clips, pull the slides back, eject the rounds in the chambers. The confusion in their eyes, the dawning horror, is sweet, sweet, sweet.

"Holy shit," says one of them. I don't even bother to register which one. In a few seconds, they're going to be nothing more than specks on the horizon.

"You're doing it wrong," I tell them. "Let me show you how to pistol-whip someone."

I spin the gun on my right at the nearest dude's head. It crashes into his temple, and I catch it on the rebound, send it swinging in a long arc towards Warriors Jacket. The second one follows, both moving like big metal pinballs, bouncing between targets. It's a goddamn festival of ouch. And in that instant, I don't care about the consequences. My city is hurting, my friends are in trouble and these fucks – these *ass-holes* – are trying to take advantage.

In seconds, they're running – or limping anyway, all four of them yelling in terror, hightailing it the fuck out of there.

"Mic drop," I mutter. Then, with a thought, I hurl the guns into the air, in opposite directions, as hard as I can. They vanish against the dark grey sky, whirling out of sight.

Africa is up on his elbow, blinking, one hand to his mouth, Annie on her knees next to him.

"Jesus, bud." I skid to my knees too. "Are you OK?"

He spits. A huge glob of blood. One of his front teeth is gone, snapped off, and his top lip is already ballooning.

"He look OK to you?" Annie says.

"M'good," Africa murmurs. "Just ... just some blood. I have worse before."

I decide not to tell him about the tooth. He'll find out soon enough, anyway.

"The hell were you thinking?" I say.

"Huh?"

"With the bike. We had it under control."

"He was gonna shoot you."

"No, he wasn't. I had the safeties locked."

"Huh?" His eyes are rolling around in his head like pachinko balls. What if he has a concussion, like Paul? Bleeding on the brain? What do we do then?

"The safeties," I tell him. "They couldn't use the guns. We were fine!"

Those wild eyes focus on me. "Then what you make them fly for?" He waves a hand around his head, like he's swatting a fly. "The guns."

"Um. Because we were about to get our asses kicked? Because you decided to play hero?" Christ, I can hardly follow this conversation.

"I was trying to make it so you don't have to show them," he mutters.

"Africa, what—?"

"You not supposed to tell people what you can do, *yaaw*? So I try and fight them off first. I didn't know you . . ." He coughs, hacks a gob of blood and phlegm onto the pavement.

"So . . . wait, hang on." I get unsteadily to my feet. "You started a fight so I wouldn't have to use my powers, even though I was using them already. And then I ended doing the exact thing you tried to stop. And you got your ass kicked for it."

Annie puts her hands on her knees, like she's just run a marathon. "Y'all both need to work on your communication."

Slowly, the reality of what I've just done settles across me. I revealed my ability. At least four people now know there's a psychokinetic in LA. I flaunted it, showing off exactly what I could, purely out of anger. If this gets back to Tanner . . . if she finds out . . .

Annie's eyes meet mine. "What's wrong? They're gone, OK?"

"It's not that." I swallow. "Annie, I . . . Please don't tell Reggie. Maybe Tanner won't find out – maybe nobody'll believe them."

"The fuck you talking about?"

"Annie, they know what I can do." The panic starting to crystallise now, jagged and brittle. "They saw. I'm sorry, I didn't mean to—"

"Yo." She reaches across, grips my shoulder, very tight. "Be cool."

"But they—"

"But nothing. Tanner isn't gonna give a fuck."

"Yes, she will."

"Look around you, baby girl." She sweeps her arm out, taking in the ruined street, the torn tarmac and wrecked buildings and burning cars. "Do you think that shit even matters any more?"

I gape at her. "Of course it does."

"Wrong. The rules changed the second the quake hit. If you gotta use your powers, then you do it. You don't even ask questions. OK?"

Somehow, I can't see Annie's argument working on Moira Tanner, or the horrifying agency that employs her. All the same, I can't help but like her for trying.

Man, what a mess.

"Did you see my tooth?" Africa says.

I grimace. "Yeah, but I think one of those dickheads stepped on it and broke it."

He makes a face, spits another gob of blood. "S'fine. I think maybe I needed a filling in that one anyway. No more dentist visit for me!"

"Pretty sure that's not how it works, dude, but you do you."

He gives me a disgusting, bloody grin, picking up his over-turned bike.

People are fucking weird, man. Drop someone in the middle of an earthquake and they will freak the fuck out, even if they suffered nothing more than a few scrapes and bruises. Pistol-whip them, knock a tooth out and they'll walk away like nothing happened.

I expected the Santa Monica Pier to be wiped out. But it's there all right, windswept ocean water clawing at it. Even the Ferris wheel is still upright, although the rollercoaster isn't. Neither are the buildings and restaurants that dot the pier. We take a hard left, heading down the beach path away from it, just three people out for an afternoon bike ride. Cold wind whips off the ocean, driving rain into my already-drenched face.

By quarter to four, we've hit the Venice Boardwalk. Or what's left of it. The strip of shitty stores, overpriced bars, bike rental places and henna tattoo shops is torn to pieces. The palm trees that line the strip between the beach and the boardwalk have been ripped up by the roots.

It's the wrecked trees that gets me more than anything. I'm sure I've already seen some today – there are plenty of palm trees in LA, all across the city. But this is the first time I've really noticed them, and there are so, so many.

More people, too, in the same dull groups as before. None of them bother us. Most don't even pay us any attention. A couple have shopping carts loaded with their belongings. That makes me think of Harry, the homeless guy who hangs around Leimert Park. I hope he's OK. He has to be, right? He'll have been out in the open, surely?

No point trying to guess. I'll just drive myself crazy. I'm already working overtime on not thinking about Moira Tanner, black site labs or spec ops teams with my name on their briefing board.

There's a road in Venice called the Speedway, which is a

stupid name, because it has an average top speed of four miles
an hour. It's even slower today: there are two troop carri-
ers, parked at an intersection and surrounded by rifle-toting
guardsmen. They don't look as we pass them, too intent on
loading people inside.

"Sir, if you could just stay calm," one of the soldiers is
saying to an irate man. "They're sending in vehicles as fast as
they can."

"You still haven't told us when that's going to be!" the
man yells back. His tie is pulled down, his upper lip crusted
with blood.

"Just stay in the vicinity."

"I don't see why we have to use the big trucks. Why can't
we drive there ourselves? I got *family* at the stadium ..."

"Sir, the APCs are the only vehicles that can get through
the streets right now." A trace of annoyance enters the soldier's
voice, but there's desperation behind it, too, as if he badly
needs the man to understand. "Just stay here, OK? We'll send
more as soon as we can."

"Where were you ten minutes ago?" I mutter, as we pass
them. Africa, riding next to me, doesn't reply.

We turn left, zigzagging up past Pacific Avenue, heading for
the little alleyway the office sits on. Paul's Boutique.

Earthquake-proof, he said. *Tanner and I fixed that up – we
didn't want Reggie in a situation where she couldn't get out.* I have
no idea what that means in practice – how do you protect a
small house when the ground beneath it goes insane?

Still, I trust Paul. He's a pain in the ass when it comes to
the details, but it's saved us more than once, and it looks like
it might have saved Reggie too.

As we approach our end of Brooks Court, right where it
crosses 7th Avenue, I see my Jeep. The goddamn Batmobile.

It's not overturned. It's not damaged – well, one of its tyres is popped, the rubber blown out, but that's it. The ground beneath it is cracked and sloping, but my shitty-ass car is just fine. Sitting there like it's a normal day, like I could hop in and take a drive.

"Yes!" I point. "Takes a lot more than a little quake to—"

Africa sucks in a horrified breath.

"Oh, fuck," Annie murmurs.

"Jesus, guys, what's with you?" I say. "It's not like I can't change a tyre."

Then I see it, too.

Paul's Boutique.

The ground around the office has all but dropped away. It's fallen three or four feet. The house, and all the houses around it, have just dropped into the earth. The Boutique has collapsed in on itself, the top floor imploded, the walls ballooning outwards into what's left of the yard. The garage is gone. Wiped out.

"Reggie." Annie's voice comes out as a horrified whisper. She abandons her bike, sprinting for the Boutique. "Reggie!"

TWENTY-FOUR

Teagan

Paul was wrong.

The words run on repeat through my mind, like a song I can't shake. He was wrong about the Boutique, about it being earthquake-proof. The stupid fucker was wrong, and Reggie is under there, under the collapsed roof and bowed-out walls and broken glass and—

I don't know who gets there first – me, Africa or Annie. But within seconds all three of us are pulling at the rubble, yelling Reggie's name, scraping the skin from our hands as we dig. Annie vaults to the top of the pile, bracing herself against what used to be part of the roof, digging in with both hands.

The chunk of wall I'm trying to lift is too heavy, my feet unable to get a purchase on the slick, sloped concrete I'm standing on. "Help me with this," I snap at Africa – only for my mind to clear, like a camera lens snapping into focus. "Actually, forget that – just stand back."

"What?"

"Annie!" I gesture at her to move. She's quicker on the uptake, skipping off the roof and skidding to a stop on the muddy ground. I send out my PK, not giving the tiniest fuck who's watching, wrapping it around the chunks of roof and drywall. They're crazy heavy, but I've got to get them off. It's 4 p.m. now, which means it's been, what, four hours since the quake? Four and a half? All that time under the rubble . . .

I close my eyes, let out a deep breath. Get past the cold and the wet and the exhaustion, and start moving things.

First, the top of the pile. I shove the rubble to the side, focusing on the bigger pieces. I don't bother to place them – just rip them away from the house, sending them crashing over into the yard behind, against the remains of the property wall. I'm more tired than I thought I was – each piece costs me, draining energy. A headache starts to bloom at the base of my skull, nausea gnawing at the stomach.

Annie puts a hand on my shoulder, resting it there. I get the sense she's doing it more for herself than for me.

"Faster, come," Africa says.

"Working on it."

"Is she down there?" Annie asks. "Her chair, maybe?"

My eyes fly open. What a fucking numbnuts I am. I'm trying to dig out the whole house, and I don't even know where Reggie is inside it. I'm wasting all this energy shifting big pieces, when there's a better way.

I inhale through my nostrils, exhale. Africa says something, but Annie cuts him off. "Let her work."

I send my PK through the house concentrating on shapes. A door handle. A fridge, I think. The office whiteboard, ripped in two. Another door, part of a wall. They've all been jumbled together, making it hard to figure out what's what. A sudden, sick fear: I might pass over Reggie's chair, mistake it for something else. She may have been knocked clear, or dragged herself under a desk, or part of her Rig. If that happens, I could burn the energy on nothing.

Right then, I get real woozy.

Under normal circumstances, I've got quite a bit in the tank before my PK gives out on me. These are not normal circumstances. The world starts to turn sideways – Annie has to grab me, hold me up. My tongue feels weird in my mouth; like there's too much space in there, like it's suddenly shrunken and can't reach the sides. It's not the worst thing I've ever felt, but it's definitely top five.

"Got it," I murmur.

"Like hell you do. You can barely stand up."

"No, I mean, I got it. Reggie's chair."

And I do. I recognise the shape now, my PK building a picture in my mind. With Annie's help, I sit down on the ground, cross-legged – my pants are already soaked, so it's not like I'm going to get any wetter. Then I start directing her and Africa, getting them to help clear the smaller bits of rubble while I concentrate on the bigger chunks. Turns out, a lot of the house is still there; it's retained its shape, as if unwilling to let the quake break it apart completely.

I move the final bits of roof and plaster, shoving them to one side. Annie and Africa look almost like they've been swallowed by the Boutique, the top of Africa's head just visible as they dig. They've got the chair now, I can feel it, and right then, I don't want them to pull it out. What if we find Reggie under there, and she's—

"She's here," Annie shouts back. "We found her!"

I let my head drop to my chest, pushing back against the headache. When I look up, Annie and Africa are halfway down the pile of rubble – and Reggie is in Africa's arms, looking as small and fragile as a newborn bird.

Her eyes are open. Unfocused, glazed . . . but open.

I collapse backwards, not giving a shit about the mud, letting out a groan of relief. Part of the garage wall is still upright. Annie props Reggie against it, and immediately goes to work. She massages the dead tissue in Reggie's legs, kneading it hard.

"Water," Reggie whispers.

Africa fumbles in his pack, holds out a bottle, forgetting for a second that Reggie can't pick it up. I don't bother correcting him – I take the water with my mind, tilting the plastic bottle to Reggie's lips. Behind us, a distant siren cuts through the hiss of the rain, coming from the north end of 7th Avenue.

Reggie sips, then starts to cough. I pull the water back too fast, spilling some down her shirt.

Her eyes flutter open. "That's the second chair I've ... managed to lose ... in under a year. Moira's going to kill me."

Africa makes a noise that might be a laugh. Even I can't help smiling, a little. We wrecked her previous chair in a police chase a few months ago, smashing it all over El Segundo Boulevard. At least this time, it wasn't our fault.

"She had it on top of her," Annie tells me.

"Quake knocked me over. Managed to pull it on top of me ... before the walls collapsed. Used ... arms."

She has to stop between words to take ragged, hitching breaths. Imagining her flat on her back, using what little strength was left in her arms to pull the chair onto her, knowing that the roof could collapse at any second ...

"Paul say the office was quake-proof," Africa says.

Reggie expression hardens. "It ... was. But this one ... bad."

"Yeah." I wipe water off my forehead. "We've noticed."

There's a laptop clutched in her one good arm. She has it braced in the crook of her elbow, like a baby.

Before I can ask why she saved it, her eyes widen. "Where's ... Paul?"

We fill her in, telling her about the job, Schmidt's plane,

the quake. "If he got any brains inside him," Annie says, "he'll go find the nearest shelter, get that broken arm seen to." Her voice is a hard wall.

"And you three?" Reggie's gotten a little bit of strength back. "You're OK?"

"Fine." I point. "What's with the laptop?"

Reggie looks down, as if seeing it for the first time. "I've got it set—" She coughs, a very weak sound. Annie moves onto the other leg, fingers digging deep into Reggie's flesh. "I've got it set to back up to my drive every fifteen minutes. I have it in . . . in case I want to show you all something in the main room. It was . . . right next to me, on my Rig. When the shaking first started, I grabbed hold of it. Pulled it with me."

"What did you find?" I ask.

The silence goes on a little too long.

All things considered, I'd rather just abandon this whole clusterfuck and go somewhere with a hot beach and cold beers. But of course, we all know what Reggie found – or the broad strokes, anyway. That means no beer until we save the world.

Reggie gathers herself. "The earthquake – both earth-quakes – were caused by a person."

And there it is.

Another long silence. I decide to say what everyone is thinking. "How sure are you? Like sort-of sure, or like really really—"

"I've got it on tape," Reggie says quietly.

"Ah. Shit."

She raises an eyebrow, and I backtrack. "Well, I mean, that's good that we know, but just, you know . . . shit. It sucks that the earthquake isn't just Mother Nature, cos . . . "

"You should stop while you're ahead," Annie mutters to me.

"Copy that."

"How did you even know where to look?" Annie asks Reggie. "Or that you needed to look in the first place?"

Reggie gathers herself. She's got a little of her breath back now. "Remember the state trooper?"

"What state trooper?"

"The one that went missing, on our side of the Arizona border. It didn't sit right. Career officer with a family and a healthy psych record, just ditching his cruiser in the middle of nowhere? Something was off."

"Yeah, but—"

"It took me a while to go digging, what with all the mission prep. How did that go, by the way? With Schmidt?"

"Teggan was on the plane when it flew off," Africa tells her.

"I'm sorry, what?"

I have to restrain myself from punching Africa on the shoulder. "Doesn't matter. State trooper. Video."

"I just kept an eye on it. Figured I'd do a little detective work. His cruiser didn't have a dash cam, but one of the last things he did before he went missing was run a plate on his computer. Vehicle registered to an Amber-Leigh Schenke, out of New Mexico."

"Who is she?"

"No idea. I couldn't dig up anything on her – my guess is, it's a fake name. Or fake registration anyway."

"I don't get it though. What made you so interested in this in the first place? It's *genuinely* not what we normally—"

Her gaze is level, surprisingly clear. "Sometimes, you get a hunch. You follow it."

Well, that's some grade-A bullshit right there. Still, I'll figure that out later. "But the local cops would know what you knew, right?" I ask her. "They'd have run the plate?"

"Correct. They'd already put out an APB. But I'm a

lot faster than them, and, if I do say so myself, able to get into places they can't. I found the car at a gas station near Cabazon."

"That was the site of the first quake," Annie says, more to herself than to us.

"Bingo. And we got lucky." She winces. "Well, lucky as can get, anyway. The station wasn't a mom-and-pop deal. That'd been the case, the footage would probably be on a videotape buried under ten tons of rubble."

I frown. "So how did you—?"

"Big national chains stream their security footage to the cloud. Wouldn't want rank and file employees having access to it, now, would we? Not when they might be stealing potato chips or whatnot."

I feel like the *rank and file employees* would probably be banging customers in the back room rather than stealing chips, but it's not the not the time to get hung up on details.

"Hold on." Annie shakes her head, like she's trying to dislodge a fly. "So they've seen the footage too?"

"Nope. Hadn't got around to reviewing it – at least, if the metadata tells me true."

"Why not?"

"Who knows? Chain of command, probably – corporate stakeholders gotta weigh in before they formally review the tape, or some such. I've taken the footage off their hands for now."

I shake my head, trying to get my thoughts back on track. "So . . . so you're saying we've got another Jake. One of my parents' rejects who grew up to be a bad guy."

" . . . Not exactly."

And she taps the laptop, still clutched tight in her arms.

I pull a piece of roof overhead to shield us from the rain,

aware that someone might be watching, and not giving a shit. With Annie's help, Reggie gets the laptop working, pulling up a video file. It's the gas station security camera, looking right across the concrete apron, out towards the pumps and the entrance from the highway. Dark clouds mass in the distance, the footage grainy and glitchy.

"Sorry about the job, by the way," Reggie mumbles.

"What do you mean?" I ask.

"When I didn't realise Schmidt had left his hotel. I'd just broken through the gas company's encryption, and I wasn't really paying attention, so—"

"For real?" Annie says.

I find my voice. "That's . . . not like you."

"Yeah. I don't get it. You always tell us that we need be completely focused on the jobs – you and Paul both." Annie bites her bottom lip, stops massaging Reggie's leg. "What gives?"

"Doesn't matter now." Reggie taps the laptop. "Fast forward. About halfway through this file."

Annie works the trackpad, Reggie directing her. "More. More. No, stop – back a little. There."

A beat-up truck cruises into view by the pumps. Before it's even come to a stop, the door pops open, and a little kid scrambles out.

"Freeze it," Reggie says.

Annie does so, just as the kid glances at the camera. The footage is a little blurry, but I get a good look at his face. No more than four or five, with an untidy mop of brown hair. Reggie taps the screen, her fingernail brushing the kid's chest.

"*Him?*" Annie says.

I start rubbing my hands together, because it feels like the blood has just stopped flowing to my fingers. "No fucking way."

"Watch," Reggie says.

The tape plays again, the kid crouching on the edge of the lot. He's joined by a blonde woman – his mom, I guess. Amber-Leigh Schenke.

The camera starts to shake. Slowly at first, then very quickly. There's no sound, but it's all too easy to imagine what it must be like.

I clear my throat. "What are we looking f—?"

The earth around the kid and his mom explodes upwards, cocooning them in a huge sphere of soil.

"What the *fuck*?" says Annie.

The camera goes dead.

"Rewind it," I say. It's a miracle I can speak at all. There's no saliva left in my mouth. None.

We watch it again. Then a third time. And as much as I'd love to believe it was a trick of a light, or a special effect, it wasn't. There's no mistake.

"Where the kid's standing?" Reggie says. "That's—"

"The epicentre," Annie mutters.

I stand, walk away. It's either that, or I'll break the laptop. Just put my fist through the screen.

Holy fucksticks, this is bad.

This is really, really bad.

It's not surprising that there's someone else like me. I exist, and Jake did, so it makes sense there'd be more. But I never, in a million years, thought it would be a kid. It couldn't be.

When my parents were first figuring out how to give people abilities, they used women with unwanted pregnancies as test subjects. Foul, on every level. It was where Jake originated – he was a reject from their programme, a foetus that they thought they'd been unsuccessful with. His mom brought him to term, and years later, he popped up on my radar. He was bad news.

He'd lost his mind somewhere along the line, and stopping him almost got me killed.

But my parents quit working with unwanted pregnancies when my mom had me, and my brother and sister. There was no reason for them to continue – not with three super-powered kids running around. But this kid has abilities, and if he's only four or five, then—

Who gave them to him?

It's not just that. At my best, I can lift a car off someone – and that's when I'm pushing it. This kid can manipulate the earth, and he just flattened most of LA.

Behind me, somewhere very far away, Annie is saying my name.

What if I have to kill him? I thought I could reason with Jake, find out who he was and why he'd had me framed for murder, but it didn't work. It was him or me. That was one of the hardest things I've ever done, and Jake was my age, a grown man. A kid? A four-year-old boy? I can't. I won't. They can't make me.

Africa is making his way towards me. I stick a hand out, warning him back.

Oh my God. The tinnitus. That weird mental static I felt, when we went out to Sandra-May's place in Watts. The sensation that someone had filled my head with water. What if it's somehow connected to the kid? To his ability?

I turn back to Reggie. "Is there any way you could be wrong?"

"Come on now," says Annie, her face pale. "You saw what's on the tape."

"Reggie. Is there *any* way?"

She shakes her head. "That's where the quake started. It isn't far from where the state trooper went missing. Even if we didn't have that, you saw how he protected himself. He's like you, Teagan."

"He is *nothing* like me." I don't mean to snarl the words, but it happens anyway.

The first quake might have been an accident – maybe he didn't know his own power. I definitely didn't, when I was that little. But it looked like he *made* it happen – it wasn't an accident. So why do it a second time? Unless . . .

Unless he wanted it to happen. Unless he *meant* to do it. Destroy Los Angeles.

What in the name of fuck are we dealing with here?

"We gotta get Reggie to a doctor," Annie says, at the same time as I ask, "Does Tanner know about this?"

Annie raises an eyebrow.

"Yeah, OK, yes, we will absolutely do that," I say. "The doctor, I mean."

"I'm fine," Reggie says.

"Maybe get a doc to decide that." Annie wipes her mouth. "You were under there for a while. You're definitely dehydrated, that's for damn sure. Maybe concussion too, along with God knows what else."

"Reggie," I say. "Does Tanner know?"

"No. The second earthquake hit right after I found out. Whole building came down on my head."

"So you're telling me . . . You're telling me that we are the only people, right now, who know that this quake was caused by an actual person? No one else knows?"

Annie squats, getting her arms under Reggie, lifting her up. Her legs are shaky, and she nearly drops her – Africa has to lumber forward to help, supporting Reggie under the shoulders.

"What happened to your *teeth*?" Reggie says to Africa, horrified.

"These *sai sai* people wanted to rob us, huh?" Africa lisps.

"I'm sorry, what?"

"We *have* to tell people," I say. "If this kid does it again—"

"We'll take you to the Speedway," Annie tells Reggie. "There were National Guard trucks. They might have a doctor."

"I'm telling you, I'm fine."

"Reggie, we have to tell *someone*—"

"*Look*," says Annie. Her voice is brittle. "We can't do shit about the kid right now. We don't know where he is, if he's even still in LA, or what. We get Reggie to a doctor, we get some food inside us, we figure out a plan. Let's go."

TWENTY-FIVE

Amber

In the movies Amber has seen, people manage to talk to each other just fine while travelling in helicopters. They're able to have whole conversations. They must have been different helicopters to this one. It's a big chopper, with a huge belly, and it is *loud*.

The pilots up at the front have headphones with huge earcups, mic stalks jutting out. Amber doesn't. Neither do the soldiers, or the thirty other people crammed into the back of the chopper. Each wall is lined with uncomfortable metal-framed seats, the passengers secured to them by rough, red straps. Every few feet, there's a circular window. Amber and Matthew are on either side of one, and she finds her gaze continually drawn to it. Despite the chaos below, she can't help but marvel at the view.

She's never been in a helicopter before. Never even been on a plane.

At some point on the road to Big Pines, there was a truck. A soldier in camo, helping her into it. A bumpy ride in the packed flatbed, a dozen people talking to her, asking her if the dozing boy in her arms was OK. When the soldiers finally let them all out, it was into the parking lot of a ruined Walmart, the destroyed blue and yellow frontage somehow still lit by flickering floodlights. And there was a chopper.

Matthew had taken in the trickle of people, the small groups of them being ushered to the helicopter.

"I thought there'd be more," he'd mumbled. "The lady at the museum said so."

Then the helicopter. Soldiers saying they needed to move people to a central location. Someone yelling about Dodger Stadium. At first, it made no sense to Amber – surely if they had helicopters, they'd want to get people further away? Then again, if you had a city full of folks in need of urgent help, you don't waste time trucking them out into the countryside. You want to bring aid to them, and preferably do it in a place they can reach themselves, if they can't get to a chopper.

And before she knew it, Amber was in the air.

Matthew is glued to the window, gawking at the view, his frustration over the earthquake temporarily forgotten. He says something to her, his voice lost in the furious whir of the blades.

"What's that, honey?"

"How long does it take to get to the stadium?" he yells.

"The soldier said twenty minutes."

She doesn't hear Matthew's reply. A shadow falls over her, and she looks up. One of the soldiers, thrusting something into her face. A clipboard, pen attached. He barks an instruction at her, one she can't make out. The other passengers have clipboards too.

Amber scans the page. Name. Family members. Next of kin. Contact numbers. The helicopter's vibrations make it hard to write legibly.

She starts to write, then stops herself, hastily scratching

out the letter D she put down next to First Name. She's *not* Diamond Taylor anymore – she has to remember that. Diamond Taylor was a con artist, and not a very good one. She's gone. It's Amber-Leigh Schenke now, and she'd damn well better remember that.

Across from her, the soldier is dealing with a woman in what used to be a neat skirt suit. The woman looks like she's in shock, refusing to take the clipboard, tears pouring down her cheeks.

Matthew yells something in her ear.

"What?"

"I *said*, I want to get closer to the ground. I need to see."

At that moment, Amber's bladder gives a horrifying wrench. The pain overrules the fear she feels of leaving her son when he wants something, and she unclips herself, looking around for a bathroom. For once, she ignores her son's angry look.

A sudden horror. What if they don't have one? Planes always do, she knows that, but military choppers might not—

There. At the far end of the interior, someone – a soldier or relief worker more quick-thinking than the others – has dragged a porta-potty on board, tied it down with thick canvas straps. Amber stumbles over to it, yanks the door open. The hollow plastic shell dulls the roar of the chopper's engines, but only a little.

When she's done, she stands and wipes herself, almost primly. The single-ply toilet paper nearly dissolves in her damp hands.

Ajay had to have known the earthquakes would happen, or something like them. How could he have made them leave the Facility? She should have confronted him, told him to find another way. Too late now. Far too late.

In a fog, she stumbles back to her seat. Matthew glares at her. "Where were you?" he yells.

Before she can answer, he says, "Tell them to go down to the ground. I wanna *see*."

She can barely hear him, has to yell her reply. "Sorry, honey, they're not going to do that."

"You're an adult," he says. In the few minutes she's been away, he's become even more impatient, anger building like steam trapped in a pipe. "They'll listen to you. Ask them."

Amber half-rises, wavers, sits back down. How can he think they'll do that? There's no way, no way at all.

She doesn't need to look at Matthew to know he's furious. Anger radiates off him. He twists to face her, straining against his own straps. "I wanna see the ground!" he yells.

There's no dirt here, she tells herself. *Nothing for him to throw.*

But there is.

Mud slicks the floor of the chopper. Everyone is dirty, their clothes crusted with it. Amber's jeans are almost black, all the way up to the knees. And on cue, as she looks down, the lumps of mud on her shoes begin to move. Trembling, like they're alive, slowly rising upwards.

He's going to do something, hurt someone, hurt *her*, unless he gets what he wants right now. She has to stop it. They are packed tight into the chopper, all these people ... even the soldiers won't know what hit them. And what if he hurts the pilot, by accident? They'll crash, plummet out of the sky. Terror paralyses her, locks her to her seat. She can't look away from the mud.

But then, it stops. Slops back onto her shoe.

She's never seen him this furious. His eyes are tiny, malignant dots of light in the darkened cabin. His shoulders tremble, his arms ramrod straight, fists clenched tight enough to whiten the skin. His mouth is set in a thin line, lower lip trembling. The air around her suddenly feels thick, stifling, like it's been turned to runny oil.

Why isn't he—?

Because he doesn't want to reveal his powers – not around other people, and definitely not around the military. Not in a helicopter, where he might cause a crash.

He can't hurt her. There's nothing he can do. The thought is so big, so impossible, that Amber doesn't know what to do with it. She's like a prisoner, held underground for years, finally being led out into the sun, blinking, flinching from the light.

And on the heels of this: satisfaction.

Twisted and strange, but still satisfaction. She handled the situation. She controlled her son. She managed to stop him from doing what he wanted. And if it happened once, then it could happen again. She—

Matthew punches her in the face.

It's not a hard punch. For all her son's powers, he's a skinny boy, almost scrawny. It glances off her cheek, rocking her head back, leaving her more dazed than hurt. It takes her by surprise, and so she doesn't get her hands up in time to deflect the second punch. This one lands right on her upper lip.

Amber's been beaten before. Sometimes they were small – a slap, a shove. Other times they were … bad. She learned very quickly which ones she could stop, and which ones she couldn't. The ones where fighting back would only make it worse. And so when instinct leads her to grab his wrists and hold on tight, she doesn't let go.

He howls, pulling as far as he can against his seat straps, trying to wrench out of her grip. When that doesn't work, he starts kicking her, sneaker-clad feet hammering her knees and thighs. He spits in her face, the glob of saliva landing on her swollen upper lip, mingling with the blood. Matthew's own cheeks are wet with tears, his mouth twisted in an animal grimace.

She's aware of bodies around her – soldiers, civilians, concerned faces, hands reaching out to hold Matthew back. Nobody appears willing to touch him, even as he kicks and scratches and bites. "*I'll kill you!*" he yells, his little-boy voice pitching higher and higher with each word. "Leggo. *Leggo me!*"

She pulls the two of them tight together, wraps her arms around him, locks him in her grip and whispers soothing words into his ear, ignoring his angry, anguished cries.

Because he *is* skinny. He *is* scrawny. And as exhausted as she is, it's easy to lock him down. Amber's breathing hard, almost gulping air, her shoulders hitching and her lip fat and throbbing. But she holds her son, holds him until he's still.

Her thoughts are a hurricane, howling and raging. This is her fault. *Of course* he'd try to hurt her, even if he couldn't use his powers. She should have seen it coming – goddamnit, she should have controlled it. She could have asked one of the soldiers, or . . . or . . .

She has to stay calm. It's just a temper tantrum, like any kid would throw. It's all part of being a mom. Another quote from one of her books – one she'd actually written down on a Post-it, stuck on her fridge – *When we are no longer able to change a situation, we are challenged to change ourselves.*

If she can hold onto him tight, show him that hurting her doesn't work, that it doesn't *always* get him what he wants . . .

He'll learn. He'll become the still child in her arms, face pressed into her shoulder. He'll see how much she loves him, and maybe she can stop him from hurting anyone else.

And he needs her, even if he doesn't realise it – no matter how smart he is. There are things she can do that he can't. He can't drive, or pay for a meal, or check into a motel. He can't even walk down the street by himself before a cop or a well-meaning passer-by asks if he's OK.

For all his powers, he's still just four years old. And she can still be his mom.

It's crazy. All of it. But that thought is easily brushed aside, a cobweb that vanishes into nothing and is forgotten almost as quickly.

There's a change in the engine pitch. Amber's stomach lurches a little – they're descending. They're *dropping*. It takes her a few stunned seconds to realise that the chopper is coming in to land.

Matthew's realised it too. He wiggles out from her grip and presses his face to the window, scanning the ground, the past few minutes already forgotten. And yet, as they swoop towards the glowing bowl of Dodger Stadium, Amber tucks the knowledge away. Hoarding it.

TWENTY-SIX

Teagan

Seven p.m on the worst day in the history of LA.

We're in the back of a troop transport, on the way to Dodger Stadium. I didn't think it was possible, but it's actually colder *inside* the truck than it is outside in the rain.

Maybe it's because we were moving before. Now we're just sitting still, crammed into the back of this troop transport, perched on freezing metal benches and trying not to move in case we accidentally elbow our neighbours in the ribs. Mine is a grouchy dude in a business suit, tie still done up. When I squashed down next to him, he gave me a look that said not to move even one inch into the space he'd carved out for himself.

I didn't have the energy to insult him properly.

Reggie got a five-second examination from a harried medic, enough to establish that she didn't have any life-threatening injuries. Maybe. Possibly. We won't know for sure until someone can give her a ten-second exam at Dodger. We've been heading toward the stadium for the past two and a bit hours, the truck regularly jerking to a halt as the soldiers clear debris out of the road.

I'm freezing, starving, and more tired than I've ever been in my whole life. And yet, somehow, I can't sleep. My body won't drop off. Africa is conked out, mouth open, leaning on Annie's shoulder. She and Africa are on the opposite side of the truck to Reggie and I, Annie tapping at Reggie's laptop, ignoring the curious, shell-shocked looks from the other survivors. "Trying to see if I can boost the range of our comms," she tells me when I ask her what she's up to.

Reggie's asleep too, snoring gently. I have to stop myself from waking her up and asking her what the secret is. I keep thinking back to the office – to the living room we'll never have another planning session in, to the roof I'll never again climb up to enjoy a sunset beer or three.

As for what I – or we – are going to do about this kid who can apparently cause earthquakes, I don't have the first clue. Keeping myself sitting up is hard enough.

Weirdly, what's getting to me the most is the lack of information. I want to know how bad it is – just how much of my city is gone. What we need is a TV, like Schmidt had on his plane. Some more words from Molly Zuckerman – that was the reporter's name, wasn't it? A strange little detail lodged in my mind. Good old Molly. She could give us the skinny from up there in her chopper. *That's right, Gina, we've learned that the earthquake was entirely natural and nothing more than a result of tectonic plates shifting. It definitely wasn't caused by a small boy with abilities beyond his control. Our sources tell us that I know absolutely fuck-all, and that I have an annoying voice and terrible hair. Back to you in the studio.*

We hit another bump in the road, the truck's huge tyres carrying us over it. Reggie snorts awake suddenly, blinking next to me. She licks cracked lips, her unfocused gaze darting around the truck's interior.

"Here." I pull out the one bottle I still have on me, half-full of water. Reggie tilts her head back, accepting the drink. Annie looks up, concerned, then flashes me a quick smile of thanks.

"Got any more?" the businessman next to me says.

"Nope. Sorry, dude."

He lapses into sullen silence.

"I never said," Reggie tells me, when she's drunk her fill. "Good job on Schmidt. That was quick thinking."

"Paul didn't think so." Man, I hope he's OK. Just because we don't see eye-to-eye on stuff doesn't mean I want him hurt. And Annie ... she's doing a good job of not showing it, but she's clearly worried about him. She's even more tense than normal, which is saying something.

"Paul doesn't know everything." She coughs. "I'm truly sorry, by the way. I should have been paying more attention to ... to what Schmidt was doing. I should have spotted how he left his hotel."

I'm about to tell her that it isn't important – however she messed up, we've got bigger things to worry about. But before I can, she says, "I knew this would happen."

"You ... knew a kid with earthquake abilities would show up?"

"I knew *someone* with abilities would, eventually. We were caught unprepared last time, and I wasn't going to let it happen again." A deep, trembling breath. "I wanted to show Moira. Prove to her that we were ready for anything."

Tanner. She won't know about the kid, that's for sure. Will she be looking for us? Trying to get us out? I doubt it. She's always been practical – chances are, she'll let the National Guard do their thing.

"You don't have shit to prove to Tanner," I tell Reggie.

"And you can't plan for everything. Besides, that's not what China Shop is for. We go out, we do jobs, we take down bad guys. Right?"

"I suppose."

The defeat in her voice rattles me, more than I want to admit. "Reggie, it's gonna be OK. This quake wasn't our fault – there's no *way* we could have known. If anything, Tanner's the one who should have known about it. We'll get to the stadium, we'll figure out what to do about the earthquake kid, then we can worry about *El Jefe*. She's not gonna get mad at us for this. How could she?"

"She won't." That same listless tone. Is it shock? Has to be. Annie will know what to do about it. I look around, trying to find some more water, half-sure that dehydration is part of the problem.

Reggie says, "She'll keep China Shop around in one form or another. No doubt about that. It'll just look ... different than before."

"What are you saying?"

"Nothing. Don't worry about it."

File that with *Stay calm* and *Your ass looks fine in that dress* under *Things that never result in the intended effect, ever.*

I'm saved from having to answer when the truck lurches, tilting upwards as it climbs over some obstacle. The back of the vehicle is open, and it looks as if it's stopped raining. I don't have the first clue where we are. Koreatown? Crenshaw? Hell, maybe even Leimert Park – if it is, I could hop off here, go see if anything's left of my house. It's probably pulverised, but at least I'd know for sure ...

"I think Moira's going to fire me," Reggie says quietly.

I blink. "Excuse me?"

"That's why I was digging into the first quake. That missing trooper. I wanted to find ... something, I don't know. I was distracted during the job, but I just ... "

"Hold on. No no no. Tanner isn't going to *fire you*. She can't."

Another sigh. "Sometimes, I forget how young you are."

"OK, number one, fuck you, and number two ... she can't fire you. You run China Shop. You're the whole reason we exist!"

"Technically, *you're* the reason we exist."

"You know exactly what I mean. And anyway, what the hell have you done to justify firing? Our jobs are going fine! Is it because of Carlos? Listen, that was as much her fault as anyone's. I even told her after—"

"Would you keep it down?" grumbles the man next to me.

"Zip it, cupcake. Reggie: you're wrong. Sorry, you just are."

"Moira and I go back twenty years now. I know exactly how she thinks. She doesn't just want good performance – she wants the right people in the right positions. Even more so now, after what happened with Carlos."

"So she was asking you to come to Washington to can you?"

"I suppose she thought she owed it to me to do it face-to-face."

"But you can't know for sure!"

"I have a pretty good idea. Just things she's said, the way she's phrased certain emails. I can read between the lines."

The idea of Reggie not being with China Shop is so dumb I can't even begin to see how it would work. "You're literally the best hacker in this country—"

The ghost of a smile. "You know that isn't true."

"The hell it is. Who the fuck is she going to get to replace you? I don't think the guy who invented the internet is available."

A thought occurs – and not a comfortable one. "Reggie, this isn't because of – I mean, there's no way Tanner would use your disability . . ."

It still feels wrong to use the word, but Reggie herself once told us that if we referred to her as differently abled one more time, she'd hack our social security files and give us that phrase as our new middle names.

In response to my question, she shakes her head. "I don't believe so. It's more about management style. I get the feeling she wants China Shop to be a little more . . . tightly run. I pushed for Africa to join our team, and I wanted to make sure she didn't regret that."

She pauses, as if choosing her words carefully. "I wanted to sell her on our creativity. That I would see things a more rigid manager wouldn't be able to. Show her we could act on our instincts, instead of just following orders." She scoffs. "God, listen to me. I've gone corporate."

"Wait a second – is this because of me? Because of that whole thing with Jake?"

"Honey, not everything is about you." But she doesn't meet my eyes.

"You tell me one thing I could have done differently in that situation. Well, OK, I probably shouldn't have thrown Annie and me out a skyscraper. And yeah, maybe I shouldn't have revealed my ability in front of Nic, but it worked out OK, didn't it? He's on board, he signed all the NDAs, no harm done. Right? And if—"

"You've been getting stronger," Reggie murmurs.

"Well . . . yeah. We knew that. Adrenaline spikes my PK. So what?"

"You think I haven't noticed how much more you can lift nowadays? The control you have? The range? You're getting more powerful, and it's starting to make people very nervous."

"People. You mean like Tanner?"

"I've kept it from her as much as I can, but she has her ways. There have been ... I guess you could call them *rumblings* in her department."

"Reggie, if you don't start talking sense—"

"There are people who work with Tanner who would prefer you back in Waco."

I let out a long, slow breath. Waco. The off-the-books Texas facility where these fuckers kept me for *years* after Wyoming. A grey hell, with endless tests and doctors and the threat of being casually murdered because someone in power thought I was too dangerous.

"Tanner wouldn't let them," I say, voice as steady as I can make it. "That's the deal, right? I work for her, she keeps me in play. And we've been doing exactly what she wants. Haven't we?"

"Tanner is getting pressure from everywhere. She has to make a change – and despite what you might think, she doesn't want you in Waco, or anywhere else but here. One option she has is to switch out the management for someone with more ... authority."

"Reggie, this is crazy. She is *not* going to fire you. I won't let her." *And I'm not letting someone else get shafted because of me.*

It's fully dark outside the truck now. We're trundling up a hill, still lurching and bouncing over torn-up rubble. There are more trucks in line behind us, headlights cutting through the gloom.

Now that I think about it, I should have known something was up. Reggie's been so distracted lately. She's been short with us, spending more and more time locked away with her Rig.

And here I was, bumbling through my weird-ass life, getting ready to ask her to tell her boss that I wanted to take time off and go to cooking school. It's like a bad joke.

There must be a strange expression on my face, because Reggie says, "What is it?"

I almost don't tell her, but then think, *Fuck it.*

"Reggie, I know it probably makes no sense to tell you this now, but I ... I want to go to cooking school."

"Cooking sc—I don't understand."

And then it all pours out of me. "I love cooking. Like, really really love it. I mean, you know that, you've eaten my food before. And I just ... I guess I just want to make it part of my life. Officially."

"You want somebody to teach you how to cook?"

"Kind of. I can already cook, but there's so much I don't know how to do. Things that might help me when I own my own restaurant. Eventually. I'd just be doing the cooking at a night school, at least at first ... "

"At first?"

I look away, then make myself meet her eyes. "You can't stop me. I need other things in my life besides ... this."

She slowly shakes her head. "Oh, h—"

"If you *oh, honey* me, I will never make your favorite brownies ever again. But I know what you were going to say anyway. You're fine with it; Tanner won't be."

She's silent for a good few seconds. "It'll be an ... uphill battle."

"Yeah, and the hill is Mount Everest. I get it."

"You could say that. Sorry, Teagan, I know it's not what you want to hear ... "

I grunt. "Doesn't matter. Pretty sure the school I wanted to go to doesn't exist any more."

"We'll find a way," she says, not unkindly. "After all, if I can play the Bard in my off-hours, then—"

"If you can what the what?"

"Play the Bard. Shakespeare?" A flicker of a smile. "I read once that the world can be separated into two groups of people: those who have played the Bard, and those who haven't."

"Cute."

"Our troupe is doing *The Taming of the Shrew* right now. Or we were. Anyway, if I can do some acting on the side, then I don't see why you shouldn't be able to do a little cooking."

Neither of us state the obvious. Reggie acts for fun. She's not planning a career change.

Somehow, that makes it worse. Reggie's more than a boss. After everything we've been through in the past couple of years, she's my friend. China Shop – her Rig, the Boutique, the job – means everything to her. Would Tanner really be so unkind as to take that away? Just to keep me in the field?

Yes. Of course she would. She'd do it without a second thought.

"Come on, motherfucker," Annie mutters. "Just a couple more minutes. Almost got you . . . "

The truck comes to a sudden, shuddering halt. A soldier appears at the rear tailgate, reaching up to pop it open. "All right, everybody out!" he yells.

It's a lot noisier out there with the truck's engine off, a buzz of voices, other trucks hissing and clunking, the roar of helicopter engines. Africa takes Reggie, hefting her in his arms and climbing down from the tailgate. The rain has started again, because of course it has.

We're in a parking lot at the north end of Dodger Stadium. If the entire baseball field is a huge V, with home plate at the bottom, we're standing roughly between the two top points.

The stadium looms above us in the cold, grey air. Most of it, anyway. The quake collapsed large sections of the bleachers, exposing concrete rebar, filling the air with the gritty taste of dust. An ad for Coors beer is torn in two – the *C* is still upright, but the *oors* part is twisted and broken.

The stadium is built on a hill. It's at the centre of a terraced parking lot – the idea being that the people seated in the cheap seats behind home plate, at the top of the bleachers, can park their car on the same level, so at least they don't have to use any stairs. I can see those seats from our parking spot. One of the sections is still largely intact, and it's bustling with people. Like half of Los Angeles is here. Choppers hover on the horizon, blinking lights against the dark sky, buzzing over the smoke from downtown.

Annie is standing off to one side with the laptop, tapping away at it, ignoring the rain pattering on the screen and keyboard. As I look over, she makes a disgusted sound, slamming the laptop closed. "Piece of shit."

"You get anywhere?" Reggie wheezes.

"I don't think so. It's the hardware, not the software."

"He'll be OK," I tell her.

Nobody has to ask who I'm talking about.

TWENTY-SEVEN

Teagan

There are more people coming into the parking lot, and huge scrums of them waiting to get into the stadium. There are lots of injuries – broken arms, legs, gashes and cuts. Everybody is soaked to the skin, shivering, with the kind of shell-shocked look you'd expect from a war zone. The soldiers shepherd us into one of the lines, just under the broken Coors ad. An oversized digital clock, somehow miraculously still working, reads 7:13.

"I came here with my dad when I was little once." Annie sounds dazed. "Dodgers-Padres. Garciaparra hit a walk-off at the bottom of the tenth."

"Don't think there's gonna be home runs here for a while," Reggie murmurs.

Africa's holding her, his arms under Reggie's knees and shoulders. "I see it like this in Sierra Leone," he says, almost to himself. "Not good."

At least the lines are moving fast. Soldiers with clipboards take names, hustle people through. Those who can't walk are pointed straight onto the field, the rest into the bleachers. "Right stands *only*," a grizzled-looking soldier bellows. "The left side of the field – yes, *my* left – is unsafe, and off limits. Walk, don't run – *hey*! Do not run! Food and water will be distributed. If you need medical attention, make yourself known at the front of the line."

You want to know something weird? The soldiers remind me of the special forces crew that tried to bring us in last year, back when we were involved in the whole Jake thing. They've got the same blank, focused way of looking at you. The same condescending voices. Who knows, maybe I'll run into Burr here, helping people check into Hotel Dodger. We can laugh about how he didn't catch me last time because I broke his finger and then almost stabbed him with a piece of glass.

When we reach the front, I get my first good look at the field beyond. The diamond and the grass surrounding it are packed with white tents, soldiers and doctors rushing between them. The bleachers are already a heaving mass of people, and despite the soldiers' best efforts, the crowds have started to spill out onto the field. Just past the far bleachers, helicopters are landing: big troop transports, touching down in the south parking lot and taking off seconds later.

One of the soldiers grabs my wrist. I'm so wired that I nearly brain him with a nearby tent pole, but he just jabs a black permanent marker at my hand, marking the back of it. I'm sure there's a reason for it, some system they've devised, but I'm fucked if I can figure it out.

"What is our plan?" Africa says. He and the others have all received similar marks.

Annie runs a hand through her hair. The damp air has frizzed it, sending it out in weird directions – mine isn't doing much better. "I'll, um – I'll take Reggie to the medical tent. Africa, Teags – you guys try find us something to eat and drink."

"Annie, I don't know if they'll give two of us enough for four people," I say.

"Figure it out," she snaps. "When you're done, I'll meet you there." She points to a section of the bleachers on our right, a relatively clear one, just beyond where third base would be.

As it turns out, we can't go our separate ways yet. The way the tents are, we're forced to walk in an uncomfortable group around the edge of the field. "Eh, Teggan," Africa whispers at me. "What is the plan?"

"Annie already told you. We'll go find some sandwiches or whatever they're dishing out."

"No no. About the boy. On the video."

"I dunno."

"We cannot just do nothing, huh? We the only ones who know. I think maybe—"

"Jesus-fuck, *Idriss*, give it a rest."

I don't mean to shout at him, but I am reaching the end of my tether, and I like to think that particular tether is pretty long.

I expect him to subside, like he always does. Instead, he gives me a weird look – almost disappointed. I turn away from him, keep trudging, feet squishing into what's left of the muddy grass. Forget food – I would sell my stomach for a pair of dry shoes.

"Medical tent's over there," Annie says, when we reach a gap. "Teagan, take Africa and – wait, did you guys hear that?"

Africa bends his head, as if listening hard. "Ya, I think so. Teggan, here." He shoves Reggie into my arms, so suddenly that I nearly drop her.

"I'm not a sack of grain," Reggie snarls.

Annie isn't listening. She's got a finger to her ear, head bent.

"Move it along," a soldier says from somewhere to my right.

"Yeah, just a second." Annie bends her head even further.

"Yo, Annie," I say. "What's—?"

Then I hear it too. Our earpieces have still been connected this whole time, although we obviously didn't need them on the bike ride down to Venice. And because we were so close, there was minimal interference. But now ... now there's a *crackle* on the line. I can barely hear it over the noise around us, but it's there.

And then, out of nowhere, a voice. Intermittent and crackly, but ...

"—can you read me, I—"

"Paul." Annie starts moving again, quick steps. "Paul!"

A few seconds of silence. Then Paul's voice, stunned. "—if you can hear me—at the—"

"I hear you!" She actually laughs. "We're in the stadium too. Where are you?"

"—west bleacher – row twenty-thr—"

Annie doesn't wait for the rest. She takes off, ignoring the three of us, heading for the bleachers.

Africa's eyes are wide. Despite our ugly exchange earlier, there's a stunned, almost goofy smile on his face.

"So," I say to Reggie. "You still wanna go to medical, or—?"

"Forget that," she mutters. "I want to see the reunion as much as you do."

We find Paul higher up in the bleachers, far back enough that he's under the angled roof, out of the rain. His arm is in a blue medical brace, his shirt is torn, and his face is covered in a thin film of dirt. None of which stops Annie nearly knocking him over. She wraps her arms around him, buries her face in his shoulder, rocking from side to side. She's making the strangest sound – a kind of gasping sob. Paul holds her tight.

At first, I don't understand why she's so emotional. Paul's ex-Navy. He can handle himself, even when he's stranded at an airport with a broken arm in the aftermath of a massive earthquake. Even I knew that. But for all of these past few hours — through all the chaos and insanity, finding the Boutique destroyed, discovering that the quake was caused by a person — which is still so terrifying I don't want to think about it — Annie's hardly mentioned Paul. She pushed all her worry down into a tiny part of herself, held it there, not letting it budge an inch this whole time.

All at once, she rips out of Paul's grip, shoves him hard enough to nearly make him stumble. "You piece of shit, don't you ever tell me to leave you again, I will slap the taste out your mouth."

" . . . OK?"

"And don't you fucking *dare* say you love me. I will break your other arm." Then she grabs him a second time, kisses him, long and hard.

"Hey there, neighbours," he says to us, when Annie finally lets him go.

"Boss!" Africa roars the word with delight. He lowers Reggie carefully onto one of the seats, thrusts his hand out to shake Paul's. Unfortunately, Paul's right arm is his injured one. When Africa realises, he snorts with laughter, claps Paul on his good shoulder. "Thought you left us, huh?"

I flash Paul a smile. "'Sup, Jasmine."

The corners of his mouth flick ever so slightly upwards. "Hey there."

"How's the head?" I say.

He shrugs. "Better. I definitely have a concussion, but they think it's minor. Or at least, they don't believe I'm going to drop dead on them."

"You sure? You were pretty out of it back there ..."

"No, I'm good. Hurts to look at lights for too long, but I think I got off easy." His eyes go wide. "The office. Did you—?"

"Toast," Annie's gone back to hugging him, her voice muffled by his shoulder.

"*What?*"

"Yeah," I say. "Guess the construction guys owe us a refund."

"I have someone," Africa says. "When we build it again, I know a company. I am friends with the CEO. He'll give us good price – it will be even better than before."

After a little more hugging, Annie gets busy, flipping open the laptop and screening the video. Paul absorbs it silently, his expression not even changing as the kid cocoons himself and his mom in dirt. When the video is done, he leans back on the plastic seats. Scratches his chin. "We're sure?"

"You saw the video," Reggie says.

"You don't think that maybe—?"

"Paul, I'm positive. It was the boy."

"Not his mother?" He glances at me. "A person Teagan's age would make sense, we saw that with Jake, but a child ..."

"Trust me, I'm as weirded out as you are," I tell him.

He lowers his eyes, and I can almost see the gears turning; the mental whiteboard, rapidly filling with mind maps and brainstorms and long, intricate lists.

"OK," he says eventually. "Everybody huddle up."

There are a few seconds of awkward silence, the rest of us glancing at one another. Mostly because we are already standing pretty close together in the narrow line of seats, and it's a little hard to figure out what he wants us to do.

He realises this. "Never mind. Our first priority is to inform Tanner. I'm guessing she doesn't know yet, right?"

Annie glances at Reggie, shakes her head.

"We'll need a satellite phone," Paul continues. "Some type of communication, anyway. There's military presence, and I'm guessing they'll have a line out."

"I will find us a phone," Africa says, squaring his shoulders.

Paul talks over him. "But before we do that, we actually have something more important to discuss."

"You literally just said informing Tanner is priority number one," I say.

"Right, right. But priority number one is actually discussing what we do when we find the boy."

"How do you mean?"

"What's our strategy?" Paul looks out over the packed stadium. "How are we going to make contact?"

"Babe, we don't even know where he is," Annie tells him.

"But we do need to find him. And that means we need a strategy for when we do. My instinct is to approach, and carefully — he might not understand his powers yet. Perhaps he even triggered the quakes by accident."

My eyes are gritty, and I have to blink a few times to clear them. "Didn't look like an accident."

"Maybe. Maybe not. But he seems young on the video. If we can talk to him, then perhaps we can neutralise this situation."

"Babe . . ."

"No, listen. Out of everyone here, who has kids? I'll tell you. Me. I'm the only one with a son."

Africa makes an *mmm* sound, as if this hadn't occurred to him.

"There are things you learn as a parent," Paul says. "Certain truths about how children act. This young man's probably scared. He probably doesn't understand what he's done, and even if he does, he might not know how to control it. And by the way, do I have to remind everybody that he's a child? We can't go in hard and fast here."

He's obviously expecting us to nod in agreement. But what the follows the speech is an uncomfortable silence. Africa and I share a glance, both of us clearly thinking the same thing.

"He's not Cole, man," Annie says gently.

God, I'm so glad she said his son's name before I had to. I *really* didn't feel like calling Paul on this. He's not just my annoying coworker right now – he's a dad, and he must be worried out of his mind. His little boy and his ex-wife might be in Arizona, but not being able to contact them has to be the worst kind of torture.

Paul closes his eyes. "I'm not saying he is."

"Really?" Annie folds her arms, but the look she gives him isn't unkind.

"Of course not. I'm just saying that I'm the only one here who actually knows what it's like to raise a boy. OK?"

"Then you know what kids can do sometimes," Annie says. "You're acting like he just . . . shit, man, isn't it just *possible* he did this on purpose? That he threw a tantrum or something?"

"Of course it's possible, but—"

"I mean, Jesus, I don't have a kid yet, but I seen plenty of 'em lose their damn minds over the smallest things. Moms not buying them ice cream. Their favourite show getting taken off Netflix."

"Right," I say. "Maybe he just lost his temper? Or his mom doesn't spank him enough? Or something?"

Annie side-eyes me. "Spank him?"

"You know what I mean. Paul, dude—"

"No." He shakes his head, firmly, like that puts it to bed. "That is not what's happening here. What he have is a little boy. You can't just assume things. And by the way, just because

I have a son does *not* mean I'm getting confused here. It gives me more insight, not less. I'm actually a little insulted that—"

"We're getting sidetracked," Reggie says. "We shouldn't make judgements until we find the boy ourselves."

"But where is he?" Africa rumbles. "We do not even know—"

"What about the epicentre?" Annie says.

Paul takes a deep breath, as if drawing a line under the awkward conversation we just had. "Makes sense. Problem is how we get there. From what I hear, it's all the way up north, in the Angeles forest."

Which is only reachable on miles and miles of broken freeways and shredded roads. That's one hell of a bike ride. Plus, the streets are almost certainly bristling with people like the ones who tried to shake us down en route to the Boutique. Or, we could try stealing an Army helicopter – we'd have about the same chance of success, and it would be a more life-affirming experience. Well, up until we all got shot.

Paul points out into the cavernous stadium. "We can't discount the possibility that he might be here."

Africa's eyebrows shoot up. "*Here?*"

"Why not? FEMA are using this as a central camp. They're already flying people in. We should check here first – with five of us, we could—"

Right then, Reggie dissolves in a fit of wheezing, hacking coughs. Her diaphragm is weak on a good day, and today is a long distance from that. Annie immediately steps over to her, helps shift her position on the seat.

Paul's face creases in a frown. "Reggie, are you—?"

"Fine." She can hardly get the word out.

"Fine, my ass," says Annie. "You need a doctor."

"Like hell I do."

"Actually, I'm with Annie on this one." I say. I don't exactly love the idea of going back into the rain, but I still want someone with an actual medical degree to give her a once-over. "You had a building fall on your head. That'll fuck up anyone's day."

Paul gets to his feet. "You're right. Of course you're right. Priority one—"

I look over my shoulder. "Dude, you really need a new system."

"Priority *one* is getting us food and water, and Reggie a sit-down with a doctor. We can't do anything if we're out of juice. And there are five of us, so we can cover a little more ground. Teagan – can you go find us some water? I saw them giving out bottles over there." He points towards where home plate would be. "Food too, if you can get it. Africa, you get Reggie to the medical tent. Annie – go with him. You can talk to the medics."

"*I* can talk to them myself," Reggie says.

Paul shakes his head, a not-unkind look on his face. "You're in bad shape. I want Annie there – she's used to working with you on a daily basis. She can step in if needed."

"What are you gonna do?" Annie asks.

"I'm going to see if I can open up a line of communication to Washington. Or at least find out where they keep the satellite phones."

He looks around at all of us. "Well, come on. Time's a-wasting. Unless anybody's got anything else to say?"

Nobody does. But as we make our way back down to ground level, the strangest thought comes into my head. The whole time Paul was talking, Reggie hardly said a word. Even before she started coughing. She just let him take the lead.

I think Moira's going to fire me.

She wants the right people in the right positions.

And I know exactly who she'd put there.

You want to know the craziest thing? Paul would be a really great choice. Even I will admit that. He might annoy the shit out of me, but he knows every part of our operation inside and out – every moment of every op, every disguise and tool and vehicle, every nook and cranny of the Boutique. Reggie's always been our boss ... but I'd be lying to myself if I didn't admit that Paul would be just as good. Maybe better.

He's not perfect. He's projecting his feelings for his son onto our little earthquake boy, for one thing, which is super-double-plus unhelpful. But the uncomfortable truth is: however much I like Reggie, however much I want her to stay, Paul Marino may be a better leader.

I take those thoughts and push them to the back of my mind. Priority one: save the world. Then we can worry about saving China Shop.

TWENTY-EIGHT

Teagan

It takes me a while to make my way to home plate. It's still raining, naturally, so I have to walk through ankle-deep, sucking mud – if the Dodger Stadium grounds crew are here, they must be losing their shit right now. All their hard work trampled under a million feet. And it does feel like a million; there's almost no space between the tents, as if the entirety of LA has been crammed into the stadium. For all I know, that's exactly what's happened.

I keep wondering if they'll ever play baseball here again – if the field can even be saved after all this. Let alone the stadium itself. Maybe they'll just tear it down and build a new one. Then again, will there even be a baseball team in Los Angeles any more? A quake like this is going to knock the state's economy off a cliff...

Thinking of the wider consequences makes my head spin. What about the restaurants I love? Not just the small mom-and-pop spots, the little Vietnamese noodle shops and taco trucks and bistros. I'm thinking about the big ones, the ones that spend their time angling for Michelin stars – spots like N/Naka, where I still haven't eaten, and probably never will. Burgers Never Say Die. Atrium. Dialogue. Shit, Howlin'

Rays! The best fried chicken I've ever eaten! All these mind-blowing restaurants that are just ... gone. And – oh man, the service staff. Waiters and dishwashers and cooks and night porters. Thousands upon thousands of people, out of work.

And there's more. Everybody thinks Los Angeles is all about the movie industry and nothing else. It definitely isn't true, but a shit-ton of people still work on movies here. After today, the global hub of film production will probably move somewhere cold and boring. Like Vancouver.

Amoeba Music? The greatest record store that ever was or ever will be? Gone. Not to mention other ones that are just as cool, like Fat Beats. And I can forget about seeing Jay Rock at the Coliseum, because the Coliseum probably doesn't exist anymore. Ditto for the Novo, the Echo, the Roxy. And all the little incidental spots that populate my life, like Ziggy's on La Tijera, where I get my hair done. The bodega on the corner of Roxton Avenue in Leimert Park, which I can never remember the name of even though I chat with Mo, the owner, all the time.

This kid's killed us. He's put a bullet through my city's brain. And he's taken up residence in my own.

Mostly, I'm pretty comfortable with who I am. I don't spend a lot of time obsessing over self-improvement, and if you don't count the four years I spent in the custody of the US government, I've never been in therapy. Who needs it? I'm not some comic-book character with a dark past and a hidden history; I know *exactly* where I come from, and why I have my ability, and I came to terms with it a long time ago. It made it easier to just chill the fuck out and enjoy life, and fill my brain with important things, like how not to burn paella.

But after Carlos, and Jake, that little core of certainty took a knock. With this kid – this child who appears to be a lot stronger than I could ever imagine – it's been sucker-punched. He didn't appear out of nowhere. Someone *gave* him his ability. But why? And who?

Where the hell did he come from?

I lower my head, and push on through the muck.

If anything, the situation inside the baseball diamond is even worse. There are fewer wounded here, but all that means is they're louder, and more likely to push you out the way as they move past. My PK gets a feel of watches, chains, wallets filled with coins, belt buckles – not to mention the world around me, plastic buckets and metal tent poles and M-16s. After someone shoves me aside for the third time, it's very tempting to just grab the nearest object and start swinging.

Paul's voice suddenly pops into my earpiece. "Testing, testing, one, two, thr—"

Static. Silence. Then Annie: "Copy th—short-range transmi—is still—"

"Yeah, think—some problems with the link. Teagan, do you—?"

"I'm here," I say, not sure whether they're going to catch it or not. It doesn't feel like it matters much.

Home plate. Near as I'll to get, anyway. Ahead of me, a soldier on an empty flatbed tries to ignore the people bustling around it. "Where's our water?" someone yells.

"For the millionth time, we've given out all we have." The soldier's distracted words are greeted with groans, angry mutters. My heart sinks. "There's more coming in, but you need to be patient."

Balls. I send out a wave of PK, looking for the familiar shape of plastic water bottles, hoping that maybe he's just stalling for time. But there aren't any in the immediate vicinity. Guess he's telling the truth.

I turn to go – and smack right into someone, face-planting their chest.

"OK, seriously," I say. "Watch where the fuck you're—"

Nic stares back at me, blinking in surprise.

TWENTY-NINE

Teagan

He looks like shit. And that's being nice.

There are dark circles under his eyes, and a huge streak of dirt down the side of his face. He's wearing an old UCLA hoodie and jeans, both of which are torn in a dozen spots. His sneakers are caked with mud.

There's a second where we just goggle at each other, then we both start speaking at once, both of us demanding to know if the other is OK, where she/he came from, if they're hurt, how long they've been here. I only stop when Nic grabs me, pulls me into a bear hug.

We're both freezing cold, soaking wet. But Nic has always given really good hugs – and right now, having him wrap his arms around me is like sitting courtside at Game Seven of the Hugging World Championships.

"This is fucked," he says.

"Yep."

After a long moment, we pull apart. "Are the guys here? China Shop?"

"Yeah. They're fine. Well, Reggie might be hurt, and Paul broke his arm."

Nic winces at that.

"But otherwise we're OK. What about you?"

"I'm good," he says. "My mom and dad, too – they're back there." He waves towards second base. "I came to get some water. Did they have—?"

"All out, apparently. I'm here with the guys though – you can always come back with me if we can't find any. Maybe they got lucky."

He nods, then leads me away from the angry crowd. There's a relatively clear spot by the wall, and we slump against it. It's not sheltered from the rain, but we're so wet that it hardly seems to matter.

Paul and Annie are still chatting in my ear, talking about the ride down from Van Nuys, which feels like a lifetime ago. I pop the earpiece out, dropping it in my pocket. I don't want to be interrupted right now.

"This is fucked," Nic says again. "They're saying it was bigger than the one in 1857. That was only a 7.9."

"Yeah, I know. I was actually in the air when the quake started. I saw it all happen."

"In the *air*?"

"Long story."

He falls silent, staring at nothing. Looking at him, all I want to do is rewind the clock. Back to the night of the paella, before any of this shit occurred.

"How'd you get here?" I ask.

"How'd *you* get here?"

"You first."

"Not surprising." He scratches at the dirt on his cheek. "They're bringing in as many people as they can – this is like a central emergency camp for FEMA. Makes sense, if they want a place people can easily get to. I'm still not sure it's a great idea, because they did the same thing in New Orleans during Katrina, with the Superdome. That went bad fast."

"Looks like it might go bad here too," I say, watching the unruly crowd. What is it with government agencies? They never fucking *learn*.

"Man, I was worried about you," he says. "When the second quake hit, I tried to message you, but I guess this one was big enough to take out the cell towers for good." He wipes his face. "I was at work – well, kind of; my mom and dad had come down to meet me for lunch, and I was showing them my new office—"

"Wait, you were worried about me?"

He gives me a strange look. "Uh . . . *yeah*. Anyway, we got out OK, the building was up to code – more or less. So we just took the stairs down to the—"

"If you were worried about me, why didn't you text?"

"I just said I did. The cell towers are down, remember?"

"No, I mean after the first quake." I probably should have led with that – my brain is all over the place, overworked and overtired. "I sent you like fifty messages, and you didn't reply to any of them."

"Um, yes, I did. I told you I was out in San Bernardino. Remember that?"

"OK, fine. *One* message. You didn't respond to any of the others."

"What does it matter?"

"What does it—? Of course it *matters*. I wanted to know if you were OK."

"I'm fine. Obviously." Nic does this thing when he's frustrated. He'll rub his leg with his right thumb, running it down the fabric of his jeans. He's doing it now. Not looking at me. "I was busy. You know, *helping out with the quake*."

"So what, you couldn't message me during a break? A little thumbs-up emoji or something? Even you have to eat sometimes, Mr Super Laywer."

I want it to come out like a joke. It just sounds bitter.

He meets my eyes. "Fine. I was pissed at you, OK?"

"What, because I wouldn't—?" I stumble over the words. "Because I didn't know how to help?" It sounds lame, even to me.

"I mean ..."

"I don't care how pissed you were, you can't just ... *ignore* me like that. You went off to San Bernardino, and—"

"The first quake was done. Nothing was going to happen."

"Says you!"

"You know what? I'm sorry." He doesn't sound even close to sorry. "I didn't understand why you wouldn't help out. I should've texted you a *thumbs-up* afterwards. Would that have made you feel better?"

"Just FYI, I *have* been helping. I messed up before, but I've figured it out. I just gotta careful when I use my PK."

"OK. How've you been using it?"

"Well, we ... I mean, I got Reggie out after the office collapsed on top of her. And even before that – these dudes tried to jump me and Annie and Africa, so I—"

"Oh, so when it's your friends, it's all good, but you won't actually help out anyone else?

"OK, that is *not* fair—"

"That's exactly how it is. Look around you," He spreads his arms. "You've got these amazing powers, and you haven't done *shit* to help. That's embarrassing, man."

"You know exactly why I have to be careful with my ability. Tanner would—"

"Would what? You think it matters any more? We got

people dying out there, we got fires, we got burst gas mains, collapsed buildings, and you're in here talking about what some FBI chick would think."

"She's not FBI."

"Then what is she? Huh? Tell me that."

"It's—" I falter. Tanner's agency or organisation or whatever it is doesn't have a name – or at least not one known to those outside the corridors of Washington. "It doesn't matter, dude. Just—"

"No seriously. What branch of the government is she from? You work for her, and you've got no idea if she even is who she says she is. Same for the whole of China Shop. My taxes go to your salary, so I wanna know. Who are these people you run with?"

"Did you seriously just pull the *I'm a taxpayer* defence? You sound like Paul right now, you know that?"

He makes a disgusted noise. "Paul. Yeah, I looked into him. Nothing but a deadbeat dad."

"Excuse me? Where the fuck do you get off—?"

"He's missed his last three child support payments, Teagan. What would you call him?

"You . . . Wait, you *investigated* him?"

"I made some inquiries. And by the way, Annie? You should see the shit she's done. The whole thing with MS-13 and that heroin wasn't even the worst of it."

"Who gives a shit?" I snarl. "She ran some drugs. She sold a few guns. She's done stuff she's not proud of. We're not talking about a . . . a . . . a fucking mass murderer here. She never killed anybody. You don't get to just sit back and judge her. And you do *not* get to go out and dig up dirt on the people I work with."

"Yeah, well. I know you don't think I care about you, Teags, but I do, so—"

"Oh, that is such bullshit."

"Nope. And see, I'm starting to think maybe I shouldn't have bothered. You don't give a shit about people. You just want to cover your own ass, so you can sit in your apartment and live your little life and not have to worry about anyone but yourself."

This can't be what he thinks. There's no way he could be this ugly.

"*Little life?*" I snarl. "You know what I've been through. You know *exactly* the kind of pressure I'm under, every single day. And you know what I do with my ability – the people I help bring down. How fucking dare you sit there and tell me it's about covering my own ass? What the fuck is that?"

Right then, I get the oddest thought. *Schmidt would get it. He'd understand.*

Jonas Schmidt, who was supposed to be one of the bad guys. Schmidt is like Nic – he wants to help, would put himself in harm's way to do so. But he lives in a world of spies and deep-cover assets and back-channel communications – a grey, shifting world where things are never simple. If I told him what I can do, how living with my ability means thinking about how I use it, all the time, and that I can't just throw it around . . . he'd understand.

Nic? Nic either doesn't want to, or can't. How could I have missed this? How could I have wanted this . . . *person* to be a part of my life?

"I don't actually care, man," Nic is saying. "I'm here, I'm fine and as soon as I get some food into me and my mom and dad, I'm gonna go back out there and *help*. You stay in here, if you want. I don't fucking care."

You know how sometimes your mind sends out a signal that overrides everything else? I'm not talking about PK. I'm talking about good old intuition, your brain's way of telling you that it's noticed something important.

It won't be able to tell you what it is – not directly. It communicates in other ways: a little prickle on the back of your neck, heightened sensation in the fingertips, a Spidey-sense tingling on the scalp.

Something I saw. Something that entered my field of vision, just for a split-second.

I glance to my left, then right. Nic is still talking, but I've tuned him out. Whatever I saw is important. I know it is.

It's a kid.

The kid.

He's walking up past the bleacher wall, on my left, at the edge of the field. Perhaps fifty yards away. There's still a ton of people around, but he's walking through a small gap between groups. He's heading directly away from my position, as if he too had visited the water point, and left when it became clear there was none to be had.

It can't be him. I've made a mistake. But then the kid looks over his shoulder, and I get a clear look at him. The shape of his face, his hair, the way he walks . . . there's no mistake. That video is seared into my mind. He's as dirty and soaked as the rest of us, wearing what was once a white T-shirt. Before I can blink, he's gone, swallowed by the crowd

Holy fucksticks. Paul was right.

Nic sighs. "I didn't mean to . . . you know, say it all like that. When this is all over, maybe we can talk, OK?"

"I gotta go." I can barely hear my own voice.

"What?"

"I'm sorry."

"Wait a second. Teagan. Teagan!"

I leave him behind, moving from a walk to a jog. My brain

is going into overdrive. The kid can't be here – there's no way, no way in hell that we'd get that lucky. I'm jumping at shadows. But I know what I saw, and more to the point, like Paul said, why *wouldn't* the kid be here? Sure, he can cause earthquakes and move soil at will, but he's not immune from the after-effects. He'd still need food, and water, and shelter. After the quake, there was probably precious little of those around, especially if he set the damn thing off in the middle of the Angeles forest. He would have looked for help, probably with his mom, and they ended up here.

A little splinter of thought: what was he *doing* in the Angeles forest in the first place? Why go there? Unless he wanted to deliberately ...

There's no way. He's four years old, he doesn't have control of his ability, and he fucked up. That's all there is to it.

The kid has vanished. I have no idea what I'm going to do when I get to him, but there is no way I'm letting him escape. "Paul, Annie, anybody, can you hear me?"

Paul's voice, sounding like it's coming from the middle of a snowstorm. "We read you, Tea—over?"

"He's here." I'm pushing through the crowd now, frantically scanning it for the kid. He's nowhere to be seen.

"Say again?"

"The boy. The one we're looking for. I just saw him, over by the leftfield wall."

A fuzz of static. Then Annie: "—sure you saw—?"

"Yes! Yes, I'm fucking sure. Get over here, right now."

Paul again. "Teagan, what's your loca—over?"

"Already said. Location is the left stadium wall. He's heading up towards the wide end of the field." Wide end? Is that even what it's actually called? My brain is a big ball of wasps right now. I'm getting the same feeling I had when I first met

Jake, the other psychokinetic, six months ago. Confusion, *awe*. It's not just that someone else with powers exists. It's that he's right here, both of us occupying the same real estate.

"Copy," Paul says. "Annie and I will meet you—confirm his last pos—"

"Goddamnit people, *move*." The group I'm pushing through don't even notice I'm there. I get a flashback to my parents' farm in Wyoming, the two or three dairy cows we had, chewing cud and staring at us with blank expressions. I turn sideways, squeezing between them and one of the tents. Too bad I can't start throwing things – *that* would shift them, all right.

"He's here now?" Africa says over the comms. "And you are abso—saw him, Teggan?"

"If someone asks me that again . . . " I hop the barrier separating the field from the bleachers. I say hop, but thanks to my short legs it's more like an embarrassing scramble.

The landing nearly topples me over, earning myself a couple of dirty, exhausted looks. Shit, where is he? I scan the bleachers.

"I do not see—anywhere," Africa says.

Paul: "Africa, stand d—find a phone, like we talked abo—handle this."

I'm running now, heading along the line of the barrier, *sorry*-ing and *excuse-me*-ing my way through the crowd. *Where are you?*

I've lost him. Maybe for good. There are thousands and thousands of people here – I might have seen him for a second or two, but actually trying to track him through this mess is too much to ask for. I come to a halt and have to bend over, a sudden stitch lancing at my side. Then I force my head up. Keep looking. Eyes darting between faces. Every child I see, boy or girl, sends electric jolts down my spine.

A minute passes. Two.

I'm on the verge of telling the crew I lost him when my earpiece bursts into life.

"Got him!" Paul's transmission is clear, at least for a second. "Heading for one of the tunnels out to the—maybe fifty yards. Annie, converge on my—"

"Copy," Annie growls. "What do we do when—?"

"Teagan, get here now. Get—" Paul's voice dissolves in a burst of static.

I can see the exit tunnel from here – or the signs for it, anyway, a gap between two of the bleachers. Is it even the right one? Fuck it – I don't care. If he's heading for an exit, that means he'll be out of the packed crowd. Easier to spot.

There must be a hundred people between me and the tunnel, but I start to run anyway, shoving through the crowd.

THIRTY

Matthew

The stadium should have been fun.

It should have been *awesome*.

When Matthew let the San Andreas fault go, the feeling had been ... *Big*, was the only word he could think of. Like he had the entire world, the whole planet, in his hand. He had some idea of how much damage there'd be. He'd caught glimpses of it at the temporary camp in Victorville, and on the chopper over to Dodger Stadium.

But he'd walked around the stadium, Amber trailing behind him, and it was lame. He wanted to see what it felt like – to be right in the middle of everything, knowing he caused it, and not a single person could have stopped him. He wanted that more anything. So why does he feel so let down?

With the amount of energy he released, the result should be more than just a big bowl full of unhappy, hungry, tired faces.

Logically, he knows why it's this way. People in California would know what to do if an earthquake hit, so they probably got under tables and stuff. They knew how not to get hurt, even during a really big one. It makes sense ... but it also makes him mad. He wants to drop the whole stadium into the ground, bury it, just so he can hear everyone screaming.

Maybe he made a mistake, setting off the San Andreas fault in the middle of the forest. He should have found somewhere with more people.

It took Amber a while to get them food. Matthew waited under one of the bleachers, where it was dry, sitting on one of the plastic bucket seats, his arms folded. Bored. That's what he was. He was bored with it all.

Once Amber returned – all she'd found was a couple of hastily made sandwiches and a single bottle of water – he'd eaten in silence, his eyes scanning the packed field. Amber had tried to talk to him as he'd chewed his sandwich listlessly, but he'd ignored her, and eventually she'd stopped.

Now, finally, he makes up his mind. The decision arrives fully formed – no point hanging around here, not when it's so dumb. "Let's go."

Amber, startled, blinks at him. "What—?"

"You have to take us out of the city."

She wants to say no. He can see it in her face. But of course, she doesn't dare – she knows what's good for her.

After a few moments, she rises, leads him back down to the field, heading for the tunnel they'd entered through. Matthew wonders if the soldiers might stop them, but the men don't even glance their way.

Out. Into the shadowy parking lot beyond the stadium, generator-powered floodlights casting pools of yellow light that split the darkness. Matthew walks without really seeing where he's going, trailing Amber, busy inside his head. OK. So San Andreas turned out to be kind of lame – not nearly as big as he thought it would be. There's plenty more he can do, as long as Amber gets them out of the city. And if she can't, or she gives him any problems, he can teach her a lesson.

Somebody's following you.

Matthew's head snaps up, and he looks back at the tunnel. There's nobody there – well, nobody but the milling, spaced-out, stupid crowd of people, none of whom are looking at him. His stomach rumbles. Maybe he's just hungry again. Yeah, that's it – hunger making him jumpy, he'll have to tell Amber to—

Then he sees the man.

He's older than Amber, bald, his arm in a sling. Pushing his way out of the tunnel. As Matthew watches, the man puts a finger to his ear, his lips moving like he's talking to someone, and looking right at him. As if . . .

He's following them. Just like Ajay said would happen.

Matthew liked Ajay. That surprised him, but only a little. Ajay was one of the few people he'd ever met who didn't treat him like a kid. When Ajay talked to him, it was as if they both knew things that didn't need to be said. They could just talk about the important stuff. Ajay had given him books and shown him documentaries and chatted about his powers like everyone had them.

Ajay had sent them away, too. Away from the School in New Mexico. Matthew had been mad at him for that. If it was anybody else, he wouldn't have gone. But Ajay said the government was coming.

In Matthew's imagination, his brain is like a giant library. Only it's not a regular library. It's a big, circular one – a huge room with clean, white walls, deep underground and filled with a million books. Matthew imagines himself standing at the centre, and he knows everything. He can reach into any book in the library, in a second. And of course he knows what the government is. He's read about them.

The government want to take him away. They're maybe the only people in the whole world who could.

And they *have* found him. Somehow, some way, they know he caused the quake.

He walks faster, catching up to his mother, grabbing her sleeve. "We gotta go," he hisses. "We gotta go now."

"Matthew, what—?"

"Come on!"

They head out across the cracked parking lot. Nearby, a young couple go from bickering with each other to a full-on shouting match, the woman yelling that she should never have come to the stadium. Hastily erected spotlights almost blind them as they move through the crowd. Amber looks back, suppresses a gasp, and Matthew knows she's seen the man, too.

What if one of the soldiers tries to stop them as they make their way across? But they barely get a second glance. They reach an access road that bisects the parking lot; most of the trees lining it have been ripped from the earth, torn roots visible. The road itself has fared better than others he's seen. It's cracked and pitted, but still flat enough for Army vehicles to rumble past. A particularly large one does so as they reach it, a huge truck with wheels the size of a person, slowly trundling across to the western edge of the parking lot.

"Honey." Amber says. "We're gonna get to the other side of that truck, OK? We're gonna walk alongside it."

He ignores her. "There." He points, his little voice breathless. "See the other trees?"

On the north side of the parking lot, the tarmac gives way to a hilly, forested park, just visible in the darkness. There's a fence, but sections of it have been shredded by the quake, along with many of the trees.

Somewhere with dirt.

With his weapons.

"No, honey, listen," Amber says. "We don't have to do that. If we double back—"

He doesn't even look at her. Just takes off running, heading for the tree line.

There are fewer cars in this part of the parking lot, fewer people. Matthew looks back. The man he saw before, the one with the broken arm, has just made it across the road that bisects the parking lot. Matthew spots two more figures behind him: two women, a short one and a tall one, both in the same dark uniforms. They're trying to cross, waiting for a small convoy of trucks to pass, yelling something at the man with the broken arm. He ignores their shouts, barrelling across the lot towards Matthew and Amber.

Finally, they reach the park. It's more an undeveloped section of the stadium property: hard-packed, hilly earth, with scraggly trees and shrubs, made even messier by the quake. Matthew starts sprinting, wanting to get in as deep as he can. Branches scratch at his arms, whipping back into Amber's body as he pushes past them. Everything is wet from the steady rain, and he can hardly see three yards in front of him.

Amber's voice is harsh, ragged. "Honey, please ... let's just ... go back, OK? We can ... "

And then a voice: "Hey, woah. Stop."

The man with the broken arm has reached them, a silhouette against the lights from the stadium. "I'm not going to hurt you."

"Leave us alone!" There's fear in Amber's voice ... and Matthew doesn't think it's because of what the government man might do. In the darkness, a small smile slides across his face.

"I know about your powers," the man says. "You made the

earthquakes happen, It's ... it's OK. You probably didn't even mean to do it. My name's Paul – Paul Marino. I work with—"

"Paul?" comes a voice from beyond the trees. One of the women in the dark uniforms.

"Over here," the man called Paul replies. He turns back to Matthew. "But you don't have to be scared any more. I work with people who can help you – they can teach you to control it. We're ... we're the good guys, I promise."

Amber steps in front of Matthew, as if trying to shield him. "Go away," she says.

He doesn't even understand why she's giving the government man a warning. The earth underneath him begins to tremble.

"You don't understand," Amber says. "You need to leave. Right now."

"I've got a boy about his age," Paul Marino says, speaking to Amber now. "His name's ... " His voice catches. "His name's Cole. He doesn't have powers ... abilities ... but it sounds like your son could use a friend."

He holds out a hand, like he's trying to shake. "I didn't mean to chase you – I wish I could have just walked up and said hello. But you don't need to worry – nobody's going to hurt you. The government can—"

What happens next happens very fast.

The two women emerge from the treeline – one tall and willowy, the other short, with spiky black hair. Matthew raises his chin, feeling the earth around him respond. Every grain of dirt, every rock, every chunk of soil, held tight in his mind's eye.

The ground around the man explodes upwards: a huge, circular wave of it, crashing down on top of him.

One of the women screams, sprinting forward. The man's

hand appears through a gap in the raging, roaring earth –
stretching for the sky, like he's appealing for help. Then it's
gone, the wave crashing in on him, forcing him into the
ground, burying him in a surge of black earth.

Then the air is filled with screams and drifting dirt, and
Matthew takes Amber's hand again, pulling her down the hill,
away from everything.

THIRTY-ONE

Teagan

Annie is on her knees in the mud. She scratches at it, throwing up huge clumps. One of her nails has broken. Snapped back, drenching her finger with blood, rivulets of wet dirt spattering her arms. She's making this awful sound – a choked, almost strangled moan.

I can't look away from it. I'm frozen to the spot, mouth open, trying to process what the fuck I just saw.

"Teagan," Annie says, her voice little more than a gasp. "Help him."

A hundred yards away, the kid and his mom – at least, I think it's his mom – vanish into another clutch of trees. He looks back at us just before he disappears. I can't see his expression from here, but I don't have to. I know the same one as before: a weird grin. An insane, twisted little smile. The same one he had when he ... when Paul ...

"*Teagan! Fucking help him!*"

I snap out of it, sprint over, skidding to my knees next to her.

"Get him out of there," she rasps. "Get him out. *Get him out!*"

I send my PK deep into the earth. Paul is there – seven or eight feet down, well within my range. It's just like back on

Schmidt's plane: I can't feel him, but I can feel the objects he
has on him. Keys, belt buckle, the metal parts of his arm sling.
His wedding band, on a chain around his neck.

But it's like trying to lift a block of concrete using just the
tips of my fingers. He won't come. The sheer weight of the
dirt holds him in place. And the objects ... they're moving,
vibrating back and forth.

He's still alive down there.

Twisting against the dirt.

Annie hasn't stopped digging. The earth is packed down
tight. Blood leaks onto the soil from her broken nail. "What's
wrong?" she snarls.

"He's not ... "

"Just pull him up!"

"I can't!"

"What do you mean you can't?"

How do I explain it to her? That this isn't about strength, or
range? There's just not enough for me to grab onto.

Annie howls, digs in even harder. She's about a foot deep
now, but the hole isn't even wide enough to fit her arms. Africa
shouts in my earpiece – I barely register his words.

If I can't pull Paul up, maybe I can get down to him. And
I can do it much faster than Annie can.

"Wait here," I say, scrambling to my feet.

"Where are you going?"

It takes every ounce of strength I have to let go of Paul's
belt buckle, his keys. To leave him where he is. *I'm coming,
man, just hold on.*

I run. Moving as my fast as my short, shitty little legs will
carry me, stumbling through the trees, ignoring Annie's confused, terrified shouts.

It takes me far too long to get to the stadium parking lot.

Thirty seconds at least. How many minutes can a person survive after being buried alive? How long can *Paul* survive? I picture him at Annie's mom's house, sitting at her dining room table, holding Annie's hand. He looked at home there. Comfortable. A man in his forties, not super-fit, probably in shock ...

I stop thinking about it. Because if I do, I'm just going to throw up.

I send my PK out in a wide arc ahead of me, and find what I'm looking for even before I burst out onto the flat surface of the parking lot. A car – a fucking Lamborghini, if you can believe it, bright yellow. Somehow, it's still upright, despite the parking lot's wrecked surface. This might be the first time I'm grateful that some dipshit in LA bought themselves a supercar. Supercars have big doors.

I grit my teeth, grab hold of the metal. A headache flares at the base of my skull as I rip the doors from their hinges. I'm expecting more resistance than I get: they're only attached with a single hinge, designed to open upwards. The term for them comes to me, and I wish it hadn't. *Suicide doors.*

I flip them through the air towards me. It doesn't look like there's anyone watching – nobody in the parking lot that I can see, just choppers taking off and landing over by the stadium. Not that I care if people sees me doing this. Let Tanner sort it out later.

"—anybody hear me?" In my ear, Africa sounds desperate. "Teggan, you OK?"

Reggie: "Paul, come—" More static. "Paul, do you read me?"

I run back through the trees, the doors trailing after me. I'm so wired that I bounce them off tree trunks several times, scarring their surfaces. Not that it matters: they are about to get a lot more fucked up than they already are.

I've lost track of how much time has passed. I don't know how long Paul has but I'm going to move as fast as I can, and get him out, and then everything . . .

Everything will be fine.

Annie doesn't look up as I approach. She's still on her knees, bent over now, arms deep in the dirt. "Move," I say, bringing the doors up and over my head.

She doesn't look round. Doesn't even register that I'm there. Her shoulders are shaking.

"Annie! Fucking *move*!"

"Wha—?" She looks over her shoulder. Her eyes are unfocused, the dirt on her face lined with tear tracks.

I drive the first door into the soil. "Out the way."

I've never used my PK to dig before. I have only the barest idea of what to do – it's not like there's a manual for this shit. I use the doors as scoops – something they are spectacularly unsuited for, thanks to their flat shape. Most of the dirt I get just slides right out again, falling back into the pit.

And Annie keeps getting in the way. No matter how many times I shout at her to move, she keeps darting back in, scrabbling at the dirt with torn fingers. I have to work around her, doing everything I can not to cut her damn head off.

I scoop dirt as fast as I can, throwing up huge piles. The headache has blossomed, pounding on my temples. *Just a few more feet. Come on. Come on!*

But it never ends.

No matter how often I plunge the doors into the dirt, there's always more of it. He's been down there for too long, far longer than anyone could survive. The thought must have made me slow down, because Annie yells at me to hurry.

I send out another wave of PK, trying to get a fix on Paul's position. To my surprise, we've almost reached him. He's no more than two feet away now. Annie seems to sense it, throwing herself down into the pit, ignoring my shouts to get out the way as she digs at the dirt. I rip the doors away – if I keep going, I'll either cut her in half, or do the same to Paul. Then I jump into the pit to join her.

It's not easy. The pit is seven feet deep now, cone-shaped, with uneven, sloping sides. As I skid to a halt at the bottom, Annie gives yell of triumph. Paul's hand is poking up out of the dirt, Annie's fingers clutching at it.

And it's not moving.

Together, she and I attack the last few inches of dirt. Paul's face starts to appear. Stark white against the black soil. His eyes are open, staring at nothing.

Annie shoves me aside. She gets her hands underneath him, and with a roar, heaves his torso, head and shoulders out of the hole. She starts giving him mouth-to-mouth, and I clear the rest of the dirt away from his chest so she can give him compressions, but . . .

I lean back against the wall of the pit, Annie a blur of frantic motion next to me. I keep seeing the kid, the sick, delighted look on his face as he sucked Paul into the ground.

"Baby." Annie's voice is husky, shredded. She hasn't stopped pumping his chest. "Baby, wake up."

I keep thinking he's going to answer her. That his eyes will spring open, that he'll explode out of the dirt, coughing and spluttering. We'll go back into the stadium, and before long he'll be laughing about what a lucky escape it was, how it's a damn good thing he was in the Navy, because they taught him how to hold his breath, giving us shit for letting the kid get away. Then we'll figure this out, rebuild the Boutique and before long Paul will be back to planning missions, while I sit on our couch and taunt him about his stupid whiteboard . . .

But no matter how hard Annie pumps on Paul's chest, or how many breaths she forces into his lungs, he doesn't wake up.

"Teagan, help me get him out."

"Annie . . ."

"No." She wipes her mouth. Her whole body is caked with dirt now. "We'll get him out. Get him to a doctor. Call Reggie, tell her we're bringing him in."

It feels like a betrayal to say my next words. And it takes everything I have to do it. "He's gone."

"The hell he is. Baby, wake up. Please. Wake up. *Wake up!*"

She's crying again. So am I now. And then, as if our conversation didn't happen, she goes back to pumping his chest. She's doing it so hard now that she's actually pushing him further down into the dirt.

I lever myself up, get my arms around Annie. She bucks me off, but I come back, refusing to let go. I'm not just doing it for her. I'm doing it for me. If I don't grab hold of something, or someone, I'm going to be swept away.

Again and again she pushes me off, until her strength gives out and all she can do is lean on Paul's body, hands still resting on his chest.

I wrap my arms around Annie and hold her tight as her words turn to sobs, as her sobs turn to screams, and her screams turn to a single, long howl, echoing out into the trees.

THIRTY-TWO

Teagan

How are you supposed to feel when someone dies?

I should know. My parents, my sister ... all dead. The ranch house going up in flames. Adam, my psychotic brother, laughing as it burned.

Afterwards, I felt ... nothing. Utter numbness. It was way, way too much to process. Too big. I felt it later, sure, when the government got its hooks into me. When the therapists and counsellors they sent my way forced the emotion to the surface, the way a diver will pry an oyster off a rock.

I'm expecting to feel the same way this time. That's my first reaction, when I stare down at Paul's white face, with its horrible blank eyes. I'm almost ready for it – ready for my brain to shut down, my body to go on autopilot. Blue screen of death. Please refer to your dealer warranty. Which means I am utterly and totally unprepared for what happens next.

A phantom fist socks me in the gut. It's an actual, phys-ical sensation: a sick ache deep in my stomach that blooms through my body like ink in water. I hug myself, bent over, a dry retch crawling its way up my throat. I'm looking at Paul as it happens, and it's followed by an urge to look away: an urge so powerful, so *everywhere*, that I nearly fall over trying to obey it. I clutch at my stomach, eyes squeezed shut, taking deep breaths that come and go without giving me any air at all. I'm shaking, trembling, like I'm a hundred years old. It's got nothing to do with the rain, or the chilly night air.

Annie's shaking too, hunched on the edge of the hole, head down. Dead still. *The kid*, I think. *We should go after him.* Oh, yeah. OK. Let's go hunt the boy who just buried Paul alive.

"Will *somebody* respond?" In my ear, Reggie sounds like she's this close to losing her shit. "Teagan, Paul, anyb—tell me what's happening out—"

She goes away, comes back, the signal fading in and out.

After a while, I stop retching. The shakes are still there, though. I have to interlace my fingers to get them to simmer down. Is it lighter in the sky now? Or is it just my imagination?

My blue-screened brain reboots into recovery mode. I lift the car doors again, thinking I can use them to at least get Paul out of the ground. Only: what then? Carry him back to the stadium? That's the sensible thing to do ... they'll have a morgue, or a tent to keep the dead in. Right?

Only: how do we get him back there? I can't float him in on the suicide doors, not without causing a panic. He's too heavy for me to carry by myself. And there is no way – at all, ever – that I'm asking Annie to carry him. It would be the worst kind of betrayal.

Call an ambulance. I am so fucking out of it that I find myself reaching for my useless phone. In the hole, Paul stares at nothing.

I can't leave him down there. Nope. Nuh-uh. No sir no ma'am no way.

Except ... what the fuck else choice do we have?

I sink to my knees next to Annie, a hand on her shoulder. Another phantom punch to my gut, this one almost as bad as the first. It takes a second for my own words to make sense. "I can't carry him out of here with my PK."

She makes a sound that is halfway between a groan and a snarl.

"I mean, I can, I could put him on one of the doors, but it's not ... I don't want to ... "

I don't want to leave him. Not like this. But the only alternative is carrying him back to the stadium ourselves, and even the thought of doing that ... carrying him like a sack of grain across that endless parking lot ...

And I can't ask Annie to bury him.

I can't tell her that we have to put him under the dirt, right after we got him out. I *won't*.

The shakes and the ache in my gut have given way to something else: lucidity. Control. My mind is suddenly agonisingly clear. It won't let me check out, no matter how desperate I am to do it. We can get a message to the people at the stadium. The National Guard, the doctors, emergency workers. Whoever is in charge. We'll have to come up with a story – tell them he fell into a hole, something like that. Or that the ground collapsed. They won't question it – why would they? They have so much on their plates, they won't even have time to. And they can come get him, pull him out ...

I tell Annie this, but all she does is shake her head. Doesn't stop. Just keeps rocking, sitting on the ground with her arms around her knees.

"Annie, please. We have to."

Long minutes go by while I talk to her. I can't believe how calm I sound. Slowly, very slowly, I make her understand. Or at least, not try and stop me.

We start walking. My arm around Annie. I try not to picture Paul's body, down in the dirt.

I'm sorry, man. I'm so fucking sorry.

The kid knew what he was doing. He knew he was about to kill someone.

And he *liked* it.

The next thing I know, we're heading back across the parking lot to the stadium. I can't even remember us walking away from the gra—from where it happened.

"We're coming in," I say, keying my comms.

A long fuzz of static. "Teagan? Is that you? What the—out there? Paul and Annie aren't answer—out of range?"

In the end, all I can think to say is, "Annie's with me."

"Did their—damaged?" Her voice is very distant now, almost inaudible.

"We'll meet you at the medical tent."

No answer. The only thing I get back is static.

It takes a while to get into the stadium. There are even more people now, crowds bottlenecking the entry tunnels, streaming in from everywhere. A dirty, heaving mass of exhausted faces and slow, shuffling bodies. We have to stand in line, despite the black slashes on the backs of our hands.

You know that whole thing about grief, where you can't understand how the world can keep ticking along after someone you love has died? I get it now. Everybody's standing around, not doing much, and they don't know that Paul is dead. They have no idea, and if they did, they wouldn't even care. The crowd is huge, like we're trying to get into a Beyoncé show. But it's quiet, dull, and even the soldiers checking us off don't give us more than a passing glance. Annie is crying again, silent tears making tracks down her dirt-smeared cheeks

Inside. Same tents, same mud. Reggie comes back in my comms, goes away again, static swallowing her. In the huge crush of bodies, every one of them radiating exhaustion and hopelessness, Annie and I get separated.

It happens almost without me noticing. I'm just concentrating on shuffling forward, trying not to get muscled out of the way, and a few seconds later she's just gone.

She was right behind me. She was right fucking here. I push though the crowd, shouting her name, squeezing between tents and bouncing off people like a pinball.

It takes me a long minute to find her, sagged against the wall of one of the tents. Staring at nothing. Face grey, mud caked on her legs on arms. When I take her hand, she doesn't resist, just lets me lead her. It's like she's gone deep inside herself.

OK. Where the fuck is the medical tent? Or . . . shit, is there more than one? I really don't feel like leading Annie on a little hike right now, but at least the thought gets me moving again. I start walking, arm around Annie's waist, heading in what I think is the right direction.

We stumble down between the tents. Every so often, I'll call out for Reggie or Africa on the comms, raising my voice over the crowd.

It's not long before we're lost. I feel like the tent should be over by third base, but I must have gotten turned around somewhere.

"Come on, A-Team," I mutter to Annie, changing our direction. It's like trying to do a three-point turn in an eighteen-wheeler. "Long way to go. We just need to—"

The ground beneath me gives way, plunging my right foot into a calf-high sinkhole of brown water. Freezing mud floods my shoe, trickling between my toes.

Paul's hand, appearing over the wave of dirt, sucked into the ground like—

I drop my head, take a deep, shaky breath. Beside me, Annie sways in place. If she goes down, I am *never* going to be able to lift her up, no matter what my superpowers are.

"Teggan – over here."

Africa's eyes are huge, his face caked with dirt. He gets an arm under Annie's on the other side, helps me lift her.

"Where you been?" he says. "We have problems with the radio. Did you find the boy? Where is the boss man? He still chasing?"

"Medical tent," I say, through gritted teeth.

"Paul is at the medical tent? I don't—"

"Us, Africa. Take us. *Now.*"

Somehow, we make it to the right tent. Somehow, Africa gets us through the soldiers manning the doors. Reggie's just inside the entrance, sprawled out on a hospital bed, covered with a ratty blanket. She looks very small, even frail, but she perks up the minute she sees us. "Oh, thank the Lord. What happened?"

I try to tell her, try to open my mouth and explain. I can't get a single word out. Not one.

A frown creases Reggie's brow. "Teagan, what's wrong?" She gives Annie a closer look, takes in the grey face, the slumped, shaking shoulders.

"Where's Paul?" she says very softly.

We don't even have to answer. Reggie's face collapses, just folds in on itself, and then Annie is on the ground, howling, and Africa has his enormous arms around her and I close my eyes and maybe if I don't open them ever again, that wouldn't be so bad.

THIRTY-THREE

Amber

"Matthew!"

Amber plunges across the scrubland, blood pounding in her ears. She can't see her son. *She can't see her son.*

And it's worse this time, because other people have seen what he can do. And this isn't like the cop from before. It's not like the earthquakes. There were witnesses. And now for the first time, Matthew isn't with her. He's on his own, and if she can't get to him, he might do it again. She's the only one who can stop it. She's the only one who can control him.

And so she runs.

The landscape is hilly scrubland, with sparse patches of trees, like an urban forest that someone gave up on long ago. The light from Dodger Stadium is nothing more than a glimmer on the horizon behind her.

In desperation, Amber heads for another stand of trees, just below the crest of a hill, forcing aside low-hanging branches. One whips back, striking her across the face, cutting a stinging line across one cheek. The rain's actually gotten worse, the drizzle turning to fat droplets. They run down Amber's forehead, blurring her vision. Her jeans are covered in wet dirt from ankle to thigh. Somewhere, she lost her denim jacket – she has no idea when that happened.

A road. There's a road. From her vantage point at the top of the hill, Amber can see right down to it. It's cracked and torn, like all the others, but if she can get to it—

Her foot snags on something in the dirt – a rock, a root. Thrown up by her son, maybe, when he caused the quake. She goes down hard, wrists snapping back as she makes contact with the shredded earth, rolling, ripping the skin off her elbows.

Amber comes to a halt against the trunk of an uprooted tree. She lies for a moment, ears ringing, chest heaving. A picture flits across her mind of the man Matthew buried, his body vanishing into the dirt, that one outstretched hand—

"*Matthew!*" This time, her shout is so loud she feels something tear in her throat: a burning sensation, like she's swallowed acid. She coughs, yells his name even louder.

A helicopter rumbles overhead, a black shadow against the sky, blowback buffeting the trees. Swaying, Amber gets to her feet. She's lost track of the road – was it on her left? No – there's nothing there but more dark scrub. Why was she trying to reach the road anyway? What made it likely that Matthew would be there?

Her eyes land on the glow of the stadium on the horizon, and it triggers a memory. The glow of light as she cracked the front door of her rooms in the School, late one night, wondering who the hell could be knocking at 3 a.m. Ajay hardly ever visited her in the rooms she shared with Matthew – when they made love, it was always in his quarters, overlooking the back of the School.

His normally neat hair was a mess. The skin around his eyes was puffy, as if he'd been weeping. He'd pushed inside the dark living room, elbowing her out of the way and closing the door behind him.

"Ajay, what—?"

"Quiet." He had a black eye – one he hadn't had the day before, when she'd last seen him. It wasn't much of a shiner – a little bruising on his cheekbone, a purpling of the skin. But it had been like a drop of ice water, trickling down her spine.

He'd seen her looking. "The Director wouldn't listen. None of them would fucking *listen*."

"Ajay, please, you're going to wake—"

He'd laughed at that, a harsh bark of a laugh with zero humour in it. "It'll be a goddamn miracle if they aren't arrested. Same for me."

"*Arrested?*"

"Wake your boy up. I'll look after him while you pack."

"Why am I . . . ? Ajay, talk to me, what's going on?"

"Just do it. I'll explain while you get your stuff."

Something in his tone made her move. She'd woken her son up – Matthew was groggy, irritated, so much so that she was worried he was going to lash out. But he'd never attacked Ajay, not once, and he let the doctor lead him into the living room. He'd sat on the couch, blinking with sleep, frowning as Amber darted around the apartment, trying to figure out what they'd need, what they dared take with them. Her toothbrush, Matthew's iPad, the few books she'd been reading, her clothes and tampons and sneakers . . .

Ajay strode to the window. He'd peeked through one of the blinds, and for a moment, Amber was overcome with just how ridiculous he looked. Like they were in a spy movie.

"Where are we going?" Matthew had asked.

"Just be ready to leave, honey." Even to her, her voice sounded unsure.

"I don't wanna go." He'd folded his arms, fully awake now. "Dr Martinez said she was going to get me some more books. And we were supposed to go to the Carlsbad Caverns soon."

"I know, honey, but Ajay says—"

"*I don't care what he says!*" Her son's anger was building, threatening to boil out of him. That had brought Ajay away from the window – he'd seen Matthew get angry, knew what could happen. He'd sat down next to him on the couch, put a hand on his shoulder. When he spoke, however, it was to Amber. Diamond, then, of course – a name she was about to lose, although she didn't know it yet.

"The government found out about the School."

"What? How?"

"We don't know. The Director isn't sure."

"Well, can't she do anything? There must be a way—"

"No. They're coming, and they're going to shut this place down."

"But *why*?"

He'd ignored the question. "You can't stay here, Di. There's a car waiting for you – a friend owed me a favour." He'd dug in his pocket, passed her what appeared to be a driving licence, and a health insurance card. "New IDs. They're not perfect – they won't pass a close look. But they'll help you get as far away as you can."

She had stared down at the cards. Her photo, a fake date of birth, a fake name. Schenke. She had a sudden urge to ask him how to pronounce it right.

"No." Matthew – still known as Lucas – had sprung off the couch, his little fists clenched. "I don't wanna go!"

"I'm sorry, Lucas, but you have to."

"I don't care if the government know about us. I'm not leaving."

It was very rare for Amber to take strength from her son, but this time, she did. She'd stepped behind him, putting down the small duffel bag she'd been shoving their clothes into, wrapped an arm around him. "He's right. We'll talk to them, work something out."

His eyes, when they found hers, were pleading. "They're going to separate you."

The ice water trickling down her spine had become a flood. "You can't know that."

Another humourless laugh. "They will. I know how these people work."

"I won't let them," her son had said. "I'll ... I'll *stop* them."

Ajay had reached out for him. "If you try, they'll just hurt you back. Maybe even kill you."

"I'll kill them!"

"And that'll make it worse for you later." He'd always been like this with Matthew: cool, unemotional, never afraid to tell him the truth. It was the only thing Matthew seemed to respond to, and it was the one thing Amber never seemed able to pull off. How was she going to manage her son without Ajay? Without the School? How could he expect her to just ... *leave*?

"There's no other way," Ajay had said. "I'm sorry, but you have to go. Tonight." He turned back to the boy. "And listen: you *can't* use your powers in front of anyone. It's just like we talked about. You have to keep you and your mom safe."

Her son had stared at him for the longest time, chewing on his lip. Then he'd nodded, as if the decision had been his to make all along. "Amber," he said, looking up at her. "Are we done packing?"

Already using her new name.

The world had seemed to tilt sideways, the ground sliding

away from her. It wasn't that the idea of going off-grid scared her – she'd spent *years* in New Mexico with no bank account, social security, any kind of record. But the sheer speed at which it had all happened. Just like that, they were having to leave the only safe place she'd ever known.

But right now, what the fuck does any of that matter? She's here, and she is going to get control of this. She is going to find her child, her *son*.

And as if the thought summoned him, she spots Matthew. He's walking out of the trees at the bottom of the slope, stepping lightly over a metal barrier onto the cracked tarmac. Amber can't see his face, but his white T-shirt is clearly visible. It's grimy and soaking by now, but still bright enough to spot in the darkness. Slowly, she gets to her feet, limping down the hill towards him.

She loses track of him within a few seconds, the white shirt vanishing as Matthew heads further onto the road. She quickens her pace, realising dimly that she twisted her ankle in the fall. It's not broken – at least, she doesn't think it is – but putting weight on it forces air out from between her teeth, like steam escaping a pipe.

Somehow, she makes it to the barrier, levers herself over. The road surface, like that of the stadium parking lot, has been damaged by the quake. It's not as bad here, though, with yards of unbroken surface – a quirk of geography protecting it, perhaps. Matthew is heading down the road, his back to her, and just beyond him—

Amber blinks. There's a helicopter parked on the street, side-on, its rotor blades still and silent. A logo emblazoned on the side: KTLA, big red letters against a white background.

The chopper pilot sits in the open cockpit door, baseball cap turned back, head bent over his phone. To his right, a woman paces, talking on her own cell. She wears a soaked green windbreaker over a flannel shirt, her dark hair pulled back in a ponytail. She looks up as Matthew approaches, frowning slightly.

There's no one else around. Amber limps towards the chopper, not sure what she plans to say, or if she even *needs* to say anything. Her only thought is to get Matthew away from them, before he does something . . .

"Can we use your chopper?" Matthew is saying to the woman when Amber arrives. The pilot looks up, puzzled annoyance crossing his face. Both he and the woman look exhausted, soaked from the rain.

The woman has her phone pressed to her right shoulder. "Um . . . are you lost? Where're your mom and dad?"

At that moment, she looks up and spots Amber. "Is this your mom? Sorry, we've got no water left – you aren't the first folks to come and ask. They'll let you into the stadium though – it's just up there."

"We need to go north," Matthew says, as if the woman hadn't spoken.

"Hi, yes, sorry." Amber puts a hand on Matthew's shoulder. "Didn't mean to bother you."

The pilot is watching them, wary, as if he expects them to try steal his chopper. There's another man, Amber sees, in the helicopter's main cabin. He's holding a professional camera, watching footage on a pop-out screen. "Nice shirt, kid," he says with a smirk, gesturing at Matthew's billowing Earthquake Exhibit T-shirt.

"Yeah, OK, excuse me." The woman puts the phone back to her ear, turns away. "Sorry, I'm here. Yes, we already tried that. It's like I said . . . "

"Matthew." Amber goes down on one knee, wincing as her ankle takes a little weight. "Let's go, OK?"

"Why? We need to head north, and they've got a helicopter."

"I know but—"

"We can't use cars," he says, sounding almost bored. "And we can't walk. So we need them to take us." He raises his voice, addressing the woman with the phone. "You gotta get us out of the city."

She doesn't even look at him. The pilot has gone back to his phone.

"Hey," Amber says, desperate to calm her son down. "Let's just . . ."

Just what? Find another helicopter?

Matthew raises his voice. "I'll make you fly us. I'll *make* you take us out of here."

"Honey, please, listen to me. I know we can't go back to the stadium, but we can't just . . ."

But it's already happening. What will he do this time? Swallow the entire helicopter? No, he'll just kill the reporter and her cameraman, maybe the pilot too . . .

Amber looks from the logo on the helicopter, to the camera, to the woman talking on her phone. And just like that, she knows what the angle is.

Doesn't matter if it's a nervous driver in Albuquerque, or a reporter in the aftermath of a Los Angeles earthquake. A con is a con.

And if there's one thing Amber knows how to do, it's run a con.

"We were in the stadium," she says. The woman flicks an annoyed glance at her, but doesn't respond. Amber almost gives into panic – she'd been banking on the reporter wanting to interview them, get some comment on the conditions inside. But her mind works the angles for her, gets her to where she needs to go.

"They kicked us out," she says loudly. "Told us we had to go somewhere else."

"Jim, give me a second." The woman puts the phone to her shoulder again, focusing on Amber. "What do you mean they kicked you out?"

"Yeah, we were there," Matthew replies, before Amber can. *Jesus, he's quick.* "They said we had to leave, because they were going to run out of food and stuff. And water."

"They're ..." Amber looks over her shoulder, as if she's worried soldiers are going to appear out of the rain. It's easy. Like muscle memory, all the old tricks ready and waiting for her. "They shot a guy. I saw it happen, he ... he was trying to get a drink of water, and they ..."

The reporter pops the phone to her ear, gaze darting between Matthew and Amber. "Jim, I'll call you back."

Her smile is dazzling, teeth achingly white. "Molly Zuckerman." She shakes Amber's hand, holding on just a little too long. "I'm with KTLA news. You saw this happen? You saw someone get shot?"

"I – yes. Yes, we did."

"Miguel!" Molly Zuckerman bangs on the side of the chopper, making the cameraman start. Some hair has come loose from her ponytail, and she brushes it back, still looking at Matthew and Amber, as if they'll run the moment she blinks. "Sorry about before. It's been a little crazy down here. You know how it is."

"So can you help us or not?" Matthew says. Amber has an urge to snap at him – he might be smart, but he's being way too demanding. If this is going to work, he needs to trust her ...

Zuckerman's smile falters slightly. Without looking away from them, she gestures at her cameraman. He's already got the camera hoisted to his shoulder, red light on. Amber's instinct is to flinch away – but then again, what does it matter? The government already knows where they are, already sent people after them.

All the same, she finds herself stepping in front of Matthew, shielding him from the camera's eye.

"OK ..." Zuckerman closes her eyes and takes a deep breath, moving her hands down to her waist as she exhales, thumbs and index fingers touching. She glances at the cameraman. "We rolling?"

He nods, and Zuckerman turns her thousand-watt smile back on Amber. "Ma'am, can you tell us exactly what you saw in Dodger—?"

"We'll talk to you if you give us a ride out of here." Amber straightens up, ignoring the stab of pain in her ankle.

"The hell you say," mutters the pilot.

A shadow crosses Zuckerman's face. "I'm just asking a few simple questions, that's all. About the stadium. Can you—?"

"I *said*. You fly us north, we'll give you your interview."

"I say we do it," says the cameraman. "We're not getting anywhere here."

"Not your call, Miguel." Zuckerman sounds annoyed now, but her eyes tell a different story. There's a hunger in them, an eagerness.

Beside Amber, Matthew has fallen silent, as if sensing what she's trying to do.

There's a risk. An *insane* risk. If the government really is on the hunt, then she's about to do something that will let them know exactly where she and her son are headed. Then again, she's lived through risk like this before. She lived through it every time she picked a mark, every time she pretended to be hurt, every time she threw herself in front of a car. Risk is in her blood.

The government won't shoot down the chopper – not one from a TV station. They might try and divert it, change the flight path ... but they'd have to do that without letting Molly Zuckerman know. And of course, even if that did happen, and the reporter agreed to it, the government couldn't just take them the moment they stepped out of the helicopter. Not while cameras are right there.

By the time the footage gets back to the station, she and Matthew will be long gone. And really, what's more dangerous? Going on foot? Through a city where the government could swoop down on them at any time? Or risking this chopper ride?

Zuckerman bites her lip. "Why north?"

"Doesn't matter," Matthew says. "We just need somewhere where the roads are still working."

The reporter blinks at him in surprise.

"Bakersfield might do," says the cameraman. "Town got hit pretty bad, but the roads are still good, s'far as I know."

A map pops into Amber's head. Bakersfield ... almost a hundred miles away, but if they could get there ...

"What's your name?" Zuckerman asks.

For a long moment, Amber doesn't know what to say.

Does she tell her they're Amber and Matthew? Does she give their real names? No – it's way too risky.

"Denise," she says, pulling the name of another doctor at the Facility. "This is ... this is Mike. Mikey."

Zuckerman's smile is back. "Pleased to meet you, Denise and Mikey. Bakersfield it is. But *only* if you answer all my questions."

"Mol, We're not a goddamn taxi service," the pilot says.

The reporter ignores him. "OK – Denise. What did you see? Tell me everything."

"No." Amber points. "We need to get out of here. We'll talk in the chopper."

Zuckerman almost growls in frustration, but glances at the cameraman. "Is that going to be OK? For sound?"

Miguel puffs out his cheeks. "Should be. Only got the one aviation adaptor, but I can lav up a headset. It'll be distorted but—"

"Good enough." Zuckerman points to the chopper. "Let's go."

THIRTY-FOUR

Teagan

A medical tent in a disaster relief camp is a shitty place to grieve. And it's *definitely* a shitty place to plan your next move.

It's noisy. Crowded. Stinks to high heaven: mud and sweat and, weirdly, the citrusy tang of orange juice. Like someone hung up a cheap air freshener. We have to crowd in close around Reggie's hospital bed, which is shoved up against a corner of the tent, the bed frame pushing against the thick, off-white fabric.

Africa is crouched down next to Annie, who has her back against the wall of the medical tent. She hasn't said a word yet – she's just sitting there, head on her arms, like she's sleeping. Africa's been trying to talk to her, but clearly it isn't going too well. The tent is loud, the air filled with shouts and groans and barked commands, which is making the argument I'm having with Reggie even more difficult than it is already.

"We can't," I tell her.

"We don't have a choice."

"Of course we have a fucking choice."

"What do you think is going to happen if you go after him right now?" Reggie's brown skin is almost grey, and the crow's feet around her eyes are even deeper than usual. "That's not smart, Teagan."

"Yeah, because what's smart is all of us staying here and trying to convince *these* people –" I wave behind me at the chaotic mess of patients, soldiers and doctors " – to let us get on the horn to Washington. Hey, hi, we're a secret government agency – no for real – and we need to jump on one of your satellite phones and call up our commander in the Pentagon so she can tell us what to do about the *kid who can cause earthquakes*."

"Will you keep your voice down?" I've never seen Reggie look this frustrated, this *angry* that she can't just climb out of her bed.

"I don't even see why we're talking about this. I'm going back out there, I'm gonna find that boy and I'm gonna—"

"What, Teagan? What are you going to d—?" Reggie coughs, her weakened lungs protesting.

"I'm gonna stop him. Obviously. Africa, back me up here."

At my question, he slowly turns his head to look at me. His face is gaunt.

"Back me up," I say. But it's getting harder and harder to put any energy into my words. Like trying to sing a high note when your vocal chords are shredded.

Africa gives a helpless shrug. "I suppose."

"Come on, dude. You can do better than that."

He says nothing. Just turns back to Annie.

"You aren't—" Reggie coughs again. "You aren't thinking strai—" The coughing intensifies, her shoulders hitching as she hacks. "Jesus *fucking* Christ."

I have never heard Reggie swear, and I have definitely never heard her take God's name in vain. Not that I'm about to bring her up on it. He hasn't exactly been doing a bang-up job lately.

It's starting to dawn on me that Paul is really gone. It feels like a hangover – like that horrible period where you're still half-asleep but you know something isn't right and you can feel it building, pushing up against your closed eyelids and clogging your sinuses and sucking all the moisture from your mouth.

I have a sudden urge to sit down, just sit and never get up again. Instead, I take a deep breath. "If we aren't going after this kid, then what the hell *are* we gonna do?"

"I didn't say we weren't going after him." Reggie lets her head fall back against the thin pillow. "I just want us to process everything first."

"What? Like Paul?"

She closes her eyes, and it strikes me then just how much effort this is taking out of her. It's using every ounce of strength she has.

"We'll mourn Paul later," she says. "I'm talking about the boy. We need to develop a way to contain him. From where I am, it appears he's like you, Teagan."

"He's nothing like me."

Annoyance slides into Reggie's voice. "You know what I mean, and don't try to pretend otherwise. Your psychokinesis affects inorganic objects only, whereas he clearly has the ability to move organic molecules. Carbon, hydrogen. Do you think he can affect *all* organic objects? Trees and leaves and such?"

"I don't know. He didn't stick around long enough to fill out the questionnaire."

"All right," she snaps. "No point focusing on the unknowns. We know for sure he can manipulate the earth – use it as a weapon. My guess is that for the most part, he's got limits, just as you do."

I gesture to the chaotic medical tent, with its doctors and

soldiers and patients swirling around us – every one of them wet from the steady rain, muddy and exhausted. "You sure about that?"

"Yeah, OK ... but I think he can only cause an earthquake in certain circumstances, like when he's above a fault line. That's what happened with the first quake, on the gas station camera."

"How can you be so sure?"

"I'm not. But the epicentre on the last quake was right above the San Andreas fault. Why go to all that trouble, if you can cause a quake anywhere?" She stares into the middle distance for a moment, thinking hard. "And he's only a child. Do you think there's a chance he doesn't know what he's doing? Maybe he reacts this way when he's scared – he might not even have meant to cause the earthquake."

I get a picture of the kid's face again. Right before he ... Right before Paul. The weird, almost smug little smile. Like he'd won a prize.

"He knows exactly what he's doing."

"How can you be sure?"

"... I just am."

Now that I've pictured the kid's face – the evil, twisted little boy grin – I can't get it out of my head. The thoughts tumble, cascade, pile on top of one another. I didn't get a chance to think much about where the kid came from before – I knew he had to have been created *after* everything went to shit in Wyoming, but I never gave a thought as to who might have done it. With my whole family gone, nobody was able to recreate my ability in another person. And God knows, the government tried.

Except ... what if they succeeded? What if, at some point during my captivity, they actually ended up creating another person with abilities? It's not like they had any incentive to keep me in the loop – I was an asset to them, a piece of government property. Still am, kind of.

Problem with that is they kept getting more and more frustrated, urging me to push myself harder, go past my limits. Why do that, if they'd succeeded? Why keep up the act? For my benefit? Fuck no. They didn't care what I thought. Whatever happened during my captivity in that windblown little facility in Waco, it didn't result in a superpowered kid.

Which doesn't change the fact that there's one of them out there, wandering around, with the ability to bury people alive.

A cold chill, shivering across my scalp. Did Tanner do this, somehow? Did she know? And if she did, if the kid really is one of hers, then what in the hell is she doing unleashing him on Los Angeles?

When I voice these thoughts to Reggie, her expression hardens. "Moira would never do that."

"Are you *sure*, though?"

"Something like this . . . it's too big. The child would be in a facility, same as you were."

"Maybe she doesn't know. Someone else in the government might be—"

"Oh, she'd know."

"She didn't know about Jake." I think back to when I first understood that Tanner had completely missed the fact of Jake's existence, after the whole mess had blown over. The idea that there were things she didn't know was intoxicating. Who's to say that she knew about this?

Reggie, apparently. "If this boy was made by our own government, Moira would be in the loop. She may have missed Jake . . . but it looks like everybody missed Jake. A government-made person with abilities would light up her radar screen like fireworks on the fourth of July. Wherever this boy came from, it wasn't us."

"Then where—?"

"We can worry about that later. Right now? We need to focus on how he can be contained."

Interesting choice of words. She's right, though. I've killed exactly one person before today, and he was trying to kill me, and he was also a grown-up, potty-trained adult with his own fully formed dreams and desires. I don't care if this kid is the Antichrist: I am *not* killing him.

"I know you want to charge out there," Reggie is saying.

"Reggie, I swear, if you're about to tell me that I have to slow down and think—"

"But I *am* going to tell you that. It's been, what, forty-five minutes since Paul? The kid is long gone by now. We don't know where he's going, what he wants, if he even wants anything. Let's at least have some kind of plan for next time."

"What about the airport?" Africa says. "We put him on the runway, huh? No dirt. No ground for him to use." He says *ground* like the word tastes foul in his mouth.

"Yeah, we gotta get him there first," I mutter.

"It's an idea," Reggie says. "But I don't think it'll work. We don't know his range, or how strong he is. He might be able to just pull earth right through the tarmac."

"Hey Teggan – what happen when you go to the forest?" Africa waves his hand above his head. "When there's no other stuff."

The forest. What he's asking is, what happens when I'm surrounded by organic objects and nothing else. What happens is that I feel all squirmy and weird, like I'm uncomfortable in my own skin.

"I can't move anything," I tell him. "But it doesn't get rid of my ability. And you'd have to *keep* me in the forest to stop me whacking you round the head."

"Could we get him on a plane, then?" Africa asks. "Keep him off the ground?"

"Maybe," says Reggie. "But there must be an easier way. I feel like we don't know enough." She thinks for a moment. "Tell me about the woman. The one who was with him – we saw on her the tape too, I think. His mother?"

It's crazy that we're having this conversation – this rational, considered, mostly calm conversation, when Paul's body is in a shallow grave not half a mile away. I exhale, trying to control my frustration. "She was kind of ahead of where he was. Most of the time, she had her back to me."

"What was she like?"

"You saw on the video. She's young."

"I know that. What else? You saw her in person."

"Kind of hard to say. I didn't get a good look. And Annie was with me. Paul would have—"

I stop, the words cutting off cold. That same feeling again: a hangover, building and building.

"The boy then." Reggie's voice is stiff. "Tell me about him."

"He was ... Well, he was a kid. I don't know what you want me to say."

"How old?"

"Again, you saw the video. Four, maybe five. Were are we going with this?"

"And clothing? What was he wearing?"

I shake my head. Reggie just stares at me, refusing to look away.

"Shoes. Pants. A shirt. A T-shirt, I mean, not like a dress shirt. It was—"

Wait a second.

Reggie and Africa must see the expression on my face. "What?" Africa says.

"Quiet." I close my eyes, trying to remember. I make myself see the kid again: that awful smile, the brown hair with the lame-ass little boy cut, the letters on the shirt . . .

I smile. "California Earthquake Exhibit."

"What's that?" Africa says.

"It's . . . it's an earthquake exhibit in California. I don't know what to tell you."

"But where?" He's on his feet now. "Here in Los Angeles?"

"His T-shirt said that?" asks Reggie. "Teagan, are you sure?"

"Pretty sure. No, *definitely* sure."

"This is good," she says, almost to herself. "We don't know where he and his mother are going, or what they want. But we do know where they've been. And I know where that exhibit is, I've seen it advertised. The Meitzen Museum, next to USC. That's not far from here."

"By car, sure," I tell her. "And we know how that's gonna go."

"Even on foot, it's probably no more than an hour away. Two, tops."

"He could have gotten that shirt anywhere."

"If you have a better idea, honey, I'm waiting to hear it. And do *not* say you're going to go back out there and go hunting for him."

"Wasn't gonna," I mutter.

"It makes sense that he went to that exhibit. If he's only just discovered this power, or didn't know he could cause quakes, then he might want to find out more. Maybe someone at the museum saw him, talked to him."

"How do you know the building's even still there? The quake might have—"

"We don't. But one of the few things we *do* know, or at least have a good reason to believe, is that he went there recently. It might give us some insight into what he's planning – if he and his mother actually *have* a plan."

She looks at each of us. "We're in uncharted territory here. Moira Tanner can't help – at least, not until I convince one of these yahoos to lend us a sat-phone. We have to help ourselves, and the way we do that is by chasing up every lead, no matter how small. Go to the museum, talk to anybody who's still there. See if they remember the boy at all – you should be able to describe him."

"Reggie, this is ... *insane*. We're going to waste hours on this, and we don't even know if there'll be anyone there. They might have been evacuated already."

"It's not a waste. It's a lead. And we won't be idle while you're gone. I'm going to do whatever I can to get a line of communication to Washington."

"And if it *does* turn out the museum is a bust?"

"Then come straight back here. We'll figure out something else."

I roll my eyes. "Fine." It's not fine, nothing in the past day has been even close to fine, but ... Reggie's right. Maybe someone at the museum did see him ...

"If we run into him again." Africa looks between Reggie and me. "The boy. What do we do?"

"We're not gonna run into him on the way to the damn museum," I tell him. "That's south of here. He was going north."

"What if we go back? Maybe he—"

Annie says, "We're gonna kill him."

They're the first words she's spoken since we got back to the stadium. They're said calmly, clearly, with zero hint of emotion. She's raised her head, looking up at us through dry, red-rimmed eyes.

"Annie ... " Reggie says.

"We're gonna take his fucking life." Spoken in the same dead tone. I've never seen Annie like this. Annie shouts and rages and gets angry. She doesn't get quiet. She doesn't have a look in her eyes like the one she has now.

I open my mouth to say that no, we aren't going to kill a kid. But I can't do it. The words won't form. How am I supposed to tell Annie, who just saw the man she loved buried alive, not to want payback? It's all very well to say he's a child, he didn't know what he was doing, we can't treat him like an adult. But right now, Annie doesn't see him as a kid. She doesn't even see him as human.

"Go," Reggie says to me and Africa. "You can head straight down South Figueroa. It'll take you right to the museum."

Africa looks sick, but nods.

"I'm coming." Annie tries to get to her feet, wobbling a little.

"Nope," Reggie says. "You're going to stay right here."

"The hell I am."

"You are not," Reggie says, emphasising each word, "ready to go back out there. You're in shock."

"I'm fine," Annie's on her feet now, but swaying, like a drunk. She reminds me of a driver trying to convince a cop that she's totally sober.

"Annabeth Ramona Cruz, you're going to stay right here. Understand?"

Annie gestures to us. "They can't do it. They don't know ... don't know how ... " She blinks, as if she forgot what she was trying to say.

"They'll come straight back." Reggie flicks her eyes towards the door, gesturing at us to leave. "Now I need you to get me some water. Can you do that?"

Annie nods and stumbles away, and once she's out of earshot Reggie says to us, "Under my pillow. There're some sandwiches. A bottle of water too, I think."

"But you just told Annie . . . Also, why are there sandwiches under your pillow? Is that code for something."

"They brought some food round earlier. I didn't feel like eating, and I had a feeling we'd need to ration. Both of you eat, get some water, use the bathroom, do whatever you got to do. Then get back out there. Paul might be gone, but China Shop isn't. Let's get moving."

THIRTY-FIVE

Teagan

It takes us a lot longer than I'd like to leave the stadium. It's not that the soldiers try to stop us – they're far more interested in the people coming in than the ones going out. But there are huge crowds now, packing the tunnels and the exits. A sea of shaken, shattered people: injured, hungry, cold, drenched from the rain.

Turns out Reggie's sandwich rationing was a damn good idea. The two mystery meat sandwiches she to gave to Africa and me tasted like squashed ass cakes, but they beat standing in the huge, unruly lines for food.

I don't even want to talk about what the stadium bathrooms were like. Let's just say I'm glad my Jordans are water-resistant.

Africa and I push our way through, *sorry*-ing and *excuse-me*-ing out of the south exit, onto the main stadium plaza. Jesus, there's a lot of people. How many before this gets out of control? I was too young to remember Hurricane Katrina, but I've read about what happened at the Superdome, and it did not sound fun.

I nearly come to a complete stop when I remember that Nic is still in there. If it does turn into the Superdome, he'll be right in the middle of it.

You know what? Better in there than out here. I don't want him anywhere near me, not while I try track down a kid who can bury people with his mind. And I don't want him outside the stadium, period. If this kid causes yet another quake, at least Nic will be somewhere that already has emergency supplies.

You just want to cover your own ass, so you can sit in your apartment and live your little life and not have to worry about anyone.

Asshole.

Has he been thinking that this whole time? That I'm not interested in helping other people? Me: the girl who's now heading *away* from food and shelter so she can stop Junior from causing the apocalypse?

Well, fuck him. I feel a sick a pleasure in imagining him safe, or safer than I am right now, anyway. *Stay with the nice soldiers, Nic. I'll be fine.*

Africa, mercifully, says nothing. Doesn't even look at me.

We head down the plaza steps into the parking lot, dodging small clusters of people. Mothers clutching babies, groups of men in thick jackets smoking cigarettes, kids running everywhere. Like the world's most fucked-up street festival. But there's a bit more space to move now, and we make our way out of the stadium grounds, heading for Chinatown. Above us, helicopters buzz back and forth, their rotors audible over the weirdly quiet streets.

It's hard going. And not just because of the terrain. I can't stop thinking of Paul. Replaying what happened over and over and over. Trying to find an angle, a way to make it come out different. But it's like the ending of *Game of Thrones*. You can wish as much as you want, but it will still suck, and it will suck for all eternity.

I'm comparing Paul's death to a fucking TV show now?

Jesus. I reach up, wipe my face, skin slick under my fingers from the rain. My eyes feel puffy, my eyelids twice their usual size.

I shouldn't be surprised at the rubble, at the cracked streets and broken buildings. I should be immune by now. But this quake is the gift that keeps on giving, and it's hard not to feel appalled at the destruction. There are no street lights – no power anywhere, except for Dodger behind us – but the night is lit by a thousand glimmering fires. The rain seems to be keeping most of them under control, but it comes with the fun side effect of chilling us to the bone.

I hug myself as we close in on the freeway, rubbing my upper arms. It looks like the Sunset Boulevard overpass has collapsed, but that's OK: we can cross the 110, which isn't elevated. It'll put us right onto Figueroa. Straight shot to downtown from there.

God, what I wouldn't give for us to still have the bikes.

We left the stadium at around 9 p.m. – amazingly, the big clock on the scoreboard was still working. I keep checking my phone, more out of habit than anything else – we've been on the move for about an hour, although it feels much longer. Africa and I walk in silence, trudging through the rain. There are groups of people on the streets, most of them heading in the direction of the stadium, looking cold and wet and exhausted. I'm a little worried they might try rob us, like the fuckwits from before. Not that it's going to end well for them – I have reached the point where I give zero fucks about using my powers in public – but I'd prefer not to. It's a relief that, for the most part, they just ignore us.

It's not long before we come across our first collapsed skyscraper.

It's crashed down onto Figueroa, utterly wrecking the buildings around it. Despite the rain, the air is choked with dust – we're probably a shit-ton of toxic chemicals. And there must be people buried under the rubble, too. *That* thought is enough to force a long, slow breath out of my lungs, a breath that really wants to be a scream of anger.

This kid. This *fucking kid*.

Africa and I come to a stop in the middle of the street, staring at the wreckage. Should I help out? See if I can pull parts of the rubble up? But there are already two or three emergency crews clambering over the building like ants, helicopters with spotlights hovering overhead. Plus, I'm not sure we have time. What's more important? Getting a few people out of the rubble? Or stopping the kid before he causes *another* earthquake that's even worse than this one?

"Let's go around," I say to Africa. He grunts, but follows me. For the first time, I clock just how quiet he is. He hasn't said anything since we left the stadium. Not a single word.

Of course, it's not just the one fallen skyscraper. At least three in the downtown area have collapsed. We keep running up against dead ends, jagged mountains of rubble, clouds of smoke and ash. The third one is the worst. It took a whole block down with it, and we can't even get close. It's a shattered mess, cloaked in thick, noxious clouds that the rain does nothing to disperse.

We beat a hasty retreat, back to Grand and 2nd. It's past 10 p.m. now. Whatever energy the mystery meat sandwiches gave us has long since been used up. I put my hands on my knees, head hanging, trying to make myself think. "OK. OK . . . if we go back to Westlake, we should be able to go round the damage."

Africa doesn't respond.

"We'll go down on the other side of the 110," I say. "Through Pico-Union. It'll take us longer, but—hey, dude. Dude!"

He's walking away. In the opposite direction from where I told him we should go.

"Uh, Africa? It's this way, man."

Africa ignores me, trudging away. Head down, arms tightly folded. What the fuck is he doing?

With a barely suppressed snarl, I take off after him, a stitch digging into my side. "Hello? Earth to Africa?"

He spits something ugly-sounding in Wolof. Then: "Just go. I will be fine."

"Um, how about no? Where do you think you're going?"

"Skid Row."

"Dude, that's— My way's a lot faster. You know that, right?"

"I'm not going to the museum. I'm going to Skid Row."

"What, you're just *going* there? Like going, and not coming back? What the fuck are you talking—"

"*Because Jeannette is there!*"

He roars it in my face. It's an Africa roar, so it's lucky my feet don't leave the concrete.

He points a trembling finger. "She is there. I go to her, and I find her. I don't care where you go, come with, what you do. But I am going to find her."

"Wait a second. Jeannette's in Skid Row? You're not homeless any more, what the hell's she doing there?"

"Oh ya." His expression turns bitter, almost contemptuous. "You say I'm not homeless. But I am always homeless man to you. We can live in big house and have all the money but we always be homeless, *yaaw*?"

"That makes *no* sense."

"You wanna know why Jeannette is in Skid Row?" He's not looking at me now, his gaze somewhere down one of the darkened, ruined streets. "She is an addict. She take meth. She smoke weed. Even when we have nice apartment, even when I have this job, she not get clean. She keep going back there to find a fix. I say to her, why? I tell her I can help her, I love her, that she must not do these things to herself. *Ce n'est pas important*.

"And she is like every addict there is. She thinks she is in control. She thinks she can quit when she want, or that she can just go away from me and come back. I am going to find her, and you cannot stop me."

Jesus.

Why the hell didn't we know about this? I've seen Africa pretty much every day – we all have. And not once does it come up that his girlfriend, the love of his life, was still a drug addict? Not a single time? And when did I even see Jeannette last?

I've met her exactly once, long before Africa came to work for us. A skeletal woman with terrified eyes, stick-thin and angry. I just kind of assumed that once Africa came to work for us ... I thought she would ...

And suddenly, I've had enough. Selfish as it is – and it is *very* selfish, the kind of impulse I normally run a mile from – we've got a *lot* of shit to deal with right now. I do not need to add Africa's relationship problems into the mix. Not when the earthquake kid is still out there.

And you know what else? I don't believe him. How many insane, made-up stories has he told us? All that bullshit about working secret service for Obama and smuggling gold in France, when he was probably nothing more than a homeless dude with an overactive imagination.

On one level, I hate these thoughts – hate how nasty and petty and pointless they are. On another, I embrace them. I am done with Africa's shit.

"Dude," I say. "I'm sorry. But we gotta go to the Meitzen

Museum. Right now. Because we are running real fucking short on time."

He shakes his head, turns away.

"Fine." I tell him, walking off. The rain has finally penetrated my Jordans, and they squelch on the muddy tarmac. "Good luck. I don't even know why you came, anyway."

I hate how nasty I sound, but I don't have the energy to care right now. Already I'm thinking ahead, planning my route. There might be more collapsed skyscrapers in the downtown core ... I should cut around them if I can, because this is taking way too—

I drop my head. A growl makes its way out of me, digging into my throat. It doesn't matter how tired I am − I can't just let Africa head off on some hero hike into the bowels of downtown Los Angeles.

"Look," I say, turning back. I have to raise my voice for him to hear me. "Right now, nobody knows *where* Jeannette is. At least go back to Dodger, OK? You'll be safe there."

He spits something angry at me in either French or Wolof, I can't tell.

"I'm trying to help you here, Africa! Don't be an idiot."

He stops. Turns to face me. A stick figure in soaking clothes, silhouetted against the glow of the distant stadium. "You wanna know why I come? Why I follow you out here?"

It's not the response I was expecting, and I have to fumble for an answer. "Because ... Reggie asked you to?"

Africa looks away for a moment, like he can't believe how dense I am. "I come because I wanna help. Same reason I leave the van at the airport, when Mister Germany arrive. Same reason I try and fight off the people who want to steal from us, when we try go to Venice Beach."

"Yeah, but—"

"*Because I want to be good at this job!*"

He roars the words. I'd call them overdramatic, if I wasn't looking him in the eyes. They are as cold and clear as the falling rain.

"Nobody ever give me nothing," he says. "I make everything for myself. I fight every time. I fight in Senegal and I fight in France and I fight here and I get nothing. But then Reggie and Mrs Tanner come find me; they say you told them I help you, and they offer me job. They offer *me* job.

"And I want to do it. I see what you can do, all the things you pick up with your powers, and I want to help. Nothing is more important."

"Oh, *come on*."

He acts like he doesn't hear me. "When you show me what you can do ... *yaaaaw*. Everything change. So I think, hey, Mister Idriss, maybe this is a real story for you." He sneezes, sending out a spray of water. "I wanted you to like me. But no matter what I do, you didn't want me there. You just talk to me like I'm stupid – like I am just an immigrant who knows nothing. None of you want me. You all treat me like idiot, every one. Especially you. *Don't worry about it, Africa. Do what I say, Africa. Stop asking questions*, yaaw?"

"I didn't mean it like that—"

"Ya, you do. I know who done what. But now, no more job."

"Of *course* you have a job. We've still got China Shop." Even as I say it, I can't help wondering if it's really true.

"Office gone," Africa replies. "*City* gone. And I think maybe, I must be gone too. I don't want it any more anyway. You are not worth it."

"Wow. That's good, Africa. Let it all out."

"You have amazing powers." There's something else in his

voice now – a bitterness. "But you don't know what you gonna do with them, huh? You not help me. You not help anyone. You nothing more than a *dëma*."

"Watch your fucking mouth." Now I'm pissed. He doesn't get to talk shit about me like that. Nobody does. My face is so flushed I'm surprised the rain doesn't steam when it hits me.

"Enough of you," he says, waving his hand as if dismissing me. "I am going to find Jeannette. You can do this on your own."

"Oh, that's how it is. Well, let me tell you something, *Africa*. You're not exactly perfect yourself."

"OK, what I do?"

"You—"

What *did* Africa do?

He was super hyped-up, all the time. He told wild stories. He kept wanting to hang out, every single day. He was loud and crazy and full-on.

And he's right: I didn't want him there. So I did everything I could to make it clear that we were not going to be real friends – and then got irritated with him when he wouldn't stop trying. Why did I do that? Because he got on my nerves? *Paul* used to get on my nerves, all the time . . . and yeah, we had our fights. But thinking about it, I never spoke to him like I spoke to Africa. Mostly because he would never have stood for it.

"What I do?" he says again.

I'm not really seeing him. What I'm seeing is another man, impaled on a steel pole, as the air chokes on smoke and heat and flame. A man begging me to save him.

Carlos.

My best friend. The whiskey-drinking mechanic and wheelman, the cackling Mexican demon who liked nothing better than hanging out and talking endless shit for hours. Who put me to bed when I was drunk, always made sure I had snacks after a job, listened when it was needed and talked when we had to fill the silence.

The Carlos who set me up to be framed for murder. Who planned for me to be collateral in his fucked-up little revenge plot. No matter how many times I tell myself he wasn't worth it, that he betrayed everything we had together, he keeps coming back.

I don't make a habit of lying – either to myself, or other people. So why don't we fucking be honest here? It's not Africa's energy, or his personality, or any of that shit. It's because every time I look at him, he reminds me of the dude he replaced.

He kisses his teeth, starts walking again.

"You're right."

I have to say it a second time before he stops. Even then, he doesn't turn around.

"I didn't mean to act the way I did," I say into the rain. "It was just . . . It's complicated. There's a *lot* that happened before you got here. And you *are* good at the job. Without you, the whole airport mission would have been toast."

Long seconds tick by.

I blink the raindrops away. "I promise you when this is all over, we'll talk, OK? We'll figure it out."

He lets out a shivering sigh. "So now you say . . . what? You cannot make it to the museum without me?"

Actually, yes, I was about to do just that. And yes, it would have been bullshit. Technically, there's no *need* for him to be here – I could easily have handled this. I debate for a second whether to bluff it out.

"You don't have to be here, if you don't want to. I can

head down there. If you really still want to go back and find
Jeannette, I won't stop you. But ... "

"But what?"

I look down. "But I'd really like the company." Now
I *am* crying. Tears pricking at my eyes. "It's been a pretty
shitty day."

He laughs, exhausted. Spent. "Ya."

We're silent for a few seconds. No sound but the pattering
rain, the distant shouts of the emergency crews. Trying to
salvage something from this giant, flaming clusterfuck.

"Jeannette is tough," he says, to himself rather than to me.
"She will be fine. So we will go to the museum."

"You don't have to," I say quickly.

"No, we must. And she is also probably away from the rain
now. She find shelter for sure."

"Where? Like an abandoned building or some shit?"

"She will have her tent. Even if an earthquake knock it
down, she just put it right back up. You think an earthquake
is worst thing for homeless people? What can it destroy for
us? Our tents are knocked down by police all the time. We
rebuild every day."

"Right. Of course." Strangely, his little speech cheers me
up, despite me being a dumbass. Harry – the homeless guy
from my neighbourhood – will probably be OK too. I'll have
to remember to say hi to him when I get back, maybe strike
up an actual conversation with him. You know, assuming we
don't die.

"Now come on." He strides past me. "We still have
long way."

We're not done talking. Not even close. But even after all
the shit I pulled, he's not leaving me alone.

That's good enough for now.

THIRTY-SIX

Teagan

Once we're actually past the hell of Downtown, we make surprisingly good time. It's around 11 p.m. when we finally hit the intersection of Figueroa and Exposition. The museum should be dead ahead.

There's a weird glow coming from deep inside the area. Not because of fires – it reminds me of how Dodger Stadium lit up the rainclouds, only not quite as bright.

We are ... Exhausted isn't the right word. I am fucking *wiped*. It is taking everything I have not to just lie down and fall asleep. Right in the rainy street, I don't care. It's not like I can be wetter or colder than I already am.

"Is that it?" Africa says.

"Think so."

There's no point saying anything else. We resume our march towards where the museum is supposed to be, in the middle of the park. Above us, a very a distant peel of thunder echoes out across the city.

As it turns out, the museum is ... gone.

We don't even have to get close to it to figure that out. Every building in the park is a collapsed ruin, and what remains of their interiors are dark. I have a rough idea of where the museum is; I'm pretty sure it's the big building at our two o'clock, the one that looks like a birthday cake that someone got really angry with.

"Shit," I murmur. Then again, we knew this might happen, I told Reggie as much. If she'd just let us head out in the same direction as the kid went, maybe we would have found something ...

Africa, however, hasn't given up. He looks around, a little more alert than before.

"What's there?" he says, pointing to the white glow. It's off to our right now, on the other side of the road from the Science Centre. There's a noise, too: generators, people shouting, the clatter of vehicle engines.

The white glow turns out to be three large, open tents, hastily erected in the middle of a huge garden. The tents are packed with tables and equipment, enormous flower beds between them. In the middle, there's a circular marble fountain.

Huge floodlights illuminate the tents, attached to big generators. There are dozens of people milling around – no, a hundred, easy. Soldiers, some of them – National Guard – but most of the occupants of the tents are civilians. They look harassed, rushing between banks of computers, kneeling under tables and messing with tangled knots of power cords, shouting instructions and scribbling on whiteboards.

ATVs – All Terrain Vehicles – zip back and forth. Big four-wheeled bikes with huge cargo trailers, hauling boxes and water tanks. Smart. Probably the quickest way of getting around right now, as long as you don't mind the godawful noise. Maybe we can steal one, to get us back to the stadium.

We stop at the edge of the park, in the darkness beyond the nearest floodlight. "What do you think, Teggan?" Africa says.

It's an oddly formal question – we haven't spoken much since our little blowup.

"I think I'd like a hot shower. Also a steak. A big-ass rib-eye, with waffle fries."

I squint into the rain. "It's not like a shelter, or a field hospital or anything."

"People from the museum, maybe?"

"Only one way to find out."

Nobody stops us as we make our way over to the nearest tent, tramping through a sad-looking bed of mangled flowers on the way. There's too much going on for anyone to notice. The few soldiers there don't even glance at us.

Being under cover is the fucking best. I don't care if these people can't help us; I'm going to figure out a way to stay here for as long as possible.

There's a metal table to our left, covered with laptops and power bricks, surrounded by people in folding chairs who are bent intently over the keyboards. I can't even begin to decipher the data on the screens; it's total gibberish, graphs and pie charts and reams of scrolling text.

I clear my throat. "So what should we—?"

"Excuse me," Africa says loudly. He's stopped someone: an older man with a mop of thinning hair, dark circles under his eyes. He's wearing muddy jeans and a knit sweater, one half of his shirt collar over the neck of the sweater. "Are you from the museum?"

"USGS?" the man says. "Thank Christ. I think we've got the link-up working – go see Gregson, she's been mapping the aftershocks. She'll help you get online."

"No no," Africa says. "We are not USGS. We are looking for—"

"You're not?" The man suddenly seems to realise that the

person talking to him is seven feet tall, and very clearly not American. He flicks his eyes over at me, which is when I real- ise we're still wearing the goddamn airport security uniforms from this morning. Added to my shower/rib-eye/waffle fries wish list: a change of clothes. Preferably a onesie with a hood, and really thick, furry Ugg booties.

"If you aren't USGS, you can't be here." He sweeps past us. "You need to leave."

"Wait." Africa reaches out for him, but he's already gone. He doesn't even stick around to check if we really do leave.

The same thing happens with the next three people we approach. Well, not the exact same thing – only one of them wants to know if we're USGS, whoever they might be. But they haven't seen a boy anywhere, can't help us, sorry. Nobody appears to be in charge, not even the older dude we stopped first. Everybody's off on their own mission, bouncing between the laptops and the racks of equipment. Crazy eyes everywhere.

It's clearly some kind of field monitoring station – one that was set up in a hurry to find out as much about the quake as possible. It's not even a cool one, like you'd see in the movies, where groups of special forces dudes are protecting Thor's hammer or something. We strolled in here way too easily for that. It's just a group of scientists, trying to be as helpful as possible, with a little bit of assistance from the National Guard.

"Let's go," I mutter to Africa, after yet another scientist utterly fails to help us. "Waste of time, just like I said. Let's hope Reggie's had better luck."

Africa ignores me, grabbing hold of a passing woman, this one in a khaki shirt with the sleeves rolled up. "Excuse me. Sorry to bother you—"

"Busy," the woman snaps.

"I know, but please." Africa jogs to keep up with her, and I follow, getting more annoyed by the second. "We are trying to find a boy, he was at the museum today. Maybe yesterday. We—"

"Go talk to Marybeth. She worked reception. Probably over by the food station now. Daniela! I need those isoseismal estimates *now*!"

Africa lets her go, his head dropping.

"We're not getting anywhere," I say, biting down on my annoyance. "Let's get back to the stadium, talk to Reggie and—"

"Who are you looking for?"

The voice comes from our left. It belongs to a young Asian woman, leaning up against a stack of plastic bins filled with thick cables. She's got a freckly face, and straggly brown hair pulled back in an unkempt ponytail. She wears a grey windbreaker over a blue polo shirt, both of which are spattered with mud.

Africa is quicker on the uptake than I am. "Are you from the museum?"

"Yeah, I was a volunteer, why?"

"We're looking for a boy. We think he came through the museum before the quake. We are trying to talk to anybody who might have seen him."

"Oh." The woman gets to her feet, which takes a lot longer than it should. "Um, I mean, we get a lot of visitors, but ... "

"But you might have seen him?" I step out from behind Africa, my heart beating a little faster.

"Maybe, yeah. What did he look like?"

I describe the kid. "He was wearing one of your shirts," I say. And I can see from the way her eyes light up that she knows who I'm talking about. I exchange a quick glance with Africa – *finally*, a little luck. This may go nowhere, but it's a start.

"The earthquake boy," the volunteer says. "Sure, he was here. He came by this morning, before . . . well, before it all happened."

"The . . . *earthquake* boy?" That cuts a little too close to the bone.

"Yeah, he was really smart, actually. Asked some amazing questions about quakes, and . . ." She trails off, her bright expression changing to a frown, taking in our sodden uniforms. "Wait a second. Why do you want to find him?"

"It's a long story. Look, what did you guys talk about? Specifically?"

She bites her lip. "I'm . . . I'm sorry, I just have to ask . . . what agency are you guys with? Because those look like TSA uniforms, so I'm . . ."

"He's my little brother," I say.

"Your brother?"

"Yeah. He would have been here with our mom. I *really* want to find him."

But I've said the wrong thing. The woman's frown deepens. "There's no way she was your mom. She couldn't have been much older than you. I'm sorry, but who *are* you guys? Why are you interested in this kid?" Looking past us now, as if trying to catch the eye of someone more senior. *Shit.*

"Hey," I say. "Hold on. Just hold on a second."

"I don't think I can help y—"

"OK, look." I step closer, dropping my voice. "We work for the government. I'm Teagan, this is Africa. What's your name?"

"Hey, Shonda!" She tries to push past me. "Can I see you for a sec?"

"No! No. Two minutes. Just give us two minutes of your time. If you don't like what we have to say, we'll get out of here, and you'll never see us again."

She comes to a stop, looking me up and down. Shonda, whoever she is, doesn't seem to have heard her yet.

"Let's just go over here." Slowly, I guide her around the boxes, out of sight of the rest of the tent. "If we do something you don't like, you can . . . you can kick me in the ovaries and run."

It gets her attention. I crouch down, making sure no one else can see us. Behind the woman, Africa hovers, looking nervous.

"What is this about?" she says. Now she sounds *really* annoyed. Maybe even a little scared.

"What's your name?"

"Mia Wong."

"Mia. OK. Hi." I lick my lips, trying to figure out what to say next.

And then I get an idea.

It's almost certainly a very bad one. It goes against everything Tanner told me. But right now, this is our only lead. I *have* to convince this person. Every second that goes by is another second closer to a third quake. To more people getting hurt. Tanner would understand. Definitely. Probably.

Fuck it. Sometimes, you just need to do what your gut tells you.

I dig in my pocket for my phone, checking around me to make sure no one else is watching. We're good. "I'm going to show you something. You have to promise that no matter what happens, you won't scream."

"*Scream?* What—?"

"Teggan," says Africa, suddenly worried. "Maybe this is not clever. Reggie did not—"

"I know, dude. But I don't think we have a choice right

now." If this woman saw our kid, talked to him, then we need to get her on-side. Fast.

"It's nothing bad," I tell Mia. "It's not going to hurt you, and I swear to God I'm not about to get naked or anything. I just . . . *Please* promise me that you'll keep quiet. At least until I can explain."

"I don't get it. Is it on your phone?"

"Mia!"

"All right, Jesus, OK, I promise I won't scream, now what— *Ohshitwhatthehellisthat?*"

That is my phone, currently floating a few inches above my hand. The sticker on the back, the unicorn smoking a joint, catches the gleam from a nearby floodlight.

"I literally just told you not to scream," I hiss. "Keep it down."

She sucks in another gulp of air, as if about to really start yelling . . . then clamps a hand over her mouth. Her eyes haven't left the floating phone.

I sigh. "You get exactly five seconds to absorb what you're seeing, and then I'm going to need you to focus, OK?"

In response, Mia whips her hand through the space between my fingers and the phone, as if checking for hidden wires. I roll my eyes, and make the phone circle my head. Then I turn it so the side is facing her, and flick the little silencer switch up and down. She squeaks. She actually squeaks. Her eyes are the size of baseballs.

"Five seconds are up." I drop the phone, pocketing it.

"How did – you – what is – I don't—"

"Mia, breathe. Under normal circumstances, we'd spend a long time talking about how it isn't physically possible and it's an optical illusion and how exactly I came by this amazing power and blah-de-blah, but I'm going to need you to stay with us, because the fate of the world is at stake."

"No. No way. Is this a fucking joke? Am I on camera right now?" She looks aghast, like I really am trying to prank her in the aftermath of an earthquake.

"It's true," Africa says solemnly.

Mia makes a very strange noise: a kind of whining hiss. Her hand is up to her face again, covering her mouth and nose. "I'm sorry," she says eventually. "No. I don't know who you are, or what you want, but I'm gonna go now."

I have to work very hard not to start yelling. "In your pockets right now, there's ..." I concentrate. "Well, not much, because womens' pants pockets are always too fucking small, but there's ... OK, a couple of coins, right pocket. Phone jammed into your left."

"That doesn't mean anything."

"Yeah, but this does." And I twitch the two coins. Make them clink together.

Mia jumps. Her feet literally leave the ground, her hand flying to her pocket – then snatching it away, like she's been burned. "What the *fuck*?"

"Yes, it is crazy," Africa says. "When I first see her do it, I think she is David Blaine, *yaaw*?"

And *still* Mia doesn't believe. I can see it in her eyes.

I look around. "See that?" I point to one of the flower beds. It's ringed by a line of low metal fencing, the kind where each section is bent into a cute arch.

Mia follows my finger. "So what?" she says, almost like she's annoyed with me. "You gonna mess with that too?"

"Got it in one." I make sure nobody else is watching, again, then flip two fence segments out of the dirt. I zip them over, ignoring Mia's still-somehow-stunned intake of breath. Then I origami them, twisting the metal into a new shape that looks like ... well, actually, I don't know what it

302   JACKSON FORD

looks like. Not as if I could make an origami swan out of it or anything.

When I'm done, I use my PK to toss it to Mia. She steps backwards, nearly falling on her ass. The impromptu sculpture slaps into the mud.

I close my eyes. Jesus, how much more of this am I going to have to—

"OK, let's say . . . " Mia licks her lips. "Let's say you really can do . . . all this."

I meet her eyes. "Yes. Let's say that."

"What do you *want*?"

"Were . . . were you not listening before? The kid. Earthquake boy. We work for the government, and we *really* need to find him."

"But why?"

"So this next part is super important. Like, next-level, life-or-death important. You saw what I just did? This kid can do something similar. Only, it's like . . . "

I swallow, trying not to think about Paul. It doesn't work. I get that same feeling, like I've been punched in the gut. All I can see is Paul's blank, staring eyes.

I make myself speak. "He can control the ground. Dirt and soil and stuff. Mia – it was him who caused the quake. Both of them."

She's already shaking her head. "No. No, that's . . . I'm sorry but no."

"Are you serious? What else do you want me to move? Seriously. Name it."

"It's OK." Africa flashes me a warning look, puts a hand on Mia's shoulder. "It's too much to take in, you know?"

"Uh-huh." Her voice is about three octaves higher than before.

"But I promise you, we are the good ones. We're not out to hurt the boy."

Annie's words lance through my mind. *We're gonna take his fucking life.*

"He maybe does not know what he's doing," Africa says. "He maybe not in control." Another lie, but I let it go. "We must find him before he hurts anyone else. If you can tell us anything about him . . . "

"His name's Matthew," she says.

Matthew. Such an ordinary name. I feel like this kid should be called Jericho. Or Cane.

"S'good." Africa says to Mia, forcing a smile. "What did you talk about, when he was here?"

"Nothing! I mean . . . he was just a really smart kid. For his age, I mean. He asked a lot about quakes."

"What did he want to know?"

She runs a trembling hand through her hair. "Pretty much everything. He was asking about fault lines, and the San Andreas, and aftershocks, and seismic data."

"A *four-year-old* asked about this stuff?" I say.

"He's gifted. One of those kids with a super-high IQ."

Oh, excellent.

"OK, think," I say. "Did the kid . . . Did Matthew say where he was going next? Maybe like another fault line? *Are* there even any others around here? Because I get the feeling he's not just going to stop at two quakes."

Mia gives her head a shake, a quick one, like a horse trying to shoo a fly. "I don't *know*, OK? Most of it was just the San Andreas, although there was a bunch of other—"

She stops. Her baseball eyes go even wider. Her still-trembling hand makes its way back to cover her mouth.

"Um. Mia?" I say.

"Cascadia," she breathes. "Oh my God."

Africa and I exchange a confused glance. "What is Cascadia?" Africa says.

"No," she says, giving a little shake of her head. "He couldn't ... I don't see how he could do it. And there's no evidence. But if he did ..."

I do not like the expression on Mia's face. I do not like it one little bit. "Yo, Mia. Cascadia. What is it?"

"The implications alone ... because ... Even if *you* have these powers or whatever, I don't see how he could ..."

"*Mia.*"

Mia looks between us. At that moment, it's as if she removes herself from the conversation. Checks out entirely, just for a second. Like she has to have a little conversation with herself. Then she draws in a weak, shaky breath.

"The Cascadia fault line. He's going to destroy the entire western seaboard."

THIRTY-SEVEN

Amber

It's almost midnight when the helicopter drops them on a vacant patch of land next to the Interstate, a few miles from Bakersfield. The cameraman turned out to be right. The town itself got hit, but not quite as badly as Los Angeles, a hundred miles south. The freeway is still mostly intact, despite being clogged with hissing, honking lines of trucks.

She barely remembers the questions Molly Zuckerman asked her. She got real vague about the soldiers not letting them enter the stadium, confused about what she saw, unsure. The reporter, Zuckerman, got more and more exasperated – especially when Matthew flat-out refused to answer any of her questions.

The whole time, Amber had been alert for a change in the chopper's direction – any sign that the government had figured out where they were. It hadn't come. Which either meant they had agents waiting for them in Bakersfield ... or they'd gotten away clean.

The chopper touches down a hundred yards from the 5, dry grass waving in the rotor backwash. "Are you going to be OK?" Zuckerman says, as she leans across to pop the chopper door. "I hate leaving you like this."

She doesn't sound like she hates leaving them. But there's no trace of betrayal in the woman's voice, no sense that she's waiting for a dozen government agents to spring their trap.

"We're good," Amber replies. "We're gonna try our luck with the trucks."

Zuckerman nods, distracted, and slides the door back. The roar of the rotor blades fills the cabin. The pilot doesn't even look at them, and Miguel the cameraman is playing with his phone. If there *are* agents ready to spring a trap, this little news crew is doing a good job of hiding it.

With a final, weak smile for Zuckerman, Amber climbs out. Matthew is right behind her. They run bent over instinctively, only straightening up once they're clear of the chopper. It lifts off with a dull roar, turns back towards LA.

Amber comes to a halt, scanning every patch of ground she can. Beside her, Matthew has picked up on her anxiety. But there are no shouts for them to stop, no phalanx of black-clad agents. Nothing but the wind, and the resigned honking from the convoy of trucks on the Interstate.

Matthew takes her hand. "That was smart."

" . . . What?"

"The interview thing. It was smart."

She gapes at him, trying to remember the last time *he* praised her. Can't do it. She gets that same burst of ridiculous pride, the same as when the professor at the museum told her she'd raised a hell of a kid.

He's calm, and she's in control. All she has to do is keep him this way. And she can do that, no sweat.

The ground is less torn up here than it was in Los Angeles, as if the quake's effects petered off the further north they got. It starts to slope before it reaches the freeway. Matthew and Amber have to scramble up the last part, hands digging into the dusty soil. *Of course, Matthew could probably create a set of steps if he wanted*, Amber thinks. She yawns suddenly, then runs a dry tongue over her lips. There was some water in the chopper, plus a bag of opened potato chips, but it wasn't close to enough.

The line of cars and trucks extends into the distance in both directions, the highway clogged, everyone trying to get out of California. The traffic is hardly moving, and the air is thick with the stench of exhaust fumes.

"Go ask them if they'll take us north," Matthew says, gesturing to the trucks.

Amber does so, buoyed by her sudden good mood. She and Matthew aren't the only ones out on the blacktop. The gaps between the massive trucks are filled with people – mostly other families, it looks like, dragging their possessions in wheeled cases or pushing them in shopping carts.

She tries the cars first, the SUVs and Priuses jammed between the trucks. But they're all full, heaving with families and belongings. No room. The few that Amber does find with space shake their heads, giving furtive glances at their door locks.

They need to get out of here. There might not have been agents waiting for them when the news chopper dropped them off, but their luck won't last long.

She starts to work her way down the line of trucks, craning her head to talk to the drivers. Same result. They're even more rude than the people in the cars. One of them openly laughs at her – a man with a fat, jowly chin and sunburnt arms. "Everybody wants a ride out of Cali, darling." He looks her up and down, smirking. "You ain't even in the top ten."

She turns away, a dull anger throbbing in her chest. She's almost tempted to tell her son to teach the man a lesson. Instead, she keeps walking. All she needs is another angle, that's all.

Except Matthew is getting more and more antsy, his shoulders tense, which worries her more than she dares let on. What she wouldn't give for their pickup. Still somewhere in the Angeles Forest, she supposes. Her son's mood weakens her resolve. Maybe they should head into town, find a car of their own there . . .

The next driver is a woman, arm dangling out window of her rig. She wears a green muscle vest, and her thick left arm and shoulder are covered with tattoos. Her face appears to be carved from granite, but she has the most incredible red hair, frizzing out around her skull like a lion's mane.

"How many y'all got?" The woman says, when Amber approaches her. Her accent is bizarre – a weird blend of Deep South and North Dakota.

"Just two. Just us."

The woman considers, then jerks her chin. "OK, come on. Ain't got all day." She reaches around, popping the passenger-side door.

Amber gapes, unsure she even heard right. Matthew doesn't hesitate. He darts around the fender and scrambles up into the vehicle.

The truck's cabin stinks of cigarettes and grease. There's junk everywhere: leftover takeout containers, magazines, at least three laptops. Behind the two bucket seats, there's a small sleeping area, a thin mattress under a mess of blankets. A mini-fridge, a tiny, crud-encrusted stove.

"Wouldn'ta let you in if there was more of you," the driver says. "Cab's cramped enough as it is. Jocelyn." She thrusts a meaty hand at Amber. Her skin is as ridged and hard as old wood, and she makes a point of shaking Matthew's hand, too. He's turned on the charm again, and he gives her a huge, toothy grin.

"I'm Denise," Amber says. "This is Mikey."

"Denise and Mikey. Well, Denise and Mikey, looks like today's your lucky day." Her smile is a little embarrassed. "Although to be honest, I wasn't going anywhere. Been sitting in this tailback for hours. Every truck heading down to LA is getting turned back, unless it's hauling food or whatever – goddamn miracle the freeway's still working, although God knows, it's gonna be one hell of a bumpy ride." She frowns. "No luggage?"

Amber's mind blanks.

"Our house fell on it," Matthew says solemnly.

Jocelyn barks a laugh. "Is that so? Maybe your day ain't too lucky after all."

Matthew nods, like it's no biggie. "We need to go north."

"Chose a good truck, then. That's where I'm headed. Not that I could turn around if I wanted to right now." Jocelyn nods towards the back of the cabin. "Make yourselves comfortable. There's plenty water if you want it. I'd go easy on the food, though – I only packed enough for one, and it's not like I had a chance to resupply in LA. Oh, hey, traffic's moving again. How about that?"

She puts the truck in gear with a thick clunk, and they start to edge forward.

THIRTY-EIGHT

Teagan

"OK, hold on," I say to Mia, trying to keep my voice as steady as I can. "When you say *destroy the entire western seaboard*, do you mean that like in a figurative sense, or . . . ?"

"But you can't," Mia murmurs, almost to herself. "It's not possible. He'd have to . . . I don't get how . . . "

"Hey," Africa says. "Mia. What is Cascadia?"

"It runs all the way up to the PNW," she says, distracted.

"PNW?" I say. "Like Pacific North-west?"

Something in Mia's eyes clears a little. Like she's back on solid ground, so to speak.

"I'll show you." She beckons us, darting around the boxes. Africa and I exchange a look, then follow.

Mia is already moving between the tables, slipping through groups of scientists. When we catch up to her, she's unrolling a map of the US across one of the tables. "Hold that," she says, pointing to a curling edge. Africa complies, giving me another confused look.

"Hey, Mimi, everything OK?" The question comes from an older man in a sweat-stained T-shirt, a plus-size version of the one the kid – Matthew – was wearing.

"Not now, Arnie," Mia says.

"You sure? Who are your fr—?"

"I said, *not now.*"

Arnie gives us an odd look, but moves off, clearly thinking he has more important things to do. *Oh, buddy. If only you knew.*

Mia clicks her fingers at me, still looking at the map. "I need a pen."

"Um . . . what?"

"A pen. Something to draw with."

"Here." Africa hands her a black Sharpie. God knows where he got *that* from.

Mia pulls the lid off with her teeth, leaving it in her mouth as she draws a line on the map. It's in the ocean, hugging the west coast, starting near the top of California. The line runs up alongside Oregon and Washington State, before crossing into Canada and finishing up by Vancouver Island.

"This —" Mia spits out the pen cap "— is the Cascadia Subduction Zone. The fault line I was talking about. It's where the Juan de Fuca and North American tectonic plates meet."

I stare at the line. "That's . . . long."

"Uh-huh," Africa says. "Why this one? Why this fault?"

Mia's eyes meet mine, and it's not hard to spot the doubt in them. It's a doubt I've seen before, plenty of times – hell, the China Shop crew had it, back when Tanner first introduced us. It's even worse here, though: Mia might only be a volunteer, but she lives in a world governed by science. If she's going to go along with us, she's going to have throw most of that out the window.

"Let's say I actually believe you," she says. "And I'm not saying I do. I don't even know why I'm showing you any of this. But if this kid can actually do what you say he can – and I'm not saying he can – then what I want to know is *why.*"

"Forgot the why," I say. "Focus on the what. What did you guys talk about at the museum? This Cascadia thing?"

"We talked a little bit about the San Andreas, but yeah, it was Cascadia –" she taps the line "– that he was interested in. He asked all these . . . all these questions about it. And we were showing him maps, and seismic data and . . . " She trails off, squeezing her eyes shut. As if she can't believe she could have been so stupid.

"What happens if he triggers it?" I say quietly.

Her brow furrows. "I already told you. The whole western seaboard goes down."

"Yeah, but what does that mean?"

"What do you mean, what does it mean? It's the Cascadia fault. What do you think it means?"

"We don't live in your world, Mia. Just lay it out for us."

"*Live in my world?*" She stares at us, genuinely shocked. "You've got this massive, *massive* fault line off the coast of California, that you live with every day, and you don't know what it is?"

"*Mia!*"

"All right, look. The Juan de Fuca plate, here – " she taps the area to the left of the line, in the Pacific " – is slowly sliding under the North American plate –" tap-tap on the right of the line, her fingernail on LA "– and all this energy has been building up for hundreds of years."

"OK," Africa says slowly. "But what does it matter? They slide under, so what? Why does that make an earthquake?"

"Because of the craton."

I tilt my head. "The what now?"

"The North American plate isn't just a single, uniform slab.." She draws a big, messy circle in the centre of America. "Here. It's a big mass of rock that was formed maybe three billion years ago, and it's geologically stable. Think of the plate as being really thick in the middle, and thin at the edges."

"Which is why we don't get quakes in Ohio," I mutter.

"Uh-huh. And the craton stops the edge of the plate from moving too far. So—"

Africa rests his oversized knuckles on the black line. "Ya, but the other plate still slides under, yaaw? So what?"

A flash of irritation in Mia's eyes. "These aren't, like, smooth sheets of paper. They're rock. They're uneven. They're crunching and grinding and going every which way. Except the thin edge of the North America plate can't really move very far because of this solid mass of rock behind it, so there's all this pressure building and building.

"The leading edge? Us? We're getting pushed upwards. A little bit at a time. And there's a lot of trapped energy down there. If it gets released . . . "

I hadn't realised how pale her face had gotten, but I sure as hell see it now. "The entire coastline would drop six feet, and shoot west thirty," she says. "All in a matter of minutes. Everywhere, from Mendocino to Vancouver."

She swallows. "It's what we call a full-margin rupture. And it's going to make all of this, all of LA, look like nothing."

"How?" Africa says, voice very low.

"Easy. LA was an 8.3. If Cascadia ruptures, like you say it will, we could be looking at anywhere from an 8.7 to a 9.2. Maybe even more."

It's times like these when I really wish I knew nothing about earthquakes. I'd rather be ignorant. Unfortunately, I've learned quite a bit of scary shit over the past couple of days, and there's one little fact that is conveniently popping to the front of my mind now. Every time you go up a point on the Richter scale, the fault releases thirty-two times more energy than before. And over a *much* bigger area.

A 9.2 . . . Holy shit.

Holy flying shitballs.

Africa has his hands out in front of him, eyes closed, like he's trying to wrap his head around it. "Wait, wait. So full margin rupture happens, the whole coast just . . . goes to the west?"

"It'll shatter the coast like a broken mirror. Massive cracks, roads destroyed, more than what happened in LA – hundreds of towns and communities completely cut off. And that isn't the worst of it."

"How in the hell is that not the worst of it?" My voice has gotten almost as high as Mia's when I showed her my PK.

"The fault line is under the ocean. The amount of water it'll displace . . . We're talking a tsunami bigger than anyone has ever seen."

"You're saying the west coast is going to get shaken to pieces . . . and then get hit by a tsunami *as well*?"

"Us, and Japan."

"What the fuck are you talking about?" I feel like I'm in an earthquake *now*, the ground shifting under my feet. "What does Japan have to do with anything?"

"This much energy, the tsunami will go in two directions. It'll annihilate the east coast of Japan. Hawaii. Maybe even Taiwan and the Philippines, not to mention just about every other Pacific island in the way. We're talking hundreds of thousands dead in a day. More."

We all fall silent, looking down at the map. There's plenty of noise around us, a shifting crowd of people, a whole chaotic city. But right now, all I can focus on is that line. The little black line that runs from California to British Columbia. It looks like nothing. Completely inconsequential. But it's like a small lump under your breast, or a cough that won't go away.

It seems impossible that humans still live on the coast. Next to this . . . this *thing*. How did we not know about this? Mia's right – it's crazy that we hadn't heard of it. That we just went on living our lives, unaware that the earth could lash out at us at any moment.

My eyes go wide. "No, hang on. Just hang on a second. This line is in the ocean."

"Ya. So?" Africa says.

"Well, he can't . . ." My brain is mush, making my thoughts hard to put into words. "I think he has to be in contact with the ground to set off a fault."

"How do you know, though?"

"It was on the footage, when he set off the first quake."

"There's *footage*?" Mia says.

I ignore her. "He kind of . . . he crouched down, or knelt down. He put his hand on the ground." The more I speak, the more excited I get. "Even if that isn't true, I'm pretty sure he's got a *range* for his ability – and it probably can't reach all the way down to the seabed. So we're OK!"

I look between them, surprised they aren't getting this. "Well, it's not as if he's gonna go scuba diving! He's like four years old. If he can't get close to the fault under the ocean, he can't trigger it. Yes? We're good. We're in the clear."

Mia does not look like we're in the clear. Mia has her hands to her face, pressed to her eyes.

"What?" I say. *Please let it be nothing. Let her have realised she left the oven on at home before the quake. Or that she forgot to pay her taxes. Let it be something normal.*

Mia looks sick. Like she's about to hurl. "The ETS zone."

"The what now?"

"Episodic Tremor and Slip. An area between the locked zone and slip zone where the mantles meet."

"Oh, great. I'm so glad you cleared that up."

"Look, fault lines aren't uniform. The pressure varies depending on where you are. There are parts where you get these long, drawn-out quakes – episodic tremors. We can't usually feel them, but they actually *increase* pressure on the locked zone – the part of the fault that can't move any more. If Matthew can create a big tremor in one of those zones, he could trigger the big one."

"*Could?*"

She gives a helpless shrug. "Maybe, yeah."

"But even if he go this BTS zone . . . " Africa says.

"ETS."

"Ya. Even if he gets to it, it's still out sea?"

" . . . ETS zones extend under the North American plate. He'll be able to reach them on land."

"OK. Fine." I lean on the table, arms akimbo, like a general considering battle plans. I can't afford to panic now, or even show it. "Right now, we don't know where he is. He might have left LA already. But we know where he's going to be." I look at Africa. "Yes? Back me up on this."

"I suppose . . ."

"Good enough." I turn to Mia. "The zone you're talking about. Where is it?"

She just gapes at me.

"OK, this is the part where you point to the map," I say.

With a trembling hand, Mia starts sketching again, circling a spot in Washington State. "ETS tremors don't happen on a schedule, but they're fairly regular. It would be a lot easier for him if he triggered a big pressure release in an area that's due for one."

My heart starts to beat faster. "Wait – you're saying that's where he's going to be? That's the ETS zone?"

But Mia isn't done. She circles another spot on the map, halfway down Oregon. A third, at the Oregon–California state line. A fourth, a little below that, in the Mendocino National Forest.

And they are *big* circles. If I had to guess, I'd say they cover hundreds of square miles each.

"These spots," she says, "are all due a slow-slip tremor. If Matthew releases enough energy in a short space of time, and if he's at the right place, it could set off Cascadia."

"So he's going to be in one of these four spots? That's what you're saying?"

"In theory ... "

"Do not *in theory* me right now. Theories aren't going to cut it. Where? Which spot would he go for?"

"If I had to guess, I'd say northern California around Mendocino, or in Washington. That's where the most pressure has built up."

Africa cuts in. "I do not understand. How does he *know* where these are?"

Mia closes her eyes, actually shudders. "I told him."

Of course she did.

And why wouldn't she? If someone asks about tectonic plates, you don't automatically assume they're going to end the world.

I tap the circle near Mendocino. "This is closest. He'd go for there, surely?"

"It might not be that simple," Mia murmurs.

"Why not?"

"The San Andreas quakes went a long way up the coast. We don't know what the roads are like up there – he might not be able to get close. That means he could go for one of the other zones."

"Which one?"

"I don't know!"

"And how close are we talking here? I'm guessing the border of each zone isn't like a hard border."

"Definitely not. But I don't know about how his ... his powers work. It might be enough for him to be at the edge of one of the ETS zones, but if he really wanted to do this, he'd probably get as close to the centre as possible – or at least, close to where we think the centre is."

"So if he has to go for one of these zone things to set off Cascadia, did he do the same with the San Andreas? With our fault line?"

She shrugs. "It's possible. The San Andreas and Cascadia faults are different – the whole of San Andreas is under our feet, not under the ocean, and it's a lot smaller. Maybe he didn't need to be right on an ETS zone to trigger it, I don't know."

"Why did he even go for San Andreas in the first place? If Cascadia was going to be such a disaster, then why start small?"

Mia stops, takes a calming breath. "I don't think he knew. About Cascadia." Her eyes go wide. "We have to tell somebody! The government, or ... "

She stands up, starts looking around, as if trying to call one of her colleagues over. I pull her back down. "Not a good idea."

"What are you talking about? Hey, Arnie! Arnie, is there—?"

"Keep your damn voice down," I hiss, even as Arnie and a couple of the other scientists look over at us.

"Teggan," Africa says. "I think they might have satellite phones here. We can tell Tanner."

"Who's Tanner?" Mia says.

I ignore her. "Dude, if we try to get hold of Tanner from here, we'll have to let everybody know about what I can do, and about what Matthew can do, and we'll be here until the end of time. Besides, right now, Reggie might be—"

"We're here already!" Africa spreads his arms, gesturing to the rest of the tent. More of the occupants are looking over at us now, exchanging confused looks. "It is the quickest way."

"Dude—"

"You already show *her* what you can do." Africa jabs a finger at Mia.

"It's not just about that."

"We do not have time to keep things secret. It's bigger than you."

Argh. It's Nic all over again – the accusation that I'm acting selfishly, refusing to help. I have to make him understand – make *both* of them understand.

"If we go and tell the soldiers or the other people here what we told Mia," I say, "we'll be running in circles for ever. They might even be hostile. By the time we get through to Tanner – *if* we ever get through to Tanner, because I sure as hell don't know how to reach her – Matthew could be halfway to setting off Cascadia."

"So what else are we supposed to—?"

"Jesus, Africa, think. *Reggie.* She said she'd keep trying to contact Tanner while we came down here. She might even have gotten through already. We hightail it back to Dodger, link up with her, tell her what we found out. She can get her people to every single one of these stupid zones."

"Who's Reggie?" Mia says. "Look, who *are* you guys?"

"File that under stuff that *definitely* doesn't matter right now. All you need to know is, Reggie's our boss, Tanner's her boss, and they're the quickest way to figuring this whole shit out."

"Gonna take us a long time to get back to the stadium," Africa says, looking sour. I don't blame him – I'm not exactly excited for the hike back either. But I know my way is the right one. It makes sense.

"I'm coming," Mia says.

"Mia," I say with what is frankly a *lot* more patience than the circumstances deserve. "This isn't a movie. You don't get to pull the whole *I'm coming with you* thing here. It's our responsibility, not yours."

She's rolling up the map, stuffing it under her arm. "One: I can help you figure out which zone he's going to end up in. Two: you don't get to show me superpowers, and then ask me to sit this one out."

"Listen, we're *really* grateful for the help, but right now—"

"Three: if you take me with you, you won't have to walk back to Dodger Stadium."

She marches over to Arnie, who is still staring at us, trying to work out what's going on. "I need your keys."

He blinks at her in astonishment.

"Don't tell me you've got a helicopter stashed some-where," I say.

"Nope. Got something better." She grins. It's the mad, almost self-righteous grin of someone totally committed to the path they've started down. It is the grin of someone has just had the laws of physics casually broken in front of them, and who has decided they are totally fine with it.

I try one more time. "*Please* listen to me. You could get hurt doing this. Maybe even killed."

"The way I see it," Mia says, "I gave the boy everything he needed. I answered all his questions. Well, we all kind of did, but ... look, the point is, I helped cause this. I'm going to help fix it."

"Mimi," Arnie says. "What exactly is—?"

"Arnie, if you call me *Mimi* one more time I will kick you in the balls."

"I can't just give you keys, Mim—Mia." Arnie draws himself up to his full height. He's surprisingly tall. "You're an intern. You're not supposed to—"

Mia sticks a finger in his face. "How about this. You give me the keys, and I won't tell anybody that I saw you watching porn on your phone in the cafeteria last week."

Arnie goes pale. "I don't know what you're talking about."

"Do you *want* everyone to know how much you like bukkake? Because I can—"

"OK!" I wedge myself between them. "I think the point's been made here. Arnie, how about you be a gem and hand Mia what she wants before she has to do any more super-awkward blackmailing, m'kay?"

"All right, all right, Jesus." Arnie glowers at me, as if he wants to demand to know who the hell we are. Then he digs in his pocket, hanging Mia a set of keys. She gives him a friendly smile as he walks off, muttering. Africa snorts.

Mia turns to us, dangling the keys. "We good?"

"Super grossed-out, but yes. What are we driving?"

Another wild grin spreads across Mia's face.

THIRTY-NINE

Teagan

Under normal circumstances, ATVs fucking rule.

I've driven them plenty of times before. We had three when I lived in Wyoming, although only one of them was usually working. After we got older, my dad taught Chloe, Adam and me how to ride them. The idea was for us to help Dad with the chores – fetching firewood, repairing fences, all that shit. But you can't give a group of teenagers access to giant, four-wheeled motorbikes without having them go tearing off into the wilderness at the earliest opportunity.

It's kind of a miracle that I'm still alive. We ramped those things a *lot*.

You know when ATVs do *not* rule? When you have to be a passenger. Also, when you have to ride them through a bumpy, torn-up, apocalyptic wasteland, and it's raining, and fucking cold, and dark as shit, and Africa doesn't know how to steer.

When we first arrived at the two ATVs, I made to climb onto the driver's seat. Africa pulled me back. "Uh-uh, Teggan. I must drive."

"Oh, really? *You* can drive an ATV?"

"I am the driver for China Shop. It's my job." *Daring* me to contradict him.

So he drives one, and Mia takes the other. These ATVs aren't like the ones my parents had. Well, they are, in that they've got four wheels and the familiar, hard, uncomfortable seats. It's just that *these* ATVs have clearly been hitting the protein shakes. The tyres are the size of extra-large pizzas, and the engines sound like God trying to win a burping contest. The unseen authority handling the Meitzen Museum staff knew their stuff, because these monsters are perfect for navigating rough terrain – and for turning my pelvis and spine to powder, because apparently, whoever bought them didn't spring for optional extras like shock absorbers. It really helps that we don't have helmets. I don't even think I *saw* a helmet.

We're ripping north, up Hoover Street. It's not the most direct route, but it has a distinct lack of smashed skyscrapers, which I always find is a plus. Africa twists the handlebars to wind us past a huge crack in the road, the back wheel nearly slipping over the edge. Ahead of us, Mia's tail lights split the night. There are fewer people out on the streets now, although some of them try and chase after us. I have no idea what they want – if they're looking for food, or to jack the ATVs, or just to say hi. I can see them shouting, see their lips moving, but can't hear a damn thing over the roar of the engines.

My imagination goes into overdrive. What if there are gangs? Like big groups of raiders you always see in post-apocalyptic movies? Big dudes in leather with spikes on their shoulders, setting up funky traps that have tripwires and pressure switches and—?

Holy fuck, I think I just drifted off. I actually fell asleep, right on the back of this snorting, snarling hell vehicle. Christ, what is the time, even? When did I last sleep? Or eat?

Doesn't matter how long it's been since I slept. I'm not drifting off again. Not when I'm on the back of an ATV with no helmet or seat belt. We haven't hit *Apocalypse Now* yet, just Apocalypse Soon, which means I don't get to fall asleep on the job.

There are a few places where the road *has* been blocked by overturned cars, or there's a crack too large for us to cross. We have to dive into the side streets, winding our way through Pico Union and Westlake. Even so, we make good time. *Really* good time. Soon, we're roaring up Vin Scully Avenue – which has surprisingly little damage – and into the stadium parking lot.

It's gotten worse in the couple hours we've been away. A *lot* worse. The crowds have grown, more people streaming in, milling around the entrance tunnels. Not exactly surprising. Even if FEMA and the National Guard weren't directing people here, the stadium is probably the only place in the city with consistent power. It's a big, glowing beacon, lighting up the clouds.

We come to a stop under a line of trees bordering the west parking lot. When Africa and Mia cut the engines, my ears keep ringing. We stink of exhaustion and exhaust fumes – and somehow, we're even wetter than we were before. I pull out my phone, half-hoping that there'll be some signal. No dice. According to the clock, it's 00:30. I've been awake for nearly eighteen hours, although my body is apparently convinced it's been eighteen thousand.

Mia dismounts her trusty steed. Without the headlights, she's a ghost, an indistinct shape in the darkness. "Your guys are *inside* the stadium?" She eyes the crowds around the entrance, over at our two o'clock. Rowdy, pissed-off, loud.

"Nah, they thought they'd just hang out in the parking lot," I say. "Make it easy for us."

"They are in the medical tent," says Africa.

Mia frowns. "You still haven't told me who you actually *are*. Are you CIA or something?"

I rub my right eye with the heel of my hand. "Call us China Shop."

"China what?"

"Never mind. We're the good guys. Come on, Africa."

I'm not even going to bother telling Mia to stay behind. She's in this now, fully committed, whether I want her to be or not. I think I knew that when I decided to show her my power – something I'm not going to apologise for, by the way. This isn't just a regular emergency; it's the dictionary definition.

We're barely ten feet from the ATVs when something occurs to me. "Give me a sec," I tell the other two.

I stride back to the quads, sending out my PK in a wide arc. It doesn't take me long to find what I'm looking for. There are flexible, plastic orange bollards dotted throughout the lot – the kind of thing that lets a driver know he can't park for shit. Checking to make sure no one nearby is paying attention, I grab the nearest one with my PK, and snap it off at the base.

"Woah," Mia says from behind me. I don't bother looking round. I work quickly, splitting the plastic cylinder lengthwise. It makes me think of a chef julienning a carrot, an image so out of place I almost laugh. But what it gives me are two long, straight chunks of plastic. In seconds, I have them twisted through the spokes of each ATV's front wheel, wrapped around the axles.

"Let's see someone steal them now," I tell the other two.

Mia shakes her head, eyes closed. She lifts a finger, like she's about to make a point, then drops it.

"I really don't know what else I can do to show you I'm on the level," I say.

"It's . . ." She clears her throat. "It's OK. It's just amazing."

"That's nothing. I once took out a police helicopter by fucking with the fuel tanks."

"You did *what*?"

"Hey, come now, no story time." Africa points at the stadium. "Let's go."

I open my mouth to tell him . . . Actually, I don't know what I was going to tell him, because right then, it happens again.

The tinnitus.

The *mental* tinnitus.

The same thing that happened in Watts, outside Annie's mom's house. My PK flickers, on and off, gone then not gone, my head filling with sloshing water. I squeeze my eyes shut, trying to get a grip on it, trying to understand what in the name of blue fuck is making this happen.

It doesn't make sense. The kid is *gone*. Even if it was me sensing some of his . . . what, after-effects? Is that what you'd call them? Even if it was, why wouldn't I have sensed it back when Paul was killed? Why now?

I force my eyes open, looking around me. But there's nothing. Not a goddamn thing.

Snap. Back to normal. Just the three of us, the ATVs, the parking lot. The trees, leaves whispering against one another. The groups of people around the stadium entrance, the chill air.

"What's wrong?" Mia asks.

"Nothing. Just a . . . just a long day." I have bigger shit to deal with right now than whatever my brain is doing. "Let's go."

But we can't get near the fucking stadium. They're not letting anyone else in.

Even with Africa trying to clear a path for us, there's no

getting through the crowds. I didn't think it would be this bad; every tunnel we try is blocked off by freaked-out soldiers who look like they're about three seconds from just opening up with their M-16s. Reggie and Annie are in there. *Nic* is in there. And if we don't get in there soon, the situation is going to get a fuck of a lot worse.

We move slowly around the stadium, trying to find a way in through the thick crowds, looking for a gap. Africa's craning his neck so hard that I'm half-convinced his head is going to pop off his shoulders. And all we see is chaos: a maddening crush of confused, angry people, fights breaking out, sullen faces and shouted words.

And you know what the worst thing is? We are three quarters of the way round the stadium before I realise we still have our earpieces.

Actually, that's not the worst. The worst is that Africa realises before I do. He starts, hand flying to his ear. "Hey," he says, way too loudly. "Anybody there?"

Mia gives him a confused look. Fortunately, I'm quicker on the uptake. "Reggie, Annie, come in."

Nothing. Not even static.

"OK," I say to Africa. "We just need to get closer. Can you—?"

He's already on it, bellowing at the crowd to make way, shouting Reggie's name on the comms, pushing for the nearest entrance. The big letters above it read GATE D, and high above that is a giant Coke ad, the witless model grinning down at us. There are soldiers too, National Guard, scared and exhausted and holding big guns.

Too late, I realise our mistake. One of them — a kid not much older than me, with a shitty goatee and wild, bugged-out eyes — sees Africa coming.

Put yourself in his shoes for a second.

You're a minimally trained National Guard soldier, deployed right in the middle of the biggest earthquake to ever hit the mainland United States, which means the biggest relief operation in our nation's history. You've been going for twelve hours straight. Maybe longer. You are currently between two groups of very pissed off people: one trying to get inside the place you've been told to guard, the other trying to get out – or at the very least, getting mightily pissed off at not having enough food and water. You are almost certainly hopped up on whatever energy drinks they dished out to keep you awake, and the last time you spoke to your loved ones was so long ago you can't even remember it.

And now, here comes a seven-foot-tall gentleman with arms the size of tree trunks, pushing his way through the crowd towards you and shouting something about *Come in*.

"*Africa!*" My words are lost in the din of the crowd. "*Stop!*"

FORTY

Teagan

Africa doesn't hear me, which means I need to use my PK to save him.

But I can already tell that it's not going to be fast enough. I've got the range, my PK is working fine ... but I don't have the reflexes. The guardsman's gun is already coming, his finger tightening on the trigger.

And at that second, a crackle in my ear. "—this is Reg—come in, over?"

Africa lets out a whoop of joy, clutches his ear. And then, like an ocean liner steering away from an iceberg, he does an about-face.

There's a horrible moment where I think the guardsman with the goatee is going to shoot him anyway. But then the gun drops, ever so slightly.

I almost collapse to the ground. I get as far resting my hands on my knees, shoulders shaking, like I just ran a marathon. Africa's voice, thundering in my ear. "Boss! We are here!"

"—Africa we—where are you?"

By this time, Africa's made his way back over to me. I interrupt his reply to Reggie by punching him very hard in the chest. He's tall enough that I have to stand on tiptoe to do it. He's lucky I didn't decide to go for his balls.

He goggles at me. "Hey, wha—?"

"Don't you ever, ever, *ever* almost get yourself almost shot again. I swear to God . . . "

Then I hug him. Wrap my arms around his torso, and squeeze as hard as I can.

"Not to interrupt or anything," Mia says, pointing at her ear, "but aren't you talking to someone?"

"Oh, yeah. Shit. Right. Reggie, are you there?"

It takes us a while to find them. They're at the edge of the east parking lot, out of the crowds. Annie is carrying Reggie, and that horrible blank expression is still on her face

"Hello!" Africa says, waving the second we spot them.

"They wouldn't listen to me," Reggie says, the moment we get within earshot. "They kicked everyone out of the medical tent – all but the worst of the wounded. It's gone to hell and back in there – we can't even get near the command tent let alone find somebody who'll let us talk to Moira."

I do my best to wade through the flood of her words. "You haven't been able to get hold of Tanner?"

"Not for lack of trying. Apparently being a government employee counts for nothing in modern-day America. Africa, who is this?"

It takes me a second to realise she's referring to Mia.

I take a deep breath. "Reggie, this is Mia. Mia, Reggie. Mia works down at the Meitzen Museum, and Reggie is my boss at China Shop. Mia knows about my PK, by the way, and I'm really sorry but I'm not sorry that I showed her, because she knows about the boy – whose name is Matthew, by the way – and she knows where he's going."

Give Reggie this: she is much better at dealing with a stream of consciousness than I am. She absorbs it all, pauses for a second, then says, "Tell me everything."

By the time we're done, her mouth is set in a thin line. It must be my imagination, but it's gotten quieter outside the stadium, as if everyone out there has suddenly realised what's at stake.

"You're sure?" Reggie asks Mia. "About the ETS zones?"

"Yes. Absolutely."

"And you don't know which zone he'd target."

"We need more information about what the roads are like up there. My guess is, it'll be the one he can most easily access. I mean, if he's just a kid ..."

"All right." Reggie's voice is way too calm. "You need to do that, and quickly. Teagan, Africa. It is *imperative* you get us a way to call Washington."

"What is Tanner gonna do when we tell her?" I ask.

"Moira has more resources than we do, and she'll understand the gravity of the situation. She can get manpower, set up road blocks, get troops to every one of these places if need be."

"This is really happening," Mia says in wonder. "All of it."

What is Tanner doing right now? Knowing her, nothing. If she thinks we're alive, she knows she won't be able to do anything for us that the federal government aren't doing already. She'll be sitting back, waiting for us to make contact as and when we get a chance, unaware that Matthew the world-wrecker is already on his way to do even more damage. If she thinks we're dead ... Well, if she thinks that, she'll still be sitting back and doing nothing.

"Reggie," I say. "Is there any other option here? What if we got you a computer? Could you—?"

She gives a hollow laugh. "With what network, darling?"

"Then we'll take you back to the museum. They might—"

"Might what? They didn't listen to me in there, so they sure as hell won't listen to me at the museum."

"But if you tell them—"

"I'm not running China Shop any more, Teagan. I'm just a crazy lady yelling about the government. No goddamn use to anyone."

"Oh come on. That's bullshit, and you know it. Annie – back me up here." But Annie isn't backing anyone up. Annie is off in her own little world. She's still supporting Reggie, but she's staring at nothing.

"Mia – could you get us a phone?" I ask. "If we go back?"

She bites her lip. But she doesn't have to answer, because I can already see how this is going to go. One of the volunteers shows up with four random people who no one knows, demanding access to a phone. Maybe we get it – maybe I *don't* have to show off my powers to convince people. But it'll take time, which we are rapidly running out of, and there's no guarantee of success. We may as well—

Wait a second.

Wait one goddamn second.

"What about the gas in the ATVs?" Africa is saying. "Is there enough to try?"

"I think so," Mia replies. "They're gonna be pissed when we get back though. Arnie wasn't supposed to—"

"We're not going back," I say.

Africa frowns. "What do you mean, we're not going back? You just asked me to . . . Why you smiling?"

Why am I smiling? I'm smiling because I know exactly who can help us. He's half an hour away, sitting in a parked plane on the tarmac at Van Nuys Airport.

He won't have left, not so soon after that insane landing his pilot pulled off, not when he still thinks he can do some good. He'll be there all right, and that ridiculous private plane of his will have power, some food, a place to finally sleep ... and a working radio. My smile cracks into a full-blown laugh.

Jonas fucking Schmidt.

"What are you laughing at?" Reggie asks pointedly. For some reason, that makes me laugh much harder, turning it into an insane cackle. Now they are all looking at me, even Annie.

"OK." I wipe my face, trying to get myself under control. "Mia, Africa: go get the ATVs. Annie: take Reggie for me. Reggie: start working on your boss voice."

"I'm sorry, what are we doing?" Mia asks.

"You ever been on a private jet?"

" ... Excuse me?"

Reggie, fortunately, is quicker on the uptake. "Teagan, are you sure? Are you *totally* sure? We don't have time to—"

"*Yes*, I'm sure." I almost start cackling again, because it's perfect. It's fucking perfect. Technically, he even owes me a favour – I promised him I wouldn't reveal he still had that list, and I've kept to that promise. "Africa, what are you waiting for? Get the ATVs."

He spreads her hands, gives me a confused look. "Teggan—"

"You know how you were talking about being good at the job? Backing me up? This is it. This is how you do it. I've just figured out how to save the freaking day, and we do *not* have time for you to start in on me with how I never listen to you, or—"

"I can't get the ATVs."

"Can't or won't?" I get in his face. "I don't *believe* this, Africa, of all the times you pick to—"

"You twisted that plastic into the wheels," Mia says. "Remember?"

My finger wavers, drops. " ... and they'll absolutely still be there because it was a genius security measure, am I right? Reggie, Annie, follow me. I'll go unlock our ride."

FORTY-ONE

Teagan

OK, half an hour was a little optimistic. I keep forgetting you can't apply the rules of regular LA traffic to a post-earthquake wasteland.

We can't use the freeways – obviously. We cut up through the Hollywood Hills into Studio City, doing a kind of weird zigzag up the map. Once again, Mia and Africa do the driving. Annie takes Reggie, wedging her between herself and Africa on one vehicle, arms wrapped around Reggie's midsection. I'm on the other ATV with Mia, doing my best to stay conscious. I almost fall asleep *again*, jerking awake a split-second before I tumble off.

This is the part of town where you live if you produce Marvel movies. The houses in the hills are mostly intact, and a few of them even have power, unseen generators clattering away. But there are other dwellings that paid for their precarious perch on the hillsides, and which are now so much kindling in the valleys below.

The Hollywood Sign . . . well, what do you think happened to the Hollywood Sign?

Since we left Dodger Stadium, my certainty about Schmidt's

plane has gotten a little bit shakier. What if he *has* left? What if they made him take off again, sent him somewhere else for . . . reasons? I'm going to end up looking stupid, and then Matthew will probably set off the biggest earthquake in human history. Nothing major.

As we pass through the Valley, I drift into a kind of waking doze, where I have just enough awareness to not fall off the ATV, but I'm not actually paying attention to anything. It's not nearly as much fun as it sounds. It feels like a weird dream, a nightmare I don't known how to wake myself up from.

The next thing I know, we're crossing onto the tarmac at Van Nuys Airport. Guess nobody's too bothered about making us put our shoes through the X-ray machine.

In the darkness, the airport doesn't look any different to when we left. The fire in the terminal building has burnt out, and the control tower still reminds me of a broken tooth. Then again, the time we were last here is a total blur anyway. In that part of the day, we didn't know how bad the damage was – not really. In that part of the day, Paul was still alive.

Africa comes to a stop as we reach the runway, Mia coasting in alongside her. "Where do we go?" he asks. Reggie and Annie both look zoned out, almost unconscious.

I squint into the darkness, trying to find Schmidt's plane. When he dropped me off, we were on the side of the runway. If the terminal building is behind us, then that means . . .

No. He wouldn't just chill by the runway – when he dropped me off, he was still quite a ways from the terminal building. If he wanted to help, like he said, he'd get closer.

Surprisingly, it's Annie who speaks first, pointing towards some glimmering lights at the other end of the runway. "Hangars. Let's try there."

And his plane *is* in one of the hangars. It's in the second one we check. Thank God. Also Buddha, and the Flying Spaghetti Monster, and whoever else happens to be listening. I almost shriek for joy when we see it.

The jet is in the centre of the floor, parked at an angle. I expected it to be surrounded by people, the relief effort, the National Guard, something. I expected to see supplies getting handed out, radio communications set up, orders being barked. What I didn't expect was to see Jonas Schmidt sitting on the steps of his plane, smoking a cigarette and looking bored. The hangar is dark, the only light coming from the interior of the plane.

He glances up as we pull into the hangar, a relieved expression on his face. The relief turns to confusion when he sees who we are, and when he spots me, his eyebrows shoot up. He stands, flicking the cigarette aside, as we come to a stop in front of him. He's wearing the same T-shirt, with the geometric tattoo visible from underneath his right sleeve.

Mia and Africa cut the engines. For a few seconds, nobody says anything. Then I give Schmidt a little wave. "Hi."

"Hello again, Mister Germany," Africa booms.

Schmidt inclines his head, a small smile on his face. "I am guessing you are not the National Guard."

It's funny. All the shit that's happened today, and I've still found myself thinking about him at odd moments. Seeing him now, remembering our conversation on the plane, before the quake hit . . .

Honestly? I thought I'd never see him again. I figured our paths just wouldn't cross. Seeing him here – healthy, *alive*, smoking a cigarette for fuck's sake – makes me more relieved than I can say.

His eyes flick over to the others, and the smile drops from his face. When he looks back to me, his expression is hard. "What do you want?"

Shit. He thinks I'm about to sell him out – that I'm about to ditch the little arrangement we made about the list. He probably thinks the Annie and Africa and the rest are my backup, although given that this also includes Reggie and a very puzzled-looking Mia, he probably thinks I should have chosen more carefully.

"This isn't about before," I say quickly. "Forget that. We don't even care anymore."

He pauses for a moment, weighing my words, then nods. He looks like I feel, haggard and drained. But his eyes land on Africa, and a tired smile flickers on his face. "*Mein Herr.* How are you and your colleague – " he nods to Annie " – enjoying your job at the Transportation Security Administration?"

"Right. You don't know who anybody is." I point to the crew. "That's Africa. Reggie. Annie. Mia, who isn't really part of China Shop but is kind of helping us out . . . "

"A pleasure." He bows his head slightly. "China Shop . . . I assume this is the name of your spy outfit?"

Shit. I don't think I mentioned our outfit's name before. I should slow down.

His gaze lands on Reggie, who is still being carried by Annie. "You are hurt?"

"I'm fine," she says. "I'm a quadriplegic – happened before the earthquake."

"Dude," I say to Schmidt. "Kind of a life or death situation here. Does your plane have power at all?"

He looks at the bright light coming from the open door, then back at me. "Yes."

"You know what I mean. Do you have comms? Radio, sat-phone, anything like that?"

"Again, I believe we have discussed this before. There is limited local radio contact, and a satellite phone."

It takes everything to stop my legs from just collapsing. Finally. Fucking *finally*.

"Perhaps this is a conversation best carried out on the plane." He strides over to Reggie. "May I take you on board?"

"Annie can carry me."

"Please, I insist." To Annie, he says, "You must have been carrying her for some time. Allow me."

"We're fine. *I'm* fine."

"My grandmother occupied a wheelchair for the last decade of her life. I am used to assisting in situations like this."

"I'm not a grandmother," Reggie mutters. But she lets Schmidt scoop her out of Annie's exhausted arms.

"Mikhail!" he shouts. *"Wir brauchen hier Hilfe."*

I'm about to follow him when a sudden thought stops me in my tracks. I grab Mia's arm – she's mid-stride, not expecting it, and as a result nearly falls on her ass.

"He doesn't know," I hiss.

"What?"

"He doesn't know about my ability. The psychokinesis."

"Isn't it telekinesis?"

"No – *psycho*. Trust me, I've been through that before. But look, I don't have time to explain this right now, but he doesn't know. And you *cannot* tell him."

"Uh . . . sure." She looks towards the plane, a strange look dawning on her face. "Wait – Jonas Schmidt?"

"Yep."

"As in, *the* Jonas Schmidt?"

"Again, yep."

"As in, CEO of—?"

"How many other Jonas Schmidts with private planes do you know?"

"Oh my God." She tugs at a strand of hair, as if trying to neaten herself. "I follow him on Twitter! I—"

"Good for you." I jog towards the stairs leading onto the plane, trying to bite down on a sudden burst of jealousy. Mikhail appears in the doorway, blinking in astonishment as he sees me. I flip him a salute.

"Thought you were planning to help out survivors and stuff," I say, as I catch up to Schmidt.

"And we have been waiting to offer it. Our last radio contact with the National Guard was over six hours ago. They said they would be sending groups here. Gerhard and the others have gone to see if they can find any in the immediate area."

"Nobody's come through?"

"*Nein.*" He ducks into the plane's body. "It is of no consequence. We will remain at their disposal here, if we are required." He lowers Reggie into a seat, barking more orders at Mikhail, who starts fetching pillows from around the cabin.

The inside of the plane is a mess. Empty food containers, a lot of beer bottles, a messy stack of what look like first aid kits. Blankets bundled up on the seats, as if Schmidt and company have been catching Zs when they can. From the snoring in the cockpit, it appears the pilot is doing just that. Annie and Africa have entered behind me, and Mia is goggling at the luxurious cabin.

"You get used to it." I say to her, like it's no big thing.

"Thank you," Reggie says, as Mikhail props a pillow under her head. "Herr Schmidt: your satellite phone, please."

Schmidt looks over at me. Again, like he's weighing up whether or not to trust us. Then he nods, spitting a barrage of instructions at Mikhail. In a few moments, the bodyguard is pressing a chunky sat-phone into Reggie's hand. I feel like there should be angelic choirs right now. Maybe Schmidt will let me dick around with the plane's sound system . . .

With Schmidt's help, Reggie manages to get the sat-phone working. A few minutes later, a crackly, monotone voice that reeks of government spook shit says, "Operator."

"Department H-2," Reggie says.

"Clearance?"

"A-409-D77."

"Party?"

"Goldfinch."

Goldfinch? I mouth at Reggie. She ignores me.

Whatever. We did it. We fucking did it. The government can take over, and I can go to sleep for a very, very long time.

"Connecting you," the operator says.

Reggie looks up at Schmidt. "As grateful as I am for your hospitality, I'll need some privacy. What I have to discuss with my commanding officer is some way above top secret."

Schmidt nods. "Of course. I will see to refreshments."

Booze. Yes. Booze good. Then a very comfortable leather seat, and a thick blanket. Those things good too.

"I'll come help," I say.

"That is really not necessary."

"Oh, I don't mind. The less I have to hear the voice of *Goldfinch*, the better. Besides, I want to make sure you aren't hiding any more of that amazing champagne."

Africa and Mia move to follow, but Reggie calls after them. "Mia, you stick around. You may need to tell our boss what you told us."

"Um ... OK? I don't how much help I can—"

"I need you to explain your data. You stay too, Annie."

I look over my shoulder, surprised. Annie is on one of the leather seats, blinking at Reggie in confusion.

"Annie?" Reggie says, pointedly.

Annie nods, then drops her eyes. "Whatever," she murmurs.

The rest of us make our way to the tiny galley at the back of the plane. On the way, Schmidt pulls me aside briefly.

"I have your word this will not change our agreement?" he murmurs.

I come round to face Schmidt, looking him in the eyes, keeping my voice as low as his. "Jonas: I couldn't give the tiniest shit about the list. None of us could. There are way, way bigger things happening right now."

There's a moment where it looks like he wants to ask me about that last bit – about the bigger things. And he *must* want to know, because what could be so major, in the middle of a huge earthquake, for us to specifically track down him and his plane?

But of course, I forgot who I'm dealing with. Schmidt understands how this all works. He understands the world that we – that *I* – live in.

"I have your word?" he says quietly.

"Yes. My word. Nobody touches you, or the list."

Africa gives us a curious look over his shoulder, probably wondering what the hell we're doing. Schmidt straightens up, squeezing my shoulder before continuing down the aisle. Part of me kind of wishes he would have squeezed a little longer.

"Hey," I say to his retreating back.

"*Ja?*"

"My name's not Jay. It's ... it's Teagan."

He nods slowly. "Then I suppose it is a pleasure to meet you, Teagan. Again."

There's a small galley at the back. Schmidt ambles over, then crouches down, rooting around in a low fridge. "It appears we have no more Krug," he says. "Perhaps some bottled beer will suffice. Budweiser?"

I look down at the line of red labels. "You've got a billion-dollar plane and *Budweiser* in your fridge?"

"A man must have his vices."

"You're *German*. I thought you people liked good beer."

"It has never been to my taste."

"In Senegal," Africa says, "We make a beer called 33 Export. It is delicious."

"Ah yes," Schmidt replies. "Although I prefer Bière La Gazelle."

"You know Gazelle?" Africa breaks out in a huge smile. "Although not even people in Senegal drink it any more. It tastes terrible."

I wink at him. "The man likes Bud, dude. What did you expect?"

"We must keep some of this for Reggie and Annie and Mia," Africa says, popping the top off his bottle.

"Plus Mikhail and Gerhard," I say. "Thirsty work, bodyguarding."

"Mikhail is more of a cocktail person," says Schmidt. "He enjoys Apple Martinis, I believe."

"Him? Really?"

"I do not understand it either."

He tilts his bottle towards us. We clink, and drink deep.

Oh my God. Oh sunny Jesus. By the power of Grayskull. You know how it is when you've had a really long day, and you go to a bar, and the first sip of beer is just ... perfect? This is that, times a billion. I couldn't give a shit if it's Bud or Gazelle or fucking armpit juice. It's all I can do not to drain the whole thing in one go.

From the distant sat-phone, Moira Tanner's voice reaches us, her words inaudible. A sudden, bitter anger wells up inside me. How dare she even *think* about firing Reggie? After everything she does for China Shop?

"You were very impressive as a TSA agent," Schmidt is saying to Africa.

"Ah, you know, it was just a game. I distract so Teggan can come on board."

The silence that follows is just a tad awkward. Schmidt scratches his stubble, staring into the distance.

"So what will happen next?" he says.

"What do you mean?"

"After your superior speaks to *her* superior. Will you leave again?"

It's a damn good question. Up until now, I'd been so fixated on getting hold of Tanner that I hadn't thought about what would happen next. It's not like Tanner *needs* us after this. She can send out her special forces teams and her helicopters and tanks and robot death machines and whatever she has tucked away, and stop this kid before he does any more damage.

Stop. There's a word. No point kidding myself, because Tanner won't waste time. Not with something as big as this. She'll kill Matthew, and give his body to the scientists in Waco. The ones who wanted to cut me open.

Another burst of that sickening, bitter anger. They're going to kill a kid. Have a sniper put a bullet in him. And why wouldn't they? He represents a clear and present danger, a proven threat, a boy who has already killed thousands and thousands of people. He's somewhere out there, in the great space between here and Canada, and he's getting ready to set off the biggest quake the world has ever seen. Of course, they're going to kill him. I can't stop it.

At least I won't have to be there. When they pull the trigger.

"I don't know," I say. "We were just supposed to get the word out about ... well, we were supposed to get the word out. Pretty sure we're not important in the greater scheme of things. They'll probably just leave us hanging."

"What is this about, Teagan?" he says quietly.

"Just some shit we gotta take care of."

"In the middle of a disaster zone? What is so important that you would come all the way back to this airport, risk everything, just to get a message to your superiors?"

Oh, I had it all wrong. Of course he'd want to know. He just picked his moment carefully.

Involving Mia was one thing. That was an emergency. Can I risk sharing what's going with Schmidt, when we've already gotten what we want? More than that: Schmidt is powerful. He's a man who could cause a shit-ton of trouble for me, Tanner, China Shop. He might already claim to know about the facility in Waco, but right now he can't prove it exists. If I show him, or let him know about Matthew, that all goes out the window.

"Understand," he says. "I am not making demands. I will not turn you away if you do not share your information – that is not how I operate."

I can't help but think how different this is to what Nic did, a few months ago, when I and the rest of China Shop showed up, asking for help. It took a long time to convince him. He wanted to throw us out of his place, until I revealed my abilities to him.

"I understand that in the world we live in, there must be secrets," Schmidt is saying. "I am merely asking as a professional courtesy."

It's a few moments before I speak again. "You're gonna have to trust me on this one. It's better if you don't know."

A sad smile. "I see. I do hope you remember my willingness to help in the future."

Jesus, even I can read the subtext on that one.

He takes a sip of beer. "So of course, you are welcome to stay here. It is not as if we are attacked by crowds of ravenous people."

"You make it sound like you're waiting for the zombies to show up."

An embarrassed smile. It makes him look a lot younger, wiping the worry lines away. "Sorry, my English. In any case, we have food, and enough water for the time being. We can wait until the *real* rescue gets here. Perhaps, if we can find some more fuel for your quad bikes, you will not mind spreading the word? In a situation like this, there cannot be enough shelters."

"On one condition. I get to sleep first. It's ... pretty rough out there."

"Of course. The seats recline fully, or you are welcome to use my bedroom if you prefer." Another faint smile. "I believe you already know where it is."

"Oh ya?" Africa says, unable to hide his evil grin.

"Fuck off, Idriss." I take a slug of beer, hoping it hides the flush I feel creeping up my cheeks. Schmidt might have meant it as a joke, but there was a split-second where I wanted to ask him to come with me.

The thought is followed by a wave of embarrassment. Who says he'd even be interested? That's a pretty big assumption, and as we all know, to assume makes asses out of u, me and everyone else. Just because he's helping – hell, just because he seems to enjoy my company – doesn't mean he's getting the same vibes I am.

Of course, that doesn't change the fact that it would feel really good to have someone's arms wrapped around me right now. And to have that someone be Jonas Schmidt ...

It can't happen. He doesn't know about my ability, which goes absolutely insane whenever I orgasm – something that initially stopped me being together with Nic, before he knew about what I could do. I'm not going to put Schmidt in

Tanner's firing line any more than he is already. Not after he's helped us out. It's not worth it, no matter what I'm feeling.

Mia walks up. "Your boss wants to talk to you," she says to me.

"Reggie?"

"No, the other. She's ... um, intense."

"That's one way of putting it."

"Is she sending the people?" Africa asks.

"Kind of. It's complicated. You'd better go talk to her."

I raise an eyebrow at Africa. That doesn't sound good.

"Here." I hand Mia my beer. "Drink this. It'll help." I point at Schmidt. "And there'd better be another one for me when I get back. I'm gonna need it."

FORTY-TWO

Teagan

It's only when I get to the back of the plane's cabin that I really start to get nervous. It's because of Annie. I expected to find her slumped over, staring into space, lost in her own private world. Instead, she's sitting up, bright eyes locked on mine. She looks like a sprinter, about to break out the blocks.

"Tanner for you," Reggie says.

I take the phone, wishing more than anything I could be back drinking beers with Mia and Africa and Schmidt. Especially Schmidt.

"What does she need *me* for?" I ask. But Reggie's face gives nothing back.

I lift the heavy sat-phone to my ear. "Teagan here."

The line shaves the top and bottom off Tanner's voice, but it loses none of its menace. "You've been busy, Ms Frost."

"You know what? Moira? I'm sorry, but I don't have the energy for your enigmatic agency operative bullshit right now. It's been a *really* long fucking day."

A while ago, I might have started off a little more polite. After all, I was planning on asking for permission to go to chef school. I needed to make sure Tanner was feeling well-disposed towards me before I asked. Not exactly a priority any more. Not when there's no longer a chef's school to attend.

"I see," she says.

"I bet you do. So, are you gonna catch this kid, or what?"

"I've been speaking with Ms McCormick, and Mia Wong, your volunteer from the Meitzen Museum. I understand the threat."

She makes everything sound so simple. I want to tell her that there is no possible way she could understand, not unless she saw it herself. "Good to know. What are you doing about it?"

"Ms Wong has agreed to speak to my analysts here in Washington. What we're going to do is use her seismic data, and combine it with the data we have here: road conditions, traffic patterns, audio and visual input. As I understand it, there are only a few of these ETS hotspots that this boy might go to – we're going to crunch the data and work out his most likely destination."

"OK. But how is that gonna help find him before he gets there?"

"It's not."

"I'm sorry?

"There's no point. We're stretched thin as it is. I don't have the manpower to set up roadblocks, even *if* we knew what route he was taking."

"You can't just figure it out?"

"Not with the available data. And not without people asking awkward questions."

"So you're just going to let this . . . this monster wander up and down the West Coast? Have you lost your fucking mind?"

"And what would you like me to do, Ms Frost? We are trying to find a single, tiny fish in a very large ocean. This isn't a normal manhunt – we are working with a shortened timescale here. We could spend hours hunting for the child, or we could—"

"Just start looking in vehicles." The cabin swims in front of me, as if the beer has gone right to my head. She can't seriously be suggesting this. She can't. "He's not exactly going to walk there, right? He must have . . . gotten a ride from somewhere, or . . ."

"Is he in a car? A truck? What if he somehow managed to talk his way onto a supply helicopter? Is he taking the Interstate, or sticking to the back roads? Perhaps he stayed in Los Angeles, or even found sea transport. *We don't know.* All we can do is make an informed prediction about where he's going to be. That's much more effective than trying to spread ourselves across an entire coastline. From what Ms Wong says, he'll almost certainly want to be deep into an ETS zone before he triggers Cascadia, which means we have a little bit of room to play with."

An uncomfortable thought surfaces: why is she telling me this? Not to be blunt, but why does she need me at all, right now?

"But you're going to stop him?" I say. "Right?"

"Yes."

"Kill him?"

A long pause. "I trust Ms McCormick. And I've been told what happened to Mr Marino."

And there it is.

"Look," I say slowly. I don't even know how I should phrase this, but I can't let it happen without at least trying to stop it. Not after what happened with Carlos. Not after I couldn't save him. I'm not letting someone else die on my watch. "He's just a kid," I say. "He's bad news, but you can't just kill him."

Annie snaps her head towards me, her eyes narrowing in fury. She has every right to be angry, but I can't just agree to murdering a kid. It's the worst thing I can imagine.

"If I could just talk to him . . ." I say.

"Ms Frost." And now there's something else in Tanner's voice. Something I haven't heard before. Not frustration, or fury. A kind of thin desperation. "We don't have a choice. With the evidence in question, we have to act. I'm not going to risk thousands of lives—"

"But we don't know where he came from! This isn't like Jake. This wasn't one of my parents' mistakes that turned out to have worked after all. *This is something new.* What if there are more kids like him?"

"That's a secondary consideration. Neutralising him is our only job here. Please understand that I don't take decisions like this lightly. I can't afford to."

Oh.

Oh, hell no.

This is why she wanted to talk to me.

It makes me want to throw up the beer I just drank. Either that, or go back to the galley and down the rest as fast as possible.

"You have got to be fucking *kidding me.*"

"If your information is accurate—"

"Do you understand what we've been through today? What we've had to deal with?" I do everything I can not to look at Annie, but it happens anyway.

"I know what you think of me," Tanner is saying. "I am aware you find dealing with me unpleasant, and that you disagree with my methods. I don't care. I am in my current role because I have the capacity to make extremely difficult decisions without regret, or remorse. This is one of them."

She takes a breath, as if steadying herself. "But if that

decision involves taking the life of a child, then I have to do everything in my power to make sure that the person who pulls the trigger is aiming at the *right* child. I will not risk shooting an innocent boy – not for anything, not for one second. Can you understand that, Ms Frost? Whatever you think of me, will you at least believe that I want to do this right?"

"And you want me to . . . what, identify him?"

"You and Ms Cruz, yes. You're the only ones who've seen this boy – well, Ms Wong too, but I believe you and Ms Cruz will suffice. Wong's a civilian, and I would prefer her involvement to be limited."

When I don't respond, she says, "We'll be sending tactical teams to all four locations, but I want you and Ms Cruz at the most likely one. You will both confirm the target. After that, my people will do the rest."

"Why both of us? And why not . . . do video, or something . . . have us confirm from here?"

Silence. And I know exactly what it means. The bitch is debating whether to tell me her reasons, or just order me to do as she says. Well, she can get fucked if she thinks I'll do that without hearing why.

She speaks in a monotone. "It's the logical approach. Having you both there in person ups the chance of you correctly identifying the boy. It eliminates the risk that you'll have to rely on video, especially when communications in some areas are still sketchy."

My mind races to catch up with her. "So why not . . . shit, I don't know, send me to one zone and Annie to another? Aren't we putting all our eggs in one basket here?"

"Not at all. There's no advantage in splitting you up – all it means is that one of you may have to use a video link.

That adds in another element, when I want to reduce them. It gives us the absolute best chance of eyeballing the target. That means both of you, on site, at the most likely location for him to trigger the fault. If it turns out our data was inaccurate, then – and *only* then – will we rely on a visual link with one of the other tactical teams. I'll be monitoring the situation from here, and adjusting tactics accordingly. Am I clear?"

There's something . . . *off* . . . about this situation. Something I can't quite see. You know, beyond the whole killing-the-kid thing. But running back our conversation in our head doesn't help – my brain is a total mess right now, weighed down with exhaustion.

"Do you understand what I'm telling you, Ms Frost?" she says.

I really wish I didn't. I would very much like to get angry, to rage and throws things and tell her she's a giant asshole for even considering this. The problem is, I don't believe it myself. And again, there's the horrible feeling that I'm being used – in a way I can't even begin to figure out.

"I need to hear it, Ms Frost. I want you on board with this."

" . . . Yeah. I understand."

"Are you ready to do what is asked of you?"

"Yes."

"Good. Get some rest, then. We'll contact you as soon as we've narrowed down the boy's likely destination."

There's a click, and the line goes dead.

Annie says, "Yo, Teagan."

" . . . Yeah?"

"You straight?"

Two words. Two simple words. A basic question that I have no idea how to respond to. Because I'm not straight at all – not even close. And yet, how the hell am I supposed to tell Annie that? She was there. She and I both saw what happened to Paul.

And what happened to LA.

"Yeah," I say. "I'm straight."

But I don't meet her eyes.

FORTY-THREE

Teagan

It feels like I've just gotten to sleep when Africa is shaking me awake. At my current level of awareness, it sounds like he's speaking Klingon.

"What?" Jesus. Trying to speak words is like trying to shit diamonds.

"I said, Tanner is sending a chopper. Few minutes."

My eyes go wide. "Wait, how long was I out for? What time is it?"

"Maybe three hours. It is almost dawn now. 5 a.m."

I push myself out of the comfy, reclined seat, nearly knocking Africa over as my feet tangled up in the blanket. "Where are we going? *How long* have I been asleep for?"

He grabs me by the shoulders, steadies me. It's a weirdly intimate gesture.

"Tanner and Mia talk a lot. They know where the boy is going. Up to Washington State."

"*Where* in Washington State? Tell me we can narrow it down. That's sort of important."

"A national park I think."

I stumble to the back of the plane, where Reggie is in

conversation with Mia and Annie. Jonas Schmidt is nowhere to be seen.

"Honey, you look terrible," Reggie says.

"Thanks, I try. What's the plan?"

"Air Force chopper'll be here in twenty. They'll take you up to Pillar Point in San Jose – apparently, the quake didn't hit it too badly. After that, you'll take a plane to Joint Base Lewis-McChord in Washington."

"But where—?"

"Olympic National Park. West of Seattle."

"It makes sense," Mia says, when she sees me about to ask for more. "It's a serious ETS hotspot. And the analyst I talked to was really good – they used all this traffic and road data to work out—"

"But are they *sure*? Wasn't one of the Cascadia hotspots in Northern California too?"

"Unlikely he'd go there," Reggie says. "It's around Mendocino, and everything west of the I5 is out of commission. He'd have to hike for days. But if he stays on the freeway, he can head all the way up to Washington."

"What about Oregon?"

"There's not a lot of pressure in that part of the fault right now," Mia says. "Like, he might be headed there, but it seems more likely he'd go further north."

Normally, sleep clarifies things. It solves problems for you, rewires your brain, makes you see a little clearer. Not this time. "Reggie, all of this ... It feels like we're rolling the dice. If we're not *sure* ..."

"Every bit of data and evidence we have points to this as the most likely outcome," Reggie says patiently. "We're in a much better position than we were before. This is the best option we have, given the circumstances."

"What are you guys gonna do?"

"We were just discussing that. I'm going to stay here, if Herr Schmidt is happy for us to do so. I want to be in reach in case Moira needs me, for whatever reason."

"Africa and I can get back on the ATVs," Mia says. "Try get the word out that there's food and water here."

I really want to think of a reason to say no to all this, because I have no desire to participate in this boy's death. But I can't think of a single one.

"Reggie," I say. "Schmidt . . . He doesn't know. About what I can do, or the kid, or . . . or any of it. I didn't tell him."

She nods, slow and careful. "Well done."

The look on her face says she knows exactly what the consequences of that choice will be. Somewhere down the line, Schmidt might call in the marker.

"I'm gonna use the bathroom," I mutter.

When I come out, a good ten minutes later, Mia is waiting for me. "Can I talk to you for a sec?"

"Sure, what's up?"

"I was just wondering what you were going to do. When this was all over."

It's a surprising question, one that rattles around my hungover brain. "You mean, if this little boy doesn't destroy the whole west coast?"

She blushes. "Well, yeah."

"Dunno. Haven't really thought that far ahead. Go see if my house is still upright, I guess. Maybe have a milkshake. Glass of bourbon. Fall asleep for a few years until it all blows over."

"Because I was thinking," she says, as if I hadn't spoken. "With your ability, you could be doing so much more."

"Yeah, I sort of work for this secret agency where we stop bad guys." I wipe my hands on my pants. "I think I'm doing OK."

"That's not what I mean. Do you have any idea how useful your ability could be in the scientific community? You can help safely transport nuclear material. Work on clean energy. Hold antimatter particles in place so we could study them. And space – Jesus, do you have any idea what it would mean? To be able to lift stuff into orbit, without relying on fuel . . . "

"Don't think I can reach that high." Which is probably why the government scientists who locked me up for six years eventually let Tanner have me. Back then, I had limited range and strength. Even now, when I'm a lot stronger than I used to be, I doubt I'd be all that useful. I *definitely* can't launch things into space.

"Even so, they could get you on the ISS." She sees my confusion. "The International Space Station, I mean. God, imagine if you could move things around *outside* the modules, without having to do a spacewalk! You could fix any problem they had. Maybe even launch probes – you'd need much less energy to do it, if they were already in orbit." Her eyes are shining. "It could change everything, having you involved."

"Thought you were an earthquake person."

She folds her hands by her waist. "Well, yeah . . . but I'm a scientist, first and foremost. And I know for a fact that every lab in the country, no matter what the field, would fall over themselves to have you. You could bring some breakthroughs forward by decades."

All I want to do is open a fucking restaurant.

I don't want to save the world or advance the cause of science or go into space. I just want to cook good food, and have other people it eat it. I want to listen to hip-hop and read books and watch movies and go explore LA.

Maybe that's short-sighted, or unambitious – selfish even – but you know what? I don't give a fuck. Everybody's entitled to fight for their dreams, and that includes me. I didn't ask for my ability, and I am getting sick and tired of being told where and how to use it, and what for.

I don't know how to begin to tell Mia this. There's too much wrapped up in it. It's too complicated, even in my own head. More than that, I just don't have it in me right now to puncture Mia's enthusiasm.

"Can't have breakthroughs if the world is broken," I tell her. "I'm gonna go do that first, then worry about the science. 'K?"

"But you'll think about it?"

"Teagan!" Annie calls from the back of the plane. "Chopper's here in five."

I flash Mia a smile, squeeze past her.

Schmidt and his bodyguards join us on the tarmac outside. The wind has picked up, and I can already hear the chopper coming in, the thick *whup-whup* in the distance. For the thousandth time, I try to think of an excuse not to go. I never thought I'd want to *stay* in Los Angeles in the aftermath of an earthquake. But right now, it seems better than the alternative.

Annie watches the approaching chopper closely. For a second time, I get that feeling of *wrongness*. She seems OK on the outside, alert and ready. But there's a weird look in her eyes.

"Pillar Point first." Someone has found Reggie a wheelchair – a very basic one, old and battered, that looks like it was used by airport staff to transport disabled people to and from the planes. "Then Lewis–McChord. Moira didn't say much about the team meeting you there, but if I know her, they'll be professionals."

"Got it." I bend down to hug her, squeezing tight.

"You'll be fine." She whispers in my ear. "I know you will."

" . . . Yeah." There's a prickling in the back of my sinuses, a thick feeling in my throat. I have to remind myself that she's not going anywhere, that she's safe where she is, surrounded by allies.

"We'll be right here when you get back," she says. "Promise." She lets me go, turning to Annie, talking quietly with her. The chopper is almost here: a big Huey, like something out of a Vietnam movie.

I shake hands with Mia, then turn to Africa.

I've been such an asshole to him, and all he wanted to do was help. To be good at his job. The thoughts freeze me in place, my hands at my sides.

Africa doesn't hesitate. He wraps me in a huge bear hug, squeezing so tight I can hardly breathe. When he lets me go, his eyes are shiny with tears.

There's not a lot else to say. Well, no, there's actually a shit-ton to say, but neither of us want to say it now. I give him another hug. I feel like if there's a chance to sneak a second one in, you should take it. You can never have enough hugs.

"You come back, *yaaw*?" he says into the top of my head.

"Always, dude."

He squeezes, lets me go. Gives me a firm nod. I return it, then look away, because otherwise I might just call the whole thing off.

"Later," I tell the bodyguards. Mikhail gives me a slow nod, his mouth set in a thin line.

And then finally: Jonas.

Standing in the rain, studying me. An unreadable expression on his face.

"Here." He passes me something. A thick fleece top, his company logo on the breast pocket. "In case it is cold where you are going."

I pull it on, almost shuddering with delight. The fleece

blocks the wind completely, even the approaching blowback from the chopper. "Thanks. For everything."

We stand for a moment, looking at each other. I expect it to feel awkward, but it doesn't. Instead, I find myself wondering how it would feel to go back inside the plane, into the bedroom, curl up in his arms.

"I would like to know your story, my friend," he says softly.

"Maybe I'll tell you one day," I reply.

He smiles. "I hope that you will."

And then the chopper is there, the thundering engines blocking out all conversation, and a soldier in dark camouflage is hopping out of the chopper body and hustling Annie and me towards it. I get one last look at the group: Reggie, her hair dancing in the blowback; Africa, still as a statue. Mia, her hands jammed in her pockets, looking uneasy. And Jonas, that small, knowing smile on his face.

The chopper door closes. Someone hands us bulky headsets, helps us put them on. My stomach gives a lurch as we leave the ground, the chopper coasting above the airport, above the city.

Heading for God knows what.

FORTY-FOUR

Teagan

Pillar Point is over three hundred miles away, but the flight feels like it takes minutes. When we arrive, I get only the briefest glimpse of the base itself. We land right on the tarmac next to a plane, and not a swanky private jet, either. This one is big, military, the kind of thing you see dropping bombs over war zones.

The soldiers don't let us linger, hustling us out of the chopper, keeping our heads down under the wash from the rotors. Before I can blink, I'm being led up the ramp at the back of the plane, to a seat along the one wall. It's a metal frame with something pretending to be a cushion bolted on top, and it feels like sitting on an armadillo.

I'm barely seated for half a second before another soldier straps me in, then turns to do the same to Annie. The ramp is going up, the plane's engines starting to rumble, even as a dozen soldiers hustle around the darkened interior, battening the hatches, trimming the mizenmast – whatever the hell happens on planes to get them in the air.

It's weird to think that I'm a part of this machine. Not the plane – the whole military-industrial complex. My boss is someone who can call on this at a moment's notice: this enormous military machine, these soldiers with their weapons and vehicles. I'm an indentured employee of the US government, to use as they see fit. But there's another side to that relationship. If they deem it necessary, if they think I need backup, they will bring the fucking thunder.

Not exactly sure how I feel about that right now.

In what feels like less than a minute, we are wheels up, my stomach lurching as the plane climbs rapidly.

"How long till we get there?" I shout to one of the soldiers.

I only just catch his words over the roar of the engines. "Maybe an hour, hour and a half."

I flash him a thumbs up, even though I'm very much not in a thumbs up mood.

I should sleep. Problem is, I'm way too wired, antsy as hell. The straps holding me to the seat are too tight, and the sick green glow from the chopper's interior lights makes everything look like it's under the ocean.

It occurs to me that I didn't tell Tanner and Reggie everything. I haven't mentioned my little PK tinnitus – the strange sensation I had from back in Watts, and again when we arrived at Dodger Stadium on the ATVs. I still don't know what caused it, or what it means.

Should I have told them? Maybe. But it's not consistent. It's only happened twice, in two vastly different circumstances.

Both times, it was in the aftermath of an earthquake. But it happened *way* after – hours later. There's no link that I can see. It may be connected to the kid, but I have no way of knowing for sure. And the kid definitely wasn't around the first time it happened in Watts.

Hey, I could just let him trigger Cascadia, then sit around and wait to see if my mind goes all wonky. Good idea. Maybe it'll let me take him down. Maybe it's a secret part of my ability, specifically designed to neutralise psychotic, super-powered children.

Yeah, OK, and maybe Ferran Adrià will reopen El Bulli and ask me to be his sous-chef.

Next to me, Annie stares at nothing.

I have to say something. I can't let her do this to herself. Then again: what do I know? Paul's death was a gut-punch for me, something I'll be seeing in my nightmares until the end of time. For Annie, it must be like the end of the world.

What would happen if I lost Nic? Or if he lost me? It wouldn't be like what Annie is going through, that's for sure. Nic and I are complicated – and the last couple of days have only made it worse. Paul and Annie have – *had* – something much simpler. She liked him. He liked her. They both realised it, and decided to be together, and like turned into love. The fact that they came from wildly different backgrounds didn't matter, and they didn't give the tiniest shit what anyone else thought.

It was the simplest, most uncomplicated love there is. You only had to take one look at them together to see it – I mean, I'm no expert on this stuff, but even I could figure that out.

And love like that ... when it's torn apart, there's nothing to fall back on. Annie can't console herself by saying he was a fling, or she was unsure about Paul, or that she'll find someone else. He *mattered* to her, in a way that I'm not sure I matter to Nic – or him to me.

And now there's only one thing she can do. One thing she believes will stop the pain.

We have to go through with this, or a lot of people are going to die. But what if Annie's nightmares become ... something worse? There's the guilt of losing Paul, which is bad enough, but what about the guilt of killing a child?

I know if I asked her this, she'd say she wouldn't feel guilty. That the kid deserves it. But what if she's wrong?

I can't stop it from happening, and I'm not even sure I should. But at the very least, I can try and talk to her. Let her know I'm around.

"Are you OK?" I shout, then immediately wish I hadn't. As conversational openings go, it lacks a certain *je ne sais quoi*.

She touches her ear, shaking her head, irritated. I look around for something to write with – pen, paper, anything. Inspiration: *you have a phone, numbnuts*. I pull it out, noting the time – 06:22. My fingers dance, opening up the email app.

I still haven't come up with a better opening gambit, so I type a simple *You OK?*, tilting the phone so Annie can see

She takes it, types back: *Fine.*

I'm here if you need to talk

Said im fine

Worried about you. Scared we are doing the wrong thing

Now there's real annoyance in her expression. She waves me away, refusing to take the phone. For fuck's sake – why is it so clear in my head, but so hard to actually say? Type? Whatever?

Annie come on . . . pls talk to me

When she read what I've written, she suddenly snatches the phone away, thumbs dancing. *I'm not talking to you about this, I don't give a duck if you want to talk . . . this is happening so just deal with it k???*

She drops the phone in my lap. Then she turns away from me, folding her arms and closing her eyes.

FORTY-FIVE

Matthew

The truck pulls off the interstate just as the sky begins to lighten in the east. Matthew wakes immediately, feeling rather than hearing the pitch of the engine change.

He sits up, blinking. Behind him on the truck's cot, Amber shifts in her sleep.

Jocelyn pulls her rig onto the shoulder, cuts the engine. She lets out a satisfied sigh as she puts the parking brake on, cricking her neck. "Oh hey, little one," she says, eyes meeting his in the rear view mirror. "Sleep OK?"

He tries to stifle a yawn, fails. Then he climbs onto the passenger seat, presses his hands to the window. Outside, the world is still.

"Careful on that glass, son," Jocelyn says, pulling out a pack of cigarettes. "You'll leave handprints."

"What time is it?"

"Oh, about seven? Quarter of?"

In the back, Amber sits up, eyes bleary.

"Are we in Portland already?" Matthew asks.

"With the roads the way they are? Honey, we're barely into Oregon. Only been in the last hour or so that the traffic has cleared a little." She yawns, exposing nicotine-brown teeth.

"So where are we? Exactly?"

"Wolf Creek. Middle of nowhere, off the 5. Don't worry, we won't be here long. Just taking a little break."

She pops the door, climbs out of the cab. She's so broad that she's actually wedged into her seat by the steering wheel, and has to wiggle her way out. Matthew follows. He's thirsty, too, his mouth desert-dry from the truck's AC.

There's just enough dawn light in the sky to see by. They're parked in a deserted rest area, well away from the Interstate. Thick trees surround them on all sides, the ground on their eastern flank sloping upwards. The shadows in the trees are ink-black. Jocelyn leans up against the truck's cab, lit cigarette in hand. They're alone in the rest area, no other vehicles nearby. There's no rain now, but the sky is still thick with clouds.

"Yep." Jocelyn exhales a cloud of smoke, careful to turn her head away from Matthew. "I love mornings like these. Nice and peaceful. Sometimes I just pull off the road and walk for while."

He's about to tell her that they need to go, they don't have time for her to give herself cancer, when he feels it.

An ETS zone.

It's a little tug at the edge of his senses – like the moment before a sunrise, when you know there's a giant ball of fire just below the horizon, but you can't see it yet. There's energy there, huge amounts of energy. It sends delicious prickles down his spine.

He thought they'd pass the one in Oregon completely, but they're right on the edge of it. What if . . . ?

He crouches down, puts his hand flat on the ground. There's

the noise of the truck's door opening and shutting as Amber joins them.

Jocelyn snickers. "Little mucky pup, your son."

"Hey, Matthew, do you want some water?" Amber calls. "I think there's juice in the truck too, if—"

"Matthew?" Jocelyn's brow furrows. "Thought his name was Mikey."

"Sorry, yes. Mikey's like a nickname. Matthew's his actual first name."

"Uh-huh. Anyway, he's a smart one, your boy. Not like my little Katy, my Sally's latest. Two years old and can't even say mama yet! Don't get me wrong, she's cute as a button, but I'm guessing talking isn't something little Mikey or Matthew or whatever had a problem with. Right?"

Matthew ignores them. The stored energy in the ETS zone is there, he can sense it. It's like an itch at a spot he can't quite reach. He has to concentrate. Dig deep. Most probably, he's not going to be able to trigger the fault from here. But oh, if he could . . .

And he can.

He can feel it. It'll take a lot of work, but he can trigger Cascadia from here. It couldn't be better. There's no one around to see him put himself inside the ball of dirt, no people from the government to stop him. They don't even know where he is. And if they did . . . so what? What are they going to do about it?

Wait. There *is* someone around.

Jocelyn is still talking, blabbering on behind him. Matthew stands, looks at her, tilting his head.

The trucker trails off. Suspicion clouds her eyes.

"No," Amber says. "Honey, please, she—"

"Shut up." He barely glances at her.

"No." She's shaking her head, stepping between him and the trucker. Matthew still hasn't told his mother about the ETS zones, or Cascadia, and she's way too stupid to figure it out on her own, but she still knows he wants to do something. "She doesn't have to – look, just let her go. Let her drive away. If we're in the right place . . . " She steals a glance over her shoulder, as if she knows she's said too much.

"Something on your mind?" Jocelyn can't quite stop the fear sneaking in. Around them, the dawn holds its breath.

Despite himself, despite the tug of the ETS zone at his senses, Matthew finds that he's curious. "Why do you care?" he asks his mom.

Amber speaks so fast that the words blur together, almost hyperventilating. "She doesn't matter. She's not important. You can save your energy for when you . . . with the . . . Whatever you want to do next. It makes you tired, right? I know it does."

He cocks his head. Maybe she's not so stupid after all.

Jocelyn stubs out her cigarette, grinding it into the dirt. "I don't know what's going on with you two," she says, pointing at Matthew, unable to keep the tremor out of her voice. "But you best mind your mom, you hear?"

And just like that, he's angry. It fills him up, boiling oil coursing through his veins.

"Don't tell me what to do," he says quietly.

"Baby, no, please—"

Jocelyn narrows her eyes. "You best calm down, boy."

"I said *don't tell me what to do*!"

Dirt erupts from behind Matthew.

He forms it into a big tentacle, like the ones octopuses have – he didn't even know he could do it until he thought about it, and the earth listens to him, like it always does. It becomes a writhing, twisting tendril of dirt, thick as a forearm, its end a churning, swollen ball of rocks and soil.

It shoots upwards, curving over him, and takes Jocelyn in the mouth. She staggers backwards, hands clawing at her face, the dirt forcing its way between her teeth.

"*Stop it!*" Amber screams at her son.

Jocelyn is making the most horrible noise – a thick, grinding sound, like a machine that hasn't been fed oil for a good long time. Her face is turning purple, the thick soil spilling out from her lips, her nostrils. Amber turns away, shaking, begging Matthew to stop. He ignores her, and keeps going. It's Jocelyn's own fault, really. And she would have died from the cigarettes soon anyway.

When it's over, after the rushing hiss of flying dirt subsides, Matthew speaks. His voice is calm again. Almost contemplative.

"It doesn't matter," he says. "We don't really need her. I think I can do it right here. There's enough energy stored up in the fault."

"Please," Amber chokes out. Her face is wet with tears. "Please, don't."

"I definitely felt something," her son says. "When I touched the ground. And I think ... I'm stronger now. It's gotten easier – I don't think I'll be as tired. Amber, come stand next to me. I'll make sure we aren't hurt."

Sobbing, pleading, Amber stumbles over to him. Matthew crouches down a second time, puts his hands flat on the ground.

Concentrates.

FORTY-SIX

Teagan

I haven't left Los Angeles for over two years. That's a condition of my employment-and-or-indentured-servitude with Tanner: I can go wherever I want as long as it's in the Greater Los Angeles area.

It only really hits me that I'm not even in California any more when Annie and I stumble out onto the tarmac at Joint Base Lewis McChord.

I've heard the name before, and I had some idea what it was – a big military installation near Tacoma, in Washington State. Makes it sound so clean, doesn't it? Turns out, military bases are an ants' nest. Huge, chaotic and *loud*. There are vehicles everywhere, trucks rumbling past with jeeps and golf-carts zipping in their wake. Squads of soldiers thunder back and forth, marching in formation. At the far end of the runway, a jet slowly turns in place, the blinking lights on the wings bright and sharp.

It is also really fucking cold, even through the thick fleece Schmidt gave me. And *wet*. And we're not talking the unenthusiastic drizzle we had in LA. The rain is a steady downpour, with big, icy drops splattering the tarmac.

The place stinks of jet fuel. The smell has a weird under-current to it, something almost floral that reminds me of weed smoke. Probably is. If I had to be a soldier in *this* shithole, I'd be constantly high off my face.

Jesus, what time is it? I haven't had a chance to look. It was 6 a.m. when we left Pillar Point, and it's fully daytime now, the sky hidden behind grey clouds. Seven o'clock? Eight? I don't know – my phone's battery has finally died.

"Move," someone barks in my ear. Annie and I are hustled off the plane's ramp, forced to make an abrupt left, heading for a low stack of buildings a few hundred yards away. Cold light glows through the windows, but I'll be more than happy to get out of the rain, and maybe stop being herded everywhere like a damn sheep.

Also get some actual food in me. It's not like our ride had an in-flight meal. One of the soldiers had a bag of jerky he shared with us, and we each got a bottle of stale-tasting water, but that was about it.

The worst? The toilet. It was a hole with chemicals in it, surrounded by a curtain. When I asked to go to the bath-room – which I had to do really loudly – one of the soldiers had to walk me there, and he actually stood outside the entire time, like I was going to steal the toilet seat or something. I wanted to ask him if he and the other guys just let down the ramp in mid-air and took a whiz when the urge arrived, but there's no way he would have heard me.

You know what? Screw this field trip. I'd rather be back in LA, hanging out on Schmidt's private jet. Hell, I'd rather be *anywhere* than here.

Abruptly, the soldier escorting me taps my shoulder, points. Another chopper is coming in for a landing a couple hundred yards away. I hardly have time to register it before we're being hustled over there. A jeep whips past us, drenching me with a thin spray of water. Not that it makes a difference – it's not like I can get any wetter. And as far as I can tell, this new chopper is identical to the one that took us from Van Nuys to Pillar Point.

The soldier at my side grabs my arm, like he's afraid I'm going to run. "*Dude.*" I wrench away. "Fucking *ow*. Get off."

A figure hops out the chopper, ducking low under the backwash from the blades. Full camo fatigues, assault rifle, helmet. I can't see his face yet, but there's something familiar about him, about the way he's running, the set of his shoulders . . .

No.

No. Fucking. Way.

There is no way Tanner would do this to me. There's sadistic, and then there's this.

The soldier comes to a halt a few feet away, an evil grin on his face.

"Hey there, freak show," he yells.

"*Burr?*"

The grin gets wider. "You miss me?"

Annie and I stare at Burr in horror. A situation which I can tell he's enjoying. A lot.

When I got accused of murder last year, Burr was part of the squad Tanner sent to bring me in. He doesn't like me, mostly because I was designed to be more useful in a war zone than him. Actually, *not liking me* doesn't quite get there. He is personally offended by the very fact that I exist, which I think is a little unfair. Most of the time, people have to meet me first before deciding that I'm an asshole.

Fortunately, Burr isn't very bright. Despite he and his squad being briefed on my abilities, the genius forgot he was wearing a wedding ring. I snapped his finger ninety degrees the wrong way. In the ensuing chaos, Carlos kicked him in the face and broke his nose.

He got the better of me in the end. After I finally took down Jake, he caught up to me, tasered me, and was all set to bring me back into the government's clutches. It was only some quick thinking by Nic that stopped it from happening. Burr was, shall we say, not exactly pleased with the outcome.

I was really hoping to never run into him again.

At least it looks like we're on the same side this time, because I very much doubt he and Tanner brought me all the way to Washington State just to off me. I send out a little tendril of PK, into his glove, sneaking in and around his fingers.

"No wedding ring this time," I yell into the wind. "Smart."

If anything, his grin gets wider. Annie looks murderous, and I don't blame her. Before he and his team found me, Burr smacked her and Paul around, trying to get information on my whereabouts.

Burr steps in close, looming over me. He's near enough now that I can hear him just fine, without him having to raise his voice too much. "I'm in command of this operation, freak show."

"Really? After what happened last time?" I widen my eyes. "Oh, I see! You're sleeping with Tanner. Does your wife know?"

But of course, I get why he's in command. Even after the injuries he sustained, he was the one who chased us down – who kept going despite the fact that Carlos smashed his nose to pieces in the escape. He's a tenacious fucker, and that's the kind of thing Tanner appreciates.

He carries on as if I hadn't spoken. "You do what I say, when I say it, we get along just fine."

He gives Annie a cheerful wave, like she's an old friend.

That does it. I step in close, snarling in his ear. "You say one word to her I will snap your fucking neck, you hear me?"

Burr doesn't flinch. "You do anything other than what I tell you to, I will shoot you in the leg and tell your boss you tried to run. You hear *me*?"

Abruptly he claps me on the back, snaps a crisp salute to my escort. "Let's go," he shouts into the wind, gesturing to the chopper.

The door is open, the interior filled with soldiers. I spot the familiar shape of assault rifles, bulbous helmets, just like Burr's. Annie and I look at each other. After a long moment, she gives a very tiny shrug.

We're almost at the chopper, doing a bent-over roadie run, when the ground starts to vibrate underneath us.

At first, I'm convinced it's the vibration from the chopper's engines. But it's too strong, too irregular. I stumble, crashing into Annie, both of us grabbing onto each other. The chopper's skids are rocking slightly, the vibration rumbling through them. On my right, a jeep screeches to a halt.

The horror in Annie's face is echoed on mine, the vibration thrumming up through our soaked shoes. This is it. Cascadia.

We're too late.

FORTY-SEVEN

Teagan

Burr grabs us, hurls us into the chopper. The second we're inside, it lurches off the ground, shooting up like someone kicked it in the ass. I grab hold of the first thing I can find, a chair support, not even bothering to get to a sitting position.

The realisation of what's happening is like a dagger through my chest. Either we didn't get to the Olympic National Park in time, or the kid found somewhere else to trigger the fault.

The inside of the chopper is hot, the air humid and sticky. It makes me feel like I'm under a thick blanket at the height of summer. The stench of fuel is stronger than ever. Every soldier in the chopper is yelling, their words inaudible under the din of the engines. There are hands on my shoulders, pulling me up onto my knees, then helping me into my seat. Annie sits opposite me, craning her neck to see out the window. What was it Mia said? *Full-margin rupture.*

The chopper banks, giving me a good look at the ground. There's still power down there, floodlights bathing the base and its vehicles in a yellow glow. I scan the runway, waiting for what I saw out of Schmidt's plane window, when the first quake hit. Waiting for the firework sparks as power lines let go. For buildings to start tearing themselves apart.

I don't see any of it. The chopper must be banking too fast – I can't get a fix on the ground.

Someone tries to put something on my head. I jerk away, almost cracking my chin on the window. It's one of the soldiers, a man with a neatly trimmed black goatee, holding a thick headset.

Hands shaking, I snatch it away, jamming the cups over my ears and adjusting the stalk mic. It must have some kind of noise-cancelling tech inside it, because the chopper's engines go from a roaring din to a low hum. Immediately, I hear bursts of chatter, distorted by static.

"Four-niner, four-niner, confirm position."

"Not detecting any—"

"—lack of activity on the ground here, confirm your—"

"Somebody tell me what the fuck is going on."

That last one is me. Either nobody hears it, or there's a button I need to push to transmit. I fumble at the cups, fingers hunting for a button or switch that may or may not exist.

"Everybody be cool." Burr's voice is loud and harsh in my ears.

"How bad is it?" Annie appears to have forgotten her hatred of him for the time being, her voice urgent.

Burr holds up a hand. There are more voices on the line, clipped and frantic, and so staticky that I can't make any of them out.

"Shaking's stopped," Burr says.

"They sure, boss?" the soldier next to me says.

"Yeah, copy," Burr replies to another voice on the line. To us, he says, "They're not sure what it was, but it wasn't the big one."

The soldier next to me, the one with the goatee, slumps back into his seat. He reaches across, and grips the hand of another soldier, a hard-looking woman with a wicked scar down her jawline. They grin at each other, wild grins, like we dodged a bullet.

"It might not have hit yet," Annie says.

"Nah," Burr replies. "They're not getting any quake activity from the actual fault. They say they'd be seeing some by now."

For a second there, I thought we were fucked. Truly and completely fucked. This is what someone must feel like after a delay stopped them getting onto a plane that crashed forty minutes after takeoff. Or someone who just, *just* missed being creamed by a speeding car at an intersection. Wide-eyed, blood rushing in my ears, the world around me curiously sharp. A nice little cocktail of adrenaline and dopamine and pure, unfiltered terror.

I finally find what I think is the transmit button, on the underside of the left ear cup. "So what was it? An aftershock from the San Andreas?"

Burr ignores my question. The familiar grin is back on his face. "Everybody, this is the freak show. Freak show, this is everybody. If I'm not available when you make a break for it, they'll be the ones shooting you in the leg. And for the record, they've been briefed on that little thing you do."

The woman with the scar catches my eyes, then rolls her own, which makes me feel a little better.

"We'll be there in a half-hour," Burr says. "Hey, freak show, you wanna do some tricks to keep us entertained? Maybe juggle something?"

"Sure. Toss me your wedding ring. Wait, that's right, you left it home. Why is that, exactly?"

The man next to me snorts, and Burr's smile falters. He looks away, the chopper banking, heading for the horizon.

FORTY-EIGHT

Amber

"Why isn't it working?"

Matthew sends huge, furious columns of dirt exploding into the air, showering him and Amber and the body of Jocelyn with hailstorms of dust and pebbles. He uproots a tree, a big Douglas Fir. Amber screams as it crashes down, the thump somehow more terrifying than what her son is doing. Matthew kicks the fallen tree upwards on a wave of rolling dirt, sends it crunching into the trunk of another, half-ripping the second one from the earth. Roots dangle, dust clouds drifting on the wind.

Amber huddles in a ball by the truck, arms over her head. And as she watches her son, something inside her . . .

Snaps.

She believed she could control him. The belief was like an old, toughened tree branch, bending against a hurricane wind. But it's been bending for too long, and it's finally broken.

She'd told herself no matter what happened, it was on her to find a way to make him better. She couldn't rely on anybody else to do it – she was his mom, and it was her responsibility. Nobody was going to do it for her – she had to step up, take the weight. Every book she'd ever read had said the same thing: nobody can help you, only *you* can help you.

As she watches her son rage, tears trickling down her cheeks, huddled on her knees amid clouds of drifting dust, Amber finally understands.

It's like the discovery of the fault lines woke up something inside him, something more malicious than before. The state trooper he buried was one thing. Even the people killed in the earthquake, and that government agent at the stadium. But the trucker was trying to *help them*. And Matthew ... he just ...

She can't control him. She never could. Maybe she might have been able to, once, but that was a long time ago. It's just like every con she's ever run. They might work, for a while, keep the money flowing in ... but it's not enough, and it'll never *be* enough.

The strangest thing: with the branch broken, with the last part of her stripped away, she feels no guilt. As her son destroys the world around them, all she feels is relief. Through her tears, Amber finds herself smiling.

Matthew drops to his knees again, hands flat on the ground. The look on his face reminds Amber of what she's seen on other children when they play: furious concentration, totally absorbed in drawing a picture or building a Lego castle. He's breathing hard through his nose, forcing air in and out in quick, harsh gusts. Abruptly, he sits, cross-legged. Streaks of dirt cover his face, his fingers black with it.

"There's not enough trapped energy here," he says. His anger has vanished, snuffed out like a candle. Now his tone is thought-ful, considered. "I got ahead of myself." In his young voice, the phrase sounds oddly formal. "And it makes sense. The closer I am, the better chance there is of letting it release. I shoulda thought about it first. That was barely a magnitude 7 quake."

He nods to himself. "Cos with San Andreas, I was right over the fault. But Cascadia's all the way out at sea, so I can only trigger it with an ETS zone. And I'll have to be right in the middle. Or as close as I can get anyway. Amber, I don't think you can drive that truck – it looks complicated. Go find us another car."

Amber doesn't move. She isn't sure if she can.

Matthew says her name again, which means he'll start hurting her soon. She doesn't know what to do about that, and isn't sure she cares. He was going to anyway, no matter what – she'd told Jocelyn to run, tried to save her. She'll be paying for that, so why not just stay huddled here? Why not enjoy a few moments of calm, blissful nothing before the pain starts?

And then the oddest thing happens. Her son climbs into her lap, nuzzling in close. Stunned, Amber finds herself wrapping her arms around him.

"Do you love me?" he asks.

Her mouth falls open. It's a question he's never asked, not once. She's not even sure he's said the word *love* before.

"Do you?"

"Of course I do." It's automatic – but then, what kind of mother doesn't love her son?

"I love you too." He nuzzles closer.

A few minutes later, he says, "Just one more, and then I'm done," he says. "I promise. I don't even think there's any more I *could* do, unless you take me to, like, South America." He giggles. "And then ... and then we can go live somewhere. We can have a house and a car and I'll even go to school and I won't hurt anybody, ever."

"It won't be the last," she tells him through her sobs. "You'll—"

"It will." He looks up at her, his eyes wide, the same blue

as hers. "I swear. Just one more, and I'll never use my power again. I'll be normal."

Incredibly, he smiles. It's the smile of a four-year-old boy, innocent and carefree and friendly. The smile of a boy in the arms of his mother.

It's all a lie. Of course it is. He wants her there to buy food and get them rides and smooth the way. But Amber is no more in control of her response than she is of . . . anything. She hugs him even tighter, lets herself fall into the feeling.

So it's a lie. So what? There's no point in fighting. No point in trying to control who he is. If she really wants to be a mom, a *good* mom, she'll have to take him as far as he needs to go.

Amber kisses her son on the forehead, helps him to his feet. It feels like she's given over control of her body to someone else, and she doesn't mind at all.

"OK," she says. "Tell me where we're going."

FORTY-NINE

Teagan

It's mid-morning by the time we reach the Olympic National Park. The sky is overcast, and it's still raining a little, but at least the sun is up behind the clouds.

All we need to do is identify Matthew. We don't have to go near him – he shouldn't even know we're there. Burr and company haven't actually explained the details of the plan to us yet, but it doesn't really matter. I know how this ends.

My stomach lifts – we're descending, the chopper banking low over the trees. The pilot puts us down in a dirt parking lot – there are big metal trash cans, a picnic table or two, the distant glint of a lake through the trees. We land with a thump, the soldier with the goatee reaching over to pop the door. The chopper interior goes from calm and still to full action in under five seconds, the soldiers hefting packs and weapons, scrambling out the door. We run, hunched over, heading for the picnic tables.

As soon as we're clear, the chopper lifts off, the pilot flashing a quick salute before vanishing over the trees.

"He's not sticking around?" I ask Burr.

"Negative. Don't want to tip our boy off when he arrives."

If he arrives. I shiver. Tanner can talk about logic and intelligence all she wants, but we are still gambling here. Trying to outsmart someone who doesn't think like we do.

The parking lot is adjacent to a campground office. What is, in fact, a campground office: a log cabin with the words WELCOME TO VANCE CREEK CAMPGROUND on a big sign above the door. The building has a huge porch, empty of chairs and tables, and a vacant carport next to it. A thick stack of metal sheets sits propped against the side of the building – I can already feel them with my PK. They're the kind of sheets you'd use for roofing on an outbuilding. Maybe the owners were planning on building a storage locker, and never got around to it.

There's a firewood shelter, like we used to have on our farm in Wyoming, but there's not a lot of wood in it. Hardly surprising – the camping season is long since done, so whoever owns this camp has probably shut up shop and gone somewhere warmer. When we're finished here, I might do the same. I'm thinking an island – one very, very far from any fault lines. An island with a cocktail bar and a hot bartender.

Trees crowd in on all sides, big Douglas Firs. A slim road slopes down from the parking lot, cutting through them. Two hundred yards away, it dog-legs right, vanishing in the shadowy forest.

"OK," Burr shouts. "Let's get to it. Santos, on the perimeter, make sure the neighbours aren't gonna complain. Grayson, De Robillard – pick your nest. Garcia, Okoro – get inside. Start setting up."

"What you gonna do?" says one of the soldiers – the woman with the scar.

He grins. "Catch up on my podcasts, Okoro. Hustle up."

She rolls her eyes again, heading for the building. When she gets there, she crouches, pulling a pick set from her pocket and going to work on the lock. I want to shout to her that I could save her the trouble, but I don't quite know how to phrase it. The other soldiers head for the forest, carrying bags of gear.

Burr turns away from Annie and me, pulling a radio off his belt. "Control, this is Delta One Commanding Officer Kyle Burr. We are on site, awaiting contact. Confirm Deltas Two, Three and Four are in position and timeline is still as discussed, over?"

"Delta One, control, copy that. Mission parameters unchanged – you have a green light. Over."

"Copy, Delta One out." He looks to Annie and me, as if noticing us for the first time.

"Your name is Kyle?" I say.

He ignores me. "OK, ladies. Head on over where Okoro and Garcia went, and I'll just need your passports and credit card details to get you checked in."

"Uh . . . yeah, what exactly is the plan here?" I say.

"Don't worry about it," Burr says, scanning the edge of the forest. "Just do what I tell you, you'll be fine, freak show."

Anger flickers across Annie's face. I get there first. "Number one," I tell Burr. "You call me freak show again, and I will find a way to break every finger I missed last time. Number two: you idiots wouldn't even be here if we hadn't blown the whistle. So let's cut the need-to-know shit."

"Little touchy there," Burr says, still smiling. But he doesn't call me *freak show*, and there's a very slight wariness to his words.

"So? How about it?" says Annie, spreading her arms.

Burr rolls his shoulders. "If this kid wants to get to the main pressure zone or whatever it is, he's gotta hike a little way into the park. Not all that far –" he points at the trees, to the northwest

"– but still a couple of hours. This camp right here is the easiest way in – or at least, the closest entrance to his target area. It lets him cover the majority of the distance by road, which is what we assume he's doing, especially if he has a parent with him."

"If we know what road he's coming in on, why hit him here?"

"Sure, we'll just open fire on a public road. Nobody'll notice."

Ugh. Fine. "What happens when he arrives?"

"Only one approach." Burr nods to the road, curving away behind the trees. "Santos'll give us a heads up if there's anybody coming. Grayson and De Robillard have the area covered from the trees. The three of us will be in the main building, with Garcia and Okoro as a secondary team."

Which is when I understand. This isn't a camp any more.

It's a sniper's alley.

"After both of you positively identify the target," Burr says, yawning. "Okoro executes."

"So, what," says Annie. "You want us to be spotters?"

Burr raises an eyebrow. "You? Please. You don't have the training. No, you and the fr—" He catches my warning look. "You'll both be alongside the team, with your own scopes. You both give a verbal OK, we'll do the rest. If we're wrong, and he hits one of the other locations, then I'll have a video feed running for you to eyeball. Any questions, class?"

Annie says nothing. Neither do I. I'm still trying to process the insanity of this situation. And trying not to think about what happens if he decides to go somewhere *other* than the four spots Tanner picked out.

"Good." Burr nods, eyes back on the forest.

"That wasn't so tough, was it?" I mutter.

His expression hardens, his eyes cold in the dawn light. "Know why I didn't want to tell you? Go on. Take a guess."

"Because you're a giant tool?"

"Cute. No, I didn't tell you cos I wanted to keep things as simple as possible. I wanted you to have exactly one thing in your minds at any one time, so your pretty little heads wouldn't get confused."

"Oh, fuck y—"

"*Because*," he says, talking over me, "the entire success of our operation depends on you positively identifying the target. We get exactly one shot at this, and I am *not* going to let it get screwed up because a couple of civilians got ideas above their station."

"Like what? What is it you think we're going to do?"

"Don't know. That's the thing about having non-military personnel involved: you haven't been trained to think under pressure. We have. So how about you let us do the thinking, and you two just do exactly what you're told?"

"I bet you say that to all the girls."

His eyes are narrow slits.

"I got family in Seattle, " he says slowly. "I've seen what you can do, moving shit all over the place, so I'm ready to believe there's a kid out there who can cause earthquakes. I am not about to let what happened in LA happen over here. Now: you got two options. You can either shut the fuck up and follow my orders, or you can shut the fuck up and follow my orders. Are we clear?"

In the silence that follows, a flock of birds rise up from the distant lake, cawing in the still air.

"Good." He jerks his chin at the camp building. "Get inside."

FIFTY

Teagan

I read somewhere once that the life of a soldier is all about long periods of waiting, followed by short bursts of terror.

I don't know if it's true for all soldiers, or for all missions. If I asked Burr, he'd probably make a bad joke about how I'd never understand it, on account of not being a real soldier boy. But judging by my limited experience of military operations – i.e. this one – it's a hundred per cent accurate.

It's now around 3 p.m. We've been in the camp building for *hours*, doing absolutely zip. The rain outside has stopped, but the air is freezing cold, even inside. I've had nothing to eat but a few rock-hard strips of beef jerky, and I am starting to get mighty antsy.

And with every minute that goes by, every moment without sight of a car or a person at the bottom of the drive, my nervousness ratchets up. The little voice in my head gets louder and louder. *They got it wrong. He's not coming. He's going somewhere else. They got it wrong. He's not coming.*

The inside of the building doubles as a general store, with racks full of camping supplies, sleeping bags, rolled-up foam mattresses and trail mix. There's a wooden counter, a chalkboard behind it covered with an untidy grid detailing trail conditions. An ancient computer – the kind with a monitor that extends back at least a foot – sits on the counter, a keyboard and well-worn mouse on a pad beside it. I got a look at the pad when I came in – it's one of those custom printed jobs, with two grinning little girls on a beach somewhere, both wearing floppy hats. Grandkids, maybe. Everything is covered in dust, the place long since shut up for the winter.

Whoever owns the campground had taken in three or four wooden picnic tables from the front deck, stashing them in a corner. Garcia and Okoro wasted no time in dragging them to the windows and setting them up so they could lie prone on top, looking out.

Okoro's rifle is surprisingly low-tech, with a flimsy grip and a thin barrel that looks as if it would blow away in a stiff breeze. But it's got a no-fucks-given vibe to it – kind of like Okoro herself. Whoever made it didn't give a shit about looking cool. All they wanted to do was make it easy to kill someone.

Garcia cracked the window very slightly, letting the barrel poke out. He and Okoro spent a while debating how to disguise what they called their nest, talking in murmurs. They settled on placing the tables at an angle, so they're exposing as little of themselves as possible while still getting a good line of sight.

Okoro's had her eyes to the scope for hours, Garcia lying alongside her. Neither of them have moved. Not a muscle. Occasionally, Garcia will mutter something to Okoro about wind direction, or temperature, or MOA and DOPE, whatever those are, which Okoro always acknowledges with a barely audible grunt.

At first, I was confused about why they'd need a sniper rifle at such close range – surely their regular assault rifles would be fine? Then again, bullets lose power with distance, so technically Okoro's even more deadly from the building than De Robillard and Grayson in the trees. The only reason they're the primary team and she's secondary is that if they miss, the boy won't know where he's being shot at from. Okoro and Garcia are a backup, nothing more.

I have no idea where De Robillard and Grayson are – no matter how often I've scanned the trees, I can't spot them, which I guess is the idea. Occasionally, one of them – Grayson, I think – will check-in with Burr, a clipped voice on the radio: "Alpha, all clear," or "This is Alpha, nothing yet."

Annie and I have been made to lie prone on one of the tables, too, at the window on the other side of the door. Instead of a sniper rifle, we each have a pair of high-definition binoculars. I personally didn't think we needed them, not this close to the parking lot, but Burr was insistent. When Santos tells us there's movement on the road leading to the camp, Annie and I will train the binoculars on the parking lot. We'll identify Matthew and . . .

And this will all be over.

"Stop fidgeting," Annie murmurs. It's the most she's said in the past four hours. Every time I've tried to talk to her, she's responded in monosyllables, never looking away from the road. All the same, the waiting is starting to get to her – she's getting restless, too, shifting her prone body more and more. She's not like Okoro, who appears to be carved from stone.

I yawn. I can't help it. I may be jittery and on edge, but my body has decided that lying prone equals sleepy time.

Annie flicks an annoyed glance at me. "They'll be here soon. Focus."

I stare into the still morning. There's a bird in the dirt of the parking lot, pecking at something on the ground. "Easy for you to say."

She gives a small sigh, still not looking away from her lenses. Something in the sigh irritates me. "What?"

"Nothing."

"*What?*"

"I said it's nothing. Relax."

"Ladies. Kill the chatter." Burr is lounging in a camp chair behind us, a leg up on his knee. He's set up a hefty-looking laptop on a second chair next to him, with video links to the other three locations.

I flip him a middle finger, hardly even realising I'm doing it. "Annie . . . you know you can talk to me, right? I'm around if you need to—"

She lowers the lenses, fixes me with a dark stare. "Need to what?"

My mouth is a lot drier than it should be. Why oh why did I think that *now* was the time to start in on this? "I just—"

"No, you know what? Shut the fuck up. I'm not actually talking about this now. Not with you."

That stings. "Hey, I was there too."

"I told you, quiet," Burr says.

I ignore him. "I'm literally the only other person who knows what it was like."

It's the wrong thing to say. It is the Olympic gold medalist of wrong things to say. It just popped out of me.

Annie's stare could drill a hole through the moon. "You have no idea," she says slowly.

"I—"

"Get this straight in your thick-ass head. This is not about you. Not everything is about *you*. You don't get to make this about *your* feelings and your story and your bullshit. You want me to tell you it's OK? Give you a fucking hug? I'm not your therapist, Teagan. I'm not Reggie, or your boy

Nic. I don't care. I just want to get this done and go home. That's it."

" . . . I'm sorry." I don't know what else to say.

"Good for you." She puts her eyes back to the lenses.

"Hey!" Burr says. "If you two don't can it, I'm gonna—"

"Dude, no one cares," I tell him, just as Annie says, "How about *you* shut the fuck up, man?"

Garcia snorts.

In the silence that follows, Annie's eyes meet mine. She's definitely still pissed at me . . . but maybe a fraction less than before.

"Just be professional," Burr grumbles. "And you, Garcia – another noise outta you . . . "

I shift position on the bench again, trying to take a little bit of the weight off my stomach. Maybe we can roll out a sleeping bag for padding – I should have looked, ages ago. I'll tell Burr to go find us some. It's not like he's doing anything useful right now . . .

I squeeze my eyes shut. I don't care about sleeping bags. I don't even care how uncomfortable how I am. I care about not murdering a child.

"Annie," I say slowly. "I don't wanna do this. He's a kid."

And of course, I made it about me. It is really hard to stay mad at Annie when she's right.

The same sigh from before, like *I'm* a kid – one who can't possibly understand. "You saw his face, same as I did. He *wanted* to hurt somebody."

"Yeah, but—"

"And are we forgetting that he caused not one but two major earthquakes all by himself? Probably 'bout to cause another one? One that's even worse?" She shakes her head. "We're gonna save lot of people here. A lot of other kids get to survive because we kill this one. Focus on that. Watch the damn road."

"It's just that . . . I feel like everybody's making out that this is simple, and it isn't."

"It is."

"What about his mom? What happens to her after we . . . we shoot him? Do we kill her too? Arrest her? On what charge? Annie, he's, like, *four* . . ."

"Don't make a difference," says Burr.

I look over my shoulder at him. He's still sitting in his camp chair, legs crossed, leaning back. Out the corner of my eye, Okoro and Garcia exchange the briefest glance.

"Thought you wanted quiet," I say.

"Yeah, well, you won't shut the fuck up anyway. And you got me intrigued. Okoro, you were in Helmand, right?"

"Uh-uh." Okoro's mouth hardly moves. "Kandahar."

"What about you, Garcia? You also in Afghanistan?"

"No, sir. Fallujah, though."

"OK. Okoro: little kid with a soccer ball approaches a checkpoint. He's got something bulky under his *shalwar*, and you can't see what it is. What do you do?"

"Has he been ordered to stop? In Pashto?"

"Dari too. He ignores the order."

"Can he see a weapon pointed at him? Are the signs around the checkpoint clear and visible?"

"Yep."

"Shoot him," Okoro says, not even changing her tone.

"Wait – *what*?" I prop myself up on my elbows, staring in horror at Okoro.

The sniper doesn't look away from her scope, just gives the barest shrug of her shoulders.

Behind me, Burr leans back, crosses his ankles. "What

Okoro is trying to say, in her own eloquent way, is that you make the call based on the information you have, and the risks the kid presents."

"He could be deaf! He could have a mental illness! Maybe he didn't hear, or his friends dared him to do it, or—"

"Or he could be carrying twenty pounds of fertiliser and nails."

"That someone *made* him carry."

"That's an assumption. All those things you just said? Assumptions. What we know, for sure, is that you are in a dangerous area known for hostile activity, approached by an unknown civilian with a suspicious bulge in his clothing. That's concrete, verifiable information, and you *have* to act on it."

"No, you don't." I hate how the words come out, all small and irritated.

"With your squad occupying the checkpoint? Plus however many other civilians around? Of course you do."

"Bullshit. You just get off on shooting people who don't speak American."

"Now that's not fair," he drawls, more amused than anything. He's unwrapping a piece of gum, long fingers moving. "I couldn't give a rat's ass what God you pray to, or what colour your skin is. You refuse to eat with your left hand? Who gives a shit?" He smirks at the pun, then grows serious. "But if you are a threat to me, my team or the people I've been ordered to protect, and you don't stop when I tell you to, then you're going down."

He pops the gum in his mouth. "Of course, I don't expect you to understand that. You can try to breed a supersoldier, but you can't give them combat judgement. That only comes through experience."

"This again," I mutter.

"What?" he says, speaking around the gum. "It's the truth."

"You know, for someone who claims he isn't prejudiced, you seem fine with hating on me for who I am."

"I don't hate you. Truly. I just think the whole supersoldier fantasy is bullshit. You can give someone all the physical and mental gifts you like, but the only thing that makes a combat professional is training and experience. That's—"

"Well, yeah. Duh."

He gives me a strange look. "What?"

"*Of course* you need training to make a soldier. I don't know why you think my ability is gonna change that."

"Way I heard it, you were supposed to replace conventional soldiers."

"Oh, you are such a douchetard, Burr."

"Is that even a word?" Garcia says.

I ignore him. "We weren't supposed to *replace conventional soldiers*, you idiot. We were supposed to stop the world needing them in the first place. Did they not brief you on this? You seem to know all these things about me, but did they not actually tell you what me and my brother and sister were made for?"

Garcia's head whips round. "There's more than one of you?"

"Guess that answers that question. There *was* more than one of me. I got the psychokinesis, Chloe got the infrared vision, Adam never needed to sleep. They tried to put all of those things in one person, but it didn't quite work out. The whole point was to create someone who could end a battle before it even started. If you shut down the enemy right at the beginning, you don't need war."

"So someone to replace soldiers," says Burr.

"*No.* It's not the same thing."

"It's literally the same thing."

"It kind of is," Okoro says, not looking up from her scope.

"Whatever. The point is, nobody actually asked *us* what we wanted. Me, my brother and sister. We were just told one day that this was what we were supposed to do, like we didn't have any choice. Well, let me set your feeble little mind at ease, Burr. I'm not going to replace you. My family's dead, and the government don't have the first fucking clue how to produce more of me. You can shoot as many kids in Afghanistan as you want."

"Yeah." Burr spits his gum back into the wrapper. "Doesn't change the fact that there *are* more of you. Like the kid making the earthquakes."

I bite my lip. "Nothing to do with me. I didn't make him. I don't even know where he comes from. And I still have absolutely no intention of getting involved in a war. You know what I'm going to do? I'm gonna go to chef school. I'm gonna learn how to work in a professional kitchen, and then I'm gonna open my own restaurant."

"You're *what*?" Annie says.

"Surprise."

"Tanner—"

"Would never let me, I know, Reggie told me the same thing. That's not actually the point, though. The point is—" I look Burr in the eyes. "The point is I don't want to be a soldier, super or not. I never did. Your job is safe, *Kyle*. Congratulations."

The cabin for silent for a long minute. Outside, the wind has picked up, the leaves of the trees rustling softly. I go back to my binoculars, scanning the road. Willing the tight feeling of worry in my chest to stay where I tell it to.

"What kind of restaurant?" Burr says.

"What do you care?"

"Just curious."

Another few seconds of silence. Then he says, "You like barbecue?"

"Yeah. So?"

"When this is done, go up to Mukilteo. North of Seattle."

"And what, exactly, is in Mukilteo?"

"Barbecue, dumbass. Diamond Knot Brewing. Best outside of Georgia. They got brisket that'll blow your—"

At that moment, his radio crackles. Santos's voice, clipped and hard.

"Delta One, Charlie. Contact."

FIFTY-ONE

Amber

They'd hitched a ride with a family in an SUV – a young couple and their baby daughter, who had taken them as far as Castle Rock, just past the Washington border. Amber had wondered if Matthew might force them to go further, use his power on them. The thought wasn't a worried one – it passed through her with a kind of cold detachment. If he wanted to hurt them, she certainly wouldn't be able to stop him.

But Matthew had let them go with a smile, then turned and asked – not told, *asked* – her to find them another ride.

They'd found an old Corolla in the parking lot of a self-storage unit, on the outskirts of town. Amber had been thinking she could track down a piece of metal to open the door, when Matthew had used a rock to smash the window. Amber had watched the glass shatter, blinking slowly. Then she'd gone to work, opening the door and clambering inside and reaching under the dash, her hands practised and quick.

Get him as far as he needs to go.

The interstate took them into dense forests, and Amber found herself calmed by the huge trees. Matthew had already told her where to go; unlike California, there was still cell

signal in Washington, and he'd wasted no time in pulling
up Google Maps on his iPad – there was still some battery
left, enough for him to spend a few minutes memorising the
directions. Matthew used the rest of it reading up on wilderness survival tips. When Amber had asked him about it, he'd
been uncharacteristically honest. "We might be quite far in
the woods for the next one." His fingers danced across the
iPad's surface. "I know we have supplies, but we should definitely know how to find water and stuff, and which berries
we can eat."

They drove for hours, well into the afternoon. The landscape became more rugged, the forest greener under the
gathering sky. Every leaf seemed to shine with an inner light,
a dark green glow, offset by the deep brown trunks and the
black shadows in the canopy. Amber thought it was the most
beautiful thing she'd ever seen.

Just one more, and I'll never use my power again.

At around three o'clock, they'd turned onto a gravel road,
winding through the dense forest. Less than half an hour
later, Matthew spotted the campground through the trees,
and a moment after that, they rounded a bend and entered the
parking lot. The Corolla's balding tyres crunch over the gravel.

"Doesn't look like there's anyone around," Amber says,
peering at the darkened building. A sign above the doors reads
WELCOME TO VANCE CREEK CAMPGROUND.

The lot is deserted, and Amber doesn't bother parking
straight. She pulls the car over at a diagonal, close to the main
building. She's suddenly aware of how much denser the forest
is here, how tall the trees are. The shadows between them shift
and move in strange, unearthly patterns. The camp building
is silent, deserted. A stack of metal sheets propped against one
side creak in the wind.

A sudden thought occurs. "Matthew, honey ... we don't have any water. For the hike."

He gestures to the main building. "We can get some in there. And if the water's off or whatever, I know how to find some in the forest." He taps the iPad again.

She's about to tell him that the building will be locked, but then, so was the car.

As far as he needs to go.

Matthew pops the door, climbing out of the car.

FIFTY-TWO

Teagan

"Is it him?"

I'm so focused on the approaching car that I don't realise Burr is right next to me until he speaks. I start in surprise, jogging my view through the scope.

The radio crackles – Grayson this time, one of the snipers. "Delta One, Alpha, we see the vehicle too. No clear view of the occupants. Over."

"Can you see inside?" Burr asks us.

"Nothing yet," Annie replies.

Let it not be them. Let be literally anybody else. Let it be the camp owner coming to check up on the place or something, I don't care.

The problem is, that will mean Matthew isn't here. It'll mean he's somewhere else, maybe getting ready to turn Cascadia loose.

The car takes an age to come to a stop. There's a woman driving it, although I can't see her face from here. Someone in the passenger seat, too. A child.

The car parks at an angle, the hood pointing at the far corner of the building. The engine cuts, leaving the camp in silence. Okoro is made of stone. Garcia too. The only sound is Burr's breathing. No – there's my own heart, thundering in my ears.

The passenger door opens. It's on the other side of the car from where I am, so I can't quite see who climbs out. But the driver's side is in full view, and as the door opens, Annie sucks in a very quick breath.

It's her. Amber-Leigh Schenke. No question about it. And there, getting out the car, his face just visible around the edge of the windshield . . .

"Delta One, Alpha. I do not have a clear line to target. He's blocked by the car."

"Don't worry." Okoro's voice is as soft as a snake sliding through grass. "I got him."

"Okoro, hold," Burr says. "Frost, can you see him?" His voice quietly urgent. No jokes now. No *freak show* jabs.

I let a long, shaky breath. A big cloud of white vapour. This is happening. This is really fucking happening.

"Cruz," Burr says to Annie. "What do you see?"

"It's him," Annie replies.

"You're sure?"

"Damn right I'm sure."

Little kid with a soccer ball approaches a checkpoint . . .

"Frost?"

There's no denying it. It's Matthew. His face is seared into my mind. He's standing dead still by the car, almost sniffing the air, gazing around the campground. He glances at the building without interest, looks away.

Four years old. Definitely no older than that. What was I like when I was four? Had I even started reading yet?

There's a coppery taste in my mouth. Bitter. I swear the pounding in my ears has gotten louder. And at the edges of my mind, Carlos, begging me to help him.

"Delta One, Alpha. Still no clear view to target. I can attempt a shot through the car itself, but—"

"Alpha, this is Delta," says Burr. "Stand down. Secondary has the target." To me: "I need an answer. I know you can see him – do we have the right kid?"

Matthew looks in my direction. I don't think he can see me, not really – but his face changes, just a little. A narrowing of the eyes, a tightening of the mouth. The fear jumps, like I've touched an electric wire. Now it's not just Carlos in my head. It's Paul, too, dropping into the earth.

Someone is going to die here. Right now. And it's going to happen because of me.

"*Frost.*"

" . . . Yes."

I don't realise I've spoken aloud at first, not until Burr says, "Again?"

"Yeah. That's him."

Burr doesn't waste time. "Okoro. Green light. Execute."

Okoro exhales very softly and squeezes the trigger.

Inside the cabin, the gunshot sounds like the end of the world.

FIFTY-THREE

Teagan

Okoro is a god-level sniper. No one lies that still and is that focused unless they've had the kind of training to make the shot, no matter what.

Problem is, *no matter what* doesn't take psychokinesis into account.

It doesn't take into account someone reaching over and, in the split-second before you fire, giving your gun barrel the tiniest little tap.

I told myself I wouldn't do it. And I kept thinking that up until the moment I did it. I knew I could end this, right here, right now – this whole fucking nightmare, all of it – just by doing nothing. And until I moved Okoro's aim a fraction of an inch off-centre, that's exactly what I planned to do.

I guess some things are hardwired into me. No matter what the stakes, no matter how important it is, I can't kill a kid.

The bullet blows a huge chunk out of the ground beyond him, setting off a landmine of dirt. He whips his head round, ducks on instinct. His mom is looking everywhere at once, eyes wide. The gunshot echoes through the trees.

"Shit." Okoro's voice is no longer soft. It's husky, ragged. She rips the bolt back, chambering another round.

Oh boy. I may not have made the best decision here.

Matthew's head whips back towards the cabin . . . and looks straight at me. Sees me. I don't why I'm the one he focuses on, but his face twists into the worst expression I've ever seen.

Anger. Hatred. *Rage.*

"Shit!" says Annie.

I yell, *"Everybody down!"*

A huge wave of earth explodes in front of the cabin. That's what it looks like: a wave. Ten feet tall, fifty across, ripping out of the ground with a sound like God clearing his throat. The kid and his mom vanish from view, and then the windows of the camp building explode inward, showering us with dirt and glass.

Annie and I roll off the table. I hit the floor hard, yelping in pain as my shoulder takes the impact. Burr is shouting orders, but I can only just make them out. Grayson's voice over the radio, urgent, heated. "Delta? Do you copy?"

The wave of dirt has become a hurricane, fragments of rock and soil ripping through the air. They're moving so fast that there are rocks embedding themselves in the walls, the smaller ones shattering completely. The racks of trail mix and sleeping bags go to pieces, toppling over, spilling their contents.

Garcia has been knocked right off the table. Okoro, however, is still there. She's hunkered down, gritting her teeth against the storm, her face scratched and bloody. Eye to the scope. I don't hear her, but I see her mouth move. "Got you, motherf—"

Something shoots through the window, and hits her in the head.

It's not a rock, or a chunk of dirt. It's more like a battering ram – one made of soil. But it's twisting and writhing, curving as it punches through the window, like a tentacle. Okoro's head snaps back, and she tumbles off her sniper nest.

I have to fix this. I sent us down this path, so I'm the one who has to find a way off it. And I need to do it before anyone else gets hurt – this whole situation is already deeply fucked.

Annie moves in a leopard crawl to cover, heading for the thick wooden counter, frantically gesturing at me to follow. I ignore her, getting to my knees, then doing a roadie run for the door. It's wide open, blown back off its hinges. My mouth and eyes fill with dust, flecks of dirt and rock shredding my skin. Like fighting through the world's worst sandstorm.

I have no idea where Burr is, what's happened to Okoro or Garcia. I just know that I've got to get out there. Nobody else has to die today.

There's another wave of earth roaring towards the building. It's even bigger than the first one. And here's me, standing in the open doorway, goggling at it like a damn tourist.

I reach out with my PK, trying to pick up something that isn't made of wood – and find the metal sheets. The roofing material, leaning up against the wall of the camp building. I grab one, send it whirling into the storm, put it right in front of me.

Just in time – the second wave hits it so hard that the impact nearly knocks me over. I have to use every ounce of PK energy to keep my little shield in place. More dirt tentacles shoot past, ripping into the wooden walls of the building.

"Wait!" I yell. I may as well be shouting at a thunderstorm. I can't see the kid, can't see anything.

I need a bigger shield. I grab more of the metal roofing, scythe it through the flying dirt, holding it up in front of me. From the sound of it, he's switched from attacking the building with the tentacles to attacking the metal. It bangs and crashes together, like the world's most fucked-up set of cymbals.

I start to walk, pushing forward against the hurricane. Five feet. Ten. I'm at the steps, now – the ones leading down from the porch. As I descend, I move the metal sheets a little, so there's a tiny gap – like a viewing port in a tank. Dirt surges through, the particles forcing their way into my mouth and nose.

But I can see the boy. I can see him!

He's still looking right at me. And now, there's another expression on his face. The anger is there, but so is curiosity. The dirt assault slows. Just a little.

The idea comes out of nowhere, the next stage in my shitty excuse for a plan. I take a deep breath, close my mouth and eyes, and use my PK to spring my shield apart. I send the metal sheets rocketing towards the kid, slice them through the barrage.

I bring the first ones down behind him, slamming them vertically into the dirt, so they stick straight up. I sprint forward, skidding to my knees in front of him. If he's still angry, if I've misjudged his curiosity, then I am fucking dead. There's no question. He'll jam one of those tentacles down my throat.

It doesn't happen. I seize my chance, slamming more of the sheets into the dirt. There are just enough to form a circle around us, a shield of metal, six feet high. It's definitely not a perfect circle, and there are plenty of small gaps, but it'll have to do.

"Woah woah *woah*!" I hold my hands out. "Stop, OK? Just stop."

Burr's team are back on their feet. I know this because I'm sensing a lot of guns being pulled from holsters, Okoro's rifle moving as someone – Garcia maybe – pulls it back into position. Which means that any second now, a hailstorm of gunfire is going to break up our little party. They won't give a shit that I'm in the way, and I don't know if my half-assed circle of roofing material is going to stop them.

I grab the guns out of the hands of whoever is holding them, wrenching them away. "No!" I shout, not knowing if they can hear me. "Just give me a second. I can fix this."

Tell that to Okoro.

I take the thought, bury it good and deep.

We're in a huge crater where the middle of the parking lot used to be. The dirt we're on is all freshly churned-up soil, dark and damp. Rocks that probably haven't seen the sky in decades lie scattered everywhere.

The first sniper team is still out there, maybe with a scope trained on us right now. I send my PK out as far as it'll go, but I can't pick any inorganic objects in the forest. They're out of my range. I have to hope they still don't have a shot. They might be moving to a better position. Which means there isn't long. Maybe no more than a few minutes.

Beyond the wall of metal, there's a panicked voice: female, high-pitched, terrified. "Matthew? Honey? Please don't hurt her! Please—"

"Be cool!" I shout – and yes, I am aware of exactly how dumb it sounds, thanks.

I've pinned the guns inside the building to the ceiling. Someone is trying to tug one of them down. I resist, locking it in place with my mind. "I just wanna talk to him."

"Who the hell are you?" the mom shouts. She's visible past the gaps in the metal wall, trying to push her way through. The car behind her – or the little bits of it I can see, anyway – looks like it just came out of a NASCAR crash.

I ignore her, and turn to face the boy.

He's still pissed off, but curiosity has gotten the better of him. He's staring at me, head cocked.

There's the sound of running feet. My PK picks up a side-arm – one I must have missed – along with zippers and a belt buckle and a metal lighter, all of them moving towards us.

"Frost, stand down!" Burr yells.

I take his gun away, ripping it out of his hands and hurling it into the forest. "Just. Give me. A second!"

"*Frost!*"

"You have powers too," the boy says.

I nod, ignoring the fact that Burr is circling the metal, looking for a wide-enough entrance. There's a scuffling sound, the mom crying out. I ignore that too. "I do."

"You're like me."

"Guess you could say that." I start to get off my knees, then stop. Right now, I'm on his level. I don't want to loom over him. I want us to talk, face to face.

My hammering heart fills my ears. This is only the second person with abilities I've spoken to since they took me out of Wyoming. The first was insane; he attacked me, and I had to kill him to defend myself. Not this time. I'm not going to let it happen. Step one: talk him down. Step two: find out where he came from. How he got his ability.

"I don't remember you from the School," he says. He's wearing little thick-laced sneakers, scuffing the dirt with his right toe.

"What school was that?" I ask.

"The one in New Mexico. There were other people with powers there, but I didn't see you."

Other people with powers.

I knew it.

I fucking knew it.

Someone figured out my parents' research. I don't know who – Tanner, someone else in government, an independent operator – but they did it. And if there are others like Matthew . . .

When you're little, you think the world revolves around you.

If you have abilities, if you're the centre of an enormous hurricane of people and demands and danger, that feels more true than ever. Why wouldn't it? You're special in a way that others can only dream of. Even if I spent my days dreaming about *not* being special, about cooking and owning my restaurant and living a vaguely normal life, I still acted like the rules didn't apply to me.

Jake was one thing. My parents made him same as they made me, even if they didn't realise they'd gotten it right. This boy . . . He's proof that there's a whole lot more.

First things first. Stop him from destroying the world. Stop anyone else from getting hurt, including him. We can figure out the details later.

"I know about Cascadia," I say.

He nods, like this isn't surprising. "You should let me go," he says, raising his eyes to the treeline.

Burr is still trying to restrain Amber. They're struggling, just beyond the metal circle. I do a quick check with my PK; still no guns in play, and I can't feel any from Grayson and De Robillard. *Keep him talking.*

"It's Matthew, right?" I force a smile onto my face. "I'm Teagan. It's nice to meet you."

He turns to look at me again. His gaze makes me feel like a zoo animal. Like he's studying me. Mia was right: this kid is smart. Much smarter than I was at his age. Much smarter than *anybody* was.

"Listen." I lick my lips, tasting dirt. "I know your ability can be scary. I know what it's like."

"It's not scary," he says. "It's fun."

"Fun . . . is a word for it," I say, trying not to let my voice betray me. "But it's also dangerous, if you don't know what you're doing. The quake in LA—"

He looks at me like I've told him the sky is purple. "Of course I know what I'm doing."

The last hope I had that maybe, just maybe, he didn't understand what he'd done fades away.

"Why?" I say. "Why would you . . . ?"

He shrugs.

It's the shrug you'd normally see in a kid who just pinched his sister, or drew on the wall with a magic marker, or stole a cookie from a plate.

I've seen some shit, OK? I have seen my family burn to death. My former best friend impaled, choking on smoke. I know the world can be an ugly, fucked-up place, and I thought I had a good idea of just how fucked up.

But that little shrug? That little *who-me* innocent rise and fall of a shoulder?

It's the most horrifying thing I've ever seen.

"Hey," he says suddenly. "Can you move buildings and stuff?"

" . . . What?"

"Like how strong is your power? What can you *not* move? I'm pretty sure you can't move people, and you can't make the earth fly, like I can."

Let Burr shoot him. Let Garcia. Give them their guns back. Give Alpha a clear shot.

And still, I don't move.

"Matthew," I say, making my voice stern. "If you trigger Cascadia, a lot of people are gonna die. Thousands. Hundreds of thousands. Do you understand that?"

He smiles. The same evil, joyous grin he made when he put Paul under the ground.

"You didn't answer me," he says. "About how much power you have."

"Just ..." I get to my feet. "Just turn around. Go back. I don't want to hurt you."

He looks at me as if pondering a very difficult question. "You can't hurt me," he says. "I can hurt you though." Stated as a simple matter of fact.

"Frost!" Burr is trying to force his way through one of the gaps now, Amber sobbing behind him.

"That's your mom, right?" I say, ignoring Burr. "You think she wants you to hurt people? Cause all those quakes?"

"I don't care what she wants. She's my mother, she's *supposed* to help me. And you still haven't answered my question about your powers."

I hold out a hand. "Matthew ... just—"

He looks right at me. Nods, as if coming to a conclusion. "I don't think I want to talk to you any more."

There's no chance for me to answer.

One second, the ground under my feet is stable. Firm. Then it's just ... gone. It flies outwards, like a pond that someone has thrown a rock into, rippling away from me. I fall, too stunned to even scream.

My brain still expects me to land on my back. When it doesn't happen – when I keep falling – it goes into overdrive. My PK supercharges, grabbing onto everything in a hundred yard radius. Every single inorganic object, inside of an instant.

None of it helps me.

Matthew creates a ten-foot-deep hole within a second, right where I was standing. I hit bottom, teeth clacking together, biting my lip. Blood fills my mouth, and stars fill my head.

There's a frozen moment where I get a glimpse of the kid, the sky above him. And the rising, circular wave of dirt, leaning over the pit.

My PK. If I can just—

The dirt crashes in.

And there's nothing but darkness.

FIFTY-FOUR

Amber

Get the gun.

It's the only thing Amber can think to do. It's a lizard-brain thought, instinctual. She doesn't even try to process what happened the other woman, the one with powers like Matthew's. She doesn't think about who she is, or where she came from. It doesn't matter now.

Get the gun. Not one of the big assault rifles – she wouldn't even know how to use one of those. No, the gun she wants is the soldier's sidearm, the one that the woman with powers threw into the forest. Amber saw where it landed, saw it skid to a halt in the ferns.

It won't help, of course. What's a single pistol going to do against a platoon of soldiers? But it's better than nothing. And maybe, just maybe, she can get Matthew away . . .

The moment the other woman vanishes into the ground – and Amber knew it was going to happen before anybody else did – she moves.

The soldier, the one who tried to stop her getting to her son, still has a hold of her. Arm around her stomach, locking her in place. He's yelling into his earpiece. "All teams, Frost is down. Open fire. Repeat, fire at will!"

As the metal barricades tumble, she rips away from him, twisting out of his grip. There's a moment where she thinks he's going to hold onto her. But a tentacle of moving dirt rips his legs out from under him.

Matthew howls, sends another wave of earth and rocks outwards. As the soldiers find their rifles again, as deafening gunfire splits the trees, Amber runs. Head tucked, bent at the waist, nearly falling as the earth bucks underneath her.

Behind her, the sound is like the end of the world.

She can't see the gun. She had it a second ago, she knows she did. But the air is full of dust, stinging her eyes, clumps of dirt raining down as Matthew attacks the soldiers. Her feet tangle up in something – roots, a rock, it doesn't matter, it sends her sprawling. She skins her palms, the wind knocked out of her by the impact. She lies gasping, chest hitching. Her fingers scrabble at the dirt—

And come down on cold metal.

She doesn't know what kind of gun it is, whether it's a Glock or a Smith & Wesson or a fucking Colt 45. She's not good with guns. She's handled them once or twice, even fired them at a range before, but she's never really cared for them. Not that it matters. Right now, the gun is the only chance she has.

She grabs it, pulls it close to her like a baby, cradling it in both hands.

This is insane. Every bit of it. The soldiers could have shot her, Matthew could have seen her running, thought she was trying to get away. She sobs, trembling as behind her, Matthew and the soldiers tear each other to pieces.

Then again, she knows exactly why she went for the gun.

It opens up another angle. One she didn't have before. Amber has spent so long running cons that the basic principles are in her bones: something she can depend on when the entire world goes to shit. Her choices here were not good. She could run . . . but that would mean leaving Matthew alone, which she would never do, never ever. He'd kill the soldiers, one by one.

A wave of frustrated, burning anger, forcing another sob out of her. Don't these people understand? You can't contain Matthew. He's too powerful. Not even the woman with powers, the other one, could stop him.

But Amber can. She knows she can. She'll get him away, get him into the forest, and then everything will be . . . fine.

Stay here. Just do nothing . . .

But she can't.

Shaking, sobbing, Amber gets to her knees. The gun held in both hands. She remembers what she has to do: check if the gun is loaded, keep her fingers away from the trigger. The noise is . . . She's never heard anything like it. Roaring, spitting gunfire. Shouts from the soldiers. And underneath it all: the crunching, thundering roar of tons of earth moving at her son's command.

Both hands, finger *away* from the trigger guard, dammit, pull back the—

A rock impacts a tree trunk above her head, gouging a huge chunk out of the wood. She ducks, flinching against the rain of sharp fragments. But her hands are moving on their own now: pulling back the slide, looking into the chamber. There's no bullet there, so she pulls back the slide the whole way, lets it go.

It takes every ounce of courage and strength she has to get to her feet. To turn around, and plunge back into that hell. Gun down, finger in the trigger guard. *Get Matthew away from here. Get him where he needs to be.*

FIFTY-FIVE

Teagan

Breathe.

Just breathe.

There is nothing to breathe.

No air, not a single molecule of it. Nothing but darkness. Heavy, stinking darkness.

I can't move – not so much as a fingertip. I'm encased in concrete. My burning chest screams at me to dig, to get myself back into open air, but I can't.

Dirt presses in on all sides. It's warm here. Not hot. Warm. Like infected flesh, like room-temperature soup. It's on my ankles, arms, face, neck. My eyelids, the inside of my nostrils.

I have to scream, or I'm going to go crazy. My mouth opens, just a little. For a second, there's hope – *movement.* Then grimy, grainy soil floods over my teeth and tongue, choking me, forcing its way into my mouth. There's no scream. Just a thin, hissing whimper. I squeeze my lips shut, knowing it'll make it worse, unable to stop it happening.

My PK. I couldn't get Paul out in time, but there's a car directly above me, isn't there? I can just reach up, rip the god-damn doors off, dig myself out. The thought is so intoxicating that it's a good few seconds before I actually do something about it, sending my PK up through the dirt like questing roots . . .

And I can feel something. The car, I think – or parts of it, anyway. But I can't *do* anything. No matter how hard I try, I can't get a grip on the car. I swing my PK around in desperation, feeling out other objects in the world above . . . but I can't even figure out what they are, much less manipulate them. The darkness and the warmth and the suffocation have turned my thoughts to mush.

My heart is going to explode. It's pounding so hard that it'll just pop like a balloon. I want it to. I'm desperate for it to happen. I can't be here, I shouldn't be here, just let me go let me go *let me go*—

Buried alive. The thought gets louder and louder and louder, until it's like someone screaming in my ear. *Buried alive! Buried alive, Teagan! Just like Paul! Not burned or shot but buried! Buried alive!*

I throw out my PK again. This time, I get even less back. My chest is on fire now, glowing red hot. For some reason, that makes me think of Sandra-May Cruz, the bottle of wine Paul brought her. A random memory, my brain scrambling for something familiar to hold onto.

Watts. The towers. The kids playing basketball. Rocko, Sandra-May's dog. The trees next to the towers, blowing in the wind.

There are tears on my face. Nowhere for them to go, so they mix with the soil. No sound now. Dead, leaden silence.

. . . Breathe . . .

The earth, crowding my nose and mouth, whispering at me to let it in . . .

Reggie, on the way to Dodger Stadium: *Sometimes, I forget*

how young you are. We were on the ATV ... No, we weren't on the ATV, we were in the truck. The ATV was after. We pulled into the parking lot. My ears were ringing, for some reason – no, that's wrong too. My *mind* was ringing. I don't know what means.

Nic. All I have to do is picture Nic, and everything will be OK. But his face becomes Jonas Schmidt, smiling, telling me he'd like to know my story. But he's not coming, nobody is coming. I'm going to die, just like Paul did, *buried alive Teagan, not burned or shot but buried!* Nobody can get to me in time.

Nic becomes Carlos, impaled on that steel bar. My chest, burning, burning, on fire, white hot ...

I don't want to think about Carlos. I don't have a choice. The thoughts are coming faster now, rushing on top of one another. I try to make myself think of my favourite things to cook – pho, steak, grilled cheese sandwiches – trying to picture the ingredients, the knife I use, my little kitchen. But I can't hold onto them. The thoughts turn to ash, just like Carlos did. No matter how hard I try, all I can see are the trees in Watts, blowing in the wind.

It's almost over.

FIFTY-SIX

Teagan

Calm now.

There's nothing I can do. Even the burning in my chest is starting to fade. I'm disappearing, melting into the darkness . . .

There's a very small version of me still screaming and raging. Pissed off at all the things she never got to do. All the sex she'll never have, the food she'll never eat, the air she'll never breathe. But she's buried buried buried, deep inside. Soon she'll be gone completely.

More images. Blurring together now. My dad's chilli. My sister's freckles. Tanner's scowl. Running through the forest in Wyoming. Driving through LA on a summer afternoon. Annie's mom in Watts. The trees moving in the wind. The strange tinnitus in my head. The parking lot of Dodger Stadium.

There's something off about those last thoughts. Not that it matters. It's quiet down here. Quiet, and warm.

The trees, moving in the wind . . .

I try to let go of the thought, but it stays. Like a splinter that won't budge, no matter how much you pick at it.

The wind . . .

Except: there was no wind.

The air in Watts was still and quiet. I remember ... I remember how hot it was. How calm. Why would the trees be moving, if there was no wind? And in the Dodger Stadium parking lot, when I got that same tinnitus in my head, wasn't I close to the trees there too? At the edge of the lot?

I know I'm seeing something important. But it's like trying to catch smoke.

Let it go. It doesn't matter.

Trees. Moving. No wind. Moving. No wind. Mov—

Fuck that. It isn't possible.

It's just the last active part of my brain, spitting up random thoughts and connections, not willing to check out yet. It's lying to me. I wasn't the one moving the trees – even *thinking* it feels stupid. I can't. They're organic molecules. They don't listen to me – they never have.

But they were. You've been getting stronger. And maybe, just maybe ...

The tinnitus. The ringing sensation in my mind. I felt it in Watts, and again in the Dodger Stadium parking lot. It was gone so quick I couldn't get a fix on it. What if ... what if I just didn't know what I was looking for?

It takes all the strength I have not to close my eyes and drift away, which is what every cell in my body wants to do.

Soil is organic matter, says the tiny part of me that refuses to die. *The stuff you're buried in? You can move it, dipshit.*

But how?

OK. Stay awake. Just fucking stay awake. Ignore the panic and the lack of air and the darkness and the heat and – *No!* Fucking stay on course, you heinous bitch.

Forget everything on the ground above. It can't help you. Just focus on what's in front of your face. It doesn't have to be big. You don't need to move the whole planet. You just need to move one tiny little piece of it . . .

I bring my PK back. I *make* it do what it's told. I make it sit in front of my face, like a dog. It's the hardest thing I've ever had to do. There's nothing to grab onto, no point of reference. Nothing to hold nothing to think about just Nic and Carlos and Annie and—

FUCK YOU. Focus.

Imagine a tangle of fine hair. A huge, loose, puffy mess. That's what it feels like. Imagine squashing it in your hand. Hardly anything there: almost no resistance.

Almost.

Because as I make my PK energy occupy the space in front of my mouth, I feel something. The barest glimmer of feedback. So brief and fleeting that I'm not even sure it's really there. It might just be my mind playing tricks.

Snatches of old songs keep floating to the top of my mind. Kendrick Lamar and NWA. Nas. De La Soul. Vince Staples and MC Eiht and Yugen Blakrok. Earth Wind & Fire tracks that my dad used to play while he cooked, the classical music my mom liked, Bach and Brahms and Beethoven. Blending into each other. Seconds left, every bit of oxygen almost gone . . .

And then, there it is. Like I had it the whole time. I can *feel* the soil. The individual granules, packed tight.

I wrap myself around them.

And push.

A headache blooms above my eyes, spreading to my temples. Burning, throbbing. But suddenly, there's no dirt against my mouth. There's a space. A little hole in the darkness.

Holy shit. I did it!

I suck in a choking, hasty breath, desperate for oxygen. But of course, I'm underground – the little hole I've created isn't a vacuum, but there's barely any air there.

Barely, however, doesn't mean none. The breath I take fills my mouth with granules of dirt, but it also clears my head – just the tiniest bit.

I need to go further. I need *more*.

I push my PK upwards. One inch at a time. Creating a tiny passage to the surface, moving soil and roots and rocks out of the way, tunnelling through the dirt like an earthworm. I can't move myself through it – I don't have nearly enough power to do that. But I can get through to some more air.

And all the while I'm thinking: *I shouldn't be able to do this. This shouldn't be possible.*

But it is. It's happening. It's really fucking happening.

I try another breath, but there's even less air than the last time. The higher I go, the more energy it takes, and the more worried I get about collapsing the tunnel. If even one chunk of soil decides to slip back, I may not have enough energy left to push it away. I'm down to seconds now, the confused jumble of memories and images getting harder and harder to turn away from.

My chest is going to explode – just rupture, ribs popping outwards. Nobody'll hear it. Nobody but me.

And then—

Then, there's no more soil.

And the tiniest crack of light slips into my prison.

I'm imagining it. I have to be. It's the last little spark from my synapses before they fizzle out for good.

But then I hear them. Voices. Shouting. Distant, muffled . . . but there.

I suck in a breath.

And oxygen floods my lungs. Incredible, amazing, wonderful oxygen.

Fuck paella. Fuck ice cream. Fuck pho and pizza and coffee and Korean BBQ and every good thing humans have invented to put in their mouths. I've never known anything to taste as sweet as air does, right now.

The burning in my chest starts to fade. The flood of thoughts slows to a trickle. The noises up top have started to resolve themselves now. It sounds like some *major* shit is going down, and I am *done* being stuck in here.

So I go to work.

I still can't move. The earth locks me in place. But I can breathe now, which means I can think. Thinking means PK. Marathon runners talk about a second wind, and it looks like psychokinetics have something similar. I've still got a tenuous grip on the soil, but I've got a much stronger grip on the inorganic objects over my head. Like, for example, the doors of the wrecked car that Matthew and his mom arrived in.

I rip them off. It doesn't take much – the hinges are fucked anyway. This trick didn't work with Paul, but it's going to work now. It has to.

Just like on Schmidt's plane, I don't have to see the doors to know their position in space. They are twisted and bent from Matthew's little temper tantrum, a good shape for digging.

I plunge them into the earth over my head, making sure to keep the little air passage open as I do so. I can't see what I'm doing, not from where I am, which means I have to go by feel. It's like trying to navigate an unfamiliar room in the dark. I grit my teeth, focusing hard, scooping the earth away above my head. Faster now. Faster. More light floods into my prison, light and noise.

I'm still alive, assholes. Get ready.

Closer now. Closer. I start laughing – insane, hysterical laughter, still gulping down the air.

And then it all goes to shit.

One of my scooping motions dislodges a thick knot of earth and roots. It collapses into my air hole, shutting off the light, choking off the air. I'm still hyperventilating, and I get another mouthful of dirt.

The sudden lack of oxygen startles me, knocks me off my game. I lose track of where the door scoops are, my PK fuzzing. In a sudden panic, I put my energy into shifting the collapsed dirt. But it's like I've been knocked back to square one, and the fear that comes is worse than before. Another fire lights in my chest, glowing, threatening to spread.

And no matter what I do, the earth won't budge. I've fallen right back into the panic. Just feet from open air, feet from safety, I've been dragged into hell.

I dig deep into my own mind. Reach to the very bottom of myself, and ask for one last push of energy.

Nothing.

FIFTY-SEVEN

Teagan

Hands.

Reaching down through the dirt, fingers brushing my face.

There's a moment where I'm dead certain I'm imagining it. But I'm not. Someone is up there, and they're digging. They're scrabbling at the dirt, letting in more bursts of light, nails scratching at my skin.

The light is followed by a trickle of air. This time, when I ask my mind for a little more, it gives it to me.

I find the wrecked doors, grab hold of them again, start to dig. More light floods in, the trees, the grey sky.

Annie.

Teeth bared, sweat pouring off her face, wrenching the dirt away.

In what seems like five seconds, my arms are free. I lever myself out of the hole, gasping, retching. Annie helps, getting her hands under my arms, grunting as she pulls.

We're in a crater, maybe four feet deep. The world is too bright, too intense. I'm sucking in great gulps of air between hacking coughs, collapsing into Annie's arms. Something bumps up against my leg – one of the car doors, I think. Out of sight, beyond the hole, Matthew is still losing his shit – huge *whump*s of shifting earth, cut through with bursts of gunfire. I can't have been under that long – a few minutes, maybe, no more, although it felt like ten years.

And I still can't breathe, because Annie is hugging me too tightly.

"I thought—" she starts. Then a sob wrenches its way out of her, a horrible, guttural groan. She's shaking too, both of us on our knees in the dirt.

She pulls away, gripping me by the shoulders, as if she wants to check if I'm still in one piece. She starts speaking, hardly stopping to breathe, the words flooding out of her. "I wanted to take out the kid but then I saw what he did to you, and I managed to get out and I couldn't let you get hurt, not like Paul, not again, not someone else, and I didn't know if I was gonna get here in time, but . . . And he's still out there fighting Burr and the rest of them . . . I wanted to help but you were down there and I couldn't . . . I couldn't . . . "

She breaks off, wrapping me in another bear hug. "You're OK," she says, like she's trying to reassure herself. "You're OK."

I am.

I'm alive.

It is half past three on a chilly, damp June day in the great state of Washington and ladies and gentlemen, *Teagan Frost is alive.*

Also dirty, stinking and mightily pissed off.

I winkle my way out of Annie's bonecrusher grip, resting my forehead on hers. "Didn't know you cared."

She makes a noise that might be a laugh.

I'm only half-joking though. She and I have had such an insane relationship. We've argued, fought, said horrible things to each other. I have literally thrown her off a building. We'd finally reached a kind of stalemate, but if I had to pick which option she'd choose between killing Matthew – the little shit who took Paul's life – and saving me ...

Annie was so laser-focused on taking out the kid. For her to choose me must have taken everything she had.

And I would've done the same for her. In a second.

I don't think I realised that until right now.

I reach down to shift the car door, still bumping up against my leg, and find it's not a door. It's an assault rifle. Annie must have brought it, and seeing it brings everything rushing back. Well, that, and the absolutely insane sounds coming from over our heads.

"Come on," I say, getting unsteadily to my feet. "World isn't gonna save itself."

We poke our heads over the rim of the crater, and my mouth falls open.

You know World War One movies? Dudes running through no man's land in the middle of a battle, with the drifting dirt and exploding mortars and total chaos? This is what it must have been like. The ground looks as if it's been shelled – huge craters, exposed roots, bouncing chunks of rock and soil. The car Matthew and his mom arrived in is almost unrecognisable. The camp building has been torn to pieces. Exposed beams, splintered walls, windows ringed with jagged shards of glass.

And off to one side of the wrecked building, maybe fifty yards away, where the woodshed used to be ...

I'm seeing things. I was looking for a little boy, but he isn't there. In his place is a giant dirt monster. A huge, shifting blob of earth and rocks and soil, maybe ten feet high. A blob that hurls boulders in all directions, surrounded by tentacles of dirt that move like liquid.

The air around us is a mess of hurtling rocks and clods of

soil, bouncing off each other. From where I am, I can see through to Burr. He's taken cover behind one of the few still-standing sections of building wall, popping up to fire at the dirt blob. There's a second where I don't understand what Matthew is doing – the dirt can't stop gunfire, surely? Then again, a whirling storm of soil and rock is probably going to deflect a bullet, and it'll make it impossible to get a clear shot.

Burr has to duck as a dirt tentacle slashes at his head, spattering against a pillar. The only reason Matthew hasn't buried him yet is because he's standing on floorboards, although I wouldn't put it past the kid to just collapse the house from underneath. The noise is like nothing I've ever heard before.

The sight of Burr clears my mind, helps make sense of what I'm seeing. It's not a dirt monster – it's Matthew, shielding himself from gunfire behind a shifting wall of earth. He's being hit on all sides – the snipers are firing from the forest, big booms cutting through the noise. Someone else – Garcia? – hunkers down behind the car, rifle in hand.

Annie pulls me back down right before a rock the size of a basketball brains me. It punches into the rim of the crater, a foot from my head, sending up a choking shower of dirt.

"Hey, Teagan?" Annie sounds like she's gotten a little bit of her mojo back. "You still wanna try talking this kid out of it?"

"I think we're past that point, don't you?"

She picks up the rifle, glances down at it, as if reminding herself how it works. "We keep hitting him. He's gotta give us an opening sooner or—"

"Better idea." Annie isn't the only one getting her mojo back. I thought I'd be out of gas by now. But I guess I had a third wind stashed behind the second one; my brain is so stoked to be alive that it's given me a *ginormous* shot of adrenaline. I can't do any real damage with the soil – I could hardly move it enough to give me an air hole. But I've still got my regular PK, and right now it's got a tenuous grip on the objects around me. Two bent and twisted car doors, and six metal roofing sheets, half-buried in the earth.

I get hold of one of the doors, flip it upright with my mind. "Magic carpet ride," I murmur.

"*What?*"

"We'll never be able to shoot our way through." I clamber onto the door, down on one knee, gripping the edges. "I'll distract him. Get you guys a clear shot."

"That's—"

"Get to Burr. Tell him the freak show's got a plan."

"Teagan – wait, Teagan!"

Putting all my energy into it, I lift the car door upwards – just like I did at Van Nuys Airport to get Paul and me onto the hangar roof. *This one's for you, Jasmine.*

"That's not a plan!" Annie yells at me.

But I'm already in the air.

FIFTY-EIGHT

Teagan

I don't get to look cool very often.

I don't have a sweet superhero costume. No catchphrase, or theme song. If I don't get coffee in the morning, I can barely form coherent sentences.

But rising up out of the earth like an avenging angel, back from the dead, with seven huge pieces of metal whirling into formation behind me?

If I do say so myself, that is *fucking* cool.

Of course, it turns out flying into what amounts to a giant sandstorm makes you cough and choke and splutter, and kind of ruins the image. It's hard to look cool when you have to hold your arm over your mouth and nose, eyes streaming.

I have no idea how long my little dose of good-to-be-alive adrenaline is going to last, so I'd better make this count. I squint against the dust, using my PK to keep my platform balanced underneath me.

Twenty feet up, I get an aerial view of the battlefield. It doesn't look any prettier from up here: a pockmarked, crater-filled hellscape. Burr, down at my eleven o'clock, crouched behind a wall. Okoro, at my three. And — yep, Garcia, sprinting over to Burr in a roadie run, only just avoiding a huge, falling pillar of dirt.

And of course: Matthew. A tiny figure surrounded by giant walls of earth, just visible through the dust. He's turned away from me – I can't see his face, but from his clenched fists, I'd say he's good and angry.

"And here we go," I murmur. Annie was wrong – I *do* have a plan. I probably should've explained it better before I left her, but it'll totally work.

I focus my PK, hold on tight and head for Matthew. Twenty feet off the ground, trailing a spinning propeller of metal.

Right then, another figure pops into my field of view. Matthew's mom: running out of the forest, head down ... holding a gun. Where the fuck did she get that? And what the hell is she planning to do, sneak up on Burr? She's going to get herself killed. Burr's an asshole but he's an asshole with special forces training, and I'm guessing he's not in a forgiving mood right now.

"How about *nope*?" I yell, sending the biggest metal sheet I've got whirling through the air towards her.

I slow it down at the last second, tilt it back. Instead of hitting her square-on, it scoops her up, like a wave lifting an unaware swimmer. I'm careful to take her weight, not just throw her, lifting her a good fifteen feet through the air and dumping her onto the ground on the other side of the wrecked camp building. She'll be bruised to hell, maybe a few broken ribs, but that's a lot better than a bullet to the face. Or a boulder – somehow, I don't think her son gives much of a shit who he's aiming at right now.

Speaking of her son ...

He hasn't seen me yet, which is good. Annie's wrong about getting an opening sooner or later – we're not going to kill this kid using luck. But if I can get all his attention, then maybe somebody gets a shot.

And after all: if you're going after someone who can bury you alive, it makes sense to attack from the air.

I rocket towards Matthew, still down on one knee, holding onto my wobbly platform for dear life. A wave of fatigue washes over me, and I have to grit my teeth to force it back. Dodging death might have gotten me an adrenaline boost, but it's not going to last long. *Make this count.*

And as if he senses I'm close, Matthew whirls round. Stares right at me.

Some kids have tempter tantrums. Others completely and totally lose their shit. Matthew is way past that. I don't think I've seen an uglier expression on anybody, adult or child, in my whole life.

But as his piggy little eyes settle on me, something else crosses his face.

Surprise.

For a second, his attacks on Burr and the others stop. A dirt tentacle dissolves, dropping to ground with a huge *whump*. A rock, freed of Matthew's mental control, impacts one of the shattered building walls.

"Up here, dickhead!" I yell.

Not exactly my strongest opening – especially since he's already noticed me. I make up for it by sending two metal sheets whizzing through the air towards him.

Give him this: he reacts fast. Two pillars of dirt erupt from in front of him and bat the sheets aside. I have to focus hard to keep hold of the metal, bring them back under control. I move sideways, circling him twenty feet off the deck, doing everything I can to keep his attention.

No point trying to control the earth myself. Just because

you've figured out you're good at shooting three-pointers does *not* mean you're ready for the NBA. I'll stick to what I know here.

My platform, the car door, dips a little. It nearly topples me right off. I bring it back, *willing* it to stay in place. But I'm losing energy fast, much quicker than I should be.

"Yeah, come on!" I yell at him. At this point, I'm not exactly thinking too hard about what I'm saying, as long as it keeps his attention on me. "Do you know how goddamn long that paella took? My plan for Nic was totally working and you *ruined* it and you don't even know what I'm talking about because you weren't there, so how about you stop before I completely lose my shit? Huh? How about it?"

He howls – a little boy howl, nearly a scream. Two rocks, each one the size of a microwave, explode out of the ground. They fly through the air like they weigh no more than softballs, both aimed straight at me.

I swing two metal sheets around to my front just in time, blocking the rocks. There's a thudding bang as they hit. The mental feedback as I take the impacts nearly makes me black out – I don't actually know how I stay upright. No sooner do I deal with the rocks than a lance of twisting dirt snakes towards me. Then a second. I dodge around them both, slicing them in half with two more metal sheets. One of them reforms – literally just comes together again, undamaged – and whips at my head. I only just manage another dodge.

And all the while I'm circling, circling. I don't know a lot about kids, but I do know this: it's hard for them to pay attention to more than one thing at a time. I don't care how smart they are. If I can just keep him focused on me ...

Hey, Teagan, do anything fun on your trip to Washington? Oh, you know, just fought a giant dirt monster while riding a hoverboard. Nothing special.

From where I am right now, I can't see any of the others –
no Burr, no Annie, no nobody.

At that moment, Matthew attacks with everything he has.
He's fast – scary fast. Rocks, big and small, hurtle through the
air towards me. *Three* dirt tentacles, right on their heels. I drop,
stomach lurching as my platform moves downwards, only just
avoiding getting brained. It takes every ounce of control I have
to block the rest, swinging my metal sheets around in front of
me and over my head. I've only got four left, three sheets and
the car door – I lost track of the others at some point, missed
them in the chaos.

Christ on a bicycle, isn't this kid tired yet? Or is he like me,
running on adrenaline?

I'm almost hyperventilating, exhaustion pulling at me. It
slows my reactions, winkles soft fingers into my grip on the
metal sheets. I force it back, dodging and ducking and weaving
in and out of the trees.

That turns out to a mega-shitty idea, because the next thing
Matthew does is collapse a tree on top of me.

There's an enormous, crunching, *ripping* sound, and then
the tree next to me fills my vision. I spin sideways, out of
control now. Branches scrape my at my arm, leaves whipping
at my face. I only just manage to not get crushed, but the tree
takes out two of my metal sheets, burying them as it collapses
to the forest floor.

And *still* no sign of Annie. She was right – this isn't a plan,
this is suicide. I am very quickly running out of juice, and it
feels like I'm trying to fight the entire planet. For the second
time today, death – the real deal, good night, game over –
claws at my mind.

But this time . . .

This time, I smile back. The adrenaline and the exhaustion

and the sheer insanity of what I'm doing all come together, ripping an cackling laugh from me, even as I try to stay afloat.

I grab hold of my car door with both hands, launch it forward. Just as the kid launches another dirt tentacle at me, I duck under it and throw myself right at him, screaming out of the sky like a meteor.

For a second, there's nothing between us. No flying rocks, no pillars of dirt. Just him and me, separated by thirty feet of air.

He reacts quickly, sending a wave of dirt that looks like the one that he threw at the camp building, after Okoro missed. I turn upwards, flying over it, letting it crash to the ground beneath me.

And right then, I see Annie.

Annie *and* Burr.

They're both sprinting as fast as they can across the broken ground, hunting for a gap in Matthew's shield. I want to yell at them that it's too soon, they're never going to get past it—

Except they are. The spinning cylinder of soil and rock that Matthew has surrounded himself with is getting patchy. It's much less solid than before. Even now Burr has his gun up, as if hunting for a clear shot. As long as I keep Matthew focused on me, he might just get it.

Of course, I may actually die before that happens. Matthew won't even have to kill me. I'll just drop dead from exhaustion.

"Come on!" I roar at Matthew, dodging yet another rock. "You want a piece of this? I've taken shits bigger than you, you little brat!"

It's working. He gives one of those little-boy-howls, sending another wave of soil lurching towards me.

Behind him, Annie gets a clear shot.

I actually see it happen. The gap appearing in the wall,

right in front of her. She drops to one knee, raises her rifle, takes aim.

And Matthew . . .

I don't know whether he hears something, or just senses it. But he spins round, eyes wide in surprise. Before Annie can take the shot, he closes the gap, shielding himself with another wall of earth that appears as if from nowhere.

Burr yells something inaudible, and both he and Annie open up. Yellow muzzle flash spits from their guns as they fire in controlled bursts. I don't know if they've seen a gap I've missed, or if they're trying to create one through sheer volume of fire, and I don't care.

I dive back in, one metal sheet left – I don't even know where the others have gone. I hurl it at Matthew's head, spinning it through the air. He knocks it aside, and I bring it right back, refusing to give, dodging left and right because through some goddamn miracle I am still riding the car door. We hit the kid on two fronts, forcing him to focus on the wall and on me.

He drops to his knees, face still twisted in that horrible grimace. It's working. It's working! Any second now, he's going to make a mistake. He'll let a gap open up in the wall, or my lone remaining metal sheet is going to get past his defences.

Through the flying dirt, his eyes meet mine.

What I see in them isn't defeat. It's not even anger. It's triumph. It's the look of a kid who just had a really cool idea.

And before I can blink, the dirt around us just . . . vaporises.

Every chunk of soil, every tentacle, every part of Matthew's wall. It fragments into tiny particles, becoming a huge, billowing cloud of choking dust. Matthew vanishes. Annie and Burr vanish. I can't see a goddamn thing.

Because of course, Matthew is smart. He might just be a kid, but he's way smarter than normal.

What do you do if you're going to lose a fight? You make it impossible for your attackers to find you.

I don't have time to appreciate the tactical genius, because right then, I lose my balance on my little hoverboard. Coughing, choking, eyes squeezed shut against the stinging dust—

I fall.

FIFTY-NINE

Matthew

They think they're smarter than him.

That's what really makes him mad. They thought he was just going to fight and fight and fight, and not see what they were doing. Like he wouldn't realise they'd try sneak up on him.

Nobody's smarter than me. Nobody.

He was smart enough to make the dust cloud when he saw what they were trying to do. They probably think he's still there, instead of where he really is: in the forest, heading away from the camp. He stays low, ducking under ferns and weaving through the trees. They would have probably just kept sending people until he got too tired to fight – and it would have been smart, because he's tired now, really tired. It would be awesome just to lie down and sleep, but he can't. Not yet ... not when he has a chance to set off the biggest earthquake the world has ever seen.

They're not going to be ready for it, not even the lady who can do the same stuff he can. The thought makes Matthew angrier still – she shouldn't have been able to get out the ground. She should have stayed *buried*.

If she's still alive after Cascadia, he'll make her *really* sorry.

He skids down a short slope on his ass, scraping his hands on a tree branch as he pulls himself up. He stops for a second at the bottom, listens for anyone coming after him. There's plenty of noise, all right – mostly shouting, and all of it behind him. He's a little too far away to have any real control over the dust cloud he made, but that's OK. Dust hangs in the air for a while, and by the time they realise he isn't there any more, he'll be long gone.

A smirk worms its way onto his face. He should have buried *himself*. He could've put himself right under the ground with just the tip of his nose poking out. It would have been tricky, all right. He would have had to position the earth *just* right, so he could breathe, and so they wouldn't see him. But it would have been awesome. Completely hidden, while they ran around trying to find him.

The ground is mostly flat now – a small clearing in the trees, with a steep drop maybe twenty feet away, on his left. He needs to get as far into the forest as he can. They won't have read as much as he has, that's for sure – they won't know the right way to go. The whole way here, he was on the iPad, reading up on the Olympic National Park, looking at YouTube videos from hikers, browsing survival tips in case they got lost. The ETS zone is to the north-west of the camp, so all he has to do is keep heading in the right direction. He'll sense it, sooner or later . . .

A rustle from above him, high in the trees. He spins round, craning his neck, expecting to see the woman who could fly. If anybody could figure out where he's gone, it'd be her – she was high up, so she might have seen him pop out the cloud of dust and go behind what was left of the building. But there's nobody – it's just the wind, hissing through the leaves.

Matthew turns – and Amber is standing right there.

She looks awful. Haggard, exhausted, dirty. But she can help him – she can go find food and water for them, while he figures out the best spot to tap into the ETS zone.

"It's this way," he says, pointing at a gap in the trees.

Amber turns, very slightly. Raises the gun she's holding, gripping it with two hands.

Points it right at him.

SIXTY

Amber

Amber has never been good at playing the long con.

Oh, she could make someone believe in her ... for a little while. Enough to get a few bucks in her pocket. But she never quite knew how to string someone along, make them believe in her and *keep* believing her. She could never read those particular angles.

But then Matthew killed the trucker, the one who helped them get out of California. Jocelyn.

It wasn't the people he might kill in a quake, who he would never meet. It wasn't someone trying to stop them, like that government agent at the stadium. Jocelyn had been nothing but good to them, and Matthew killed her anyway.

It had broken something inside Amber. She was wrong to think of it as a branch, finally snapping against a hurricane wind. It was more like ... like a stone, thrown at a window – one which doesn't quite break through. The glass cracks and spiderwebs. The light passing through it bounces in strange directions, changing what's on the other side.

And Amber had seen the angle.

She knew what she had to do.

She would never be able to control Matthew; she was a fool for trying. He was too powerful, too suspicious of her. But there was another way ... and it needed every bit of skill she had.

That was what the soldiers hadn't understood, and the woman, the one like Matthew – the one who'd lifted her into the air, dumped her on the other side of the camp building. You *couldn't* take him down by force – not head on. You had to con him, make him believe you were on his side, until you reached the only time where he'd be completely focused – when he'd be utterly oblivious to the world around him.

Right before he caused an earthquake.

As they'd driven up to Washington, Amber had turned the thought over in her head. It had felt awful, poisonous, like holding a rotten fruit in her hands. She'd wondered if there was any other way she could do it – it felt insanely risky, waiting until he was on the verge of causing another quake – but she came to the conclusion that it was the only way.

To save the world, to save herself, Amber would need to pull off the con of her life.

She thought about waiting until he was asleep, but she had a sense that he wouldn't sleep until it was done. And she wasn't sure she could do it – stand over her sleeping son, in the dark, and murder him. And if she messed it up ...

Driving them off the road was another option. She was in control of the car, after all. But that would kill her as well as him, and if she didn't get it exactly right, he might survive. The consequences were too awful to contemplate.

Nobody else could do this. Only her. It was her responsibility. It made her feel sick, turning her stomach, but that didn't stop it being true.

Things might have been different. If she hadn't slept around like she had, if she'd never ended up at the School, if, if, if. Her whole life has been a series of missed chances, opportunities she didn't take – or ones she took that she shouldn't have. It was crazy to think this would be any different.

She'd take Matthew where he needed to go. She wouldn't fight him. She'd wait until the moment he was locked in, focused on releasing the fault line, and then . . .

That had nearly made her throw up, right there in the driver's seat of that hotwired car. The *how*.

A rock would be best, she supposed – there'd be some of them around, surely? It felt almost poetic – her earth-moving son killed by a rock to the head. That had been the most horrible thought of all. But she couldn't think what else to do.

Then they reached the campground, the soldiers ambushed them, and Amber saw the gun go flying off into the trees. She hadn't planned for that to happen; it was if God had decided to make it a little easier for her.

And yet, she's still messed it up.

He knew the moment he'd spotted her holding the gun. She could see it in his eyes. She should have kept it hidden, made an excuse, *anything*. Too late now.

The shouts of the soldiers are very distant now. The wind rustles the trees above them, whispering to the leaves.

And to Amber's amazement, Matthew does nothing.

Just stares at her, aiming the gun at him.

He's surprised, she realises. *He never expected me to do it.*

For perhaps the only time in Matthew's whole life, she has the drop on him.

Amber holds the gun carefully in both hands, hardly shaking at all.

He's a murderer. A demon. Something horrible that *she* helped create. She could blame the Facility all she wanted – maybe he would have turned out differently if she'd never gone there. But he still came from her. She has to kill him.

He's my son.

The gun is pointed right at his chest. Her finger tightens on the trigger.

Do it.

His eyes are huge. Stunned. Uncomprehending. He doesn't look like a monster. Like someone who would kill thousands of people. He looks like a scared, confused child. One who needs his mother.

Right then, all Amber can think about is the moment they placed him in her arms for the first time. She doesn't want to, can't afford to, but it's impossible not to go right back to the way she felt. The wave of uncontrolled joy and terror, the stunned realisation that she had made this – this truly beautiful thing. If only she could have frozen time at that moment ...

Before he began to kill. Before he became what he is now.

DO IT!

The rock that hits her is the size of a basketball. The second is only slightly smaller. They connect on either side of her rib cage, crushing it, launched hard enough to turn the organs inside to pulp. Amber jerks, the gun slipping out of her fingers. She tilts her chin up, and coughs a huge spray of blood. Matthew steps back to avoid it, his eyes narrowed in triumphant slits.

Amber feels no pain: just a sudden, strange lightness. As she drops to her knees, the rocks falling away, she becomes aware of how hard it is to exhale. There's a breath held tight in her lungs that she can no longer push out. That's OK. She's become very used to holding her breath. All she has to do is ...

But her legs won't move. Her body has stopped listening to her.

The colour begins to leach out of the world. Amber topples sideways, her head hitting soft moss, the blood from the enormous wounds in her sides soaked up by the good forest soil. She blinks, tries to speak, say her son's name.

He isn't even looking at her. He's running, heading for the trees on the far side of the clearing.

Strangely, the way her body feels now is familiar. When she'd throw herself in front of a slow-moving car during a con, it always felt a little like this. No matter how carefully you timed it, there was always that stunned moment as you lay on the ground, that moment where the connection between your body and your brain shorted, sputtering like live wires ripped from a socket.

No. Diamond Taylor was the one who felt like that. Diamond Taylor threw herself in front of cars, and she got back up afterwards. What's happened to Amber-Leigh Schenke is much, much worse. And Amber-Leigh Schenke – she understands this now, the thought flowing through her mind like ink through water – is going to die.

Amber blinks again – it feels like it takes a long time. When she opens her eyes, the gun is there.

It fell right next her. Less than a foot from her chest. Without fully understanding what she's doing, she reaches for it, her numb fingers brushing the barrel.

No noise now. Nothing but the soft rush of blood in her ears. There's no pain, and that's good.

Amber-Leigh Schenke is dead. Diamond Taylor is still alive.

Diamond the con artist.

Diamond, who could never find a way out, who was born in Barelas and would die in Barelas and would spend the time between living a life that no self-help book in the world could fix.

Diamond, who might still be able to pull off her long con after all.

Somehow, she gets her hands around the gun. It's only when she aims at her retreating son's back that she registers how hard she's shaking. Her arms shudder with the effort. She still can't exhale, can't get enough strength in her chest.

She's looking down a long, dark tunnel. She doesn't know how she entered it – perhaps it's always been there, and she just couldn't see it until now. At the very far end, a million miles away, her son is about to disappear into the trees.

Diamond doesn't realise she's squeezed the trigger until the gun jerks in her hands.

In the distance, Matthew – *Lucas, his name is Lucas* – falls. His arms fly out on either side of him, his back arching as his feet leave the ground. A split second later, he's gone. Tumbling into the trees.

Diamond's world is silent. Dark. She closes her eyes, just for a moment, just to rest them.

And finally, she exhales.

SIXTY-ONE

Teagan

Ow.

Fucking ... *ooooowwww.*

I don't know if you've ever fallen flat onto your back from height, but it sucks. I've gotten pretty good at reading the signals from my body over the years, and right now, it's saying: *I am going to be bitching about what you've done to me for a long time, and you totally deserve it, you monster.*

I stare up at the sky, blinking. It takes me a second to process that I can actually *see* the sky – it's not hidden behind a huge dust cloud any more. I try to sit up, and get another message from my body: *don't you fucking dare – I'm still mad at you.*

To try calm it down, I wiggle my big toes. I'm bracing myself for the inevitable lightning bolt of pain that will tell me I've broken something important, but it doesn't come. Ditto for my fingers. And the fact that I can actually move them means I haven't broken my stupid neck.

Slowly, I prop myself up on my elbows. It feels like it takes my head a long time to swing all the way up.

Here's the one advantage of fighting a kid who can attack you with earth: his attacks create a lot of churned-up ground to break your fall. I wouldn't call it a soft landing, exactly, but it's not a hard one, either.

Ladies and gentlemen, Teagan Frost is alive.

Just.

There's still a ton of dust in the air, but it's starting to settle. The whole camp is a churned-up nightmare. I landed a few feet away from the destroyed woodshed – one of my trusty metal roofing sheets sticks up out of the ground, like a flag. Maybe I'll take one home with me as a souvenir.

The camp building has no roof left, of course. Hardly any walls either. A toppled-over rack of trail snacks hangs out a smashed window frame, the packages swinging in the breeze. Dazedly, I wonder if destruction by superpowers is covered under the owners' insurance policy.

Turns out, trying to look everywhere at once is a terrible idea. I might not have broken anything, but my neck is ... not happy with me. After I'm done wallowing in agony for a few moments, I open my eyes to see Burr. He's a few feet away, in a tight huddle with Okoro and Garcia. Okoro looks dazed, a huge gash on the side of her face still leaking blood. But her eyes are focused, her gaze steady as Burr points towards the forest.

I can't hear what they're saying. There's nothing in my ears but a steady ringing. I squeeze my eyes shut, and slowly, the voices begin to fade in.

"... north by north-west," Burr is saying. "Garcia, get on the horn. I want helos in the air from McChord, as many as they can spare. If they've got drones on-base, I want them too."

Okoro steps to one side slightly. Annie is standing behind her.

The relief that floods through me when I see her is like a drink of ice-cold water.

Annie's still holding her rifle. Her face and clothes – that damn TSA uniform, same one I'm still wearing – are smeared with dirt. She's scanning the trees, as if looking for—

Shit – the kid!

He's nowhere to be seen, which means he got away. I try to get to my feet, but my body decides this is a terrible idea and drops me right back down.

Annie and Burr are getting into it now. "You need us out there," Annie says.

"The hell we do. You're a civilian. I want you – "

Burr frowns as he spots Annie's rifle. He grabs it from her, twisting the barrel away from him. She tries to fight, but then Okoro puts a hand on her shoulder, hissing something in her ear.

OK, sick of being an innocent bystander. And how dare these assholes try tell Annie to butt out, after she and I saved the day? The kid is still out there, and they're going to need as much manpower as they can get.

On instinct, I reach out to the rifle with my PK, thinking I should put it back in Annie's hands—

And get nothing.

I am tapped. Out of juice. Donezo Washington.

Ah, fuck.

Annie spots me. She pushes past Burr, almost falling as she stumbles across the torn-up ground. She yells my name, skids to her knees next to me. "We gonna get you an ambulance, OK? Just—"

"I'm all right," I tell her, vaguely surprised I'm still able to speak.

She wipes her face. "Jesus. That was—"

"Yeah. I know."

"Frost." Burr walks up, looking murderous. "Both of you, get inside."

He points to the wreck of the camp building. I'm about to say that it doesn't exactly have an *inside* any more, but Annie gets in first. "Hell no. You don't get to cut us out of this."

"Sure I do. Get your ass to cover, wait for extraction."

"Uh, hello?" I wave – an act that makes the muscles in my arm file a formal complaint. "Do you not think maybe having someone who can move shit would be useful? You know, like it just was two minutes ago?"

The familiar smirk creeps across his face. "You're out of gas, Frost."

"I'm good." I spit a glob of dirt-flecked saliva. "Let's do this."

"Really?" He taps a heavy, black flashlight, squirrelled away on his belt. "Move my torch."

"I—"

"Go on. You bump it even a little, I'll let you come with us."

I stare back at him, waiting for my PK to kick in. After a few seconds, I drop my head. "Fuck you."

"Thought so."

"That shit don't matter, man." Annie speaks through gritted teeth. "He's still out there."

And then Burr does the damndest thing. He drops to one knee, looking intently between us.

"You guys did good," he says, his voice a low monotone. "For real." He glances at me. "That was quick thinking, with the . . . you know." He wobbles his hand in the air, imitating my little hoverboard trick.

"Yeah." Annie still sounds furious. "So let us come with you. We can help."

"Frost is done, and you're a civilian. Both of you are. You're not gonna be any use out there. We'll find him, and this time, we'll nuke his ass with a hell-fire missile from thirty thousand feet. See him try block that shit."

Burr looks at me again. I'm expecting the usual scorn, the almost amused contempt. Instead, there's something else there. Not respect exactly – it's more like he's seeing me for the first time.

Huh. He doesn't know that I bumped Okoro's rifle, right before she shot at Matthew. He must think she missed – if he thought otherwise, he'd be a lot more pissed off. Christ, what does Okoro think? Does she know? I look past Burr, but the sniper is turned away from me, deep in discussion with a shaken Garcia. In the distance, a helicopter is approaching, the *whup-whup* coming in above the trees.

Annie is still furious. "No, see, that is some bullshit. We—"

"Annie." I put a hand on her arm. "It's OK."

"Are you *serious*?"

" . . . He's right."

And he is. Without my PK, I am next to useless. The fear is coming back now, the fury that I let the kid get away – that *we* let him get away. But it doesn't change the fact that I would be precisely zero help right now. And while Annie can definitely handle a weapon, she doesn't have the training for this kind of thing.

Annie glowers, her shoulders tight. But she doesn't shake me off.

"How the hell did you get out?" Burr says to me. His voice is even lower than before.

Oh yeah. Shit. Jeez. I can move soil with my mind now. Organic molecules.

It's hard to process. Even as it was happening, I didn't believe it. It's been one of the big limits of my ability my entire life, and I just proved it can be done. It takes adrenaline and terror and a major panic response . . . but it's possible.

My ability is changing. Growing. I can lift more than I

used to. I can reach further. And apparently, the old limits no longer apply.

No response from the soil now, of course. I can't feel it. I can't feel anything. I am, as Burr put it, out of gas.

"He didn't drop me in too deep," I lie. "I dug myself out."

He shakes his head. "That's insane."

"Nope. That's telekinesis, Kyle."

I've always called it psychokinesis, not telekinesis. But what the hell: when life gives you a shot at a Tenacious D joke, you take it. Even if it means compromising your standards.

Fuck me, what a day.

Burr gives me a final, guarded nod. Then he gets to his feet, gesturing to the others, pointing at the forest.

As the soldiers fan out, the helicopter appears above the treeline, a dark shape against the grey sky. I reach out for Annie, putting my arm around her shoulders. After a moment, she lifts me up.

SIXTY-TWO

Matthew

Tree trunks loom in his path. Branches try to snag him. The ground slopes and undulates, threatening to trip him. But even as he runs, Matthew's thoughts are clear.

Amber almost shot him.

If he hadn't forgotten about the little slope at the edge of the clearing and fallen over, she would have.

He should've gone back, made sure she was dead, maybe even hit her in the head with one of the rocks. But he'd fallen right off the edge of the clearing, almost in the same instant that the gunshot rang out. He'd panicked. The bullet passed by *this close* to him, and it was only the fall that made it miss. He'd landed hard, but was up and running in the same instant, his feet flying. His face and hands were scratched to hell, but he barely noticed.

This whole time, Amber was planning to shoot him. He taught her a lesson though. A big one. He's surprised to find that he's not angry any more – more annoyed than anything else, mostly because it'll be harder to get adults to do what he wants now. After he sets off Cascadia, he'll have to find someone else. Another Amber. No problem – there'll be more than enough opportunity later.

And with that, he dismisses Amber from his thoughts.

Those soldiers, and the lady with the powers. They're still alive, probably, and they'll catch him eventually – at least, if all he does is run.

And the solution is obvious, isn't it? He can try and fight them off, but there's a better way. If they can't see him, they can't catch him. If they can't follow his path, they can't find him.

As Matthew runs, he sends his power out in a wide arc behind him. He doesn't have all that much range, really – not unless he's on top of a fault line, which amplifies what he can do, lets him reach a lot further than normal. But he's still able to use the soil up to about fifty feet out, and he *uses* it. He swings it in all directions, spreading it as far as he can. It'll leave a trail, sure … but it'll be a big one, wide and dispersed, and if he's clever – if he zigzags and goes in unexpected directions – they won't be able to track him nearly as accurately.

Behind him, he continues destroying the forest, uprooting trees and detonating clods of earth, left and right, irregular patterns designed to confuse any pursuers. As he reaches the other side of the ridge, he cuts a hard left, using his hands to help him balance on the steep slope, wincing as a jagged rock grazes his palm. He reaches back with his mind as far it will go, and rips open a great hole in the earth.

Voices. Just on the other side of the ridge, shockingly close. "Delta Commander, do you copy? Over."

A burst of static from a radio, followed by an angry voice, spitting words Matthew can't make out. His trick didn't work. Somehow, they've found him. They weren't supposed to do that. He stills, clenching small fists by his sides. He'll bury them. He'll bury them all.

"Copy that. We're maybe two klicks into the woods. Heading north by north-east. We'll keep you posted. Out."

He's about to send out a tidal wave of dirt, perhaps rip the ground out from underneath them and bury them deep, when he stops. He's vulnerable here, and these men have guns. They've seen what he can do, and at this close range, there's a chance they could fire off a few shots before he kills them. He has no desire to die – especially not when Cascadia is so close.

And there's another way. A smarter one.

Quickly and quietly, he moves the dirt under his feet. He slips beneath the soil as if dropping into water, the granules of soil and rock and clumps of root simply sliding past him. At the very last instant, he closes his eyes, tilting his head back so just the tip of his nose shows above the surface. With a soft, rolling hiss, the dirt hides his face from the world.

Other kids would be scared about being buried this way. But they aren't as smart as him. Why should he be scared? He can tell the earth what to do. Other people might freak out if you put them in the ground, but not him.

He reaches out, sending up a few bombs of dirt further away, deep in the trees. Let them follow his trail. He won't be able to send the bombs any further, and they'll wonder why he stopped ... but at least then, they won't be in his imme-diate area.

Muffled sounds reach him. Crunching footsteps, hushed commands, the soft clanking of equipment as it shifts across hips and backs. Matthew waits. It's possible they might find him – notice the one tiny slip of flesh he has to keep above the ground to stay breathing. If that happens, he'll bury them, and accept the risk that they might try shoot him. There's only so much he can do.

But the footsteps are already moving away. Matthew waits, very still. Breathing, in and out through his nose, ever so softly.

And before long, the forest is quiet again.

Dead still, under the earth. One hour, two. It takes everything Matthew has to control his annoyance, his desire to hunt down the men chasing him.

He occupies himself by imagining what will happen to them when he triggers Cascadia. They'll be crushed to pieces. Drowned in a tidal wave. Maybe they'll be in a building when it happens, and die from a gas explosion. He pictures their torn bodies, which makes him forget for a while that he has to be still.

Eventually, when he's absolutely sure he's alone, he lifts himself out of the dirt. Slowly, carefully, listening hard. Waiting for a shout of alarm. Nothing. The forest is darker now, more shadowy, and the only sound is the wind in the trees.

He did it.

They can't hurt him. They can't do a thing to him. If he hears them first, he'll just hide himself away. If they surprise him, he'll kill them. For real this time.

There's the fluttering of wings above him as some bird takes flight. He shivers, suddenly cold. It was surprisingly warm under the ground, but the open air of the forest has a chill to it. His sweater – he'll need it if he's going to—

The sweater is still in the car, back at the campground. Amber was supposed to bring it with them.

Matthew pouts, hugging himself. His breath forms a very light cloud in front of him.

Whatever. It's not like he's going to be out here long, anyway. Just long enough to trigger Cascadia, and then he can make his way back. He'll find a new Amber. And there are plenty of other fault lines – none as big as Cascadia, sure, but they'll still be fun to set off. And what about volcanoes? He hasn't even *started* thinking about volcanoes! The thought sends an electric bolt up his spine, makes him grin momentarily. He'll have to find out. Even if it's a no, there's other, smaller stuff he could do: messing with building foundations, bursting dams . . .

His thoughts land on the woman with the powers. The one he thought he'd killed. If she existed, others will too. Maybe they could work together.

First things first. Cascadia.

Only: where is it?

The ETS zone was a little way into the park. He'll have to get pretty far in to trigger it, but it shouldn't take him all that long to get to a point where he has a strong enough connection. The zone was to the north-west from the campground, maybe a three hour hike.

But where is the campground? And which way is north-west?

Matthew turns in a small circle, heart beating a little faster. His annoyance grows. This is dumb. He knows which direction the ETS zone is in. It's just over there, past that grove of shrubs.

He sets off, picking his way across the uneven ground. He's thirsty, his throat a little dry. He clears the grove, the branches scratching at his bare arms. It's actually gotten colder, and the tops of the trees are darker now, less distinct. A bird calls out in the dusk, startling him.

The ground is getting hard to see now. His foot tangles in a clutch of roots, and he almost falls. Suddenly, he's breathing hard, clutching at himself as he fights for balance. He puts a tiny hand against one of the big tree trunks, and his skin comes away wet.

OK. So he doesn't know where the ETS zone is, or which direction he should go. It's cool. All he has to do is concentrate, and he'll be able to feel it calling out to him, even if he isn't close enough to release the pressure. That's how it's supposed to work, right? The very first fault – that little one when they were driving into LA – called to him. Didn't it?

You were close. You were right next to it when that happened.

He kneels, placing his palms flat on the damp earth. For a moment, he thinks he feels it ... but it's just the regular ground, the dirt, the usual stuff. Boring. Stupid.

Amber had the maps, the sweaters. The food and water. She was supposed to bring it all.

With a growl, he tears a chunk out of the ground, a boulder the size of a motorbike. He hurls it into the trees, listens to it break apart with a giant crunch. More birds take flight, cawing in alarm. Matthew jerks, as if shocked, then abruptly starts walking again. He'll just keep heading in the same direction, and everything will be fine. He's bound to come across the ETS eventually, and then—

Wait. The direction he's walking in now ... is that the same as before? He'd tripped, or almost tripped, and he'd gotten turned around He needs to turn right a little. That's definitely north-west.

Stumbling. Hands out in front of him. He can hardly see them now, let alone the ground. More than once, he's certain he hears voices in the trees, and whirls, ready to defend himself. But there's nobody there. He just ends up losing his direction again.

"They don't understand," he mutters, not realising how hard he's shivering. "I have to do this. I *want* to."

He takes another step – and his shoe fills with water. Icy, shocking. He yelps, yanking his foot out of the unseen puddle, and sits down hard on the cold forest floor. Then he lashes out, shredding the earth in a fifty-foot radius, ripping and tearing, hurling up clouds of dirt. A tree topples over with a crunching bang, loud enough to make him whimper.

He needs to see where he's going. That's it. He'll just ... get higher.

In moments, he's rising on a column of earth, half-crouched on it, wobbling for balance. It's hard – much harder than anything he's ever done. The column snakes up past the canopy, bearing him on it, his teeth gritted. Despite the cold, sweat slicks his forehead.

He turns in a small circle, fists clenched at his sides. The tree canopy stretches away in all directions, a dark, undulating sea of leaves and branches. He can't see the campground, of course. He can't see anything. Even the stars are hidden behind low clouds.

Dizzy. Really dizzy, all of a sudden. As carefully as he can, Matthew lowers himself back to ground level. In his mind, he's taking it slow. In reality, the column of earth drops in big, lurching increments, nearly throwing him off. He sits on the ground, panting, then scrambles to his feet and starts to run. He's very cold now – running will keep his heat up. He read that somewhere, didn't he? But where?

A tree rears in front of him, its trunk death-black against the dark backdrop of the forest. He swerves around it, ripping it up by the roots almost as an afterthought. He reaches out, hunting, desperate for contact with the ETS zone. He's only just aware that he's started crying, tears dribbling down his cheeks. He can't even remember which direction he's supposed to head in now. All he knows is that he has to keep going.

Somewhere, very distant, a bird calls.

SIXTY-THREE

Teagan

The funeral for Paul is held at the United States Naval Academy Cemetery in Annapolis, Maryland. There's a small memorial service held later in the Naval Academy Chapel, too.

We hold one of our own.

At *our* place.

Well, kind of our place. Paul's Boutique is gone, of course. We talk about having the get-together up at his ex-wife's place in San Diego, but that idea doesn't last long. Annie saw her at the funeral, and she was ... not good. Neither was his son, Cole. Mostly because the way he died is next-level top secret. They don't know what China Shop Movers really was (*is, dammit, is*), and they think he was killed when the office collapsed.

Of course, Annie's not doing so well herself.

We decided to hold the memorial at the last place we all hung out together – Sandra-May Cruz's house. Watts got hit just as hard as everywhere else, but her home is still mostly intact, although part of the back kitchen wall has collapsed, and there are cracks snaking through the rest of the house. There's no power, either. Plenty of places in the city haven't had it restored yet, and spots like Watts and Compton are definitely low on the list. Some things never change.

Not that Sandra-May gives a shit. She's found a generator, had one of her neighbours hook it up, filled the house with food – God knows where she got it all from. As far as I can tell, she invited damn near every single person in Watts. She's zooming around the house now, making sure everyone has enough to eat and drink, her dog Rocko trailing at her heels. She drags her wheeled oxygen cart, her emphysema barely slowing her down. I get the feeling she's a little scared to stop moving. I catch her at odd moments, looking out one of the broken windows, gazing at nothing.

I'm in the packed living room, squashed up against one of the house's few unbroken windows, drinking a warm beer. People keep giving them to me – Bud Lites and Coors, pressed into my hands whenever I get halfway down a bottle. I'm drunk – getting there, anyway. God, I wish Africa was here – he's the kind of person who is really good at parties.

Nobody knows where he is. Shortly after the chopper lifted off from Van Nuys with Annie and me onboard, he stole one of the ATVs and took off. I assume he went to look for Jeannette – probably figured there was nothing more for him to do. I've thought about heading to Skid Row, or to his apartment, trying to find him. I haven't gotten up the energy to do it yet.

I hope he's OK.

It's *loud* in here. Voices raised to the damn roof. People with paper plates of pizza and nachos and sandwiches, waving beers in the air; somebody passing around a bottle of whiskey. It's still cool outside, but there's no rain – and inside the house, it's hot enough to slick my skin with sweat.

When I was growing up in Wyoming, I used to fantasise

about going to parties like this. Teenage parties, kids packed in tight, drunk and sweating and making out. This isn't exactly how I saw it go down.

There's a big photo of Paul propped in one corner, in full Navy uniform. Taken maybe ten years ago, when he was just starting to lose his hair, grinning at the photographer like an idiot. Sandra-May has placed lit candles around it, and I smile to myself when I imagine him telling us that it's probably a major fire hazard. Earlier, somebody asked Sandra-May why we were celebrating some old white Army dude; the earful she gave him would have charred concrete.

The booze suddenly gets me, flooding my skull and turning the room woozy. I push off the window, start to wind my way through the crowd. I get a few curious glances – little white girl, hanging around a party in Watts – but nobody hassles me.

Even if I wasn't welcome here, I don't really feel like going back to the place I'm staying – a miraculously still-functioning two-star hotel in Pomona. It's crazy far out of LA – almost forty miles from my own place. But it's packed out, so I can only imagine the strings Tanner had to pull to get rooms for me and Reggie. Hard bed. Antiseptic bathroom. No kitchen. Not that I'm complaining, really: my apartment in Leimert Park is a no-go. It's . . . not destroyed, exactly, but it's in real bad shape. Huge cracks in the walls and ceiling, windows broken. And I swear to God it's actually tilting a little to one side. I gathered as much of my stuff as I could, as many clothes and cookbooks and records as the Batmobile would take, and got the fuck out.

It sucks. I *liked* that apartment.

At least I still have my car. The Batmobile lives. I found it back where I left it, outside the remains of the Boutique. Took me a while to get back there, but seeing that damn Jeep was the fucking best.

It's been about two weeks since our little adventure in Washington. Cascadia has not gone off.

I have no idea how ... but I think we saved the world.

They never found the kid. Tanner pulled in every favour she could: satellite imagery, infrared scanning, dedicated tracker teams. Drones and choppers, like Burr said. They scoured that forest for two weeks, and found nada.

And that probably sounds weird, doesn't it? All those resources, all those eyes, and the kid still never pops up? Yeah, I thought it was strange too. Strange, and scary.

When you have a stomach bug that won't quit, or a strange rash on your arm, you start Googling for solutions – even when you know shouldn't. When you have a psychotic four-year-old who could end the world at any moment and who is missing in the woods, you do the same thing.

We still can't find people who are lost at sea, or stumbling around on the ice at the north and south poles. And they aren't covered by a thick tree canopy. There's a reason why people who get lost in the woods stay lost – even hikers who wander off the path, and who are desperately trying to get back to civilisation. And if that's not convincing enough, let me share a little nugget I dug up a few days ago.

In 2009, a three-year-old named Joshua Childers wandered away from his family into the Mark Twain National Forest in Missouri. He wasn't even wearing pants – just shirt, shoes and a diaper. Now: think about this for a second. The kid's three. Tiny legs. Can't get far. Probably bawling his eyes out. Desperately wants to be found. And there was a huge manhunt to pull that off. Layup, right? Well, guess how long it took to find little Josh? Who was still alive and kicking when they got him, by the way.

Fifty-two hours.

Over *two freaking days*.

Now up the stakes. A target who doesn't want to be found. Who is way, way more intelligent than most kids his age. And who has abilities that would make disguising his trail very easy.

UAVs – Unmanned Aerial Vehicles, the big Predator drones – have thermal imaging, sure. But they struggle seeing through dense tree canopy, and telling the difference between a human and, say, a coyote. You could fly some smaller drones through the trees of course, but the problem is that most drones rely on GPS, and signals get real weak in the woods. I hear the guys at MIT lent Burr and company a couple of special drones which *don't* use GPS . . . but they only had a couple. Not nearly enough.

So it's about manpower. Boots on the ground. And in this case, manpower came up short.

So yeah: it's been a pretty terrifying few days. But the longer we went without a catastrophe, the easier it got. Here's what I think: I think the woods just swallowed that boy, like he made the earth swallow me, and Paul. If he *is* still out there, he hasn't gotten close to the ETS zone.

Good fucking riddance.

We're still trying to untangle just who his mom was. We don't know where she came from, how she landed up with a superpowered kid. More importantly, we don't know *why* she helped Matthew. That's the thing that gets me the most. Matthew was psychotic. It was all a game to him. But what I can't figure out is why his mom – his *parent* – would not only let that happen, but actually help him.

It's not as simple as genetics – as if I would ever consider genetics to be simple. Psychos like Matthew don't come along often. A mother-son pairing? That's lottery odds. So what was her deal?

It doesn't exactly simplify things that she was found dead in the forest. Crushed by rocks. It means that Matthew turned against her, right when he probably needed her most.

Too much for today. Too much for any day.

I wind my way into the kitchen, which is nice and bright and airy thanks to the collapsed back wall. Probably isn't a very safe room, especially if we get any lingering aftershocks, but it's still packed with people. Annie is at the kitchen table, beer in hand, hunched over it protectively, speaking to a large guy with dreads who I don't recognise.

We haven't talked about what happened at the Vance Campground.

It should be easy. She saved my life, coming to help me when she had a real chance to get revenge on Matthew. I've tried to thank her a billion times, check in on her, let her know I'm around if she wants to talk. She doesn't. It's like she's trying to pretend the whole thing – including helping me out – didn't happen.

Annie and I have never been all that close. But over the past few months, ever since Carlos died, we've become . . . not friendly, exactly, but at least nicer to each other. We don't get on each other's nerves like we used to. Then she saved me, and I thought . . .

Well, I don't know what I thought. I didn't expect us to be bosom buddies suddenly, but I didn't expect to get frozen out, either. It feels like we've taken a massive step back, and I have to keep reminding myself to give her space.

Looking at Annie now, seeing the tightness in her shoulders, the way she grips her beer bottle like she's trying to crush it to powder, makes me think: *fuck it*. I'm booze-brave, more than ready to have it out. If I can't get her to talk about it, at least I can let her know that we're still cool. I wipe my mouth, taking a step towards her.

And stop. Because, even drunk, what am I going to say to her that I haven't said a billion times already?

No, seriously: what? What combination of words is going to get her to open up, and even if that actually does happen, what then? She collapses in floods of tears, and we hug it out, and she's suddenly miraculously OK? That's not how this shit works.

As if sensing my thoughts, Annie looks up. I thought she was drunk, way more than me, but in that instant, her eyes are completely clear. Patchy, red, set in a face that looks ten years older than it did two weeks ago, but clear.

She gives a little shake of the head. Almost invisible – the guy she's talking to doesn't even notice the movement, just keeps blabbering on. I stand, swaying in place, the urge to say something growing and fading with every in-out breath. Does she think I'm going to be pushed away by a little head-shake? But if I *do* say something ... and she *still* doesn't listen ... ?

Then she raises her bottle, tilts it in my direction. Gives me the smallest ghost of a smile.

I make myself smile back, returning the toast.

Then I get the fuck out of there and into the backyard before I do something stupid.

The rear of Sandra-May's house is much smaller than the front yard. An uneven rectangle of slightly scruffy grass, running onto a low wall which lets me see right into the property opposite. That house is in even worse shape, one whole side collapsed, the windows dark and dead.

LA is getting itself together a little faster than I would have thought. Dodger Stadium was a clusterfuck – and came very, very close to being a full-on New Orleans Superdome situation. Fortunately, it didn't. If the soldiers had been police, motherfuckers would have ended up getting shot. But the

National Guard are soldiers, and soldiers are trained not to fire at things unless they really do pose a threat. That much, at least, I learned from Burr and Okoro. So Dodger was on the edge for a while, but it never truly got to disaster territory.

As for the rest of the city, it turns out FEMA actually learned *some* lessons from Hurricane Katrina. Congress threw a shit-ton of money at the problem – both during, and after. Especially when the California reps reminded them just how much money the state itself makes for the country. A few billion dollars in emergency funding gets a lot of things done. As does a shit-ton of private funding from Facebook, Apple, Google and just about every other tech company in the state. Give them this: they know a good PR opportunity when they see one.

Of course, the authorities still would have fucked it up in some way – they're the government, after all, and I have very close and personal knowledge of them fucking things up. Fortunately, a day or two after the quake, Japan arrived.

Here's the thing about the Japanese government. They are *really* good at fixing earthquake damage. Remember Fukushima? Quake, tsunami, nuclear meltdown? That was a 9.0. There were plenty of big freeways near the plant – freeways that got wrecked by the quake – and the Japanese authorities fixed most of them as good as new *in under a week*. I looked up the before and after photos – the roads are better than they were before the quake hit. Japan does not screw around.

Admittedly, our little 9.3 is a bigger job. It's been slow-going. But it's surprising just how much has been achieved, even after two weeks. Several freeways are still down ... but there are also plenty that can now handle traffic. It's going to take a long time for LA to feel normal again. Maybe years. But it's a lot better than it was a month ago.

Whole sections of the city still don't have power. But it could have been much worse – at least the fires were contained. The debris was cleaned up – or pushed to one side anyway, so cars could get past. The population plummeted in the days following the quake, but people have slowly been moving back.

We are not a post-apocalyptic wasteland. We are not *Mad Max*, or *San Andreas*. We're a city that took the biggest punch the earth can throw . . . and we're slowly getting back off the mat.

After our little adventure in Washington State, Tanner put us up in a hotel in Seattle. A *good* one, with a bed bigger than my living room. Weirdly, I didn't want to be there at first – I wanted to get back after the kid. I'd positively identified him. I'd tried to talk to him, and it almost got me killed. But as Burr put it: what the fuck was I planning on contributing? He had his own people combing the woods, along with the entirety of the Air Force's drone complement, and I was being ordered to butt the fuck out. They'd find the kid, observe from a distance, and take him out. Gives me shivers just to think about it, but it's a good strategy.

I could have gone out there, I guess. I don't see how in the hell they were going to stop me. Instead, I put on the complimentary bathrobe, the one so big it went down to my feet, and completely wrecked the room service menu, ordering everything remotely good. Then I got blackout drunk.

When I woke up, I stayed in bed for a long time, trying to process the fact that I can move organic matter. Something I *had no idea I could do*.

I practiced. Wouldn't you? Tried moving some flowers in a vase. I got the same sensation – that tinnitus again – but I couldn't actually move them. I needed adrenaline. Or fear. Or anger. Something. At that particular moment, all I had was bone-numbing exhaustion.

Annie stayed in her room. Whenever I knocked on the door, she just told me to go away.

I spent a lot of time walking around Seattle, trying to get my head straight. Ate at restaurants whose names I don't remember. Got drunk at bars. Talked to strangers and waved off dudes trying to pick me up and waited for the world to end.

It didn't. And after a while, Tanner sent us down to LA. The way today is going, I kind of wish I was back in that fluffy bathrobe, drunk out of my mind on overpriced minibar champagne.

I rest my arms on the low wall, beer dangling, and let out a low sigh.

"Hello there."

Reggie makes me jump. She's off to one side, by the corner of the lot. Her new chair is a slim, motorised model in hospital-white; it doesn't look like much, but apparently it handles dirt and grass just fine. It's nothing on the beast she had before, but as she pointed out to me, she doesn't have a Rig to drive any more. Reggie's chair: another casualty of that fucking kid. Along with just about everything else in this city.

"Scared the shit out of me," I mutter, but without much feeling.

"Oh good. Thought I was losing my touch."

I snort, despite myself. "Yeah. Even without your old super-powered stealth chair. I never used to hear that thing coming."

She bursts out laughing, wheezing a little. "That piece of junk? Good riddance. You would not believe how often I had to plug it in to charge."

"Don't worry, we'll get you a new one. If you're really nice to me, I'll make it fly. You can have a floating chair, like the bald dude from the X-Men."

"Or MODOK."

"Who?"

"One of their bad guys? MODOK? Mental Organism Designed Only for Killing?"

"That cannot be his name."

"Of course it is. You're half my age, how have you not heard of him?"

"Not a big comic book person."

"Really?" She looks genuinely surprised. "Your education in the classics is lacking, young padawan."

"That one I do know. Don't you *young padawan* me. And is that really the guy's name? Like someone actually wrote that, and people took it seriously?"

"Of course."

"And you'd rather be *him* than baldie?"

"Professor X, yes. And of course. MODOK's a big head in a floating chair. Describes me perfectly."

This time, my laugh is genuine. Even so, there's a sense that the little chit-chat we're having is like skating on ice over a very dark, deep pond. We've got a shit-ton to discuss, and it feels as if neither of us really wants to go there yet.

I lift my bottle to my lips, right as I realise she doesn't have anything. "Hey, what are you drinking?"

"Hmm?"

"The Coors is pretty nasty, but I think I saw some Buds in there somewhere – at least you can drink those. Oh wait, you're wine, huh? I'll get you—"

"Already got someone fetching me some."

"Oh. Cool, cool."

The silence between us isn't as comfortable as I thought it would be.

She shakes her head. "I'm glad you're OK, darling. I heard about how the boy . . . " She clears her throat. "How he did to you what he did to Paul."

I haven't told her – haven't told anyone – about my sudden ability to move organic molecules. Don't plan to either, not until I've got a handle on it myself.

"Yeah," I say, draining the last of my beer. "Not fun."

"That's one way of describing it." Reggie's voice is a little harsher than before, more uneven. She's not looking at me, gazing at some point in the distance. She blinks, then says, "Hell of a thing, you getting out in time."

"Yeah," I say, not meeting her eyes. "Annie helped."

"Did she now?"

What was it she said, back when we were first arriving at Dodger? *You think I haven't noticed how much more you can lift nowadays? How much more control you have? You're getting more powerful, and it's starting to make people very nervous.*

"Um. So." I straighten up. "Whoever you sent to get you a drink obviously couldn't find their ass with both hands, so I'm gonna—"

Reggie glances over my shoulder. "No need."

I turn, and Moira Tanner is standing right behind me.

SIXTY-FOUR

Teagan

It's the first time I've seen her in two years. I've spoken to her on the phone, gotten text messages from her, heard her commands relayed through Reggie. Seeing her here, standing in Sandra-May Cruz's backyard, is like having a storybook monster suddenly pop into existence at the foot of your bed.

She's dressed for DC, not Los Angeles. Leather flats. Dark, tailored suit over a white shirt, buttoned to the neck. No jewellery, not even an American flag lapel pin. Matter of fact, I'm pretty sure she was wearing the exact same outfit when she sat across from me at the Facility in Waco all those years ago, and told me that I was going to be working for her. It's easy to picture her closet, nothing but five or six copies of the exact same suit. Maybe a dark blue one for the office Christmas party.

She has the blank, neutral face of an Easter Island statue. Long angles and hard bones, eyes the colour of old ice. Her hair is pulled back into a severe bun. There's more grey there since the last time I saw her, but only a little. If the folks in the house were wondering why there was a Navy dude's picture in Sandra-May's living room, they must have bugged the fuck out when Moira Tanner walked through the door.

Then again, given her aura of instant death, my guess is nobody said shit.

"Good afternoon, Ms Frost," she says, leaning on the surname. After the whole thing with Jake and Carlos, I asked her to stop using my birth name. Well, *asked* isn't quite right. I more or less told her, then hung up on her.

I find my voice, which was curled up in stunned surprise somewhere in my stomach. "You too."

She's holding two Buds. In her elegant piano-player fingers, the bottles look like a joke. She glances down at them, then passes one to Reggie, the one with a straw in it to make it easier for her to drink from.

"Apologies," she says. "If I'd known you were joining us, I would have fetched a third one." She looks down at her own beer, as if she can't quite fathom how it landed up in her hand. "I represented us at the funeral, of course. And originally I wasn't planning to come today, but I needed to be in Los Angeles anyway. I want us to meet as a team, talk about how we move forward. And offer Ms Cruz my support, of course."

"That's cool. So hey, listen, you can't fire Reggie."

Reggie, halfway through a sip, chokes on her beer.

Tanner raises an eyebrow. "I beg your pardon?"

"I know you were planning on firing her because you didn't think she was doing a good job or whatever, and you absolutely can't do that. It's a stupid idea."

Tanner frowns. "I don't—"

"If you fire her, then you'll have to fire me, too. I won't work with anybody but Reggie. She's the best computer person you've got, don't try to tell me otherwise—" Reggie tries to interrupt, but there's no way I'm going to let her cut me off. "—and I know there was that whole thing with Schmidt and the car arriving and Reggie not realising he'd left the hotel, but that's only because she was checking out the earthquake thing, and if she hadn't done that then we still wouldn't know the kid did it and Cascadia would have gone off, so when you think about it it's actually really lucky."

Tanner tilts her head, examining me. Like I'm an organism under a microscope.

"Anyway," I say. "That's all I wanted to say. No firing. Reggie, I mean. She stays, or I go."

Reggie clears her throat loudly, looks away. From inside the house, there's the crash of a dropped bottle, followed by a gale of laughter and applause.

"Let me be clear on something." Tanner's voice is like a calm sea, with black shapes swimming just beneath the surface. "Any conversation Ms McCormick and I are going to have will be conducted in private, with all the proper protocol being observed. You will not—"

"Will not what? Defend my friend?"

"Teagan," Reggie says. "This is *not* the time."

"You didn't come to LA for Paul's thing." I wave at the house. "You don't give a shit about Paul. You came down here to can Reggie. Or am I wrong?"

Tanner looks away. "I don't discuss personnel decisions with—"

Which is all the information I need. I turn to Reggie. "Wow. Your old Army buddy's a cunt."

Reggie gapes at me. Tanner's teeth are gritted so hard I'm surprised her jaw doesn't implode.

I don't care. All the anger and horror and fear I've dealt with in the past two weeks is coming up for air.

"You are way, way out of line," Reggie says.

"Actually, you know what?" I put a hand on the top of her chair. "I'm kind of done with giving you pep talks, Reggie. Because here's the thing: she obviously knows about how you discovered the earthquake boy, and she has to know about all the stuff after. You were the one who kept us all going. You had the smarts to make us go to the museum. We wouldn't be here if it wasn't for you. She *knows* that, and she still wants you gone? And you're just gonna sit there and take it?"

On second thought, asking a quadriplegic if she's going to *sit there* is probably not the best idea. Oh well.

"Ms Frost," Tanner says slowly. "You're going to go back inside. You're going to drink your beer, and you're going to forget you ever saw me today."

"Do you *get off* on talking like this? Like you're gonna vanish the second my back is turned or something? What are you, fucking Batman?"

"I am not—"

"She's right," Reggie says.

Tanner and I both look at her.

"Who?" I say. "Which one of us is right?"

Reggie doesn't look at me. Instead, she tilts her chin up, eyes locking on Tanner's.

"Moira," she says slowly. "I know you believe I don't have a hold on this operation. But if it weren't for me, we simply would never have known about the boy. And beyond that ..."

She pauses, as if gathering herself. I know exactly why. If there's one thing I've gotten to know about Reggie McCormick, it's that she has a real issue with talking herself up.

"After Paul was killed," she continues, "I helped keep the team together. I did it without having the immediate ability to contact you and ask for orders."

Tanner says nothing.

"If I hadn't done my job, we would be in a different situation right now. You and I don't always think alike, Moira, but that's something we should use. It shouldn't be something you view as a problem."

"That's right, go on, tell her." I nod enthusiastically. It's only a second later that I realise Reggie's done.

Tanner is silent for a good fifteen seconds. Not speaking. Not moving. Just looking at Reggie. And Reggie stares right back at her, as if daring her to try argue this. If it wouldn't look and feel really weird, I'd give her a little punch on the shoulder.

Eventually, Tanner takes a deep breath, lets it out. "Very well. We'll continue as before, with the team structure intact."

Forget punching Reggie on the shoulder. I feel like doing a victory dance. Reggie gives Tanner a small smile, nods her thanks.

"We still need to have a formal debrief," Tanner tells Reggie.

"Wait a second," I say. "How did you guys not know about the kid?"

"Teagan, *enough* now," Reggie says.

"No, she doesn't get off that easy. First she completely drops the ball on Jake, and then this kid appears out of nowhere, and—"

"Stop."

Tanner's voice is soft, so soft I shouldn't be able to hear it over the noise from the house, but I do.

Her eyes on me, she bends down to speak to Reggie. "Would you give me a minute with Ms Frost, please?"

After a moment, Reggie nods. As she wheels past me, she nudges me with her shoulder. I find it, squeeze hard.

"I'll see you folks inside," Reggie says. Nestling her beer in the chair's cup-holder, she trundles smoothly across the grass towards the back door.

It's the first time I've been alone with Tanner in ... shit, literally years. It is exactly as uncomfortable as it was the first time.

All the same, I'm not about to back down. "If you're

planning on giving me the runaround about me not being able to understand how this works ... "

Tanner closes her eyes for a moment, as if steadying herself. When she opens them, there's a different look on her face. It's like she's drawn a line under the previous conversation.

"First off, I wanted to say I think you did the right thing by bringing Mia Wong into the fold."

Her praise takes me off guard, especially given the little rumble we just had. "The scientist? From the museum?"

"That's right. It can't have been an easy decision – you're obviously aware of how seriously I take breaches of classified information. But ... in this case, it was the right call. It resulted in actionable intelligence, and led us directly to the boy who called himself Matthew Schenke. I'm willing to give it a pass. This time."

"How nice of you. What happens to her now? Guantanomo Bay?"

"Hardly. She's signed the same NDAs as Mr Kouamé did."

Africa. "OK? And?"

"She's agreed to a small retainer fee as a scientific advisor. I don't think you'll need her on the team full-time, but she's a bright girl. It would be good to have her around."

"Yeah, well." I can't think of what else to say to that, so I settle for, "You're welcome."

I'm planning to steer us back on track, ask her why she didn't know about Matthew before he wrecked California, when she says, "You will notice that I have not yet mentioned your actions at the Vance Creek Campground."

"My *actions*?"

"Indeed. The boy had to die." Said like she was ordering a cup of coffee. "Once you'd positively identified him, the course was clear. He was far too dangerous – and we were already running a major risk letting him get that close to Cascadia. And then there you were, trying to prevent my team from doing their jobs."

"Hey, your sniper *missed*."

"Master Sergeant Okoro missed because you moved her rifle barrel, Ms Frost. And don't insult me by pretending you didn't. It is simply impossible for someone with Okoro's skill and experience and temperament to miss at that range – or so unlikely as to be effectively impossible."

The retort I had ready dies on my lips. Tanner fills the silence herself. "And tell me: what did you gain from confronting the boy? What information did you extract?"

"That there was a school in New Mexico. And there were other kids like him – or other people, anyway, he didn't say how old they were. How can you tell me that information wasn't useful?"

"Oh, it's very useful. It's also the kind of thing we could have easily uncovered ourselves, after the boy was dead. Okoro's instructions were to kill *him*, not his mother. She was not considered a threat, and we believe she would have given up the information readily." Her voice is a low monotone, dull as a torturer's knife. "You performed admirably in the immediate aftermath of the earthquake, I will grant you that. But you put yourself and your colleagues in danger because you forgot what you were supposed to be doing. And then you see fit to question my decisions in front of other employees?"

"Oh, fuck you." I get in close, anger overriding the fear. "I'm so sick and tired of being treated like a little kid. Like I can't understand, and I should just let the grown-ups take charge and decide what's best for me. You do it. Reggie does it. Even Paul, he ... " I stop, stunned at the lump in my throat. Choking off the words.

"You can't understand," Tanner says softly.

"And there it is. Same old shit."

"It's not personal. I would say the same thing to Ms Cruz. Ms McCormick. Even Mr Marino, were he here. None of you have the capacity to gather intelligence in a meaningful way."

"Do you *ever* say anything nice? Or did they remove that part of your brain at birth?"

She at least has the good grace to wince, very slightly. "I admit, the phrasing there could have been better."

"Yeah, no kidding."

"But I want you to understand this. It's *imperative* you understand it. Gathering actionable intel is *hard*. I've been doing it for decades, and it has only gotten more difficult. Our intelligence community is simply not set up to deal with people who have abilities like yours. It is a big, grinding battleship, and we are asking it to do a three-point turn so it can track a tiny thing made of shadows. That's part of the reason you've been so useful in the first place – because the enemies of this country can't see you coming, either. But it works both ways. You have no idea – the battles I've fought, the politics I've had to play. Just to convince my superiors to keep you in the field."

"And I'm supposed to be grateful?"

"A little gratitude wouldn't hurt, yes. But let's not get distracted. So there was a school in New Mexico, containing other individuals with abilities. Was it an actual school? Or was this just the boy's way of thinking of it? Where was it? If it's still there – and I very much doubt it is – where did it come from? What shell corporations funded it? Who owns them? Is there a paper trail? More importantly: how? That psychokinetic you faced a few months ago – Jake – was one thing. There's a logical explanation for where he came from. There is no logical explanation for a young boy who can cause earthquakes. It goes far beyond your parents' research – something

completely new. And the other people at this *school*? What can
they do? And why would someone set up a facility to develop
them in the first place? What's the end game here? If you can
answer these questions – if you can answer even one – then I'll
never bother you again. I'll let you do as you please."

I can't help but look back towards the house, as if Reggie is
going to come to my aid. She's at the kitchen table with Annie.
The dreadlocked dude from before is there, too, in the middle
of some story or other.

I turn back to Tanner. "So what you're saying is, I'm just a
little cog in your intelligence machine."

She sighs. "Once again, you have completely misinterpreted
what I said. You're not just a cog. You're *the* cog. You are the
central gear around which all of this turns. You are our entry-
point into this world."

"Oh, come *on*." I fold my arms. "I break into safes and crack
locks and lift people onto roofs and plant tracking devices and
shit. Little stuff."

"For your information, everything you've done has fur-
thered the security of this country. I don't waste my assets,
Ms Frost – something you should know by now. I don't
bother with the *little stuff*. In any case, that was before. Things
are very different now. And you *cannot* just throw yourself
into situations without thinking it through. You are far
too important. Especially now that your abilities extend to
organic matter."

Her words take a second to sink in. I try very hard to keep
my face neutral . . . and fail spectacularly.

"What are you talking about?" I say.

"Ms Frost, you were underground longer than Mr Marino
was – whatever your talents, they do not include the ability to
hold your breath longer than a former Navy man."

"Yeah, but I—"

"I have already told you, Ms Frost." She's dead still. Even her lips hardly move. "Don't insult my intelligence."

Oh.

I get it.

Back on Schmidt's plane, when Tanner first told me that Annie and I were going to Washington State. There was something off about what she was saying – a weird element to it I couldn't put my finger on.

She claimed that it made logistical sense for Annie and me to be together at at least one of the ETS zone sites. That it would be better than us patching in by video, having us ID the kid remotely. It sounded strange then, and now I know why. She *wanted* me up there.

She must have known about my newfound ability before I did – but how? And how could she have known it would show itself in Washington?

Crap. If she knows, then other people in the government know, too. If she isn't able to protect me any more, then I have a real fucking problem.

"I suspected your ability had changed as you'd gotten older," Tanner says. "No, don't interrupt. I didn't know how – or by how much. I certainly didn't know you had the power to affect organic molecules."

The confusion must show on my face, because a hint of a smile creeps onto hers. That's how she likes it – when she knows more than everybody else.

"I took a risk, Ms Frost. A calculated risk. I had no idea what the outcome might be, but I wanted to see if your new abilities would present themselves. I'm pleased to say they did."

"No. You're wrong. I don't—"

"You can rest easy, by the way. At present, Ms McCormick and I are the only ones who know. It's going to stay that way."

She doesn't have to say the last part. I can hear it just fine. *It's going to stay that way . . . as long as you continue to do what I say.*

Tanner purses her lips. "And you are definitely far too important to be spending your time at culinary school."

I blink. Did I mention that to her? The last few weeks have been a blur, but I'm sure I would remember if . . .

She shakes her head, as if shooing away a fly. "I would be a very poor intelligence operative if I didn't understand what it was my assets wanted."

" . . . Why can't I? What difference does it make?"

"Because I know you, Ms Frost. You would launch yourself at it, to the exclusion of everything else. Your work with China Shop would suffer, and I can't allow that. Not with so much at stake."

"Oh, bullshit. You can't just . . . just run my life like this. Anyway, I'll do it on my own time. I'll pay for it. If I'm allowed a life outside of China Shop, then I should be allowed this." I hate that I'm bargaining with her, doing it without meaning to. "Everybody thinks they know what's best for me. Nobody's ever asked me what *I* want."

"Tell me," Tanner says quietly. "If you could have stopped Matthew Schenke from ever reaching California, but in doing so you'd be required to give up your dream of being a chef for ever, would you have done it?"

"So I'm just selfish now? That's what you're saying?"

The very slightest smile. "Ms Frost, you're putting words in my mouth. Think of it this way. Jonas Schmidt – who you seem to have developed quite a bond with, by the way – turned his plane around when the San Andreas fault went off, at considerable risk to himself. What do you think his answer to my question would be, if he was in your shoes?"

I don't reply. Which is a good thing, because I'm not sure I could do it without swearing. A lot.

"We're not finished with this," I tell her.

"I have no doubt. And in case you'd thought I wouldn't mention it, we are going to have a *thorough* debrief on the Schmidt operation. But, for the foreseeable future, you and I are going to continue working together."

"Might be a pretty boring job." I spread my arms, gesturing to the rest of the world. "LA isn't exactly what it used to be. My guess is the world's super-criminals will probably take their shit elsewhere."

"On the contrary, our targets may flock to Los Angeles. A damaged place is always profitable, if you don't care about damaging it further.

Would you be kind enough to – ah, never mind. There she is."

Reggie's obviously been watching, keeping half an eye on us. She's wheeling her way back out from the kitchen. "They're doing Jäger shots," she says to me.

"Oh, Jesus."

"Yep. Believe they told me that if you don't join them, Annie is going to sit on you while her cousin pours it down your throat."

"I'll do one if she does one," I say, jerking my finger at Tanner, who looks like I've just invited her to go skinny-dipping in a pool of pee.

"She's more a wine gal," Reggie says. Tanner has turned away from us, hands clasped behind her back. Surveying the empty yard, as if examining captured territory.

"Of course she is. Care to get shitfaced with us?"

"You go on ahead. I'll come over in a bit." She looks over at Tanner – and this time, there's no fear in her eyes. "We've got a lot to talk about."

Halfway across the yard, my phone buzzes in the pocket of my jeans.

Phone service is still spotty, but they've managed to get a basic version of it back online. And I know without looking exactly who is texting me. He's sent so many messages over the past few days that I can probably figure out what he's saying, without reading it.

I pause for a moment, hand wavering over the pocket of my baggy cargo pants. Then I let it go, head back inside. I probably need to be a lot more drunk before I deal with that. Actually, before I deal with anything. My little chat with Tanner has left me feeling like there's still an earthquake happening, the ground shaking under my feet.

It isn't just Annie doing shots. It's about ten people, and they all cheer when I duck into the kitchen. I was introduced to a few of them earlier, but I've already forgotten their names. Hands reach for me, pull me into the circle, squashing me down on a chair next to Annie. She looks over at me, the grin on her face at odds with her red-rimmed eyes. She's drunk now, not quite able to focus on me.

I reach over, wrap my arms around her. "I love you, Annie. You know that, right?"

She mumbles something in my ear, impossible to make out over the loud voices.

But she squeezes back.

Someone shoves a whiskey glass filled with a double shot of black liquid into my hand. Everybody has one, and everybody shoves their own forward into a giant communal toast. It's a miracle we don't break any of them.

As the horrible concoction nukes the inside of my mouth, there's a commotion from the front of the house. Shouts. Laughter. The *blat* of an engine – and not a car engine either.

Annie's eyes meet mine. "The fuck?" she mumbles.

The front porch is crowded with people. Ditto for the yard. They're all cheering and laughing at ... *something* out front. I've lost track of Annie somewhere between kitchen and porch, but I push my way through the crowd. I can't see a damn thing, and it doesn't help that I'm about half a foot shorter than anybody here. It's only when I get to the front fence that I finally see what's causing the ruckus.

Africa.

Fucking Africa.

He's standing on the ATV he stole, arms spread like he's conducting an orchestra, a smile on his face the size of California. He's guffawing with laughter, calling out people in the crowd, pointing. There's a woman by the ATV, looking around, standing awkwardly while Africa soaks in the applause. She's stick-thin, with scraggly red hair and a pinched, nervous face.

Jeannette. The stupid son of a bitch found her.

He catches sight of me, and the smile gets so big it threatens to crack his face in two. "*Teggan!*" He roars. "You *dëma*! You made it, huh?"

I can't help smiling back.

How in the blue hell did he know that Paul's memorial was today? How did he know where to come? And how in the name of all that is good does he already know everyone here?

Actually, you know what? It doesn't matter. I'm sure he'll tell me the story before long.

Some of it might even be true.

SIXTY-FIVE

Teagan

Later.

I'm sitting on the front porch, not really thinking about anything. I'm drunk, but not nearly as badly as I should be. It's like the beers and Jäger and – tequila? Yes, tequila – just went right through me.

There are still voices in the house, but they're quieter now. Slowly, the crowds drifted away, people leaving in twos or threes. I went to the bathroom at one point, and came back to find just about everybody engaged in a massive clean-up operation, black trash bags appearing from nowhere, people stacking plates and sweeping up the odd broken glass. Rocko, Sandra-May's enormous dog, ran around barking and pretending he was being useful. About the only person not helping was Annie, who was passed out on a couch, snoring like a beast. Sandra-May was in the middle of it all, saying she hoped it wasn't too much of a bother, she and Reggie directing operations, Reggie immediately calling me over to gather empty beer bottles. It made me think of the day after the first quake, when Paul asked for help cleaning up the Boutique, and I had to excuse myself for a few minutes to get my shit together.

I yawn suddenly, huge and wide. I have no idea how I'm getting back to the hotel. I left my Jeep parked there – somehow, I knew driving myself would be a bad idea today. One of Sandra-May's neighbours picked us up, a huge man in a white T-shirt who bumped trap music all the way over, but I haven't seen him in hours. Christ, what time is it? I dig in pocket for my phone.

Onscreen is that text message. The one I ignored.

The one from Nic.

I let out a long, slow breath. Stare at the notification. *Hey just checking in. Are you doing OK?? I still feel like . . .*

Without really wanting to, I flick open the message, read the rest . . . *We left things on a bad note . . . would love to chat if you around . . .*

He knows I'm still in LA. I didn't just leave him hanging. When cell service came back a few days ago, the first thing to arrive was a deluge of texts from him. I let him know where I was, and what was happening, although for obvious reasons I didn't tell him about Washington. He knows about Paul, too . . . although I haven't told him how he died.

My texts were brief, to the point. I didn't trust myself to write anything longer.

He's still in LA. He's had no word about when the District Attorney's office will reopen, but he says it's a when, not an if. He's been helping out with quake clean-up, because of course he has. Amazingly, his apartment made it through. The place has spotty power, but is apparently liveable.

Without wanting to, I scroll up past the chain of messages.

Hey do you want to meet up? There's a cafe in Sawtelle that's open . . .

Just checking in to see how you doing :) . . .

It'd be really good to see you sometime . . .

I wasn't really thinking straight at Dodger, just wanted to let you know where my head is at . . .

It's been a while since I messaged him. A couple days, at least. I should probably check in with him – I might not know where we stand, exactly, but I don't want to just ghost him.

I'm probably too drunk to be messaging him, but I start tapping anyway. *I'm OK. Just at Annie's place for Paul's party*

I send the message, still staring at the screen. Should I say more? Not that it matters – he's probably asleep by now, so I'll only get the reply in the—

Nope. There are those three little dots. Then: *Oh shit forgot that was tonight :(sorry*

No worries, we good

You still there? How you getting home tonight?

Ha. Interesting question. Before I can write a response, he sends another message: *You welcome to stay at my place if you want lmk*

Oh, Nic.

You know what surprised me the most, after I got back from Washington? When I finally had time to think about Nic, I discovered I wasn't mad. I thought I would be. What he said after the first quake, and then again at Dodger Stadium, cut deep.

But I found myself thinking about how he must have seen it. In the past few months, he'd discovered that superpowers exist – and that someone he was close to, a person he wanted to be with, had a piece of it. Finding out shit like that will do a number on you, and the mind has a way of forcing the world to reorder itself so it all makes sense.

Nic's generous. He helps people. And I guess on some level, he couldn't understand why I wouldn't just use my ability after the quakes hit. I thought he was being an asshole . . . but it's not quite that simple. Took me more than a few sleepless nights staring at the ceiling of my hotel room to figure it out, but I got there. And it's pretty clear that he doesn't feel so good about how he acted, either, hence the attempts to try and patch things up.

A month ago, I would have jumped at the chance to stay at his place. It was everything I wanted. Now ...

There's a chunk of soil a few feet away – maybe one Rocko kicked up from stampeding around the yard. I focus in on it, pushing past the drunken haze, sending out my PK. There's the very faintest hint of contact, like soft lips brushing a shoulder ...

Then nothing.

I'm changing. In more ways than one. I'm not just stronger. I'm better. I'm ... evolving, I guess is the word. And doing it in ways that no one – not Tanner, not Reggie, not my parents or anybody else – could have predicted.

I'm OK for tonight :) I type. *Thx though*

The three dots of his reply stay on my screen for a good two minutes.

No worries . . . get home safe OK? Maybe chat tomorrow?

Sure. Will msg.

I rest my chin in my palm, staring at nothing. My eyes flicker shut, and for a second, sleep nearly gets its hooks into me. Not quite yet, though. I straighten up, roll my shoulders, wincing as my neck bones creak.

My thumb moves before I can stop it, calling up Instagram on my phone. Data in LA is still kind of glitchy, but it's been getting better, and the app boots up fine. I started a burner account recently – *@PaellaBitch*. I've made sure it has every appearance of a fake. No posts, no profile pic, and a random list of follows, everything from porn accounts to motivational

speakers to anime memes. There's only one other account I'm
interested in though, and I don't think he'll notice I've followed him. When you have 1.2 million followers, you don't
tend to pay much attention to them.

@JonasSchmidtCEO spent quite a bit of time in LA. Not a
lot of shots of him specifically – just his crew, doling out food
and bottles of water, plus plenty of Stories showing videos of
his plane, sharing its location at Van Nuys Airport. Eventually,
though, FEMA took over. I don't know how he got back to
Germany, but there was a gap of a few days, and then normal
service resumed. Gym videos. Photos taken at conferences.
Shots of his staff, the description always talking about what
they do, and why they're awesome at it.

My finger hovers over the latest one – a selfie of him with
one of his employees. His CFO, the description reads. A
thirty-something woman rocking spiky red hair and a huge
grin, her arm around Jonas. He's wearing aviator shades, a
tight black T-shirt.

I pause, then double-tap to like. A little red heart appears
below the pic.

It already has 1,871 of them, so there's no danger of him
noticing one more.

I kill the app before I do something stupid. Like start scrolling. Again.

I don't need another person in my life to be complete. I have
my friends, and my job, and my ability. My city. Food I haven't
tried yet, music I haven't listened to, awful Reddit threads I
still need to read. I don't need Jonas.

But just because you don't need something, doesn't mean
you don't still want it.

The door behind me opens, and the familiar sound of
Sandra-May's laboured breath reaches me. "Well, hey," she

says. "Didn't realise you were still with us." Under the porch light, she looks small and tired.

"Yeah." It takes me a second to clear my head. "No, I think I'm gonna run in a minute. It was a great party though."

"Run?" She cocks an eye at me. "You ain't going anywhere. You're bunking right here. Couch is pretty comfy."

"But—"

"No buts. Dell can drive you home in the morning."

I'm on the verge of protesting, but then I think how sweet it would be to collapse on a couch. Close my eyes. Drift off.

"Is there anything else to clean up inside?" I say.

"I think we're good."

"You got it. And thanks, then. For letting me crash. I'll cook breakfast, OK?"

She starts to protest, but this time, it's me who cuts her off. "Nope. That's my condition. Otherwise I'll *walk* back to Pomona."

"Deal."

The silence that follows starts comfortable, but goes on a little bit too long.

I start to rise. "Well, good n—"

"Paul didn't die in the quake, did he?"

She's stooped, breathing hard. But her eyes are bright. Alert.

I open my mouth to tell her that of course he did ... but I don't have it in me. Not after everything that's happened.

"I knew, from the way my Annie was tonight. This wasn't nature. He was killed by something ... preventable, I guess is the word. He was a good man. An honest one. Fair few of those around, I don't mind telling you. And you know how good he was to my Annie." She breathes a shaky sigh, and under the porch light, her cheeks glisten with tears. "God, I wish he was here."

"Mrs Cr—Sandra-May . . ."

"I need to ask you something." Her voice is suddenly hard. "And you'd better answer straight. Was it drugs? Were y'all involved in some drug thing?"

"What? No . . ."

"Guns? Gang nonsense, anything like that?"

"Of course not!"

"Is my Annie involved in something that hurts people? In any way at all?"

I hold up my hands, just to give myself time to get my thoughts in order.

"Paul would never hurt anybody," I tell her, forgetting to use the past tense. "Neither would Annie. Or me. We're not criminals."

There's a long pause where she just stares at me. And I know what's going to happen next: she's going to push. She'll make me tell her, and I don't know if I can lie. But I can't tell her the truth, either – not without bringing the wrath of Tanner down on my head.

But then she nods. "I get it. You don't think you should be the one to spill it. I suppose Annie will, when she's ready. Just promise me one thing."

"Of . . . of course."

"You keep her safe. You don't let her get hurt. She's already been through enough, and she's going to need a lot more help after this. So you watch out for her. Understand?"

Slowly, I nod. Not wanting to admit how relieved I am.

Sandra-May gives me a slow smile, then starts to move back into the house. I push myself up, thinking I should get while the getting's good.

And then I spot something . . . a little weird.

Actually, a lot weird.

Across the street from Sandra-May's front yard are the Watts Towers. The big, alien-spaceship-looking sculptures, rising out of the cul-de-sac. The houses around them are in bad shape, some even knocked over completely. But the towers . . . they're undamaged. Ditto for the wall around them. Those tall, fragile, airy constructions of rebar and concrete are still there. I didn't even notice before – our arrival at Sandra-May's was a blur of people and trays of food and boxes of beer. But they're still there. Undamaged.

"What?" Sandra-May says. She follows my gaze. "The towers?"

"Yeah. I thought they'd be . . ."

She huffs a laugh. "Let me tell you a little something about the Watts Towers. See, they were built over a period of thirty years by one man. One single man, bit by bit. Simon Rodia, his name was – although back in Italy they called him Sabato Rodia." She sees my expression. "Don't worry. It's not a long history lesson."

"OK?"

"Anyway, Rodia used nothing more than seashells and bits of glass, held together with mortar. And in the fifties, the city decided that the towers were a hazard – if a quake happened, they'd fall over and kill people. Personally, I don't think they gave a tin shit about the folks in Watts – they just didn't want any of 'em having a nice piece of art nearby. We didn't hold with that, made them do a test. They brought in a crane, tied steel cables to the towers. Ten thousand pounds of force. And they couldn't budge them – not one inch."

"Why? That doesn't make sense."

"No idea. Only person who could tell you is dear old Simon Rodia, and he's long gone."

She spots the disbelief on my face, and laughs. "You can

look it up on your phone. It's all documented – photos and everything. Takes more than a couple little earthquakes to knock down the towers."

"Kind of an obvious lesson, isn't it?"

She shrugs. "Gets me through the day. I'll leave a comforter on the couch for you, and there's extra blankets in the hall closet if you get cold. I'll see you in the morning, and I do believe I'll hold you to that breakfast."

She goes inside, shutting the door quietly behind her.

The neighbourhood around me is quiet ... but not silent. A few doors down, there's a barbecue going on – a group talking in low voices, the sizzle of meat on a grill, a charred scent in the air. On the far side of the towers, on Santa Ana, a car drives past. Moving slow, negotiating the cracked road. Its lights illuminate a group of kids, out way past their bedtimes, chasing each other in some game. On the corner of the triangular park the towers stand in, two women talk over the glowing light of a cigarette, laughing at some unheard joke. In the distance, a dog barks – and underneath the sound, very faint, the soft hum of Los Angeles traffic. Nothing like it was before the quake – but still there, all the same.

Yeah. Definitely an obvious lesson.

Which doesn't stop it being true.

I put my phone back in my pocket. Then I lift my tired body up off the porch, and step inside, closing the door behind me.

SIXTY-SIX

The Director

Seven days earlier. Olympic National Park, Washington.

A pickup truck pulls into an empty parking lot on the shore of Lake Cushman, not too far from the Vance Campground.

The truck is a big Ford F150, double-cab, with huge tyres for negotiating uneven roads. It comes to a stop, the driver parking it neatly between the lines. In the silence that follows, the trees crowding the lake seem to bend a little closer.

The Director is in her mid-twenties, with a willowy figure and an oval face dotted with acne scars. Her blonde hair is tied back in a neat ponytail. She wears a polo-neck sweater under a North Face vest, with hiking pants and thick, chunky boots.

"Listen, you go ahead," says the man in the passenger seat. He's a little older than she is, with thick black hair going very slightly grey at the temples. "I'll watch the little monster."

The girl in the backseat giggles. "I'm not a monster."

That earns a smile from the Director – but suddenly, a worry line crinkles her forehead. "Olivia, you're sure about this?" she says.

The girl blinks at her from behind owlish glasses. She's a plump five-year-old, slightly stubby fingers clutching an iPad. Her feet, clad in comfy child-size Crocs, dangle off the big backseat.

"Positive," she says. She spins the iPad to face the Director, fingers dancing effortlessly to bring up a satellite map. "Here. Just take the trail in for ... hmmm ... for three miles. It'll work, I swear."

The Director pats her knee. "Thanks, sweetie. I'll see you in a little bit, OK? Ajay's got some snacks if you want."

"Are they Pringles?"

The man named Ajay rolls his eyes. "Olivia. You know we don't eat those."

"Why?"

Ajay gets a kiss on the cheek from the Director. She hops out the car, grabbing her daypack from the cargo well. It's a bright, cold day, overcast but not dull. There isn't another soul around.

The Director hefts her pack, heading for the far side of the parking lot, the painted white blaze marking the start of the trail. The trees close in on her, swallowing her from view.

Olivia has almost never been wrong before. She could look at two other kids playing baseball, study them for a moment, and tell you that the pitch after next would break a window – and which one it would be. You'd put her in front of an office building, tell her about the companies that occupied it, and she'd say whether the next person who came out the front doors would be a man or a woman. And the one after that. And the one after that.

The child was a wonder. She was easily the most successful test subject at the Facility, and she delighted in using her powers. She was capable of things that seemed, to the casual observer, like predicting the future. What it actually was, was probability. Given enough information, Olivia could parse the likely outcomes of any situation. She was most precise when the information was purely mathematical – even this young, the girl had a grasp of numbers that was just unbelievable. But she could look at any real-world situation, and make a very educated guess at the outcome.

She could, for instance, be told what occurred at the Vance Campground a few days before. She could be given access to maps. Photos of the surrounding forest. Details on the terrain, the vegetation and animal life, the weather. Then she'd look up, blinking behind her thick glasses, and calmly pronounce that the boy who could cause earthquakes was still alive.

Even then, it was something of a gamble. The girl would only give a general area where the boy would be. It was small, but it would still take days to search.

Unless, of course, the searcher had the genetic ability to see things in the infrared spectrum, with far more precision and at a much greater distance than even the most advanced military technology.

Unless she could pick out warm bodies in the undergrowth from miles away, as easily as someone spotting a friend across a crowded room.

Olivia had helped in other ways, too. The US Army had declared the Olympic National Park off-limits while they conducted their search – nobody in, or out. But the park was almost one and a half thousand square miles in size, and not even the Army could watch every access point. Olivia had worked out that this particular trailhead – the one the Director has just taken – would have the best chance of being unguarded on this particular day. The Army searchers would have moved on, heading deeper into the park.

It was a risk, of course. A big one. Then again, the Director is carrying no weapons. She's just a hiker, out for a stroll.

And of course, she can see them coming long before they can see her.

A few hours later, the Director stops at the top of a small rise, checking a map on her phone. Looks around her. When she was a child, she couldn't see that far – fifty yards, maybe, no more. But she's gotten a lot stronger since then. She slowly turns, noting the glowing red form of a bear, snuffling in the undergrowth half a mile away. The squirrels scrabbling across the tree trunks. The deer, drinking from a stream – a very faint glow in her vision, nearly a mile hence. She's especially alert for large human shapes in the distance – the special forces tracker teams, still hunting. But it's a huge area for them to cover, and she can't see anybody.

At her two o'clock, there's a tiny blob of heat energy. One that might be a raccoon, or a small coyote, or something else altogether.

She takes a drink of water from her pack, then sets off again, moving off the path and into the dense forest, keeping a lazy eye on the bear shape so she can give it a wide berth.

She's always loved walking. Ever since she was a kid, when she and her brother and sister had a thousand acres of unspoiled Wyoming wilderness to play in. She'd often ditch them and go for rambles – that's what she thought of them as, rambles, a word her dad had once used which had never left her. She wishes her dad was here now. He'd appreciate what she was trying to do.

And what are you trying to do?

Even now, she has her doubts. It has taken so much faith for her to proceed this far – not just in Olivia, or Ajay, or the other doctors. It's taken faith in herself. In her mission.

The Facility had been the easy part. Once she had the funds in place, and the right people, it all came together. There were challenges of course – the boy, for a start. His desire to hurt those around him, to see what it would feel like, took some serious thinking to overcome.

But the challenges *had* been overcome. And the Director had started to think a little bigger. She'd begun to imagine what would happen if people like her and the children and her brother could walk freely, not hiding their abilities, safe in the knowledge that no one could hurt them.

Of course, for that, she needed money. Plenty of it was available – Olivia proved as deft at predicting the stock market as she did at predicting where a baseball would end up after it was hit. But it was far too slow. It would take years to raise the kind of funds needed without attracting attention – years of careful planning, shell companies, an intricate network of investments. Years of trying to outsmart the federal government, not making too much too quickly, staying under the radar.

And then, one day, she'd had a revelation – one so startling she'd sat bolt upright in bed, causing Ajay to spill his morning coffee next to her.

She'd started feeding Olivia more data. Much more. Asking what would happen to the economy and the market under certain scenarios. How the financial world would react following war. Disease. Terrorist attack.

Or if a massive earthquake were to strike somewhere in the United States.

Olivia, ever eager to please, had sucked it all up like a sponge. With her help, they'd modelled a scenario, down to the last variable. They'd worked out where to place their funds, investing in places no one would think to put their money. Setting up a massive, interconnected web of holdings that would sit, dormant, until a specific event thought to be entirely out of human control set them in motion. Then they would grow, and grow, and grow some more.

Causing the specific event – the earthquake – was where the Director had taken a huge leap of faith. No one knew what would happen if the boy were to come across a fault line. He might not sense it at all, or sense it but be unable to do anything about it.

The Director had spent long nights in conversation with Ajay. She'd consulted Olivia repeatedly (without telling her the full picture – she was only five, after all). She'd watched the boy from her office window. Wondering how someone so young could be so cruel.

She had a strong sense that he couldn't be forced to do it. If they dragged him to a fault line, he might just refuse to help, or lie to them. He would have to find his own way, believe it was his idea . . .

She could guarantee that he'd cross the San Andreas fault – that part was easy. It was practically impossible to enter Los Angeles *without* doing so. But the rest of the plan was less certain. It required Ajay convincing the mother and her son to run. It required the Director to trust her instincts as much as she trusted Olivia's mind.

She knew there was a chance that the boy would disappoint them, and she planned accordingly. She was already in the process of moving the Facility, changing their identities – if the boy was caught, she didn't want it coming back on her. She's become used to this kind of subterfuge, the subtle ways to stay out of the government's eye. She's been doing it for a very long time.

All the same, she had a good feeling about the plan. When you wanted to create a new world, you had to believe in your ideas.

The Director had wondered why the loss of life in the earthquakes didn't bother her. She supposed it was because most of the people in the affected area would despise her, and Olivia, and anyone else with abilities.

She didn't especially wish them dead. They simply didn't matter to her. If there'd been an easier way to achieve her goals, one without loss of life, she'd probably have taken it. But there wasn't, so she didn't.

Of course, things hadn't gone completely to plan. They'd factored in the Director's sister, and her little government-owned crew, but not even Olivia could account for everything. Humans weren't always predictable. Cascadia had not gone off, which meant that their stock market gains hadn't been as huge as she'd hoped.

All the same, they were substantial. Her dream, of a new world for her and her kind, was closer than it had ever been – and who knew where the next few months would take them?

The thought of her sister gives the Director pause. Teagan thinks she's dead, of course. Along with their brother, Adam.

The Director isn't sure how she feels about that. It's a necessity of course. There's no way they could pull this off if Emily (Teagan, as she calls herself now) knew about it. But it doesn't stop the little pang in the heart, the pang of one sister missing another. The pang of lost years.

Off the trail, the woods are hard going. It takes the Director a little while to get close to her target. And it's no animal, that's for sure. It senses her coming, tries to hide, but it can't move very fast and it's far too weak.

The boy is hidden in the hollow of a dead tree, curled against one of the roots. He's smeared with dirt, shivering, scrawny, pale as snow. His hair is a wild mess, and he gazes up at the Director through haunted, half-mad eyes.

The Director crouches down, keeping her distance. "Hi, Lucas. Do you remember me?"

It takes him a few seconds to answer. "The l-lady from the School."

"That's right. I'm Chloe. I've come to take you home."

A few moments later, he's gathered in her arms, his freezing face pressed to her warm neck. She rocks him, soothing him, as he starts to cry. Around them, the forest breathes, slow and sure.

When he's calmed down a little, she hefts him, and begins her walk back out the woods. A couple of hours later, some signal bars appear on her phone, and she dials Ajay. He picks up on the first ring.

"I've got him," she says. "Tell the monster she was spot on. No, I'm coming back. Keep it warm for us. Oh – and do me a favour? Call Adam. Tell him he can drop the homeless act. We don't need to watch Teagan any more."

She hangs up, kisses her charge gently on the head.

"Almost home," she whispers.

ACKNOWLEDGEMENTS

Hey. Teagan here.

Jackson Ford is a lazy asshole, and forgot to do his acknowledgements. It's cool though, *I'll* write the thank yous, it's not like I've got anything else going on right now.

However! Since Jackson left it to me to finish what he started, I get to do it my own way. And since all my amazing, hysterical hip-hop-related in-jokes were forcibly removed during editing, I'm getting my own back here. This isn't part of the story, and no one actually reads book thank yous anyway, so nobody can stop me.

I thought long and hard about this, and decided the best way to do it would be to give everybody a Wu Tang Clan nickname. Shut up, it's a great idea. And you fuckers are lucky I'm in a good mood, or at least one of you would have ended up as Blue Raspberry. Google her.

First up: Ed "The RZA" Wilson. Jackson's agent, the man with the plan, the guy who makes sure things actually get done around here. Without Ed, none of this happens. Also, the world would have a lot more negronis and dog-patterned trousers to go around.

Equally important: Emily "The GZA" Byron. Her editing mind is as sharp as a liquid sword. We couldn't have done it without her. She also got rid of the ninja unicorn assassin from another dimension that showed up for the final battle, so yeah: she's good at her job.

Emily got an assist from Bradley "Method Man" Englert. New York's finest. Thanks, homie.

Joanna "Inspectah Deck" Kramer brought this book from error-filled manuscript through to the thing you hold today. She bombs atomically.

Steve "U-God" Panton, for once again putting together a cover that makes the ladies melt and the fellas get jealous. Seriously: my covers look fucking great.

Saxon "Cappadonna" Bullock, who helped fix all of Jackson's continuity errors, spelling mistakes and shitty writing. He did a great job, too. Even if he thinks it's preferable to write Tupac, instead of 2Pac. Don't ever fight with me on rap trivia, man. You'll get your ass kicked.

Nazia "Ghostface Killah" Khatun and Ellen "Raekwon" Wright: the dynamic duo who promoted the hell out of this book. Also to Madeleine "Masta Killa" Hall, with the mad marketing moves.

Finally . . . oh. Shit.

OK, so, here's the thing. The other main person I have to thank is Tim Holman, who runs Orbit Books, and is Jackson's publisher. There is only one core Wu Tang member left, and as much as I crack jokes, I'm not sure I can get away with calling the actual boss of this whole operation Ol' Dirty Bastard. Tim: you're fantastic, we love you and please don't fire us.

A few more people. One of the most overlooked parts of this operation is the Hachette Audio division. They do a time-intensive, difficult job creating audiobooks, and I want to thank them here. You really, *really* need to hear the audiobook of *The Girl Who Could Move Sh*t With Her Mind* (the book before this one, in case you're keeping score). They crushed it. Go listen. I'm hoping most of them come back for another go. A big thank you to Lauren Patten, Graham Halstead, Michelle Figueroa, Pavel Rivera and Louise Newton.

Jackson Ford talked to two highly qualified academics for this book, and then did his usual trick of messing up every bit of useful info they gave him. They are not to blame for any of it. A big thank you to Kit Miyamoto, for breaking down Jackson's misconceptions about earthquakes, and Nick Wogan, for helping him figure out the ETS zones.

As we all know, Jackson couldn't find his ass with both hands and a map, let alone accurately depict Los Angeles. So thank you to Alisha Grauso. Jackson's LA connect, his fact-checker extraordinaire, the one person standing between him and God knows how many lawsuits.

George Kelly and Werner Schutz read this book when it was still just a pile of dog-eared pages covered in mayonnaise and earwax. That they actually sent it back with some helpful comments blows me away. Or, hell, maybe they just really like mayo and earwax. Whatever turns you on, guys.

And let me get serious for a second, OK? While this book was being written, we lost two incredible musicians here in Los Angeles. Darrell Fields, aka Mr Guitar, of Skid Row, a huge advocate for the city's homeless as well as a peerless player. And Ermias Ashgedom, aka Nipsey Hussle, one of the greatest rappers ever, entrepreneur, activist, LA ambassador and a true marathon OG. You will both be missed, and my city is a little darker without you.

extras

orbit
www.orbitbooks.net

extras

about the author

Jackson Ford has never been to Los Angeles. The closest he's come is visiting Las Vegas for a Celine Dion concert, where he also got drunk and lost his advance money for this book at the Bellagio. That's what happens when you try play roulette at the craps table. He is the creator of the Frost Files, and the character of Teagan Frost – who, by the way, absolutely did not write this bio, and anybody who says she did is a liar.

Find out more about Jackson Ford and other Orbit authors by registering for the free monthly news-letter at www.orbitbooks.net.

if you enjoyed
RANDOM SH*T FLYING
THROUGH THE AIR
look out for
THE LAST SMILE IN
SUNDER CITY

by

Luke Arnold

I'm Fetch Phillips, just like it says on the window. There are a few things you should know before you hire me:

1. Sobriety costs extra.
2. My services are confidential —
the cops can never make me talk.
3. I don't work for humans.

It's nothing personal — I'm human myself. But after what happened, humans don't need my help. Not like every other creature who had the magic ripped out of them when the Coda came . . .

I just want one real case. One chance to do something good. Because it's my fault the magic is never coming back.

"Do some good," she'd said.

Well, I'd tried, hadn't I? Every case of my career had been tiresome and ultimately pointless. Like when Mrs Habbot hired me to find her missing dog. Two weeks of work, three broken bones, then the old bat died before I could collect my pay, leaving a blind and incontinent poodle in my care for two months. Just long enough for me to fall in love with the damned mutt before he also kicked the big one.

Rest in peace, Pompo.

Then there was my short-lived stint as Aaron King's bodyguard. Paid in full, not a bruise on my body, but listening to that rich fop whine about his inheritance was four and a half days of agony. I'm still picking his complaints out of my ears with tweezers.

After a string of similarly useless jobs, I was in my office, half-asleep, three-quarters drunk and all out of coffee. That was almost enough. The coffee. Just enough reason to stop the whole stupid game for good. I stood up from my desk and opened the door.

Not the first door. The first door out of my office is the one with the little glass window that reads *Fetch Phillips: Man for Hire* and leads through the waiting room into the hall.

No. I opened the second door. The one that leads to nothing but a patch of empty air five floors over Main Street. This door had been used by the previous owner but I'd never stepped out of it myself. Not yet, anyway.

The autumn wind slapped my cheeks as I dangled my toes off the edge and looked down at Sunder City. Six years since it all fell apart. Six years of stumbling around, hoping I would trip over some way to make up for all those stupid mistakes.

Why did she ever think I could make a damned bit of difference?

Ring.

The candlestick phone rattled its bells like a beggar asking for change. I watched, wondering whether it would be more trouble to answer it or eat it.

Ring.

Ring.

"Hello?"

"Am I speaking to Mr Phillips?"

"You are."

"This is Principal Simon Burbage of Ridgerock Academy. Would you be free to drop by this afternoon? I believe I am in need of your assistance."

I knew the address but he spelled it out anyway. Our meeting would be after school, once the kids had gone home, but he wanted me to arrive a little earlier.

"If possible, come over at half past two. There is a presentation you might be interested in."

I agreed to the earlier time and the line went dead.

The wind slapped my face again. This time, I allowed the cold air into my lungs and it pushed out the night. My eyelids scraped open. My blood began to thaw. I rubbed a hand across my face and it was rough and dry like a slab of salted meat.

A client. A case. One that might actually mean something.

I grabbed my wallet, lighter, brass knuckles and knife and I kicked the second door closed.

There was a gap in the clouds after a week of rain and the streets, for a change, looked clean. I was hoping I did too. It was my first job offer in over a fortnight and I needed to make it stick. I wore a patched gray suit, white shirt, black tie, my best pair of boots and the navy, fur-lined coat that was practically a part of me.

Ridgerock Academy was made up of three single-story blocks of concrete behind a wire fence. The largest building was decorated with a painfully colorful mural of smiling faces, sunbeams and stars.

A security guard waited with a pot of coffee and a paper-thin smile. She had eyes that were ready to roll and the unashamed love of a little bit of power. When she asked for my name, I gave it.

"Fetch Phillips. Here to see the Principal."

I traded my ID for an unimpressed grunt.

"Assembly hall. Straight up the path, red doors to the left."

It wasn't my school and I'd never been there before, but the grounds were smeared with a thick coat of nostalgia; the unforgettable aroma of grass-stains, snotty sleeves, fear, confusion and week-old peanut-butter sandwiches.

The red doors were streaked with the accidental graffiti of wayward finger-paint. I pulled them open, took a moment to adjust to the darkness and slipped inside as quietly as I could.

The huge gymnasium doubled as an auditorium. Chairs were stacked neatly on one side, sports equipment spread out around the other. In the middle, warm light from a projector cut through the darkness and highlighted a smooth, white screen. Particles of dust swirled above a hundred hushed kids who whispered to each other from their seats on the floor. I slid up to the back, leaned against the wall and waited for whatever was to come.

A girl squealed. Some boys laughed. Then a mousy man with white hair and large spectacles moved into the light.

"Settle down, please. The presentation is about to begin."

I recognized his voice from the phone call.

"Yes, Mr Burbage," the children sang out in unison. The Principal approached the projector and the spotlight cut hard lines into his face. Students stirred with excitement as he unboxed a reel of film and loaded it on to the sprocket. The speakers crackled and an over-articulated voice rang out.

"The Opus is proud to present . . ."

I choked on my breath mid-inhalation. The Opus were my old employers and we didn't part company on the friendliest of terms. If this is what Burbage wanted me to see, then he must have known some of my story. I didn't like that at all.

" . . . *My Body and Me: Growing Up After the Coda.*"

I started to fidget, pulling at a loose thread on my sleeve. The voice-over switched to a male announcer who spoke with that fake, friendly tone I associate with salesmen, con-artists and crooked cops.

"Hello, everyone! We're here to talk about your body. Now, don't get uncomfortable, your body is something truly special and it's important that you know why."

One of the kids groaned, hoping for a laugh but not finding it. I wasn't the only one feeling nervous.

"Everyone's body is different, and that's fine. Being

different means being special, and we are all special in our own unique way."

Two cartoon children came up on the screen: a boy and a girl. They waved to the kids in the audience like they were old friends.

"You might have something on your body that your friends don't have. Or maybe they have something *you* don't. These differences can be confusing if you don't understand where they came from."

The little cartoon characters played along with the voice-over, shrugging in confusion as question marks appeared above their heads. Then they started to transform.

"Maybe your friend has pointy teeth."

The girl character opened her mouth to reveal sharp fangs.

"Maybe you have stumps on the top of your back."

The animated boy turned around to present two lumps, emerging from his shoulder blades.

"You could be covered in beautiful brown fur or have more eyes than your classmates. Do you have shiny skin? Great long legs? Maybe even a tail? Whatever you are, *who*ever you are, you are special. And you are like this for a reason."

The image changed to a landscape: mountains, rivers and plains, all painted in the style of an innocent picture book. Even though the movie made a great effort to hide it, I knew damn well that this story wasn't a happy one.

"Since the beginning of time, our world has gained its power from a natural energy that we call *magic*. Magic was part of almost every creature that walked the lands. Wizards could use it to perform spells. Dragons and Gryphons flew through the air. Elves stayed young and beautiful for centuries. Every creature was in tune with the spirit of the world and it made them different. Special. Magical.

"But six years ago, maybe before some of you were even born, there was an incident."

The thread came loose on my sleeve as I pulled too hard. I wrapped it tight around my finger.

"One species was not connected to the magic of the planet: the Humans. They were envious of the power they saw around them, so they tried to change things."

A familiar pain stabbed the left side of my chest, so I reached into my jacket for my medicine: a packet of Clayfield Heavies. Clayfields are a mass-produced version of a painkiller that people in these parts have used for centuries. Essentially, they're pieces of bark from a recus tree, trimmed to the size of a toothpick. I slid one thin twig between my teeth and bit down as the film rolled on.

"To remedy their natural inferiority, the Humans made machines. They invented a wide variety of weapons, tools and strange devices, but it wasn't enough. They knew their machines would never be as powerful as the magical creatures around them.

"Then, the Humans heard a legend that told of a sacred mountain where the magical river inside the planet rose up to meet the surface; a doorway that led right into the heart of the world. This ancient myth gave the Humans an idea."

The image flipped to an army of angry soldiers brandishing swords and torches and pushing a giant drill.

"Seeking to capture the natural magic of the planet for themselves, the Human Army invaded the mountain and defeated its protectors. Then, hoping that they could use the power of the river for their own desires, they plugged their machines straight into the soul of our world."

I watched the simple animation play out the events that have come to be known as the *Coda*.

The children watched in silence as the cartoon army moved their forces on to the mountain. On screen, it looked as simple as sliding a chess piece across a board. They didn't hear the screams. They didn't smell the fires. They didn't see the bloodshed. The bodies.

They didn't see me.

"The Human Army sent their machines into the mountain but when they tried to harness the power of the river, something far more terrible happened. The shimmering river of magic turned from mist to solid crystal. It froze. The heart of the world stopped beating and every magical creature felt the change."

I could taste bile in my mouth.

"Dragons plummeted from the sky. Elves aged centuries in seconds. Werewolves' bodies became unstable and left them deformed. The magic drained from the creatures of the world. From all of us. And it has stayed that way ever since."

In the darkness, I saw heads turn. Tiny little bodies examined themselves, then turned to inspect their neighbors. Their entire world was now covered in a sadness that the rest of us had been seeing for the last six years.

"You may still bear the greatness of what you once were. Wings, fangs, claws and tails are your gifts from the great river. They herald back to your ancestors and are nothing to be ashamed of."

I bit down on the Clayfield too hard and it snapped in half. Somewhere in the crowd, a kid was crying.

"Remember, you may not be magic, but you are still . . . special."

The film ripped off the projector and spun around the wheel, wildly clicking a dozen times before finally coming to a stop. Burbage flicked on the lights but the children stayed silent as stone.

"Thank you for your attention. If you have any questions about your body, your species or life before the Coda, your parents and teachers will be happy to talk them through with you."

As Burbage wrapped up the presentation, I tried my best to sink into the wall behind me. A stream of sweat had settled on my brow and I dabbed at it with an old handkerchief. When I looked up, an inquisitive pair of eyes were examining me.

They were foggy green with tiny pinprick pupils: Elvish. Young. The face was old, though. Elvish skin has no elasticity. Not anymore. The bags under the boy's eyes were worthy of a decade without sleep, but he couldn't have been more than five. His hair was white and lifeless and his tiny frame was all crooked. He wore no real expression, just looked right into my soul.

And I swear,

He knew.

Enter the monthly

Orbit sweepstakes at

www.orbitloot.com

With a different prize every month,
from advance copies of books by
your favourite authors to exclusive
merchandise packs,
**we think you'll find something
you love.**